BROKEN SHELVES BOOK 2

# LIVING FOR *truth*

## DAISY WREN

Edited by Brit and Jen at The Author Experience

Cover design by Brit at The Author Experience

For rights and permissions, please contact:

daisywren.author@gmail.com

Paperback ISBN: 979-8-9917189-0-5

Never settle for less than you deserve.
Someone's "too broken" will be someone else's dream
come true.

# AUTHOR'S NOTE

This book contains explicit on page content and is not suitable for anyone under the age of eighteen.

This book discusses topics that may be triggering for some readers such as: body shaming, infertility, miscarriage, verbal abuse, emotional neglect, religious trauma, and brief mention of child abuse (not on page).

Reader discretion is advised.

"My Kinda Lover" - Remastered 2010
by Billy Squire
"I'm Yours" by Jason Mraz
"ROOM FOR 2" by Benson Boon
"Starving" by Hailee Steinfeld, Grey, Zedd
"To Be With You" - 2021 Remastered by Mr. Big
"Kiss Me" by Sixpence None The Richer
"Message In A Bottle" (Taylor's Version) (From
The Vault) by Taylor Swift
"Love Is Like a Butterfly" by Dolly Parton
"gentle" by Lexi Jayde
"Beautiful Things" by Benson Boone
"Please Notice" by Christian Leave
"Would You Be So Kind" by dodie
"Cut To The Feeling" by Carly Rae Jepsen
"A Lot More Free" by Max McNown

# GLOSSARY

**"Broke My Shelf":** A term used primarily in the ex-Mormon community that describes the final event or aspect that made them want to leave the religion.

**"Watch" List (Bishopric):** A list of members who are inactive or members the church is concerned about. Oftentimes, this includes people who aren't actively participating in discussions or people who don't fit the "standard" for Mormon members.

**(Church) Records:** A demographic data study of the members of the church.

**(Temple) Recommend:** A special card which grants you access to the temple and the rituals performed there. In order to receive the recommend you have to go through a temple interview.

**FLDS Church:** The Fundamentalist Church of Jesus Christ of Latter-Day Saints, a religious sect of fundamentalist Mormonism whose members still practice polygamy. They claim to not be connected to The Church of Jesus Christ of Latter-Day Saints.

**Holy Ghost:** One of the three members of the Mormon Godhead (known as a Trinity in other religions). The Holy Ghost is supposed to act as one's conscience and is given to someone after they have been baptized.

**Mission Call:** An assignment to a specific area where the person will travel and share the religion's basic teachings to people who haven't heard of it before or are interested in learning more.

**Mission President:** The leader assigned to a specific proselytizing area. Most mission presidents are wealthy, and all of them are men. They are in charge of the missionaries in that area.

**Missionaries:** Generally, 18-20 year old men and 19-21 year old women who are sent to specific areas for 18-24 months in order to proselyte and increase membership numbers.

**Missionary Training Center:** A center where missionaries are sent to learn how to be missionaries before they're sent to their assigned areas. There are nine locations throughout the world, but the largest is in Provo, Utah.

**Priesthood:** The power to act in God's name on the earth. Given only to worthy men, starting at the age of twelve.

**Remnants Movement (Snufferites):** The Remnant movement is about establishing a more grassroots experience of the Restoration than the Church of Jesus Christ of Latter-day Saints offers. That means less leadership and organization and a bigger emphasis on individual expressions of revelation. Receiving personal visits from angels and Christ is an important part of Remnant beliefs. The name "Remnant" refers to their idea of remaining in the full covenant, i.e., not the misled state they believe the Church of Jesus Christ is in. (*www.mormonr.org*)

**Sacrament Meeting:** An hour long meeting where members eat bread and drink water to renew the covenants they made during their baptism. This is also where most ward business is announced.

**Sealing Ceremony:** Usually happens on a wedding day but can be performed later. It's a ceremony that bonds people for time and all eternity.

**Second Counselor in the Bishopric:** All organizations in the church are made of three members, with a president, first counselor, and second counselor. The Bishopric is the head entity of the ward and holds more power than other ward members but less than the Stake Presidency.

**Spiritual Giant:** Someone deemed to be more spiritual than the average member. This person has held many high profile callings and is usually listened to more than others.

**Stake:** Each area is broken up into different sections. A stake is a larger collection of wards and branches (branches are smaller wards).

**Stake Patriarch:** A man given the power to give a patriarchal blessing in order to "guide" the recipient in future decisions (essentially a fortune teller). Once a man is ordained as a patriarch, he's a patriarch for life.

**Stake President:** The leader of the Stake Presidency.

**Temple Interview:** An interview of worthiness where the bishop and the stake president determine whether or not a person is eligible to receive a temple recommend.

**Temple Sealer:** A man authorized to perform a temple sealing.

**Ward:** A congregation of members led by the bishop.

**Zone Leader:** A missionary appointed by the mission president to lead all of the missionaries in a specific area.

# PROLOGUE

*Hannah*

My phone pings again, probably my coworkers wondering when I'll be coming back to work. I wish I had an answer.

How much time are you supposed to take after your entire world gets flipped on its axis? How much of a grieving period is allowed when you're grieving the loss of someone who was supposed to be the love of your life?

How long am I allowed to grieve the seven babies I never even got to hold? People say it's easier because I never got to meet them.

They're wrong.

I still *felt* them. I still *loved* them. I carried them in my body. They were *part of me*. Even for a blip in time. Losing them was like losing parts of myself, and those are parts I will never get back.

I'm about to close my eyes and go back to the blissful void of sleep, where I don't have to think about my reality, when there's a soft knock on the door.

"Hannah, I have food for you. Your favorite! Chicken and dumplings," Mom's voice calls out, and I sigh, shoving the covers off and making it to the door in two steps.

I live in my childhood room again. Where the walls are no longer the bright teal of my youth but a pale sage green that's actually quite lovely. The full-size wrought iron bed is still the same, creaking when I move, especially now that I weigh more than I did as a teenager. My bookshelves are still here but empty since I haven't unpacked my belongings yet. It doesn't look like my childhood room at all, thank goodness.

It's still in my childhood home, though. Where my "concerned" mom keeps trying to "cheer me up" by doing things I don't actually like.

I don't like chicken and dumplings—that's *her* favorite. Dumplings always feel too mushy and taste like I'm chewing on raw dough. But she wouldn't know it isn't my favorite because she doesn't know *me*.

I open the door and take the tray from her, muttering a "thanks" then turning back to my bed. I don't bother to close the door. There's no point when she doesn't understand what personal space is.

"How long are you going to lock yourself up in this room, Hannah? You need to get out and go do something. It's the only way you'll feel better," Mom says, leaning against the door frame.

I wish she'd just leave me alone.

I shrug. "I have to go back to work sometime soon."

She sighs—so much disappointment in such a small sound—but nods her head then closes the door for me, leaving me alone.

I discard the untouched meal and turn on the TV for background noise to drown out my own thoughts. I should call my therapist again. I should get back to work and move on with my life.

I shouldn't let my soon-to-be ex-husband have so much control over my emotions.

But that can be future-me's problem. Current me will be laying in bed the rest of the day and wondering where it all went wrong.

# Chapter I

*Hannah*

I've been warned about strangers and the dangers they present since I was a child.

*Don't talk to strangers.*

*Especially strangers on the internet!*

*They'll kidnap you!*

*They'll steal your identity!*

*They'll sell you into a sex trafficking ring!*

No wonder I have anxiety.

Now, I'm an unwed—technically divorced—twenty-six-year-old, and people are encouraging me to get on dating apps or setting me up with their cousin's best friend's dog sitter.

Someone who's well-adjusted might think, "Twenty-six? That's so young to be divorced already!"

When you live in Utah and grow up Mormon, the norm is to get married straight out of high school—which I did—and pop out your first kid nine months from your wedding day—which I didn't, though not for a lack of trying.

Divorce isn't as common as one would think. People usually just stay in unhappy marriages and pretend everything is peachy keen, especially in Mormon culture.

My ex-husband was adamant we weren't meant to be, even though we were married for almost eight years, and I wanted to make the marriage work. In the end, he initiated the separation and sent the papers, and I didn't have any fight left in me.

That's how I ended up on yet *another* date with a "sweet boy who would be just perfect for you!" according to my mom's best friend.

*Twenty-seven-year-old Brody Smith. Dora's grandson's old mission companion, oldest child of six, served his mission in Peru, just graduated from Brigham Young University with his MBA.*

His "dating resume" plays on a constant loop in my head, as if it's different from any other BYU boy. They even tend to look the same.

Blue eyes, blonde hair perfectly gelled up in the front and tapered on the sides, and a clean-shaven face. He's wearing a short sleeve, blue button-up with khaki chinos and brown dress shoes, all of which are probably from Target or Zara. He's not... unattractive *per se*, but he's just... unoriginal. I don't feel anything towards him.

Well, that's not entirely true. I don't feel anything *positive* towards him.

He's been rambling for fifteen minutes about crypto currency. It started with me asking who he admires most, and his answer?

"Every smart person I admire in the world, and those I semi-fear, is focused on the concept of crypto."

I tuned him out after he started talking about beaver markets or bear markets or something. It's times like these I wish I could openly drink alcohol because I think it would make this conversation significantly less painful.

Why can't I drink alcohol openly at twenty-six? Well, it's against Mormon rules. My first experience with alcohol was six months ago when Liam handed me divorce papers as he walked out of our shared apartment, bags in hand. I went straight to the liquor store, bought a box of cheap wine, and drank half of it in one night.

The hangover after wasn't fun, but it numbed the pain of ending what I thought would be an eternal love, at least for the night.

My phone buzzes, and I glance down to see a text from an unknown number. My brow furrows as I read the message.



"Hannah, are you listening to me?"

I look up at Brody with a faux apologetic smile. "I'm so sorry, Brody. It was *so* riveting to listen to you talk about the bear market—"

"It's BULL market."

"Right, *bull* market. My brother just texted me to remind me it's my turn to let out our parents' dog," I lie with an exaggerated pout, grabbing my purse and standing from the table. Do my parents have a dog? No. But he doesn't know that.

"Oh. Okay. Well, call me sometime, and I can help set you up with your own crypto account. Maybe we can finish this date," he purrs as he stands and wraps his arms around my waist, pulling me into an awkward embrace.

I force a smile that probably looks more like a grimace. "Sure."

Apparently—and unfortunately—he takes it as his cue to kiss me goodbye. Somehow his lips are dry *and* greasy from the burger he practically inhaled. I suppress a gag as his tongue tries to weasel its way into my mouth in the middle of this restaurant.

My phone *pings* with another text, and I push him away gently.

*Saved by the bell.* "Bye, Brody."

"Bye, beautiful."

*Gross.* I roll my eyes as soon as I turn away from him and walk as fast as I can out of the restaurant and to my car.

Don't get me wrong, it's nice to be complimented, but I got the impression he'd try to dry hump me to orgasm—for him, not me—then ghost me because I don't fit the "vibe" of his future wife or some bullshit like that.

**Unknown:** I hope I didn't hurt your feelings. You're a super cool guy and smokin' hot, totally out of my league, but we just aren't compatible. We're at different places in our lives.

I smirk as I read the message. *Way to try to save this guy's ego, unknown texter.*

**Hannah**: I think you have the wrong number.

**Unknown:** This is Morgan. Is this not Blake?

**Hannah:** Nope. Sorry.

**Unknown:** Prove it.

**Hannah**: Excuse me?

**Unknown:** Send me a pic so I know you're not Blake playing games.

**Hannah**: Absolutely not. I'm not sending my picture to a random stranger.

**Unknown**: Then how do I know you're not Blake?

As a woman on the dating scene, this Morgan lady should understand why I'm not going to just send my picture to random strangers.

I get into my car, turn on my "bad date" playlist, and let Taylor Swift and Carrie Underwood soothe my soul with music about men who have done them wrong.

**Hannah**: My name is Hannah, I WAS just on a date but with a dude named Brody who talked for fifteen minutes about the importance of crypto currency then tried to stick his greasy tongue in my mouth. You don't have to believe me, but trust me, I'd rather be Blake.

**Unknown:** Alright, I believe you. I don't think anyone would make that up lol.

I huff out a laugh and place my phone in the cup holder as I make my escape.

When I pull up in front of the place I call home, I take a deep breath and plaster on a smile before I walk inside.

Unfortunately for me, I had to move back into my childhood home. I didn't want to have to live with four other girls in order to make rent. Living at home lets me save money and build up a nest egg for when I eventually do move out.

My mom, Shelly, is sitting in her usual spot on the couch watching a Hallmark movie and scrolling through her phone when I walk in.

I don't really look like her. Or my dad, for that matter. Mom has long, brown hair she streaks with blonde highlights, blue eyes, and a pointed nose she always seems to be looking down. My dad's bald, save for a thin ring of graying hair shaped like a "U" around his head, and has brown eyes. Sometimes I wonder if I was adopted because I don't have much in common with them, and I don't feel like we have a familial bond. It's like we're all business partners who meet for nightly business meetings they call "family dinner."

"Hannah." She looks at the time. "Oh, you're home early. Did the date not go well?"

"It went okay. I don't think we'll go out again." Better to keep it short and simple. I don't need her telling her friends *another* one of my dates didn't go anywhere.

Who am I kidding? She'll tell them anyway, even if I don't say a damn thing.

"Oh." She frowns. "That's a shame. Brody seems like such a nice boy. You know, your biological clock is ticking, Hannah."

My jaw tenses, like it always does when this conversation happens. "I know, Mom. It's not like I'm not trying.

I can't magically make the perfect man appear in front of me on one knee." *It's not my fault my body didn't want to cooperate and keep a child, either. Or did she forget the multiple miscarriages I had?*

"Well, maybe you need to be less picky. I mean, what was wrong with Brody? He comes from a good, faithful family. He served a mission, is temple worthy, has a degree and a good job."

I want to say: "He didn't ask me a single question about myself. He looked disgusted when I ordered a burger instead of a salad like he suggested and could only talk about crypto currency."

Instead, I say, "There was just no chemistry between us."

Mom sighs disappointedly. "Well, maybe if you focused a little more on taking better care of yourself there would be some chemistry."

*Alright, I'm not going there tonight.*

"Right. Okay, well, I'm going to go... somewhere else. Goodnight."

As I make it to the bottom of the stairs, she calls out, "You need to stop being so sensitive! I love you, and I'm worried about you!"

I pretend I don't hear her.

As soon as I'm in my room, I flop on the bed and scream into my pillow. Of course she thinks it's because of my body. It can't be any other reason other than I'm picky, I'm not trying, or I'm fat.

My mom acts like I wasn't married for eight years. Like I'm just *refusing* to get married even though my divorce was only finalized three months ago. Everyone expects me to just... move on from an eight-year relationship like it meant nothing to me.

I stand and look at myself in the full length mirror on my closet door. I felt pretty when I put on my favorite blush pink bodysuit underneath a black and white daisy print mid calf-length skirt. I thought the black wedges I paired the outfit with made my calves look good, but now the ugly thoughts are creeping in and showing me what everyone else sees.

A double chin.

Flabby arms.

Big boobs weighed down by gravity.

A pudgy stomach with an apron belly covered in stretch marks.

Thighs littered with cellulite that rub together and chafe when I walk.

Dirty blonde hair chopped to just below my chin—a post-divorce impulsive cut.

Hazel eyes.

I'm not the thin, perky, blue-eyed, blonde girl of everyone's dreams.

But if someone doesn't want me for me, then I don't want them.

# Chapter 2

*Morgan*

Another date, another fail. Why is it so hard to find someone to date?

Oh, I know. I live in Utah, the Mormon capital of the world.

Literally. Their headquarters are in Salt Lake.

Here, no one wants to be with a guy who already has a school-aged kid. They're all too focused on starting their own families, and they see my sweet Alyssa as baggage they don't want to carry.

Not to mention I'm not part of their little "book club," so that's another mark against me.

The gay and bi guys are apparently allergic to commitment, and the women seem averse to being a step-mom to a kid who can form her own thoughts. I think if Aly were a baby, it might be different, but I can't change her age.

I'm too old to play this fucking dating game.

Cocky as it sounds, I thought people would be jumping at the chance to date a former wide receiver for the

Denver Mustangs, but I guess when you aren't a Super Bowl champion, the NFL title kind of loses the allure, especially coupled with the single dad factor.

Blake was nice enough, but when I asked him if he wanted kids, he said, "I think kids are the worst. They're loud, they're gross, and they don't have boundaries. I'm too selfish to want to take care of someone else." Which is valid. If you don't want kids, you don't want kids. And it's okay to be selfish and not want to take care of a whole-ass human.

But I already have a kid, and I will not be giving her up for someone else. She and I are a package deal.

I finished the date because I'm not a total ass, but there's no way there'll be a second.

Bagel, my gray striped cat, ambles over and curls up on my lap. He always knows when I need some extra cuddles. I got him when Aly was barely a year old, thinking it would be great to have her grow up with a furry little buddy. He's very calm, and he's been the perfect companion for us.

Unlike his asshole little brother, Bean.

Bean was just a kitten when we found him behind the flower shop two years ago, and Alyssa refused to leave him there. He was so tiny, and his cries were so sad, I relented. We took him to a vet and got him started on his vaccines, and he and Bagel seemed to hit it off. He was calm for the first week, then he became a little black void of chaos. He likes Alyssa but hates me and everyone else.

I reflect on my date while I stroke Bagel's fur, my lips tipping up when I remember I wasn't the only one on a bad date.

At least my date didn't kiss me with a greasy hamburger mouth.

What a wild coincidence that I accidentally texted the wrong number and that number just so happens to belong to a girl who also went on a bad date.

Maybe it's a sign from the universe I should get to know Hannah. Or maybe I'm just lonely as fuck and want someone new to talk to.

Either way, I text her again.

> **Morgan:** I'm sorry your date didn't go well.

The three dots appear, disappear, and reappear a few times until she finally responds.

> **Hannah:** Thanks? Same goes to you, I guess.

> **Hannah:** But tbh, you could use some new excuses. He's out of your league? How original. *eyeroll emoji*

Okay, rude.
But she's right. It wasn't very original.

> **Morgan:** Ok, fine.

**Morgan**: It was totally unoriginal. BUT I wasn't lying. Blake is cool and hot and way out of my league.

**Hannah**: Then why didn't it work out?

God knows why I want to tell a complete stranger the failings of my love life.

Hannah seems… nosy. Straightforward. Sassy.

It's a refreshing change from people pitying me for being a single dad. But she doesn't know that about me yet.

**Morgan**: He lives his life based on astrology and I… don't? I guess that's the simple answer.

**Morgan:** For example, I asked him out, and he said we would have to wait for the full moon because it's the best time for starting romance.

**Hannah**: …Alright, that's a little odd.

**Hannah**: I can see how that would be off-putting if you're not into that

**Hannah**: It's like dating someone outside of your religion if you're super religious

**Morgan**: Exactly. We also just have different life goals and aspirations.

**Morgan**: Why didn't your date work out?

**Morgan:** Other than the greasy tongue thing

**Hannah:** Do you want my reason or what my mom thinks?

**Morgan:** Your reason, obviously. Who cares what your mom thinks?

**Hannah**: Everyone cares what my mom thinks.

**Hannah**: He didn't ask me a single thing about myself. He told me I should order a salad, not a burger, and then he talked about cryptocurrency the entire time.

**Morgan**: What an asshole.

**Morgan**: Why would he care about what you eat?

I watch as, once again, the three dots appear and disappear. After five minutes, I assume she's just going to stop talking to me. I don't know why that disappoints me so much.

**Hannah**: I don't know. Because I'm a woman?

**Morgan**: It's probably because he's got a small dick.

**Hannah**: OMG, you did not just say that!!!

**Hannah:** You're probably not wrong.

**Hannah**: But I wouldn't know, and I will never find out.

**Morgan:** Good. He probably can't find the clit anyway.

**Hannah:** Why do men struggle with that? It's not like it's difficult.

**Morgan:** Good question. I ask myself that all the time.

**Hannah:** It will go down in the history books as one of the many mysteries of the world.

**Hannah**: How did you end up texting the wrong number if you were already on a date with the guy?

**Morgan:** Blake and I were talking through Hinge, and he didn't want to exchange numbers until we met in person. I don't know why I texted you AGAIN, though. I guess I was hoping maybe we could be friends. I don't have many.

**Hannah:** That makes sense. I understand not having many friends too, unfortunately.

**Hannah**: What if I didn't respond?

**Morgan:** I would have left you alone. I don't try to force things that aren't supposed to happen.

**Hannah:** You mean… you let the UNIVERSE decide?

**Morgan**: uuuuuggggghhhh NO! Lol.

**Morgan**: But I can't MAKE you text back, so why would I keep bothering you?

**Hannah:** Fair point.

**Hannah:** I need to get to sleep, but you can text me again sometime, I guess. I could always use a new friend.

**Morgan:** Same. Thank you. Sweet dreams, friend. :)

**Hannah:** Back at ya :)

I check the time and realize it *is* getting kind of late. It's Saturday, and the shop's closed tomorrow, but Aly gets up early no matter what day it is, so I should call it a night.

I swipe through some potential matches on Hinge, but no one really stands out. There's been no... spark with anyone. I'm starting to wonder if I'm destined to be a single dad forever.

I go through the motions of getting ready for bed, check in on my baby girl who's not a baby anymore, and lay down in the massive king-sized bed that feels extra empty tonight.

I'm tired of being lonely.

I'm tired of not being able to share Alyssa's milestones and troubles, and I'm tired of not having someone to lay in bed with and debrief about our days.

I don't want random hookups and flings anymore.

I want a life partner.

# CHAPTER 3

*Hannah*

I hate Sundays.

I've hated them for as long as I can remember.

*But Sunday is for brunch and relaxing.*

Not when you grow up Mormon—*sorry*—a "Member of the Church of Jesus Christ of Latter-Day Saints."

In the few instances I've met someone who hasn't heard of the cult I grew up in, I consider them extremely lucky. Lucky they didn't have to sit on scratchy, uncomfortable benches and listen to the same lessons and speeches and stories about someone losing their keys and an almighty being taking the time to help them find them because they "prayed." *Invest in one of those tracking tiles for yours and God's sake.*

They're lucky because when they turned eight, they didn't have to put on a white jumpsuit and be dunked under water in front of their whole family and then be told that if you sin, you're going to hell.

Lucky because when they turned twelve, they didn't have to sit in a class for two hours—an hour now—every Sunday and be told their body was going to be what leads young men to sin.

Lucky that at eighteen, they weren't forced into a new group of young single adults whose sole purpose is to get married and "multiply and replenish the earth."

I stopped believing in this sham of a religion about two years ago in the midst of my fifth miscarriage, after my best friend told me the true history, and I started learning about the fallacies in the doctrine. I haven't stopped coming to church because I don't know how to do that without causing a scene, especially now that I'm living with my parents again.

I haven't talked to anyone other than my cousin Emma and my best friend, Sage, about it.

Emma moved to California with her best friend's family a couple years after graduating high school. She's living her best ex-mo life.

Even our cousin Elli left the church and is traveling the country with her boyfriend on his music tour.

I want to be free like them. Emma told me I could come live with her and her bestie if I wanted to, but I don't want to step on anyone's toes. I think the familiarity of church helped during the divorce, but now it's more of a pain in the ass than it is helpful. I *dread* going.

"Sister Layton, will you read the next scriptures for us please?"

*Shit.*

I really need to stop letting my thoughts wander when I should be paying attention. Where were we?

My only church friend, Lucy, discreetly points to where the last person left off, and I mouth a "thank you" to her.

"Of course, Sister Mayfield." I clear my throat and read *Doctrine and Covenants* chapter eighteen, verses fifteen and sixteen.

"Thank you, Sister Layton. Any thoughts you'd like to add along with that?"

I politely shake my head, and she moves on with the lesson.

Lucy leans over to me. "You okay? You looked like you were in a completely different world."

*I fucking wish.*

"I'm okay, thank you. Just tired." I check the time on my phone and realize I still have thirty minutes before I can get out of here and internally groan.

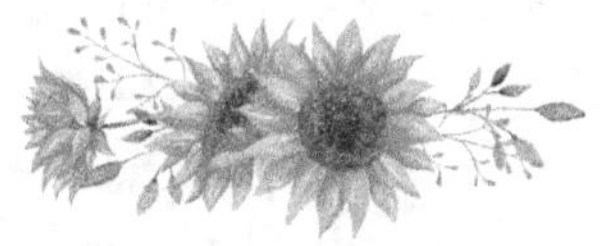

As soon as "amen" is murmured at the end of the closing prayer, I book it out of the Relief Society room so I can make a quick exit.

Squeezing through the crowded halls makes my escape take longer than I want, which means the second counselor in the bishopric, Brother Bragg, is able to grab my attention and call me into a meeting.

I hate these meetings. It's like a job interview, but instead of them asking you questions, they're telling you "God called you to this position" and questioning your worthiness.

The offices smell like old men and look exactly the same. White walls, carpet halfway up the walls, big oak desk and a brown office chair. Pictures of Jesus and the nearest temple and a filing cabinet behind the desk.

"Sister Layton. How've you been?" Brother Bragg asks, leaning back in his oversized office chair.

He looks like a villain, to be honest. Like most of the other members of the bishopric, he's a portly white man with a bald head and clean-shaven face. His nose is sharp, and his brown eyes lack any real warmth, though he puts on a good show. He's wearing a crisp, black suit with the standard white collared shirt underneath and a blue checked tie.

"I've been good. How about you? How is Sister Bragg?" I reply, hoping I can distract him so I won't have to answer any more personal questions.

"She's good. Kyle is getting married next weekend to a nice girl from Logan, so that'll be good. Hopefully we'll have a grandchild next year!"

I force a smile. "That would be great for you."

"Yes, very." His face changes from polite casualness to serious. "Now, Hannah, I noticed we haven't had you in for a temple interview yet, and your recommend expired a few months ago. The bishopric wanted to reach out and make sure everything was going okay, that you weren't straying off the path or needing some extra guidance."

*Damn it.*

I was hoping they didn't actually keep track of stuff like that. That I could slip under the radar and eventually just slip away without consequences.

I can't answer the temple questions honestly without raising questions and being put on their "watch" list. Not that I want to go to the temple anyway. That place is creepy as hell, and I've never felt any semblance of peace there.

"I've been very busy with work, and it must have slipped my mind," I say, hoping he drops it.

"Well, we can do it right now if you have the time? Then we just need to get in contact with the stake president to schedule a meeting after."

I would rather kiss burger lips again than do this stupid interview. Luckily for me, I have an excellent reason why I can't.

"I would love to, but we're having a family dinner tonight, and I have to get home to make the jello salad."

Brother Bragg nods like he's trying to decide if he can force me to stay. Finally, he sighs and says, "Family is the most important thing. But you make sure you schedule an appointment to get your recommend renewed. It's the only place you can go to be close to God."

I should get an award for not rolling my eyes. I smile politely and nod, then he lets me leave with a firm handshake.

I wasn't lying about family dinner. I was only half lying about the jello salad; we made it this morning. Everyone is coming to watch my brother, Jake, open his mission call.

When I pull up to the house, I already see Uncle Kent and Aunt Louise's van parked in the driveway, which means Elli's parents are going to interrogate me about their daughter's life.

Elli and her parents had a falling out because she left the church and started dating Wes, a tattooed, pierced, long-haired musician. They blame her for Izzy, her little sister, also wanting to leave the church.

Now, Izzy's the only person in their family who talks to Elli, so they resort to asking me sly questions to see if I'll give them more information than Izzy does.

I won't. My loyalty lies with my cousin, not with her mom.

I open the door to pure chaos.

"Oh, Hannah! Good. You're late, but you're here. I need you to get the tablecloth from the closet. The green one with the embroidered flowers. It needs to go on the table. Oh! We need to put the leaf in the table so it will be big enough. Then, you can fill water pitchers and wash the fruit," my mom chitters, flitting from the stove to the sink.

I hate it when she does this. She stresses herself out when she hosts. Then, *I* get a task list a mile long just because I live here. I spent the day cleaning the house yesterday before my date, and now I'm doing the last minute prepwork while my dad and brother sit around.

"Got it, Mom. Sorry I'm late, Brother Bragg wanted to meet with me for a minute. Hi, Aunt Louise, Uncle Kent." I wave to my aunt and uncle, who are helping in the kitchen and sitting on the couch with my dad, respectively.

My mom stops in her tracks and turns to me. "Why did he want to meet with you?"

I shrug. "Just checking in."

She eyes me skeptically but drops it quickly and goes back to running around. I make my way down the hall and into the linen closet to grab the tablecloth, and when I come back, Uncle Kent and my dad, Mitch, are putting the leaf in the table. I lay the tablecloth on it and make sure it's even on all sides.

I walk to the pantry to grab the pitchers for the water when Izzy comes and grabs them from me. "Hey, Han. Let me fill these, you can wash the fruit."

"Thanks, Izzy. You're the best." I give her arm a gentle squeeze.

The place fills with more aunts, uncles, and cousins in the next hour, and our house barely fits the mass of bodies. Heaven forbid someone opens a mission call in private.

My mom has eight siblings, and if they're all able to attend family gatherings, they do so along with their plethora of kids. My mom, Aunt Pam, and Aunt Alice are the only ones with two kids, everyone else has at least five. Alice doesn't really hang around the family anymore because she left the church a long time ago. I miss her, but I get it.

Today, only two of my mom's siblings are here; the rest of them will likely be at the farewell. Aunt Pam, her husband, John, and their son, Nathan, and Uncle Kent and his family. Pam and my mom are super close. Pam's like a second mom to me. At least, she was until she started distancing herself from not only me, but the whole family for some reason. It probably has to do with the sect of Mormonism she and John joined. While the whole religion is made up, there are different variations people sometimes branch off to, usually led by another white man who claims to have been chosen by God.

The most well-known sect is The Fundamentalist Church of Jesus Christ of Latter-Day Saints, or FLDS, which is a group that still practices polygamy and has had documentaries made about them. The group Pam and John joined is called the Remnant Movement. I don't know what exactly they believe because I haven't done my research.

My dad has three sisters who live close by—Anna, Sheila, and Lisa—so they're here, too, along with my grandparents on both sides.

I sit next to Izzy while we eat, trying to avoid my grandpa's questions about my divorce. We chat about my work, her boyfriend, Luke, and her plans after graduation in a little less than two months.

"Luke and I both got into Utah Tech, Utah Valley, and The University of Texas at Austin and San Antonio. It's just a matter of where we want to live. The plus side of me going to UVU is in-state tuition and being able to live at home, but I don't know if I want to do that with everything that's happened. If I move to Texas, I could probably live with Elli and commute, which isn't ideal. But it might be worth it to get away from here."

"If Wes is on the road, Elli might need someone to stay at her apartment anyway, so that might work out. It's cool you guys will be going somewhere together, though," I say, feeling a bit jealous of her.

I wish I could move away from here and start over.

Before Izzy can respond, my dad announces Jake is going to be opening his mission call now, and the chatter in the room stops.

I pull my phone out of my dress pocket to record and notice an unread text.

**Morgan:** Happy Sunday, Hannah. I hope it's relaxing and fun!

I can't help the smile on my face, it's nice to have a friend even if I have no idea who she is.

**Hannah:** Happy Sunday to you, too. Relaxing? Not so much. Fun? Eeeehhhh. It's alright. How is your Sunday going?

**Morgan:** Do you have work or something? It's been very relaxing. I've been reading and lounging around with my cat.

**Hannah:** No work, just unpleasant activities. That sounds lovely. What book are you reading? What's your cat's name?

**Morgan:** That's no fun! I'm reading Pride and Prejudice. His name is Bagel.

Morgan sends me a picture of a well worn copy of the book sitting against a gray striped cat curled into a ball.

> **Hannah:** Awwww, cute kitty! That's a good book! And it looks well-loved. Have you read it before?

> **Morgan**: Bagel is the sweetest, unlike his asshole brother. It's my go-to when I want an easy read. Helps calm me down, you know?

> **Morgan:** And besides, who doesn't want to swoon over Mr. Darcy? Book boyfriends never disappoint.

I hold in my laugh because Jake is reading his mission call, and people are recording. I tune back in just in time to hear him say "...called to serve in the Cape Verde Praia Mission, Portuguese speaking."

The whole room erupts into cheers and sounds of wonder.

I have very strong—negative—opinions on missions, so I don't cheer or "ooo" and "ahh" for my brother. I give him a thumbs up and a forced smile when he looks at me.

**Hannah:** Amen to that. I'd take a book boyfriend over a real one any day. Why is his brother an asshole?

**Morgan**: Bean hates me. And despises anything on the counter. Or the shelves. Or the coffee table.

**Hannah**: Maybe he's just misunderstood?

**Morgan:** No, he's not misunderstood. He's just an asshole. I rescued him from an alley, and he repays me by biting my nipple if I'm shirtless.

**Hannah:** LOL stop.

The chuckle slips out this time, and Izzy nudges my arm. "Who's got you laughing?"

"Oh, just someone telling me about their cats." I shrug, putting my phone in the pocket of my dress.

"A boooy?" Izzy waggles her eyebrows, always the chaos stirrer.

"Ew, no. A girl. She texted the wrong number, and we kind of hit it off as friends."

"Hmmm. Interesting how things work out." Izzy shrugs, then goes back to texting.

I'm about to do the same, but her mom comes to sit by me instead.

"Hannah." Louise gives me a curt nod. I swear her face is always in a permanent frown.

"Aunt Louise. How is Spencer doing?" I ask, knowing the topic of her son on his mission is safe territory.

"Oh, just wonderful," she gushes, her lips tipping in a rare smile, happy to talk about her favorite child. "He's a zone leader now and has baptized ten people in the last two months! We couldn't be more proud of him and the work he's doing. How firm he is in the gospel." Her eyes dart to Izzy disapprovingly. "Have you heard from Elliana recently?"

I internally groan. I knew this would happen, yet I'm still surprised.

I plaster on my best smile. "We chat occasionally. Wes's stop in Salt Lake is next month, so it'll be good to see them."

Her nose wrinkles like Wes's name smells bad. "She never mentioned stopping in Salt Lake."

"You haven't talked to her since Spencer left so how would you know?" Izzy murmurs, still looking at her phone.

Aunt Louise's face turns a shade of red, but instead of responding to Izzy, she excuses herself and walks away.

"She really hasn't spoken to Elli in almost nine months?" I whisper to Izzy once her mom's out of earshot.

Izzy looks at me and shakes her head sadly. "Every time I bring Elli up, or try to get my mom to talk to her, she shuts me down or pretends she doesn't hear me. It's like Elli doesn't exist. She's too stubborn and hard-headed to apologize, and Elli's set a clear boundary."

"That sucks, Izzy. I'm sorry."

"It is what it is. I—"

"Isabelle. Time to go," Louise barks, interrupting Izzy.

Izzy's posture stiffens, and the light playfulness that usually surrounds her dims.

"See you later, Han," Izzy says, leaning in for a hug.

I squeeze her tight and whisper in her ear, "Text me if you need anything, okay?"

Izzy nods once before she leaves, and my heart breaks a little bit for her. I wish I could do something to help her, but I wouldn't know how. I only hope she can escape before the light in her dims completely.

The rest of the party goes on as it usually does with people congratulating Jake and saying how proud they are of him.

I'm proud of him, too, but not because he's going to be playing white savior to the people of Cape Verde. I'm proud of how hard he's worked in school and how kind he is to everyone.

Mormon missions are nothing but a waste of time and money for those who go.

My Grandpa Walter, the patriarch of the Monson family, hobbles over to me and wraps me in a hug that's surprisingly strong for such a frail, old man. He always smells like pine and cedar—the nostalgic smells of working in his workshop.

"How are you holding up, my dear?" His voice always has a bit of a melodic lilt to it, like at any minute, he's about to burst into song—which wouldn't be surprising in the least.

I plaster on my best fake smile and look at him as best I can seeing as he hasn't released me from his vice grip. "I'm hanging in there. Thanks, Grandpa."

He hums, then steps back to put a hand on my shoulder and look me in the eyes. Sometimes, I swear he can see straight through to my soul. He's what people call a "spiritual giant." He and my grandma, Eileen, have been mission presidents twice. He's currently a stake patriarch—a Mormon version of a fortune teller—and a temple sealer. He's known for his words of wisdom, musical talents, and storytelling abilities.

"Liam was but a bump in the road to an extraordinary love, my dear Hannah. You'll find someone whose dreams and values match your own, just as long as you remain true to who you are and never falter. Live for truth, and the right man will see the way you shine." He ends his speech with a solemn nod.

"Thanks, Grandpa," I whisper, tears brimming my eyes for many reasons. I know he means what he says, but he doesn't know my truths don't align with his own anymore. He wouldn't tell me to live for truth if he knew I didn't live, breathe, eat, sleep, and shit the gospel anymore. If he knew my thoughts about Joseph Smith being a pedophile con artist who made his money by telling elaborate stories. If he ever finds out, he'll be extremely disappointed. It's a big reason why I haven't publicly left, why I keep up the ruse.

"I love you, Hannah. Don't hesitate to come visit. The garden will need tending soon, and I know how much you love weeding." He gives me a playful nudge that evokes a genuine laugh.

I do love his garden. It's gotten significantly smaller in recent years because he can't keep up with it. When I was with Liam, we lived on the other side of town from my grandparents, and I'd spend my random days off helping in the garden and doing yard work when I could.

"I love you, too. Don't hurt yourself trying to do it alone. You call if you need help."

He scoffs. "I'm spry as a spring chicken. I still have many years left in me."

I don't believe him. His knees are both terrible, though he never uses his cane, but I don't say that or point it out.

They're the last to leave, and I help my mom clean up the remaining food, trash, and put the extra chairs and table leaf away. Then, I make my way down to my room to recharge my social battery before I work tomorrow.

I didn't respond to Morgan's last text—I wasn't looking for a lecture from my mom about being glued to my phone—so I'm surprised to see another text from her.

**Morgan:** What do you do for work?

**Morgan:** Also, sorry if I'm bothering you. I could use some friends, and you seem to be pretty chill, but please tell me to fuck off if you need me to lol.

**Hannah:** You're not bothering me :) I could use a friend, too. Sorry I didn't respond, I was at a family gathering lol.

**Hannah:** I'm a librarian. What about you?

**Morgan:** That's cool! I own a flower shop.

**Hannah:** Really? That's fun! What's your shop name? How did you get into that?

**Morgan:** Fowler's Flowers. Original, I know. I've always thought plants were cool, and I worked at a flower shop in high school. I like the language of flowers and wanted to be part of that.

**Hannah:** That's very cute lol. The language of flowers?

**Morgan:** Thank you! Oh, yeah. Like red camellias are for romance, pink ones mean the person is longing for the other, and white means that person thinks you're adorable.

**Hannah:** Wow. Who knew flowers could mean something other than "sorry I forgot our anniversary two days ago?"

**Morgan:** Has that… happened a lot?

**Hannah:** My ex only bought me flowers when he thought he messed up. And he always got me red roses because he thought they were my favorite.

**Morgan:** At least he chose one that means love, I guess. If those aren't your favorite, then what are?

**Hannah:** Sunflowers and daffodils.

**Morgan:** Ah, excellent choices. Sunflowers represent a long life and lasting happiness, and daffodils represent rebirth and new beginnings.

**Hannah:** Hm. Maybe if he'd gotten me sunflowers our relationship would have been happy, rather than depressing as fuck.

**Morgan:** lol maybe. I hope the next person you date brings you flowers you actually like.

**Hannah:** Thank you.

> **Morgan:** It's been good talking with you, Hannah. I've got an early morning tomorrow, so I'm going to go to sleep. Sweet dreams

I glance over at the clock and realize it's almost ten. I'm usually asleep by now because I have the early shift at the library on Mondays.

> **Hannah:** Thank you. You, too!

After I send the text, I put my phone on "do not disturb" and settle under the covers. I hope this friendship doesn't fizzle out.

# CHAPTER 4

*Morgan*

It's been almost two weeks since I accidentally texted Hannah, and to be honest, I think I'm crushing a little on the stranger. I have no idea what she looks like, but—at least through text—she's funny, witty, smart, and kind.

We text pretty much every day, just checking in, and sending each other random pictures. She sends me pictures of interesting books she finds in the library, and I send her pictures of the arrangements I make.

It's nice.

But I want to meet her in person.

I'm working up the courage to ask her to hang out, but I haven't figured out a way to bring it up organically.

The bell above the shop's door rings, and I walk around the back counter to greet the customer. I stop in my tracks when my eyes land on one of the prettiest women I've ever seen.

She's probably about five-foot-seven, dirty blonde hair cut in a bob just above her shoulders, and is curvy as all get-out. The black jumpsuit she's wearing hugs her in all the right places, showcasing her wide hips perfect for grabbing and thighs that would feel so fucking good wrapped around my head.

I take a deep breath to calm myself because I shouldn't be having sex fantasies about a customer, let alone one I haven't even spoken to.

But then she turns her hazel eyes framed with round gold wire glasses on me and gives me a soft smile with luscious lips covered in a glossy pink hue, and my breath stutters.

I clear my throat and put on a smile to hopefully cover the fact I was totally ogling her. "Hey there, welcome in. Is there something specific you're looking for today?"

"Hi. I'm actually looking for..." She shakes her head. "Never mind, sorry. I'm just here to pick up an order for Mitch."

"Ah, yes, I just finished wrapping it. Follow me, and I'll get you checked out." I walk back to the counter, and the blonde goddess follows me, her eyes taking in the premade bouquets, the various potted plants for sale, and the wall of buckets housing individual flowers for a "do-it-yourself" bouquet experience.

"Everything in here is so lovely," she says as I round the counter and grab the bouquet of roses from the fridge.

She eyes the jewelry on the counter, her gaze snagging on the peach moonstone crystal butterfly necklace. She reverently traces a finger over the pink crystal and gold chain before placing her hands back at her sides and perusing the rest of the jewelry.

"Thank you, my sister's my silent business partner, and she likes to make sure it looks 'aesthetically pleasing.'

I'm not complaining though, I'd rather focus on the flowers. She's also the one who makes the jewelry."

"It's all gorgeous."

"Yeah, she's pretty talented. Mitch paid online when he ordered, so I'll just need a signature here." I turn the iPad around, and she uses her pointer finger to scribble a signature.

"Perfect," I say, handing over the bouquet and wishing this interaction wasn't so quick. It feels unprofessional to ask for her number or make a move, so I don't. I'll just have to hope she comes back sometime. "You're all set. Is there anything else I can help you with?"

She pulls her bottom lip between her teeth, glancing around the store again, looking like she's going to ask a question, but she stops and shakes her head again. "No, I think that's everything. Thank you so much for your help."

"Anytime. I hope to see you again soon." I try to add a little flirtation to my smile, but I'm not sure it comes across that way.

"I'm sure I'll be back. Have a wonderful day." She smiles at me, then turns and walks to the door.

"You too!" I try—and fail—not to watch her walk away. When the bell dings, signaling her departure, I turn back to the iPad to see if I can put a name to the face. The only legible part is the "H" at the beginning of her signature. The rest is all scribbly.

The "H" reminds me of Hannah. The girl I'm crushing on who I've never met. How ironic I have a crush on a girl I've only talked to through text with no idea what she looks like and another crush on a girl I only had a two minute interaction with but no clue what her name is.

I'm a hopeless romantic at heart. I fall fast and hard and then get my heart broken. It's been a pattern since I was in junior high, and apparently I haven't grown out of it.

It's why it was so hard to be in the NFL. When I was playing football, people wanted to be with me for status and benefits, not because of *me*. I also didn't have a lot of time for deep connections because of the practice schedule, but I tried my best.

It's why it's hard now as a thirty-six year old man to just jump into a relationship without vetting people thoroughly. It's not just my heart that could get broken if I attach myself to someone. If I introduce someone to Alyssa, and then they disappear, it would break her heart, too.

The bell above the door rings again, and I take a deep breath and plaster on my customer service smile.

No time for life complications when there are people who need flowers.

"But I promise to clean the litter box for a week! Come on, Dad. Every other girl in the class will be there," Aly whines, twirling her spaghetti around her fork.

"Bub, you're supposed to do that anyway. That's your contribution. You know the rules. I'm more than happy to let you go to the party and have a late night but no sleepovers."

"Ugh! You're the worst!" She stands from the table, storms out of the kitchen, and up to her room, slamming the door and rattling the wall.

Bean meows in solidarity with his favorite person before following her. I hear him scratch at the door, Aly opens it for him then shuts it again.

This isn't the first time we've had this conversation, and I know it won't be the last, but it gets more and more exhausting every single time.

I try not to scare her, but I want her to be informed about the dangers of the world, and the reality is sleepovers aren't safe. Too many children have been sexually abused at the hands of "kind" parents or siblings, and I won't risk my daughter's safety.

I gather our plates, cover her half eaten spaghetti, put it in the fridge, load the dishwasher, and then walk over to her door.

I knock gently then call out, "Aly? Can we talk for a minute?"

"No. I'm not ready to talk to you," she calls back.

"Okay. You know where to find me when you are. I love you."

She doesn't say it back, but that's okay. I've taught her she doesn't have to say it back, and she doesn't have to talk to me if she doesn't want to. It sucks because I just want to fix it, but I also want her to be able to have her space if she needs it.

I walk downstairs, plopping myself on the couch, and Bagel follows me, settling on my lap as soon as I sit down. I lay my head back and go through the highs and lows of the day.

The high for today was creating a bouquet for a high school kid who was taking flowers to his very first girlfriend. He was so nervous but so sweet.

The low was hurting Aly's feelings. I always hate fighting with her; it breaks my heart.

Another low was not getting the name of that gorgeous woman at the shop.

*My butterfly.*

That's what I've been calling her in my head. Beautiful, graceful, and flying away before I could catch her.

Thinking about her makes me think of Hannah, so I pull my phone from my pocket and open our text thread. We haven't talked much today, so I type out a quick message.

**Morgan:** Happy Friday! Quick question. Would it be unprofessional to get someone's number at work?

**Hannah:** Happy Friday to you, too. I don't think so, as long as you're not creepy about it.

**Morgan:** Damn. The most stunning girl came in today, and I didn't even get her name.

**Hannah:** A girl? Huh. That's a bummer. Maybe she'll come in again, and you can get it next time?

My brow furrows. Why would me being interested in a girl confuse Hann—OH! Right. When I originally texted her, it was about Blake.

**Morgan:** Ah, I'm bi. I like men and women, no need to be confused lol. I hope she comes in again, but it's all good if not.

**Morgan:** What have you been up to today?

**Hannah:** Oooooooh. Okay. That makes sense.

**Hannah:** It's my mom's birthday, so we went to lunch, and then she and my dad left town for a week-long getaway, so I took them to the airport.

**Morgan:** Party at your place, then? ;)

**Hannah:** LOL right. I work tomorrow, but Sunday will be a nice break. I don't have to go to church to keep up the image with my parents, and I'm not sure what I want to do with myself.

**Morgan:** Are you part of the Mormon book club? Why would you need to keep the image that you're going to church?

**Hannah:** Unfortunately, I am part of it. I don't want to be even more of a disappointment to my parents. I'm already divorced at 26, I don't want to disappoint them by leaving the church, too.

**Morgan:** That seems like a heavy expectation to carry.

**Morgan:** What would your ideal Sunday be, if you didn't have to go to church?

**Hannah:** Hmm… I really want to try this place in Salt Lake that is supposed to have the best brunch. But they only have it on Sundays.

**Morgan:** Are you talking about Silver Spoon?

**Hannah:** Yes! I've also heard it's hard to get into. And it'd be kind of awkward to go by myself, you know? I don't know who would come with me.

My good friend, Charlie, works at Silver Spoon, so I know I could get a last minute reservation for this Sunday.

Would Hannah even want to go with me? It's a fifty-fifty shot. I've been dying to meet her in person, and this is the perfect way to bring it up.

**Morgan:** You can totally say no, but…

**Morgan:** I can get a reservation for this Sunday at Silver Spoon, if you'd be interested in going.

**Morgan:** With me, I mean. Go to brunch with me?

**Hannah:** Are you being serious?

**Morgan:** Deadly. I'd love to get to know you in person. I wasn't sure how to bring it up without being weird, and I think this is as good a time as any.

I watch the text bubble pop up and go away multiple times before she finally responds, and I swear to God my heart almost stops when she says,

> **Hannah:** That sounds great. I would love to go to brunch with you! Just text me the time, and I'll be there.

> **Morgan:** Hell yes! I'm very excited to meet you in person.

I fist pump the air, proud of myself for taking the leap and so damn excited to meet her.

"Dad, why are you hitting the air?" Alyssa startles me, making me jump a little, which makes Bagel jump to the back of the couch.

"I'm just excited about meeting a friend. Are you ready to talk now?" I pocket my phone, making sure I can give my number one girl my undivided attention.

She nods and sits next to me on the couch. She takes a deep breath before she calmly tells me she's upset she's not able to go to the sleepover. She feels like the odd one out in school because she can never sleep over at her friends' houses. She understands the concern for safety, but she doesn't like feeling like an outsider.

Her beautiful blue eyes gloss over with tears, and my heart cracks like it does every time she cries. "I feel like a weirdo at school because it seems like everyone in my class has these big, happy families with a mom and a dad and siblings. I love you, Dad, but sometimes I wish I had a mom or sister I could talk to about things."

"I'm sure your mom would be willing to talk to you about whatever you want, Bub," I try to placate.

Aly shakes her head. "I've tried calling her three times this week and sent her a bunch of texts, and she doesn't respond. She sent a text that said, 'Busy! Talk soon,' and that was it."

My heart breaks for my sweet girl. My anger towards her mother is usually kept at bay, but right now I'm seeing red.

Whitney has made it clear she has no desire to be a full-time mom, but I never thought she'd brush off her own daughter like that. It makes my blood boil that she doesn't seem to give a fuck about her daughter.

Aly is going to hit puberty soon, and while I've educated myself and have sisters and a mom who are more than happy to help with that stuff, it still doesn't replace Whitney. If Whitney weren't in the picture at all, I think it would be easier, but instead, she's flitted in and out of Aly's life for years.

The first year of my baby girl's life, Whitney and I tried to make it work. But we quickly found a romantic relationship between us was not compatible. We tried to live together and co-parent, but I was still playing football at the time, and my schedule wouldn't allow me to be home to help her. My mom helped where she could, but it was still really hard on Whitney.

When Aly was three, Whitney decided she didn't want to be a full-time mom and only wanted her every other weekend. That was the year I tore my meniscus and had to retire. I was thirty and planning on retiring after the season anyway. I tore it during a preseason game, so I didn't even get to play my last season. That was fine with me because it meant I could be with Aly more. My parents followed us from Colorado to Utah so I could raise Aly with my family. Whitney's family also lives in Utah, which is one of the biggest reasons we decided to move here. My sisters were already living here, and Whitney and I both wanted Aly to grow up surrounded by family.

Whitney's family was so disappointed in her for having a baby out of wedlock they refused to even meet their granddaughter. Aly doesn't know who her maternal grandparents are, and I doubt she ever will.

When Aly turned five, Whitney stopped taking her every other weekend and started taking her twice a year for a week. That only lasted until she was six. Now, Aly's lucky if she sees her once a year for a couple of hours. Whitney refuses to answer my calls or texts, but I didn't think she'd go so far as to ignore her own daughter.

"I'm so sorry, Bubs. It's not cool for your mom to ignore you. You know you can always talk to your aunts or grandma about things you don't want to talk to me about."

She sniffs. "I know. I'm sorry I was angry at dinner and called you the worst. You're not the worst." She burrows into my side, wrapping her little arms around me and laying her head by my heart.

"It's okay to be angry, honey. It's okay to be mad and sad and any other emotion you may have. I'll always be here when you've calmed down and are ready to talk." I kiss the top of her head.

"I love you, Dad."

"I love you, too, Bubs."

# Chapter 5

## Hannah

Usually, I dread Sundays. I hate the thought of having to put on a mask and sit through two hours of droning meetings that repeat the same things over and over again.

When I was married, it wasn't so terrible to go to church because we were assigned the nursery-aged kids—eighteen months to three years old—and I spent most of my time just hanging out with them.

When I moved back home, and my mom insisted I go back to the single young adults ward, I started to hate going to church again. I hate feeling like an old lady, even though I'm only twenty-six. The ward I'm in is filled with fresh-faced eighteen-year-olds who have just graduated high school, or twenty-one-year-olds who just got back from their missions and are looking for their eternal companion. There are a few older people, but most of them are also women. The men who are over the age of twenty-five are looking for a fresh-faced eighteen-year-old. No one wants to date the newly divorced, fat girl.

That's fine with me, though. I don't think I want to get married again, at least not anytime soon.

After seeing Elli's parents practically disown her, I'm even more scared to skip church on Sundays because I have nowhere to go if my parents kick me out without imposing on someone else.

I'd like to think that wouldn't happen, but I don't know at this point.

Today, I'm not dreading Sunday. I'm excited to hang out with a new friend and eat some delicious food.

I tried to meet her in person on Friday when I went to pick up Mom's flowers from Dad, but the only person at the shop was the attractive giant who looked out of place amongst the delicate flowers.

When Dad asked me to pick up the bouquet he ordered, I was reluctant. First of all, why get flowers if they're just leaving for vacation? Second, I just finished my afternoon shift at the library and was looking forward to coming home.

But when he sent me the name of the shop, I recognized it instantly. I thought it would be the perfect time to meet Morgan in person without having to plan a meetup.

I was disappointed she wasn't there, but I didn't have the nerve to ask the disgustingly attractive man where she was. Maybe Morgan is the sister he mentioned?

Either way, I couldn't get out of there fast enough. I haven't been interested in anyone since Liam, but even I can admit the guy at the counter was hot. The way he was looking at me made me nervous. Not in a creepy way but in an appreciative way that made my cheeks flame. I was grateful I put on my favorite jumpsuit so I at least felt confident in myself.

I was relieved when Morgan mentioned getting brunch today so I didn't have to think of a plan to meet in person. I'm nervous, sure, but I'm more excited to get to know a new friend. We seem to have a lot in common, and I'm excited to see if this friendship works outside of the digital world.

I stare at my closet, willing an outfit to fly out and put itself on my body instead of having to pick it out myself.

Unfortunately, I possess no magic, so that doesn't work.

What does one wear to brunch to meet a new friend?

The Silver Spoon isn't *fancy*, but it's not like an IHOP. I also want to make sure I feel confident because if I feel uncomfortable, I'm not going to be great company.

I eye the outfit I wore on my date with Brody. The one I was wearing when Morgan first texted me. It feels like a full-circle moment if I wear the outfit I was wearing when this all started, so I slip on the buttery soft, blush pink bodysuit and the black floral skirt. Pulling out my black wedges, I slip them on, then go to my jewelry box and put on my usual jewelry. I hop over to the bathroom and add a thin layer of light pink lip stain to my lips and double-check that there are no mascara smudges under my eyes.

I bounce up the stairs and make sure the front door is locked before I hop in my car and plug the address into my navigation system. I may have lived in Utah my whole life, but Downtown Salt Lake isn't a place I have memorized, nor is it my favorite place to drive.

A thirty-minute drive later, I park in a parking lot down the street from the restaurant, and make the one-block trek to the entrance. It's the third week of April, which means it's about sixty degrees today, but it could change tomorrow. We've been known to get snow in June sometimes.

The Silver Spoon is on a street of historical houses turned into businesses. It's nestled in between a quaint little crystal shop, and a nail/hair/eyelash salon combo. The Colonial-Georgian style house is navy blue on the outside, with four sets of windows painted white. There's a balcony under the upper right corner window that holds brightly colored flowers. The name of the restaurant is painted in swooping cursive letters on a sign that hangs from the balcony.

When I walk in, the hostess stand is right at the entrance in front of a partition blocking off the main dining room.

The inside is painted a light blue with gold accents, and there's floral wallpaper in the little waiting area.

"Welcome to the Silver Spoon. Do you have a reservation?" the pink-haired hostess asks me with a bright smile. Her name tag says her name is Greta.

"I think the reservation is under Morgan Fowler?" I should have double-checked. I should have checked to see if she's here, too. Now I feel kind of silly.

"Oh! Perfect. Morgan's already here. Let me take you over," Greta says, leading the way around the partition.

The dining room has dark hardwood floors, bright floral wallpaper, and mismatched multi-colored tables, giving it an eclectic feel. Some of the chairs are velvet, others are colorfully painted wood, and the tables are all different shapes. Pretty much every table is full of patrons enjoying various brunch foods, and my mouth waters as I see the options I'll get to choose from.

Greta leads me to a table in the back corner, where the man from the flower shop is sitting. I jolt, wondering if this is some weird setup from Morgan. Or maybe Morgan's just in the bathroom and forgot to tell me her brother was coming?

Either way, I'm flustered and confused, and I'm sure my face is as red as an apple.

His skin is a caramel beige, like he spends a lot of time in the sun, but it also looks like it could be his natural skin shade.

He's *buff*. His blue button-up shirt is stretched tight across his broad shoulders and snug against his bulging biceps. They don't look like the muscles I see on gym bros in pictures, but you can tell he works out.

Flower Guy looks confused but also a little pleased, as he stands—good Lord, he's tall—and pulls out my chair. Greta leaves us with menus and a chipper, "Enjoy your meal!"

I sit, he sits, neither of us look at the menus in front of us.We stare at each other in awkward silence.

"I can't believe—"

"What's going—"

We both speak at the same time and laugh awkwardly. He runs a hand through his sandy brown hair. It's longer on the top and faded on the sides, but he doesn't have the top gelled to perfection, just kind of tousled and half-styled, but it works somehow. His beard is neatly trimmed and pairs nicely with his haircut.

"You go ahead." His voice is deep and kind, but there's a hint of authority there, too, that threatens to send a shiver down my spine. His moss-green eyes hold an intensity that's both hard to look at and hard to look away from.

I clear my throat. "I'm confused about what you're doing here. I thought I was meeting Morgan."

His brows furrow. "I *am* Morgan."

"Pardon?" That can't be true.

"I own Fowler's Flowers. I'm who you've been texting for two weeks." He grabs his phone and shows me our text thread.

"But I thought Morgan was a woman..." I feel really, really stupid right now. How did I not know?

Morgan smirks. "I am most definitely *not* a woman. But I can see how things might have been a tinge confusing. I never explicitly said I was a man, and me being bi probably didn't clarify things."

"I'm so embarrassed. I should go—" I grab my purse and go to stand, but I'm stopped by one of Morgan's large hands gently settling on mine.

"Please." His eyes are pleading. "Please stay. I was going to say earlier how it must be fate the cute girl from Friday is actually you."

I slowly lower back into my chair and place my purse at my feet. "What do you mean?"

Morgan scrubs a hand down his face, his cheeks turning a little pink. "*You* are the customer whose number I wanted to get. I've felt a little silly for having a crush on a girl I've never met, *and* a girl whose name I didn't know. It's a one in a million chance you're the same person."

"You're being serious?"

"Deadly, Hannah," he says with such conviction I have no choice but to believe him.

"I just—but you—look at you!" I blurt just as the waiter comes over.

He gives us a tentative smile. "Howdy. I'm Cody, and I'll be your server today. Can I start you out with something to drink?"

I quickly glance at the drink menu and order a vanilla oat milk latte. I don't drink coffee regularly, too scared my mom will find out. Morgan orders a caramel latte and some mini Dutch baby pancakes for a starter. I hope he plans to share.

"What were you saying before we were interrupted?" Morgan turns his piercing gaze on me.

"I was just pointing out it's weird someone as handsome as you is interested in someone like me. I don't get it."

Morgan's eyebrows shoot into his hairline. I've always been blunt. There's no point in beating around the bush with certain things—this in particular. It's unlikely a man who looks like Morgan—all tanned skin, gorgeous eyes, blinding smile, muscles for days, and friendly as hell—would be interested in a plus-size divorcee who spends most of her time with books and still lives with her parents.

I continue, "My divorce was only finalized three months ago, and although I've been forced into dating again by my mother, I don't know if I'm ready to have something serious. My heart's still tattered to bits and trusting someone with it isn't easy for me."

"I don't understand how you don't see how fucking beautiful you are, Hannah. Not only are you physically stunning—which I thought as soon as you walked into my shop—but your personality is beautiful. I know it's only been two weeks, and we've only talked through text, but I've had more fun texting you than I have on real dates. I'm not trying to propose right now, but I want to get to know you. I can understand needing time after a heartbreak like yours. At the very least, I'd like to be friends."

# Chapter 6

## Morgan

I hold my breath as I wait for Hannah to respond.

I'm not lying, *per se*. I *do* want to be friends. But I also want so much more. When I saw her walk into the dining room, I swear the whole restaurant faded away, and it was just her and me.

A goddess gracing me—a mere mortal—with her presence.

Am I being dramatic? Absolutely. I've always been one for theatrics. But the fact the two women I haven't stopped thinking about are the *same person?* That's got to be fate.

Hannah chews her plush bottom lip anxiously as she considers my spiel. God, what I wouldn't do to be able to reach across the table and hold her hand, to touch her somehow.

"I think I'd like to be friends. If that's okay?" Her full cheeks blush again, and I'm dying to feel their heat under my palm.

But I will take the gift she's given me and be friends.

I can definitely be *just* friends with my dream girl.

*Pull yourself together, man. You just met her.*

"I would love nothing more." My smile is genuine, though I feel a little like I've been sacked on the field. "Now, down to important business. Since I've been here before, I'm more than happy to order what I think is best if you don't want to make a decision about food. And since I asked you to come, I will be paying, and I will not take no for an answer."

Hannah rolls her eyes. "Fine, but next time we hang out, I'm paying. Go ahead and order, I don't know what to choose."

"Whatever the lady wants." I don't think I could smile wider if I tried. She's already thinking about the next time we'll hang out! This bodes well for my plan to win her trust and, hopefully, her heart. "Do you have any allergies or preferences?"

"No allergies. I'm not a fan of fish, but that's the only thing I can think of."

"Perfect, I know just what to get then."

Cody comes back with our coffees and our baby pancakes with a bunch of different toppings, and Hannah's eyes light up with interest. They look absolutely delicious.

*Almost as delicious as the woman across from me.*

No! Friends don't think like that.

"Alright, have we decided what to have for the main course?" Cody asks, a notepad in hand.

"We're going to have the eggs cochon, the steak gorgonzola flatbread, and two cinnamon rolls, please. We'll be splitting all of it, so if we could have some empty plates that would be great."

"Fantastic!" Cody clicks his pen and takes our menus. "It should be out soon. Enjoy the Dutch babies."

"Thank you," Hannah says politely. I push the plate of pancakes over to her, and she hesitantly takes one and fills it with some raspberries, blueberries, and a dollop of whipped cream.

She takes a bite, humming happily as the flavors melt on her tongue. "That's really good. The pancake is soft on the inside but crisp on the outside, and the sweetness from the whipped cream balances the tart from the berries."

"Yeah, they're one of my favorites," I say absently as I watch her little pink tongue dart out and lick a falling drop of whipped cream.

This whole "being just friends" thing is going to be extremely difficult if I can't even watch her eat a fucking pancake without getting turned on. I feel like a pervert.

"So," her melodic voice brings me back to the present, "how did you get a reservation on such short notice?"

"My friend Charlie is the manager here. We dated for like a week, but it was an amicable break up, and he said whenever I need a reservation, to give him a call."

"Oh, well, that's cool. Do you..." she trails off before shaking her head—something I've noticed she does a lot, like she's censoring herself—and continuing, "So you come here a lot?"

It takes everything in me not to smirk because I think my new *friend* might be jealous. "Not very often, but it's Alyssa's favorite place, so we try to come once every few months on dates."

Hannah freezes, and I realize my mistake immediately. I haven't told her about my daughter, so I can only imagine what she's thinking.

"Alyssa is my nine-year-old daughter. I take her on dates pretty often to show her how she should be treated when she starts dating. Plus, it gives us time to spend together and catch up outside of the monotony of our everyday life."

Hannah's shoulders sag in what I imagine is relief. "Oh. That's actually really sweet. She's one lucky girl."

"Are you upset I never mentioned her before?" I don't think she is, but I want to make sure.

She shakes her head. "No, not at all. I was just worried you were married or something. It doesn't change how I see you, other than I get to add 'good dad' to the list of characteristics I like." She takes a sip of her coffee. "Wait. If she's nine, how old are you? If you don't mind me asking."

"Not at all. I'm thirty-six." Which has me wondering, "How old are you?"

Hannah's cheeks pink again. "I'm twenty-six, almost twenty-seven."

I blink. "When did you get married?"

"At eighteen. Four months out of high school. He was in the single young adult ward I went to after graduation, and it was a whirlwind romance, I guess." She shrugs like that's normal. Which, I guess, in Utah it probably is.

"You don't want to be friends with a twenty-six-year-old divorcée anymore, do you?" she tries to joke, but it lands flat.

Of–fucking–course I still want to be friends with her! Well, *more than* friends, but friends for now until she knows she can trust me and she understands I won't break her heart. It's not like she's sixteen, and I'm twenty-six—that would be creepy as hell. We're both well into adulthood.

"I'm still excited as fuck to be your friend, Hannah. I personally think age is just a number past a certain point in your life, and since both of our prefrontal cortexes are fully developed, I don't see why we can't be friends. Unless you're freaked out by me being a single dad?"

"No, it doesn't bother me. It actually makes me like you more." Her smile is soft but genuine, and it makes my stomach flutter. I'm glad revealing I'm a single dad didn't scare her away.

Cody brings our food, and we eat while we talk. I hoard every new piece of information she gives like they're gems, and I'm a dragon. I hang on every single word that comes out of her exquisite mouth, and by the end of brunch, I'm certain of one thing.

Hannah is my future, and I'll wait as long as I have to for her to see that.

# CHAPTER 7

*Hannah*

S omehow, I made it home safely even though my mind was *not* on the road in front of me. It was on the information I learned at brunch, and now my brain won't stop going over it all.

Morgan is a *man*. Not just any man, but *the hot* man from the flower shop. That he owns. He has a daughter. He's ten years older than me. He's charming, understanding, funny, and very patient with my indecisive, blunt self.

And what did I do? I friend-zoned him.

Why would I do that? He was very clearly interested in me romantically for some reason I don't understand, so why didn't I just jump in?

Oh, I remember.

My ex-husband did a number on my self-esteem and gave me hella trust issues.

I was so embarrassed when Morgan asked how old I was when I got married. Looking back now, it was *really* weird for Liam to be so interested in an eighteen-year-old as a twenty-two-year-old. We dated for all of two months before he proposed, and two months after that we were married.

Because of the church's strict dating rules, Liam was my first real boyfriend. I wasn't allowed to date anyone exclusively until I turned eighteen. I didn't have a lot of prior experience with boys or dating, so when I was approached by a handsome returned missionary, I didn't know better. All I knew was that I was supposed to get married.

We got married and moved into BYU married housing so I could get my Masters of Library Science and he could get his MBA. He would make comments about how if I got pregnant, I'd probably have to quit school to be a stay-at-home mom, and I was okay with that. So when I got pregnant four months after our wedding, I was prepared to finish the semester, give birth, then stay home with the baby while he worked and went to school.

Except I miscarried at ten weeks. The doctors didn't have a reason for me other than, "Sometimes these things happened." I was *devastated.* I told Liam I didn't want to try again for at least six months, and he agreed.

Fast forward seven years and six miscarriages later. I was on multiple medications for depression, anxiety, and hormonal imbalances, which—coupled with the stress from the miscarriages—made me gain a lot of weight, and Liam said he no longer found me attractive. I was never a skinny girl, but my curves were more accepted before I got pregnant. He wanted me to look like the eighteen-year-old I was when we met. He wanted someone who could carry his biological children and have them "naturally." He shot down my ideas of IVF and adoption whenever I brought them up. I didn't think my body—or mind, for that matter—could handle another miscarriage.

He blamed me for each one. He told me it was my fault because I didn't "have enough faith," and I was "selfish" for wanting a degree instead of a family.

Then, he changed his tune when asking for a divorce. He said he didn't want kids at all anymore, and since I did, our marriage wasn't compatible.

I heard he's dating someone seriously now, but I don't know for sure since he blocked me on all social media. Not that I want to look. As much as I probably *should* for how shitty he treated me, I don't hate him. I mourned the loss of my first love and then realized during the last three years of our marriage, I was with a stranger. We had sex maybe twice a month, always quick and with the lights off, and we never went on dates. He was always working late or going to the golf course with his buddies if the weather was good.

It's possible he could have been cheating on me, but it doesn't matter now, does it? He left me, and now I'm all alone picking up the shattered pieces of my heart.

So yes, it's hard for me to trust Morgan has good intentions. He might like the idea of me now, but is it because I'm younger than him and easy prey?

The logical part of my brain knows he's not that kind of guy. He didn't even know my age until brunch, and he didn't know I was a hot mess until today either.

As I unlock the door, my phone pings, and my stomach flutters a little when Morgan's name pops up.

> **Morgan:** I hope you made it home safely. I had a REALLY great time today, even if there was a little miscommunication to begin with lol. Anyway, let me know next time you need some space from your house, and we can plan something! I want to hang out again soon.

I can't be having flutters for a man I barely know! I can't be thinking about making an excuse to see him soon because I enjoy his company and his conversation. Not to mention, he's a damn God among men with his looks.

Comparing him to Liam is wrong, I know, but it's like comparing an apple to a steak. Liam was attractive in a boyish, clean-cut Mormon way. Morgan is attractive in a more rugged, mature way that makes me want to drool.

> **Hannah:** I had a REALLY great time, too, once the shock wore off lol. I'm always looking for reasons to not be here.

I wanted to say, "I'm free every night this week, so let's hang out!" But he has a daughter who is clearly his priority.

*Which is another* really *attractive thing about him.*

You'd think I'd be turned off by the fact he has a nine-year-old, but if anything, it makes me more attracted to him.

The way he talked about Alyssa made it clear she is his world, and she will always come first. I have a lot of questions about his situation but none feel appropriate to ask right now.

It's barely two o'clock, and I don't know what to do with myself. Usually, I'd just be getting home from church and helping my mom with dinner, playing board games with Jake, or reading. Those were the only acceptable activities we could do on "the Lord's day."

Jake's on a weekend trip with his friends, so for the first time in a very, very long time, I have the house to myself.

I don't know what to do with myself.

As I'm changing into a pair of joggers and an oversized t-shirt, my phone pings again.

**Morgan:** It sounds like we should have extended our brunch, then! Any plans for the rest of the day?

**Hannah:** I think I'm going to read? Or maybe catch up on that new reality show where people sit in the cubes and determine whether or not they want to date someone without seeing them.

**Morgan:** Oooh, that's a good show. Do you think you could ever do something like that?

I think about it for a second before I reply.

**Hannah:** Honestly? Probably not. Not because I don't think I could date someone without seeing them, but I'd be worried about them not liking what they see for me. I can't exactly be like "Hey, I'm fat, btw." Because that defeats the whole purpose. What about you?

**Morgan:** I would 100% be able to fall in love without seeing what someone looks like.

**Morgan:** I think anyone would fall in love with your personality, and your beauty would just be a bonus for them.

Even though he can't see me, my cheeks heat to one-thousand degrees at his compliment. I still can't wrap my head around the fact he finds me attractive.

It's taken me a while to accept my body and the way it's changed the last few years, and while I don't always love my body, I don't hate it. I can appreciate it's gone through a lot.

> **Hannah:** Thank you, Morgan. That's very sweet of you to say.

> **Morgan:** You're welcome, Hannah. I wasn't trying to be sweet, I was just being honest. I have to go get Aly from my parents, so I'll talk to you later. :) Have a good rest of your day!

> **Hannah:** You too.

I lock my phone and flop back onto the couch. I don't know what I'm supposed to do about him, but something tells me he's not going to lay off the charm with me.

I just hope my heart won't suffer.

# CHAPTER 8

*Morgan*

I don't bother knocking on my parents' door when I get to their house to pick up Aly. They always leave it unlocked for me when she's spending time here, and if it's locked, I have a key.

Laughter floats from the kitchen as I breach the entryway, and the sound has a smile tipping up the corners of my lips. Aly's been struggling a lot lately with the stuff with her mom, but my parents always know how to boost her mood, and for that I'm grateful.

As silently as I can, I take off my shoes and make my way down the hall to the kitchen. As I peek around the corner, my dad, Axel, bends over the counter with his reading glasses perched on his nose. He is grumbling under his breath while he rolls out what I assume is cookie dough.

"Papa!" Aly giggles. "You're pressing it too hard. You're going to make our cookies too thin, and then they won't be soft!"

"I'm trying my best, Sissy, but I'm just too strong to do it gently." He stops rolling and flexes his muscles, causing Aly to giggle again and my mom, Iris, to roll her eyes.

"Here, Papa, I'll show you how to do it gently." Aly sets down her own rolling pin and makes her way around the counter, but before she can get to my dad, she sees me and smiles. "Hi, Dad! We're making sugar cookies."

I walk fully into the kitchen and stand by my mom. "I see that, Bub. It sounds like your Papa needs some baking lessons," I tease.

"Don't antagonize your father, Morgan," my mom says with a gentle swat to my arm. "How was brunch with your friend?"

Aly has her hands on my dad's and is gently explaining how to use the right pressure to get the best thickness for the dough, and my heart melts at their interaction.

Axel Fowler is not a small man. At six-foot-four and two-hundred-twenty pounds, he towers over my nine-year-old daughter. He's always been a man of few words, but his actions speak to how good his heart is. Like right now, he could have let Aly and my mom make cookies alone, but he wanted to spend time with his granddaughter, so he's doing something completely out of the ordinary for him to put a smile on her face.

"It was good," I reply to my mom, never taking my eyes off of my daughter.

"You seem different than when you dropped her off, so I'm not buying that it was just 'good.'" She sniffs.

I glance at her, then back over to Aly and my dad, then back at Mom and motion for her to follow me out on the patio. She sets her rolling pin down, washes her hands, and warns Aly not to eat any more dough before she meets me outside.

Their house has enough rooms for all of my siblings and me to sleep over for major holidays, and their backyard is big enough for a game of flag football. The patio is covered, so we can still have a place to sit outside and enjoy the rain without getting drenched when the weather allows. It's currently coated in a layer of my daughter's chalk art from earlier today.

"Aly's getting really good at drawing, isn't she?" I ask, settling into an Adirondack chair.

"Yes, she's very talented. Don't try to stall, young man," Mom chides, settling in next to me.

"I told you I was going to meet the girl I accidentally texted two weeks ago." Mom nods in agreement. "Well, turns out she's also the gorgeous girl from the flower shop."

My mom's mouth drops wide open on a gasp, then she cackles what we've dubbed her "witch" laugh, smacking her knee. "What are the chances of that?!"

I can't help but chuckle too, her laugh is contagious. "Yeah, it's crazy. She also assumed I was a woman because I initially texted her about going on a date with a man."

That makes her laugh even harder, tears streaming down her face. "Oh, Morgan. That's so funny. I needed a laugh today. What did she say when she saw you?"

"She thought the sister I mentioned at the shop was setting her up on a date. I cleared it up pretty fast, but she was still a little apprehensive at first."

"Well, that's understandable. I would be too if I was expecting a woman and you showed up instead." She wipes at the few errant tears that have fallen out of her eyes. "What's got you buzzing like a bee then?"

I'm unsure if I want to tell her. I love my mom, but she's got a habit of trying to play matchmaker, and I don't want her meddling in this. It's too fragile. But then again, she's always been there to help me with my relationship troubles.

I take a big breath, hoping I'm not creating more of an issue. "She's the one."

My mom narrows her eyes at me. "What do you mean?"

"You've always told me to trust my gut. I knew the minute I saw her today. The more we got to know each other, the more I realized she's it for me. I haven't been able to stop thinking about her—the 'virtual' her or the 'flower shop' her. She's got a lot of trauma from her ex-husband, so we agreed to just be friends for now, but I'm hoping she'll feel the same way."

"Oh, honey." My mom sets her hand on my knee. "I'm not going to tell you what you're feeling isn't true, because I'm not you. But I will tell you that if you're already so far gone for this girl, you've got to protect your heart. She may never feel the same way you do."

I know this, and I know she's right, but I just... I just *know.* I know in my soul Hannah and I belong together. I may fall in love fast, but it's always been a more lustful, overwhelming, can't eat, can't sleep kind of love.

What I feel for Hannah feels like snuggling up in a warm blanket on a rainy day and listening to the rain pitter patter on the window while I read my favorite book. The feeling only grew the more time I spent with her. And I know—I *know* it's crazy as hell. Especially for someone my age. But maybe that's why I trust the feeling. I've been around long enough to discern one feeling from another.

"I know, Mom. I have to look out for Aly, too. So Hannah and I will be friends, and whatever happens, happens."

"You're destined for a great love, Morgan. I've always known that. Please don't settle for anything less." Mom squeezes my knee and then stands. "We better make sure your daughter and father haven't eaten all of my dough."

I stand and follow her inside, where Aly is telling my dad about her new island in Critter Trails. I don't personally understand that particular video game, but Aly loves it, so I listen while she tells me about it. From what I gathered, there's no plot to the game. You create islands and trade things with other villagers.

"Alright, Aly girl, let's get these cookies in the oven so you and your dad can get going. I'll send you home with the frosting so you can decorate them." My mom uses a spatula to move the shaped dough pieces onto a baking sheet.

"Okay, Gigi, I'm going to go wash my hands. Dad, can I go get my GameSky so I can show Papa my new island?"

"Sure thing, Bub. I'll help your Gigi clean up."

"Thank you!" Aly's voice echoes down the hallway as she darts to the bathroom.

"Did you have fun at Gigi and Papa's?" I ask Aly later that night while we're eating dinner.

She's back to pushing her food around her plate, and a small frown has settled on her face. "Yeah, Gigi helped me draw with chalk, and Papa liked seeing my new island."

I set my fork down and reach across the table to place my hand on hers. "What's up, buttercup? You seemed so happy earlier with Gigi and Papa. Did something happen?"

She looks up at me, and her bottom lip wobbles. "I texted Mom to ask her if I could see her on Mother's Day in a few weeks, and she said, 'Sorry, Alyssa, I'm busy that day, maybe another time.'" She sighs. "I'm her only daughter. Doesn't she want to see me?"

"I think it's time I have a chat with your mom, Bub. I know you didn't want me to, but if she's not going to hold up her end of the bargain, that's not fair to you." My voice, luckily, doesn't betray just how angry I am with Whitney. She's going to get an earful from me.

Aly doesn't say anything, just nods her agreement and starts pushing her food around her plate again.

After a few minutes where she hasn't even taken a bite, she gently sets her fork down. "I'm not that hungry. Can I go play some video games until bedtime?"

"Sure thing, Bub. Just cover your plate in plastic wrap and put your fork in the dishwasher, please."

She does as she's asked, and Bean follows her as she makes her way to her room.

I take my time washing the dishes from dinner while I contemplate what I'm going to say to Whitney. I hope she answers because if she doesn't, I don't know how I'm going to fix this. I didn't want to tell Aly this, but I'm going to threaten to take full custody and not allow visitation if Whitney doesn't get her shit together and start spending time with her daughter. I'd have a pretty good case since she hasn't seen her in almost a year.

I knock on Aly's door, and when I get the clear to come in, I poke my head in and say, "I'm going to be in my office if you need anything, okay?" All I get in response is a quick thumbs up, but I'll count that as a win.

I head into the third bedroom, which I've made into an office, and sit down at my desk. I don't come in here very often, since I don't like to bring work home with me, so it's pretty empty. All that's in here is a bookshelf filled with books, an "L" shaped desk with my laptop on it, and my office chair. I have a picture of Aly and me in the hospital from the day she was born on my desk, and I smile at the memory of the best day of my life.

Then, I put on my game face because it's time to call her mother.

I click Whitney's contact number and listen to it ring once, twice, three times before Whitney answers with a tinny, "This is Whitney."

"Whitney, it's Morgan. We need to talk about Alyssa." I'm not going to waste time with pleasantries. I'm even more irritated that she doesn't have my number saved.

It's so silent for a minute, I think she hung up, but then she clears her throat. "Morgan. How are you?" Her voice wobbles a bit.

"I'm fine, Whitney. Know who isn't fine? Our daughter. She's cried twice in the last week because her mom won't talk to her."

I can practically hear her eyes roll as she says, "Oh, please, she's being dramatic. I've talked with her plenty. Sorry I can't be at her beck and call day in and day out. I have a life of my own, Morgan."

My jaw tenses, and I remind myself fighting with her won't do Aly any good, even if I have some choice words for her.

"It's been almost a year since you've spent any time with her in person. If you don't start upholding the custody agreement, I'm going to petition for full custody, and then you'll never see her," I threaten.

Whitney gasps. "How *dare* you threaten me? That would hurt Alyssa more in the long run."

I shrug, even though she can't see me. "I disagree. Her mother refusing to see or talk to her is hurting her. If I have full custody, she'll at least know there's no hope of you popping in and out of her life. She needs consistency, Whitney. If you're not going to be in her life consistently, I think it's best if you're not in her life at all."

There's a long silence before I hear her huff. "Fine. She wanted to see me for Mother's Day. I have something on

Sunday, but we can go to lunch on Saturday. I'll come pick her up at ten and spend the day with her."

"Fine. You have to text or call her to let her know. I'm not going to be the messenger for you. If you cancel or don't show up, you don't get any more chances. Do better for our daughter."

I don't bother with a proper goodbye to her, I just hang up the phone. As soon as I do, my screen lights up with a text from my butterfly. I smile when I see her name but immediately scowl when I see the contents of the message.

**Hannah:** Even though she's not even in the state, my mother is still hovering. She's apparently set me up on a date for Friday.

**Morgan:** How did she do that on vacation?

**Hannah:** They ran into an old family friend at the resort they're staying at, and it just so happens their son moved to Salt Lake to go to the U for medical school. So now I'm supposed to go meet ANOTHER literal stranger for dinner.

The thought of Hannah out with another man makes me itch with jealousy. Especially a man who's going to be a fucking *doctor*. I just own a fucking flowershop. What if she and this doctor dude hit it off and fall in love?

> **Morgan:** You don't seem super excited by the prospect of dating a doctor.

> **Hannah:** I don't care what he does for work. I keep telling my mom I don't want to do the blind date thing anymore. She just won't listen until I either have a mental breakdown or get a boyfriend.

Before I can even think about what I'm doing, I press the call button.

"Hello?" Hannah answers with a question in her voice.

How is it possible I missed her so much when I just saw her a few hours ago?

"What if I pretend to be your boyfriend?" I blurt out.

"What?"

"If you had a boyfriend, your mom would back off, right? So let me pretend to be your boyfriend. It would give you time to breathe and not have to suffer through any more blind dates."

She's silent for a minute before asking, "Why would you want to do that?"

*I would get to spend more time with you, maybe get to hold your hand. Show you you can trust me, and hopefully you'll fall in love with me.*

I don't say that even though it's the truth.

"It would be an excuse to hang out with you more and get to know you better. Plus, I want you to be happy."

"I don't know if this is a good idea..." She sounds like she's trying to convince herself of that, not me.

"It's the best idea. Tell your mom you're busy on Friday because your boyfriend is taking you on a date and you no longer need to be set up on blind dates."

"She's going to have a hard time believing it unless you physically come pick me up."

"Done. Send me your address, and I'll pick you up at seven."

"You're serious?"

"Wear something like you did today. Nice but not fancy."

"I can't tell if you're joking." She lets out an awkward laugh.

"Hannah, I'm dead serious. I'm taking you out on Friday. To your mom, it'll be a date. To us, it'll just be two friends hanging out." I hate the word *friends* right now.

Hannah sighs. "Fine. Be prepared to be asked a million and one questions."

"I'm prepared. I'll see you Friday. Goodnight, Hannah."

"Goodnight, Morgan." She hangs up before I do.

Aly knocks on the door, so I do my best to wipe the smile off my face, but it's damn hard when I'm this excited to take Hannah out on a date. I just have to remind myself that for her, this is fake. This is a means to an end for her, but if I can show her how good of a fake boyfriend I am, maybe she'll want me to be her real one.

My daughter steps through the door already in her pajamas, and a glance at the clock tells me it's almost bedtime.

"I just came to say goodnight. Mom texted and said she's taking me to lunch the day before Mother's Day." She twists her pajama shirt anxiously in her hands. "Can you help me pick out a gift for her?"

I smile softly. "Of course, Bubs. Why don't you make a list of things you think she'd like, and we'll pick something together?"

"Okay. Thanks, Dad. I'm going to go to bed. I love you." She rounds the desk and wraps her arms around my neck in a tight hug.

I engulf her in my own arms, relishing these moments before she decides she's too old for hugs. "I love you too, Aly. Sweet dreams, sweet girl."

# CHAPTER 9

## Hannah

My mom, as expected, didn't believe I had a boyfriend. I told her I wouldn't be going out with Doctor Blaine because I had a date with my boyfriend, and she laughed right in my face.

I can't say I'm surprised, but it hurt nonetheless.

I told her to cancel the date anyway and that Morgan is going to come over and pick me up so I can introduce them. I told her we met at the flower shop when I picked up her bouquet from Dad, and we've been talking ever since. She's skeptical, but I think she'll buy it when he comes over.

At least, I hope she will.

I'm not going to lie, this whole thing is weird for me. I didn't think Morgan was being serious, but I was also slightly relieved when he offered. I'm still a little skeptical we can pretend to date and still remain friends, but at this point I'm willing to do anything to stop the never-ending awkward first dates that don't lead anywhere.

I'm also well aware if he acts like my boyfriend, my heart is going to fall in love with this man, and then it'll end, and I'll be devastated because none of it was real.

I'll just have to constantly remind myself it's not real, and I can't get attached.

I've just finished applying my lip tint when the doorbell rings, and my stomach drops straight out of my body and onto the floor. I take a stabilizing breath to calm my nerves and head up the stairs.

My parents are sitting out on the back patio, so I answer the door, and Morgan's smile is blinding.

"Hi, Hannah. You look very nice tonight." He bends down and gives me a peck on the cheek, making them heat, and a zing of something travel down my spine.

"Thank you. So do you. Come on in, let's get this over with." I motion for him to come in, and he grabs my hand, intertwining our fingers. I look up at him with a puzzled expression.

"Gotta sell that we're dating. Is this okay?" He strokes his thumb gently back and forth. The action shouldn't make me swoon, but it does.

Lost for words, I simply nod, and he squeezes my hand in response. Why does something so simple make my stomach flutter so much? My brain is acting like I've never held hands with someone before.

*You* like *like him,* the voice in my head taunts.

I *can't* like him like that. I can't move on so soon after having my heart broken.

I block that voice out.

We walk out to the back patio, where my parents are sitting on the swinging bench and scrolling on their phones. No idea why they came outside to ignore the magnificent pastel colors of the setting sun, but to each their own, I guess.

My mom nudges my dad, and they both put down their phones when they hear the back door close. My mom appraises my outfit, my dad appraises Morgan.

I've got on a black, form-fitting midi skirt with a slit up to my knee on one side and a plain, pink rib knit short sleeve shirt. I put the same wedges on as Sunday, and I have to say, I feel pretty.

Until my mom says, "Are you sure you're comfortable in that?"

I'm about to respond, but Morgan cuts me off, "I think she looks lovely and comfortable. It's nice to meet you, Mr. and Mrs. Layton. I'm Morgan Fowler."

My dad's mouth is agape. "Morgan *Fowler*? Like, the former wide receiver for the Denver Mustangs, Morgan Fowler? Owner of Fowler's Flowers?"

"One and the same, Mr. Layton." Morgan's cheeks turn a tinge pink at the attention. I didn't know he played football, and I sure as hell didn't know he played professionally.

"Please, call me Mitch. I can't believe I didn't recognize you right away! Shame your career ended because of that injury. They haven't won a Super Bowl since you retired," my dad continues.

Morgan shrugs. "It happened at the right time for me. I was planning on retiring after that season anyway, so it worked out well for me and my daughter."

My mom's head whips towards Morgan. "You have a daughter?"

"Yes, ma'am. Alyssa—she's nine and the light of my life." Morgan's so proud of his daughter. I love that about him. She's not some dirty secret or shameful thing.

"How... interesting," Mom says, evidently unhappy with that tidbit of information. I also don't think she likes that Morgan has my dad's stamp of approval because he played football.

"How did a man like you end up with my daughter?" my dad asks. I know he didn't necessarily mean for it to sound like an insult, but the way he words it makes me want to crawl into a hole. Like it's *totally* impossible for a guy like Morgan to be remotely interested in me.

"I own Fowler's Flowers, and Hannah came in to grab a bouquet. It was an instant connection." Morgan looks at me with a soft expression, and I give him a small smile in return.

"Hmm. You own a flower shop?" Mom asks, her voice full of disdain.

I don't know what stick crawled up her ass, but if she's going to continue to give Morgan an attitude, I'm going to riot.

Dad, oblivious as usual to Mom's mood, pipes up, "That's where I got your flowers from, Shelly. I've been wanting to check it out and meet Morgan since they did that story when the shop first opened. It was all over the news a few years ago." He turns back to Morgan. "I don't buy flowers much but thought I would this year for Shelly, use it as a chance to finally check it out. I was so disappointed I got stuck in a meeting and had to ask Hannah to pick them up. Guess I should be patted on the back instead, huh?" Dad nudges my mom's shoulder playfully, and she just shoots him a glare.

"I'll forever be grateful Hannah was the one to pick them up." Morgan checks his watch. "Well, it was nice to meet both of you, and I hate to cut this short, but we have a reservation to keep. I promise to bring Hannah back in one piece."

"Bye, guys. No need to wait up," I say with a small wave.

Just as we make it to the door, my mom shouts, "Remember, Hannah. The Holy Ghost goes to bed at midnight."

God, I haven't heard her say that to me since I was a teenager.

When we make it to Morgan's green RAV4, he opens my door for me and helps me in. Once he's settled in the driver's seat, he turns to me with a puzzled grin. "What was that about?"

"The ghost thing?"

"Yeah, the ghost thing."

"When you get baptized into the church, you get 'the gift of the Holy Ghost,' which is supposed to be like your conscience, essentially. Apparently this ghost goes to bed at midnight, so it can't help you make good choices after that." It's actually pretty embarrassing having to explain that phrase to someone. It's something I grew up with, so I've never thought about how weird it is.

Morgan laughs, loud, uninhibited, and so joyful it sends goosebumps skittering up my arms. It's contagious, and soon I'm laughing too as he pulls out of the driveway.

"That's weird as hell, Han. But also absolutely hilarious," Morgan says, shaking his head.

"Yeah, a lot of things Mormons say or do are. Or just plain creepy." I try to ignore the flutter in my belly at the nickname he used so easily. I also try to ignore the way his arm flexes as he puts his car into the right gear. I try to ignore how *big* his hands are on the gear shift.

I fail at all of those things.

It's going to be a long night if I'm already this flustered.

# Chapter 10

## Morgan

I feel like a kid on Christmas morning as we make our way to Salt Lake. I know it's *technically* a fake date since we're just trying to get her mom off her back. I'm going to treat this as a real date though and use this as an opportunity to show her how she deserves to be treated.

Even though this is fake, my nerves and excitement are real. How could I not be nervous when the girl of my dreams is sitting in my passenger seat looking like a vision?

It was an impulsive decision to kiss her cheek when I saw her, and my lips are still tingling from the brief contact. Then, when I grabbed her hand, I half expected fucking sparkles or some magical glow when ours fingers interlocked. Why? Because it felt like pure magic holding her hand.

I can't even imagine what would happen if we kissed. It would probably feel like taking a bite of your favorite dessert. Decadent, delicious, and impossible to stop after one. Making love to her would feel like a baptism, a cleansing of my soul that would erase every other person I've touched until it's only her.

Of course, that won't be happening—at least not anytime soon—but a guy can dream.

Hannah brings me back to reality with a gentle, "Where are you taking me?"

"Have you ever been to Fondue Frenzy?"

"Oooh. No! That's the place where you get a big pot of cheese, right?" Her excitement is contagious. I'm glad I chose this place.

I chuckle. "Among other things. They have a whole three course meal experience we'll be enjoying tonight."

Hannah does a little happy dance then sighs. "Ugh, I love cheese. Liam, my ex, never wanted to venture out and try new places. He was content with fast food joints or the three other restaurants we frequented." I glance over and notice she's frowning. "Now that I think about it, he never really took me out the last three years of our marriage. I think he was embarrassed by me."

My fingers tighten on the gearshift, and my jaw clenches. I *cannot* fathom how anyone would be embarrassed by this woman. "That's so boring. I can't imagine not trying new places. I love the places I love, but sometimes you just have to try something new." And then, because I apparently like upsetting myself, I ask, "Why would he be embarrassed of you?"

"Because I gained a lot of weight after..." she trails off, like she doesn't want to finish the thought. Damn, I'm so curious, but I won't force her. She clears her throat. "After some medical issues, he didn't like that my body wasn't the same as when I was eighteen."

Well, fuck him all the way to hell. "That's awful, Han. I'm so sorry. You deserve much better than that."

"Thank you," she whispers. "I like that you're calling me Han. I've never had a nickname. Well, other than 'babe.'"

"'Babe' is so unoriginal. My nicknames for significant others are never that boring."

"What would you call me if we were, you know, *actually* dating?" she questions.

I pause like I'm thinking really hard, but the truth is I already know. I've been calling her "Butterfly" in my head since the flower shop. Then there's the obvious "my love." But it's a bit soon for that.

"'Butterfly' or 'sunflower,'" I finally say, grateful we're almost to the restaurant so I can turn and see her reaction.

"Why those?"

"Butterflies are hard to catch, delicate, and absolutely stunning. I thought of the nickname when you left the shop because it felt like you slipped right through my fingers. Sunflowers are a symbol for resilience and can grow in adverse conditions. You've gone through a lot of shit and are still bright and beautiful."

I pull into the parking lot of the restaurant and turn in time to catch the flush from her cheeks work its way down her neck and disappear beneath the modest neckline of her shirt. I'm dying to know if it goes all the way to her chest.

"Those are very nice nicknames. I don't have one for you, though," Hannah finally says.

I grin. "That's okay, Han. You'll think of something, I'm sure. Now come on, let's go get some cheese."

I round the car and open her door before she can respond. I don't hold her hand this time, even though I want to. There's no reason we have to pretend to be dating here. We're just two pals hanging out, eating cheese.

We're halfway to the door when Hannah stops in her tracks.

"What's wrong?" I'm immediately looking around for any signs of danger and follow her gaze to a yellow Dodge Charger.

"That's Liam's car."

"It could be someone else's?" I suggest, but she would know better than I do.

She shakes her head, her hair flying around her face. "I know it's his because of the stupid vanity plate I begged him not to get."

I glance down at the license plate that says "HEIS-RZN" and frown. "What does it mean?"

"'He is risen.' Like, Jesus is risen. I told him it was douchey because it's a double entendre, but he just waggled his eyebrows and said, 'Yeah it is.'" She pitches her voice lower to mimic his and then cringes.

I can't help the laugh that bursts out of me. "Of course he would say that. What would you like to do? Would you like to go somewhere else?"

She squares her shoulders. "No. I'm not letting him ruin this like he's ruined so many other things. I just hope you're prepared to act like a doting boyfriend on the off chance we run into him."

She has no fucking idea how ready I am. "Then let's go, Butterfly." The nickname just slips out, but I don't take it back or apologize. I hold my hand out for her, ready for her to decline. To my utter delight, she clasps my fingers in hers, and we walk into the restaurant.

Once we're inside, she glances around, but the lighting is low, and most of the booths are arranged in a semi-circle, giving the illusion of complete privacy for a romantic, intimate dining experience.

"Welcome to Fondue Frenzy. Do you have a reservation?" The woman at the front is dressed in a black button up and black slacks, and her name tag reads "Shondra."

"Yes, two for Fowler," I respond, giving Hannah's hand a reassuring squeeze.

"Ah yes, Mr. Fowler. Let me show you to your table." She grabs two menus and leads us around the hostess stand to the main dining area, where most of the booths are filled with couples out on their own dates.

We're led to a booth by a window that looks out onto the bustling streets of Salt Lake City. I allow Hannah to slide in first, and I follow, leaving a friendly amount of space between us.

Shondra lays the menus down. "Your server, Katie, will be with you momentarily to grab your drink orders." She then scurries off back to do her job.

I pick up the menu and look at the drinks. "Their cocktails are amazing. Oh, wait, do you drink? I won't drink if you don't want to."

Hannah shrugs. "I'm not technically supposed to drink, but I have before. I think tonight is a good excuse to let loose a little bit. Which cocktail do you suggest?"

I already know which one I would suggest. "Love Potion. I personally really enjoy their French Kiss cocktail, but for someone who hasn't had a lot of alcohol, Love Potion would be good."

Hannah *giggles,* and it makes my heart threaten to burst. "Why are they all so sensual? I mean, Love Potion? French Kiss? Cupid's Cup? Part-Time Lover? Hanky Panky? I'm surprised there's no Sex on the Beach on the menu."

"There's a bar over on thirteenth that has a whole slew of dirty cocktails and shots. If raunchy, sexual alcoholic beverages are your thing, I'm more than happy to take you."

"I have always wanted to try a Wet Pussy shot. See what the hype is about," she says just as the waitress comes over.

Thank *God* because hearing the word "pussy" come out of Hannah's mouth makes me think of other scenarios she could say it in. We order our drinks—a French Kiss for me and a Love Potion for her—and Hannah lets me order the meal, keeping in mind she doesn't like fish.

Katie writes it all down and promises our first course of cheese fondue will be out soon, then as she turns to walk away, she runs right into another patron.

"Oh, I'm so sorry, sir," Katie says.

"Maybe just watch where you're going next time," the man snaps, and I watch Hannah stiffen at his voice.

I think she's upset he's being rude to Katie for no reason until her eyes meet mine, and she mouths, "*That's Liam.*"

Then I hear a familiar voice say, "Come *on,* Liam. I want to get back to your place."

My head snaps towards the voice, and when Katie finally escapes, I say, "Whitney?"

# Chapter 11

## Hannah

The blonde woman snaps her gaze toward Morgan and so does Liam.

Liam does a double take to me and says, "Hannah?"

The blonde—*Whitney*—says, "Morgan?"

Since he's the only one who hasn't been mentioned, I say calmly, "Liam?"

Liam shakes his head. "What are you doing here?"

Whitney says the same thing to Morgan at the same time.

Morgan looks at me, and I subtly nod my head, so he says, "We're on a date. Presumably *you two* are also on a date?"

Whitney squares her shoulders, but before she can say anything, Liam says incredulously, "*You* are on a *date*? With *him?*"

I shrink back at the way he spits the words, like they taste sour in his mouth. The last thing I want right now is a confrontation with my ex-husband, but Morgan slides his arm around me and squeezes my hip in a comforting gesture.

"I don't know why it's so hard to believe, but yes, we're on a date," Morgan says confidently.

"Who is this guy, Whit?" Liam slides his arm possessively around Whitney, who's glaring daggers at Morgan.

"This is my ex, Morgan," Whitney explains through gritted teeth.

"We also share a whole child, but yeah, we dated." Morgan drops that bomb like he's talking about the weather, and my mouth pops open in an "o."

*So this is Aly's mom. His ex. A permanent fixture in his life.*

Jealousy and inadequacy start to rear their ugly heads, but I tamp them down. This is a fake date. Morgan and Whitney aren't together. *We* aren't together. I have no reason to be jealous. The way he talks about Aly, it's clear she's the best thing that's happened to him, and Whitney was part of that, whether I like it or not.

Liam's head whips to Whitney so fast I'm surprised it didn't snap. "You have a *kid?*"

I'm suddenly very interested in this conversation. Liam made it clear at the end of our marriage he would never want kids, so the fact his date didn't disclose that little tidbit is probably making his blood boil.

"Well, I don't have full custody. He won't—she doesn't—" Whitney stutters.

"I can't believe you have a child, Whit. You didn't think to mention that *once* in the four months we've been together?" Liam's tone is harsh. It's one I didn't hear often, but it was the one that stung the most. He used it when he was blaming me for the miscarriages we experienced and when he told me he no longer wanted to work on our marriage.

Whitney looks—rightfully—chastised, and Morgan butts in, "Not to worry, man. She hasn't seen her in over a year, so she's not very involved in our daughter's life."

Whitney looks like a tomato about to burst. "I've been busy."

Morgan snorts. "Sure. I can see that. Whatever, that's between you, me, and Aly. We can arrange a time for the three of us to chat later. If you don't mind, it seems Katie has our drinks and is trying to get past you. I'd like to enjoy this evening with my girlfriend."

My stomach flutters, and I tamp down that shit because I'm not his real girlfriend. But to sell the lie, he gazes at me like I'm his whole world and squeezes my hip again.

Katie apologizes to Liam and Whitney, sets down our drinks, then leaves.

Liam eyes my drink with clear revulsion. "So you're an alcoholic now?"

"What I am is none of your business anymore. But no, I'm not. One drink does not an alcoholic make," I say, proud my voice came out strong instead of shaky.

"Were you ever going to tell me you were seriously dating someone? Has my daughter met her? Are you bringing a parade of women around her?" Whitney spits.

"I haven't introduced Aly to Hannah, and who I date is none of your business. If you would like to have a civil conversation, then we can have one at a later time." Morgan's voice leaves no room for argument. It's authoritative and calm, and even though the situation is *not* sexy, I feel a small spark of something in my lower belly.

"Fine. Let's go, Liam." Whitney tugs his arm, leading him away from our table.

He doesn't say anything but leaves with a look of utter disgust on his face, like the mere sight of me repulses him.

I slump when they're no longer in our sight, and Morgan takes a long sip of his cocktail.

"Well, that was fun. Super great first date," he quips sarcastically.

"I feel like I've aged ten years," I joke back.

He barks a laugh and kisses my forehead. Then Katie is back with our first course.

I don't have time to dwell on the intimate gesture or the fact no one was around to see it.

Morgan and I don't really talk as we dip and munch. When the cheese is almost gone, we both sit back so we can have some room for our main course and then dessert.

"So," I start, twirling my finger around the rim of my drink glass. "That's Alyssa's mom?"

Morgan nods. "That's her, unfortunately."

"That seems a bit harsh." I don't know why I feel the need to defend her.

He sighs. "You're right. That was uncalled for, but I wasn't lying when I said she hasn't seen her in over a year. She barely even answers Aly's texts and calls. It's like she decided having a kid wasn't what she wanted so she just abandoned her. I'm upset because she's hurting my daughter, and she doesn't give a fuck."

My stomach plummets and tears threaten to spring to my eyes for Aly. I don't have a good relationship with my mom at all, but I can't imagine being abandoned like that. "That's really, really shitty. I'm so sorry you and Aly have been dealing with that." I squeeze his arm in what I hope is a comforting gesture.

"Thank you, it's not easy to watch Aly feel like she's not loved. My mom and sisters try their best to be there for her and give her all the girl time they can, but it's not the same. And it's hard to not be able to celebrate or commiserate Aly's highs and lows with a partner who loves Aly as much as I do, you know?"

"I don't know, honestly. I was never far enough along to get to that point." I slap a hand over my mouth, cursing the lack of filter on me. This isn't about me right now, it's about him!

Morgan's eyebrows knit together, and he turns his body to face me in our little booth, grabbing my hand. "I'm not going to pry about that, especially right now, but just know I'm sorry."

I blink back tears at the sincerity in his voice. Not many people know about the miscarriages, but everyone always says the same thing.

*"They're in a better place."*

*"They were too pure for this Earth."*

*"They'll be waiting for you in the Celestial Kingdom."*

What people don't realize is those things don't mean much, especially when you're like me and aren't sure there's an afterlife. I don't know if I'll get to see my babies again. And how can there be a better place than in my arms? Does the God Mormons believe in not find me worthy to have a child?

When Liam told me it was my fault for not being worthy enough to carry a child, I took it to heart and doubled down on being the "perfect" member. I did the service, I read my scriptures, I prayed twice a day on my knees, and still, nothing was good enough.

I realize now maybe it wasn't *me* who was unworthy of having a child. Maybe if God is real, he was just showing me Liam's true colors so I wouldn't be stuck with a narcissistic asshole for eternity.

The fact Morgan didn't fill me with fake platitudes or hollow words means more than he will ever know.

"Thank you. It's still really fresh and hard to discuss, but hopefully someday I'll be ready to talk about it." I give him a sad smile and squeeze the hand holding mine.

"I hope one day you'll see how incredibly strong I think you are, Han. I hope one day you'll trust me."

I don't tell him that I already kind of do trust him. The fact scares the ever-loving shit out of me.

I just hope my trust isn't misplaced.

# CHAPTER 12

## *Morgan*

After the cheese, we had the main course: different types of marinated meat cooked on a cast iron skillet along with a side salad and an assortment of vegetables.

Now, we have our dessert—chocolate fondue. I chose the turtle fondue with candied pecans because it's fucking delicious.

I didn't think this through very well though.

I already toed the invisible line by kissing Hannah on the forehead when no one else was around. I could play it as a "just in case they're watching" gesture, but the truth is, I wanted to.

But now, I'm crossing all sorts of friendship boundaries with the direction my thoughts are going.

I didn't think I'd get turned on watching Hannah wrap her plump lips around a chocolate covered strawberry or enjoy the little hums she makes after a particularly good bite. I didn't think about how difficult it would be to stop myself from wiping a smear of chocolate from her lips.

I can picture it clearly. I'd wipe that smear with my thumb, bring it to my mouth, and suck it off, mixing the sweetness of the chocolate with the sweetness that is Hannah. Her eyes would darken with desire, and I'd say, "I think I need another taste," and cup her face gently before bringing my lips to hers, savoring what I'm sure would be the most immaculate flavor combination.

Or, I'd press my chocolate covered thumb to those pillowy lips, and she'd suck it into her delectable mouth, swirling her tongue around the tip of my thumb like she would around the tip of my cock. I'd pull it out with a pop, and then I'd lean in and ravish her mouth like I would her pussy.

*Fuck, am I a pervert?*

I might be. Because she sees us as friends, and I see us naked in bed together.

I stifle a groan and shift myself, grateful my dark pants hide the semi I'm sporting. Good thing Hannah is distracted dipping a cream puff in the chocolate.

"You good, Morgan?" she asks while swirling the pastry in fondue.

"Yeah, why do you ask?"

"You seem a little antsy. We can leave whenever you're ready. I know you probably need to get Aly, too." Hannah shoves the whole chocolate covered cream puff in her mouth, making her cheeks puff up a little like an adorable chipmunk.

I clear my throat. "I'm good. Just trying to figure out what I want to try next. There're so many options." I stab a piece of pineapple from the tray with the skewer and swirl it around. "As for Aly, she's sleeping over at my sister's tonight."

"That's so fun. I have a lot of fond memories of sleeping at my Aunt Pam's house when I was a kid." She half frowns then shakes her head. "Anyway, do you have any other siblings?"

I don't press on the subject change, though I really, *really* want to. I want to know why she gets so sad sometimes, what goes on in that pretty head of hers.

"I have two older sisters, a twin sister, and a younger brother. Olivia, Alice, Sarah, and Kendall. Kendall and I are the only ones not married, and I'm the only one with a child. Olivia helps me run the shop and creates all the crystal jewelry."

"That's so cool! I've always wondered what it'd be like to have more siblings than just Jake. There's such a big gap between us, so we aren't very close. Are you close with all of your siblings?"

I chuckle. "Yeah, we're a tight-knit group. My mom never forced us to be close, which is nice, but we all kind of got there on our own. When shit hit the fan with Whitney, they were the only thing holding me together. I wouldn't have survived without them—I still wouldn't be able to."

Hannah gives me a soft smile. "I love that. What are your parents' names?"

"Iris and Axel."

"Oh," Hannah sighs wistfully. "Iris is a lovely name."

"She's a good mom. I would be totally lost without her."

"That must be nice," she says a little sadly.

I give in to the urge to place a hand on her thigh and squeeze, hopefully in a comforting gesture.

"I'm sure they'd love to meet you. My mom has welcomed everyone else's partners with open arms." My eyes widen when I realize what I implied. "Not that we're partners. Just friends. But she's a mama bear and loves fiercely."

Hannah's cheeks flush, and she just nods. I mentally smack myself in the head.

It's awkward for a few minutes until Katie comes with the check, and then we decide it's time to head out. Hannah argues with me about paying, saying since it's a fake date—*ouch*—we should split it.

I level her with a serious look and say, "If we were actually dating, I would pay the check. So let me pretend for a minute, okay?"

She acquiesces but still grumbles that she's paying next time. Just like at brunch, I can't help but smile because she *still* wants there to be a next time.

On the drive to her place, we don't really chat. But it's a comfortable silence as we listen to an up-and-coming indie musician's station. I get her back home at precisely ten-thirty-five, well before midnight, so hopefully that scores me some points with her mom.

I walk her to the door, and even though this isn't a real date, the anticipation of a goodnight kiss is palpable, and I wonder if she wants me to kiss her.

Hannah fiddles with her keys but doesn't make a move to unlock the door.

"Thank you for tonight. After the drama at the beginning, I had a really great time," she says, almost shyly.

"You're welcome. Thank you for agreeing to come. I had an amazing time. Let's do it again soon, yeah?" I ball my fingers into a fist to stop myself from tucking a strand of hair behind her ear, cupping her cheek, and finally figuring out what her lips feel like against mine.

She stares up at me with her hazel eyes and nods. "I'd like to do it again soon."

"Good," I whisper, the tension in the air thickening. Just as I'm about to make my move and completely obliterate the boundaries of our arrangement, she steps back and puts her key in the door.

"Text me when you get home so I know you're safe." It's not a question but a demand, and dammit if it doesn't make me like her more.

"I will. Goodnight, Hannah." I step down off the porch.

"Goodnight, Morgan." Hannah steps inside her house, and I hear the *click* of the lock engaging.

I blow out a frustrated breath as I get in the car and pull out of the driveway.

Things are surface level with Hannah—I know that—but I'm already struggling to stay patient while I wait until she's ready. Pushing her won't get me anywhere other than further from her. It was one date. One *fake* date. At least in her eyes. But she wants to see me again, and I count that as a win.

I just wish whoever's writing the story of my life would hurry the fuck up and get to the part where I can kiss her already.

# Chapter 13

*Hannah*

I shut the front door and slump against it, heart beating wildly.

I thought he was going to kiss me.

I think I wanted him to.

But at the same time, that would make things too complicated, and I don't have my heart or head in the right place to handle the complexities that are Morgan Fowler and my feelings.

I toe off my shoes and put my purse on the hook by the door then go to make my way downstairs when my mom startles me.

"Have a good time?" she asks callously, and my skin prickles with awareness. Something's off.

"I did. It was really good," I say carefully.

She makes some noise of affirmation. "See anyone you know?"

My stomach plummets—right out of my body and onto the floor, ready to be trampled.

"Not that I'm aware of."

"That's not what Liam said." She pauses whatever show she's watching and stands, crossing her arms across her chest.

*Shit. What did that asshole say?*

"Why were you speaking to Liam?" I try to keep my voice steady and brace myself for the blow about to come. Where my ex is involved, it can't be anything good.

It shouldn't surprise me my mother keeps in contact with him, she always thought he was the best part about me. They used to team up with each other to get me to do whatever they wanted.

"He called me." Mom watches my every little expression for a tell, but she won't find one because I perfected my mask of indifference years ago. "He said he saw you out with your *boyfriend,* and he was worried you were becoming an alcoholic."

I just *barely* hold back an eye roll. I had *one* drink, but of course they think it means I have a problem.

"I'm not becoming an alcoholic. He's not worried about me, Mom; he's being petty because he's upset his ex-wife is dating his new girlfriend's ex-boyfriend."

My mom's eyebrows shoot to her hairline, obviously Liam didn't mention that piece of gossip to her.

Good.

"Well, *I'm* concerned. Is Morgan forcing you to drink alcohol? What if he had drugged your drink, Hannah? Taken advantage of you?"

Imagine that. She's never been concerned that one of the many *strangers* I went out with would drug my drink because they were all active Mormons. The *one* guy I choose to go out with for myself, who isn't Mormon, she decides is trying to drug me.

She continues before I can reply, "I looked him up since Dad seemed to be obsessed with him. He's *thirty-six*, Hannah! He has a child. He's a millionaire from his time playing professionally. What could he possibly want with you?"

My mouth physically drops open at that, and to my utter horror, tears brim in my eyes. "I cannot believe you just said that. I'm not having this conversation with you. I'm going to bed."

"Hannah, no, wait. That came out wrong. I—"

"No, Mother. I think it came out just as you intended. I'm ending this conversation before we say something else we can't take back," I grit out, practically running down the stairs.

Jake is downstairs on the couch with two of his friends, playing a video game in the family room when I rush past toward my bedroom.

"Why is your sister still living at home?" I hear one of his friends ask.

"She just got divorced," Jake says blandly.

"I don't blame the guy, who would want to be with such a—"

"Watch what you say about my sister, or I'll knock your teeth out. She's gone through a lot of crap, and she doesn't need judgments from you jerkoffs," Jake barks, effectively shutting up his friends.

More tears flow down my cheeks at his act of protectiveness. We've never been particularly close, but I always hoped he knew I'd have his back if he needed it, and it seems he has mine.

I go quickly through my shower and skincare and slip into some pajamas before I settle into bed and decide to scroll through social media.

When I pick up my phone, there's a text from Morgan.

**Morgan:** I got home safe and sound.

**Morgan:** I also want you to know it means a lot to me you said that. I hope the rest of your night is good.

**Hannah:** I'm glad you got home safely. Do people not usually want to know their friends get home okay?

I frown when I type the word "friends." It feels… wrong. It feels like too small of a word for what we are, but what other word would I use?

**Morgan:** Some people just don't show it in little ways like that.

**Hannah:** Huh. Interesting.

> **Hannah:** What are your big plans while Aly's not there?

> **Morgan:** Lol no big plans. It's not like I need extra sleep since she's almost ten and sleeps through the night. I usually use nights like this to catch up on work without feeling like I'm ignoring her, maybe go on a date.

Jealousy stirs in my gut at the thought of him going out with other people. I have no reason to be jealous. He has every right to go out on dates. I have no claim on him. Before I can say anything, another text comes in.

> **Morgan:** I haven't gone out with anyone since the night I first texted you, and I have no interest in doing so while I'm in a relationship. Fake or not.

> **Hannah:** Now I just feel like I'm making you lose out on something with this fake dating stuff.

**Morgan:** Hannah, I promise I'm not missing out on anything.

**Hannah:** If you start feeling that way will you tell me please?

**Morgan:** I promise, I won't feel that way.

**Hannah:** Please.

**Morgan:** UGH. Pushy woman. FINE. I'll tell you if it happens.

**Morgan:** But it won't.

**Hannah:** Thank you.

**Hannah:** In other news, Liam called my mom tonight.

**Morgan:** WHAT?! What did he say?

**Hannah:** That he's "worried" about me because he thinks I'm an alcoholic.

**Morgan:** … you had ONE drink. How does that make you an alcoholic?

**Hannah:** That's Mormons for ya. One sip of alcohol makes you an alcoholic, and apparently, you were trying to drug my drink to take advantage of me.

The three dots appear, disappear, reappear, and disappear again before Morgan's name is lighting up my phone with a phone call.

"Um, hello?" I answer.

"You know I'd *never, ever* drug you, right?" his voice sounds almost panicked.

"Of course I know that. My mom is just dramatic and judgmental."

He sighs in relief. "Good. I want you to feel safe with me, Hannah. I would remove my own pinkie if I ever made you feel uncomfortable."

"That feels a little dramatic." I giggle.

"I'm dead serious, Butterfly." Fuck, my heart stutters at the use of the nickname. I love it.

"I feel safe with you, Morgan. I promise."

"What else happened with your mom?" he asks, and I hear the creak of what must be a chair or something on his end of the phone.

I sigh, settling into my own bed. "Same old things. She looked you up, apparently, and thinks that because you're rich, ten years older than me, and have a kid you couldn't possibly have any interest in me."

"What exactly is she implying?" Morgan sounds annoyed, which makes me feel better because I always feel like I'm being dramatic in regards to my mom.

"That I'm a gold digger? Or you're a human trafficking mastermind? I don't know because I didn't stick around for that conversation."

"Well I'm not a human trafficking mastermind. Are you a gold digger?" Though his voice conveys he's teasing, I feel the need to make sure he knows I'm not.

"I know nothing about football, so it never occurred to me that you'd be wealthy because that stuff isn't important to me. Obviously, you and Aly have a stable income to live off of, and that's all that really matters in my opinion."

"I know you're not a gold digger, Han. I was just teasing. I'm sorry your mom is being that way." He pauses. "Is the age thing starting to bug you? Or the fact I have a kid?"

I pause to truly think about it because I want to answer him honestly. This feels like a pivotal moment in our non-relationship.

"Honestly? No, it doesn't bother me. It's like you said at brunch: we aren't sixteen and twenty-six. You haven't known me as a child. It's not weird for me. It also doesn't bother me that you have a kid. I haven't seen you interact with Aly, but I've heard you talk about her. It's obvious she's your world, and you're an amazing father."

Morgan lets out a long breath, like he was holding it the whole time I was talking. "I'm relieved to hear that, Butterfly, because I don't think I could walk away now."

My heart starts beating rapidly. "Walk away from what?"

"From us. Our... friendship." It sounds like he forces the word "friendship" out like it physically pains him.

I can relate.

"Right. Me either. It feels like I've known you forever but not long enough at the same time," I say. It's easier to admit these things when he's not staring at me with his gorgeous green eyes.

"I feel the same way, Butterfly. I should probably get some sleep, gotta work at the shop tomorrow."

I glance at the clock and see it's almost midnight.

"Right. Have a good sleep, Morgan."

"Goodnight, Han. I look forward to seeing you again."

"Goodnight."

Then, he hangs up, and I'm left with a lot more questions about what the *hell* is happening inside my heart.

# Chapter 14

*Hannah*

My mom hasn't spoken to me in the three days since Friday. I've been treading lightly so I don't upset her, but I haven't exactly felt the desire to chat with her either.

I'm waiting for the inevitable conversation with my dad where he tells me *I* hurt her feelings, and *I* need to apologize because she's sad.

Or she'll just ignore it and pretend everything is fine.

My guess is, since my birthday is in two days, it'll be the latter. Mom can't resist a big birthday celebration, even if I don't want one.

Luckily for me, work is a good distraction from everything happening in my personal life. We're finalizing our summer programs right now, so I've been making sure the schedules match and confirming the dates with our guest speakers..

I dial the number for the local plant nursery, and the owner answers with a rushed, "Botanical Bliss, Santana speaking."

"Hey, Santana, it's Hannah over at the public library. I was just calling to confirm your participation in our summer program. It looks like we have your slot scheduled for Thursdays at two o'clock. Does that still work for you?"

Santana lets out a strangled sound that's more like a half sob half laugh. "I'm so sorry, Hannah. I'm not going to be able to participate in the summer program this year. There's a lot of stuff happening in my personal life."

"Totally understandable. No need to worry, we have plenty of options we can fall back on. I hope whatever you're dealing with isn't too bad." We *don't* have a lot of options to fall back on. Santana was one of two options, and the other nursery is owned by an older gentleman who has no volume control.

"Thank you for understanding. I have to run. Good luck with the program." The line goes dead before I can say anything.

I set the phone down, take off my glasses, and rub at my temples. I don't know what we're supposed to do now, but it's my job to figure it out.

My best friend and coworker, Sage, comes into the office, takes one look at me, and immediately walks out.

If I didn't know her so well, I'd think she was pissed that I look stressed, but she'll be back in a few minutes with a water bottle and some type of food because she knows I haven't taken a lunch break yet.

Sure enough, five minutes later she waltzes through the door with two water bottles, two wrapped sandwiches, two bags of chips, and two chocolate chip cookies about to tumble out of her arms.

"I know you haven't eaten yet, so we're taking our lunch breaks, and then you can tell me what's happening," Sage demands, setting half of the spoils on my side of the desk, then settling in with hers on the other side.

"Thanks, Sage." I give her a small, grateful smile, and we eat in silence.

Sage Oldham is five-foot-three, has wavy, mushroom brown hair she keeps cut in a seventies shag, beige skin, and piercing blue eyes. She's a plus size girl like me, but she's the kind of plus size where she has big boobs, a big ass, and a smaller waist. She's a lovely hourglass shape where I tend to be more round. She also has a penchant for loud patterns, bright lipstick, and colored mascara.

We've been best friends since college, and she's the only person I tell everything to. We finished our MLS together at BYU, then both ended up landing jobs at the Salt Lake City Public Library, one of the largest libraries in the state. We've been friends for almost as long as I've been—*was*—married. She was integral in how I survived the divorce and also a big reason why I started questioning the church I was raised in.

Sage grew up in the Mormon church, just like me, but when we hit our third year of undergrad, she started questioning things. At BYU, you're forced to take a religion class each semester as part of your required credits, and some of the things Sage learned didn't sit right with her. It took a few years, but after the research she presented me with, I couldn't argue it away anymore.

The church is a money hungry, misogynistic, lying, racist cult.

I told her I couldn't leave without upsetting Liam, but then the divorce happened. She's already removed her records, and she's been urging me to do the same, but I just can't bring myself to do it while I'm living with my parents.

I will one day, but today is not that day.

"So, tell me what's going on. I know your mom is being a bitch, and you're all befuddled over Morgan, but is there anything else?" Sage asks once she's finished her sandwich.

As soon as I got to work the day after Morgan offered to be my fake boyfriend, I spilled everything—the texting, brunch, how hot he is, his daughter, that he's the hot flower shop guy, his offer—to Sage so she could talk me out of it.

She didn't, though, because she's obsessed with drama that isn't her own, and she thinks this is "good for the plot," the little traitor.

"Botanical Bliss can't do Thursdays anymore. Santana's had some personal stuff come up, so now I have to find a replacement. Not a lot of places are willing to close early to come teach classes for free at the library."

Sage taps her hot pink painted nails on the desk as she contemplates, then gives me a smile that *screams* mischief. It's the same smile she used when she said we should leave gummy bears on Liam's car in the hot August sun after he said he wanted a divorce.

"Well, I personally think it would be *lovely* to have someone come teach a class on, I don't know, the *language of flowers*. Or a bouquet design class. But who do we know that owns a flower shop?" She dramatically taps her chin in contemplation, and my stomach twists.

"No idea." I play along.

"Oh darn," she sighs. "If only one of us had a hunky boyfriend who owned a flower shop willing to do us this favor."

I roll my eyes. "He's not my boyfriend."

Sage pins me with a "get real" look. "So sorry. *Fake* boyfriend."

When I don't immediately take her bait, she continues, "Think about it, babe. A former sports dude turned florist? It would get so many people in here—so many people who could donate to fund other programs. Plus, a little bit of eye candy wouldn't be so bad, right?"

"Fine, I'll ask him, but don't hold your breath. He's got a lot going on with his daughter."

Sage claps excitedly. "Yay! This is way better than some lady coming to talk to us about the fertilization process of plants."

"Don't be rude, Sage. I'm sure lots of people would have loved that! Besides, Morgan hasn't agreed to anything. He could still say no."

Sage smirks. "But he won't."

I don't want to agree with her, but I do.

Later that day when I get home, my mom is fussing around the kitchen. I'm still avoiding her, so I start to head downstairs.

"Hannah, come here please," my mom demands, and I internally groan and stomp my feet like a petulant child. I don't want to deal with her right now.

I pad over to the kitchen island and lean against the cool marble. "Yes?"

My mom stops her frantic stirring of whatever's on the stove. "Will I need to tell the restaurant we'll have six people or just five?"

Confused, I ask, "What?"

She huffs, then faces me fully. "For your birthday dinner. Is your friend and his daughter joining us?"

*Friend. Ha.* If only she knew how right she was.

"I don't know."

"Well, ask him, unless he's not celebrating with us. Which would be strange since he's your boyfriend." To anyone else, the words might sound casual, maybe a little worried. To me? They're an obvious threat. A dig at my relationship because she doesn't believe he could actually like me.

"I'll ask him when I see him tomorrow." I lift my chin, trying to come off as confident and nonchalant.

I didn't want to bring up my birthday because I didn't want him to feel obligated to get me anything since we're *just friends.*

"Good. Dinner will be done in an hour." Mom turns back to the stove, effectively dismissing me until the proverbial dinner bell rings.

Good thing I already planned on talking to Morgan tomorrow, I guess.

# Chapter 15

*Morgan*

**Hannah:** Can I stop by the shop after my shift? There's something I want to talk to you about.

**Morgan:** Sure. I'll be here until closing.

Waiting for Hannah to show up at the shop is like waiting for cookies to bake. You *know* something good is coming, but the wait is agonizing.

It's been four days since our "date" and late night phone conversation, and I've been champing at the bit to see her again or at least have another phone call. We've been busy with work, so sporadic texts are all we've had time for.

God, I sound like a sad puppy when its owner goes to work.

The bell above the door dings, and I put on my customer service smile, but as soon as I see the head of honey blonde hair, my smile widens because my girl is here.

Not *my girl*. My friend—the girl I'm head over heels for—Hannah.

And she looks like a dream. She's wearing another jumpsuit, but this one is a light green with a daisy pattern on it. It's a spaghetti strap top, so she's got on a thin white shirt underneath to make it work appropriate, and she's paired it with adorable white sneakers.

*God, she's so pretty.*

When she sees me, she offers a small smile and fixes her glasses, even though they weren't askew.

She's nervous, I can tell. But why?

*Oh no. She's going to end our arrangement.*

Panic claws at my throat, but I do my best not to show it.

"Hey, Han. How's it going?" I greet, leaning against the counter as casually as I can.

"It's... going. Um, how are you?" Hannah again fixes her not-askew glasses, then tucks and untucks a strand of hair from behind her ear.

"I'm good, thanks. You said you wanted to talk about something? Let's head to my office, and we can chat there. I'm just going to put up the closed for lunch sign." Better to get to the nitty gritty immediately.

I head toward the front door, despite Hannah's protest of, "Oh, no you don't have to close for me."

Once the lock is engaged and the sign is up, I head to the back. I look Hannah in the eye as I say, "You always deserve my undivided attention."

Her cheeks flush a rose pink, and I internally fist-bump myself. "My office is this way." I lead her around the checkout counter and to the narrow hallway behind it that hosts a restroom, supply closet, and my office.

It's not much, just a desk, a rolling chair, a couch, a shelf, and a filing cabinet where I keep all the necessary legal documents I need. I don't spend a lot of time here because I prefer to be out at the counter. Olivia handles most of the paperwork from her home office.

I motion for Hannah to sit on the small couch. I sit next to her, but that's a mistake because we're not small people, and now our thighs are almost touching.

"What's up?" I toss an arm over the back of the couch so I can face her a bit more.

Hannah takes a deep breath. "I know this is kind of short notice, but the library needs to fill a Thursday afternoon slot for our summer program. We originally had a plant nursery scheduled, but the owner can't commit anymore, and my friend Sage and I were wondering if *you* would be willing to come? Maybe talk about the language of flowers or lead a bouquet design workshop or talk about the different needs of different flowers.

"We can't pay, unfortunately, and I know closing early once a week might not be a financially sound decision, which is understandable, so this might be a really dumb idea—"

"Hannah," I cut her off, gently placing my hand on hers, "I'd really enjoy doing that. How long does the program last?" How could she possibly think I'd say no? Especially when it means I'd be guaranteed to see her once a week?

"The program starts the last week of May and goes to the second week of August."

"Done. I'll see if Olivia would be willing to watch the store, and if she can't, I think the high school kids I employ would be able to for a few hours. Thursdays aren't our busiest day so it should be fine."

Hannah's shoulders slump in what I imagine is relief. "Thank you, Morgan. You're really saving my bacon. I owe you one."

Oh, I can think of *many* ways to cash in my favor. But not all of them are appropriate right now so I'll put that in my pocket for later.

"You're welcome. Is that all you wanted to talk to me about?" I'm tempted to reach out and run a silky strand of hair through my fingers, just to touch her in some small way.

"No, I uh, was wondering what you were doing to-morrow night?" She winces on the last word.

Hope ignites in my chest. Is *she* asking *me* on a date? "I don't have any plans. Why?"

"I know it's *very* short notice, but my birthday dinner is tomorrow, and my mom made some—"

"Wait, *what?* Your birthday is tomorrow? Why didn't you tell me?" I'm kind of hurt she didn't let me know. Why wouldn't she tell me?

Hannah shifts uncomfortably, her thigh inching clos-er to mine. "Well, we're still getting to know each other, and I didn't want you to feel obligated to get me a gift or anything."

Okay, that makes sense. Still. "Your boyfriend should know your birthday."

"I know," she says sheepishly. "Which is why if you can't make it tomorrow, I understand. My mom also wanted to know if Aly was coming, too."

I think Aly meeting Hannah alone would be fine. But I'm not subjecting Aly to the judgmental stare of Shelly Layton until Hannah and I are serious for real.

"Aly can go to my parents' house. I think it'd be better if it was just me for tomorrow."

"I agree. I don't want my mom to scrutinize and judge Aly just for existing. Aly deserves better than that." Hannah pulls out her phone and types a text to her mom. "Alright. We're meeting at Hughes in Farmington at seven. Is that okay?"

"I'll be there at six-forty-five," I tease and that finally pulls a smile from her.

"I believe you. Please don't feel obligated to get me a present."

Too late. I already know what I'm going to give her, and she's going to love it.

"Oh boy," she sighs. "You're going to anyway, aren't you?"

I nod, and she scowls at me, but it holds no heat. All it does is make me think how adorable she is. I want to pull her into my lap and tickle her to make her giggle. I want to give her kisses all over her angelic face until she's begging me to stop.

Some day, I won't have to hold myself back. Hopefully.

She leaves after a few more minutes, and it's like the room is a little dimmer without her sunshine.

# CHAPTER 16

*Hannah*

I woke up this morning to a "Happy Birthday" banner and my favorite breakfast of baked french toast and perfectly crisp bacon smothered in vanilla syrup. Breakfast was silent and awkward with Jake filling most of the silence with talk of his end-of-school-year projects.

When I got to work, Sage had my favorite cheese pretzel and dirty chai latte from the German bakery a few blocks over. She gifted them to me along with a gift card for a size-inclusive lingerie store.

"Ya know, in case you need to buy something sexy for a date with Morgan," she explained with the most deceptively innocent expression when I looked at her confused.

Considering I haven't bought nor worn regular underwear in almost a decade, I wouldn't even know where to begin with lingerie. I'm fine in my church issued garments because they're familiar and easier than trying to buy new underwear. I know I'll need to get normal underwear eventually, though.

After saying thank you, I started my day.

Now I'm shelving books with the gift card burning a hole inside my purse. My mind floats to images of me buying a bold red set, and Morgan slowly peeling away my clothes to reveal the delicate lace underneath.

What would he think of the lingerie? Would he like my body in the lace? Or would he want to tear it away and just get down to business?

Something tells me he'd want to go slow. He'd want to take his time and—

*Why am I thinking about this?*

I look around to see I'm alone, thank goodness. I wipe my hands on my clothes to dry the clamminess, willing the heat in my cheeks to cool down.

When I get home, I change out of my sensible black work pants and plain white collared shirt with a brown sweater vest and into a dress I bought as a birthday gift to myself. Blue with a square neckline, fluttery sleeves, and hitting just above my knees.

As I examine myself in the mirror, my mind automatically wonders what Morgan is going to think.

As if he's been summoned, he texts me.

**Morgan:** What colors are you wearing?

**Hannah:** Um, blue?

**Morgan:** What shade?

**Hannah:** …cerulean?

**Morgan:** Perfect. I'll see you there.

**Hannah:** See you soon.

Confused, I touch up my makeup and head upstairs to meet my parents and Jake.

My mom comes out of her room and frowns when she sees my dress. "Are you wearing garments?"

I self consciously tug at the hem of the dress, even though I quadruple checked that it would cover the god-forsaken article of clothing. "Yes."

"Did you roll them up? You know that's not allowed." Mom scowls, but before she can further her lecture, Jake runs up the stairs, and my dad emerges from his office.

"Alright, let's get going so I can get home before the start of the baseball game," my dad grumbles, heading straight for the garage.

I'm this close to telling them we don't need to go at all if it's such an inconvenience. I'd rather go to dinner with just Morgan, anyway.

But that would cause more problems, so I keep my mouth shut and slide into the backseat of my dad's brand new, black SUV.

The drive to Hughes is silent, except for the radio playing some sort of talk radio station that my dad's obsessed with.

When we arrive, I see Morgan's already parked. As he sees us exit the car, he climbs out of his and walks over carrying a bouquet of flowers and a small pink box.

*I told him no gifts!*

"Happy birthday, Han." He grins, wrapping me in a bear hug. He smells *really* good, like the flower shop mixed with something spicy, but I can't really determine the exact smell.

"Thank you, Morgan." I pull back and notice he has on a white button up with little blue flowers on it that match my dress perfectly.

He looks so good.

"Mr. and Mrs. Layton, it's good to see you again." He nods at my parents, then extends his hand to Jake. "Hey man, I'm Morgan. You must be Jake. Nice to meet you."

Jake, ever the people-person, takes his hand enthusiastically. "Nice to meet you too."

Then, Morgan's attention is back on me. "I know you said no gifts, but I couldn't help it." He holds out the bouquet of red carnations mixed with sunflowers and a small light purple flower I don't recognize. I wouldn't think the colors would mesh well, but they look stunning.

Morgan hands over the small box, so I pass the bouquet to my mom who looks like she's smelled something bad. She's probably upset he didn't give me roses or something "fancier."

Morgan looks like a little kid on Christmas, bouncing lightly on the balls of his feet as he watches me pull the silky ribbon bow apart. I give it to Morgan, who puts it in his pocket, then carefully open the box. I gasp when I see the peach colored crystal butterfly nestled in the cotton.

My eyes find Morgan's. "You remembered?"

If I'm not mistaken, the tips of his ears turn a little pink. "Of course I did. That was the first time we met, and I remember every moment. Can I help you put it on?"

Stunned, I simply nod and hand him the delicate gold chain. I turn around and hold my hair up as best I can while he slips the necklace around my neck, and his surprisingly nimble fingers clasp it behind me.

I pretend the slight touch of his fingers doesn't leave goosebumps on my arms. I disregard the fluttering in my stomach and the way the world seems to condense into this two-foot square where only we exist. I ignore the fact that my heart is already too invested in this thing between us even though it's only been a few weeks, and it's supposed to be fake.

Nothing about this moment feels fake.

"We're going to be late for our reservation," my mom snaps, turning on her heel and striding towards the restaurant, still gripping my bouquet.

Jake and my dad fall into step with her, and Morgan places his hand on my lower back as we follow them.

I forgot we'd actually have to interact with my parents, and now my stomach isn't fluttering with twitterpated butterflies but anxiety. I want to believe my mom won't use this as an interrogation, but I'm not holding out hope. My dad will only want to talk football, and Jake will give input where he deems necessary.

When we get inside the waiting area of the restaurant, it's pretty cramped, so we all have to stand relatively close together. Morgan is squeezed flush against my back.

He leans down and whispers quietly so only I can hear, "You look absolutely stunning, Butterfly."

"Thank you. You look pretty great yourself. And thank you so much for the flowers and the necklace. I love it." It's the first piece of jewelry I've been gifted that I *actually* like. Even my engagement ring from Liam wasn't my taste, but I didn't want to seem ungrateful.

"I knew at the shop it was meant to be yours. I'm just glad I finally had a sensible reason to give it to you."

Before I can ask what he means by "sensible reason" the hostess is calling for our party and leading us to a table in the back of the restaurant.

We sit and the waitress takes our drink orders. Then my mom clears her throat, folds her hands in front of her, and to my horror, asks, "So, Morgan, why are you a single dad?"

# CHAPTER 17

*Morgan*

I don't think anyone has ever asked me that question in such a direct way before, and it makes me want to laugh.

I glance over at Hannah, who is hiding her face behind her hands, and it makes me want to laugh even more because she's probably embarrassed by her mom.

I came prepared for outlandish questions, though that's not one I was expecting.

"Well," I start, "I met Alyssa's mom when I was still in the NFL. We were only casually seeing each other when she got pregnant, and she decided to keep the baby. I didn't want my child growing up without a father, so I was as involved as I could be, and we even tried to make a romantic relationship work for a while. I tore my meniscus and had to retire early when Alyssa was three. By then, her mom decided she didn't want to have full custody so we agreed to joint custody, but I'm the primary parent."

Shelly looks skeptical, but I have no reason to lie to her.

"Shame about your injury and early retirement. I think you could've won the Mustangs a Super Bowl title," Mitch says, shaking his head like it's some horrible tragedy instead of an unfortunate accident that ended up being the best thing for me and my daughter.

Don't get me wrong, I loved football. I still love it, but having it be my life while raising a toddler was *hard*. Aly took the top spot on my priority list the minute I heard her heartbeat at the first OB appointment. While I loved my time in the NFL, I'm glad to be done so I can focus on my girl.

"I think they'll get there eventually." I want to get the focus off of me and onto Hannah since it's her big day, so I turn to her. "How are the preparations for the summer program?"

"They're good. We were able to finalize our guest slots yesterday, and sign-ups have been overwhelming in the best way. We're excited to—"

"What summer program?" Shelly cuts in.

"The library's summer program." Hannah lights up as she explains, "It's really cool, actually. We have different people coming in each day to talk about their jobs and businesses, as well as doing activities with people. We have National Park rangers coming, a marine biologist, entomologist, and—"

"That just sounds like career day at an elementary school." Shelly frowns.

Before Hannah can speak up and explain that it's not at all like career day, our waitress comes to take our orders. Once those are placed, there's silence at the table.

Hannah's mom gave her a scathing look when Hannah ordered pasta, even though Shelly "helpfully" suggested one of the salads instead.

I wonder if this is how it always is for Hannah, and if it is, my heart aches for my sweet Butterfly. I can't imagine Shelly was the most comforting maternal figure in the midst of the divorce.

"How does a former NFL wide receiver become a florist?" Jake asks from across the table. It sounds genuine, which I'm grateful for.

"I used to work at a flower shop during the football off-season in high school so I could earn extra cash in case I didn't get a football scholarship. The owner of the shop, Miss Agatha, was a quiet woman who barely spoke, but when she did, she was full of wise words. She told me she didn't need to speak as much in the flower shop because flowers had their own language. I thought she was a little crazy at first, but she gave me a book published in 1960 that explained how every flower had a different meaning.

"For some reason, it fascinated me, and I decided if I didn't get to play professional football, I'd want to open up my own flower shop so I could teach other people about the language of flowers. When I retired, I knew it was what I wanted to do. Luckily for me, the previous owner of the shop I now own was looking to sell, so I jumped on the opportunity." That was a long answer to such a small question.

"Wow, that's pretty cool. So if I wanted to tell a girl I liked her, what kind of flowers would I give her?" Jake asks, and Shelly shoots an exasperated look his way.

"Well, it depends. If you want to just tell her you think she's pretty, you could go with gardenias or yellow tulips. If you're in love with her and want her to know, go with yellow daffodils, red chrysanthemums, or asters. Wisteria means 'will you dance with me?' so that would be a good one, too." I watch as Hannah's eyes dart to the bouquet I gifted her.

Did I purposefully leave out red carnations, sunflowers, and purple limonium? Absolutely. I can't give away all my secrets.

Jake takes out his phone and jots down the ones I suggested, and Shelly gives me a look so scorching I'm surprised I don't burst into flames.

"Who on earth would you be buying flowers for? Your focus should be on your mission. Not a girl," Shelly scolds Jake, and the tips of his ears turn pink.

"No one," Jake mumbles, slumping in his chair. I feel bad for the kid. If he does really like this girl, leaving for two years with little contact would be heartbreaking.

Our food arrives, and we eat in relative silence, which is new for me. Meals with my family, even at a restaurant, are loud and filled with laughter and chatting. I don't understand why they all came out to eat if they're not going to talk to each other.

Watching Shelly and Mitch's interactions—or lack thereof—makes me think they don't actually like each other, let alone love each other. Is this the kind of relationship Hannah and Jake have to model their own romantic relationships off of? If so, it's no wonder Hannah is so hesitant to be in a relationship. Especially after the way her marriage ended.

"When do you leave for your mission, Jake?" I can't take the silence anymore.

"Middle of August is when I report to the Missionary Training Center in Provo."

"And where are you headed, again? I think Hannah told me, but I can't remember." Hannah never told me, but I'll do anything to keep the conversation flowing.

Before Jake can answer, Shelly does it for him, "Cape Verde. Portuguese speaking. He's *so* excited. Aren't you Jacob?"

Jake cringes at the use of his full name and puts on a smile that's so fake it should be painted on. "Thrilled."

"We don't know what we'll do with all the free time we'll have now that Jake will be gone, and Hannah's working so much. It's not like we have any grandchildren to keep us busy." Shelly looks pointedly at Hannah.

Hannah, though her body stiffens, calmly replies, "You can get a dog."

Shelly rears back as if she's been slapped, and I almost burst out laughing. I take a sip of my lemonade to stop the sound from breaking free.

"Well since you and Morgan are so serious now, I'm sure Allison would be happy to hang out at her future grandma's house," Shelly snaps.

"Her name is Alyssa. And I haven't met her yet, so she won't be hanging out with you anytime soon. Sorry, Mom," Hannah replies.

"What do you mean you haven't met her yet? Are you not serious about my daughter?" Shelly turns her sharp, blue-eyed gaze on me.

"I'm quite serious about your daughter, Mrs. Layton. Alyssa is at a vulnerable age, and change is hard for her. I planned on asking Hannah to come over and meet her in the next few weeks, actually. I just haven't gotten around to it." I don't mention Aly will be introduced to Hannah as my friend. Until Hannah is ready to be more, that's fine, but I want her and Aly to spend time together and get to know one another without the pressure of a romantic relationship between us.

Shelly makes a sound of acknowledgement but doesn't press the issue any further.

By the time we're done with our main courses, everyone is too uncomfortable to stick around for dessert, so Mitch pays the bill, and we all awkwardly make our way to our cars.

"Thanks for coming, sorry it sucked," Hannah whispers. We're walking a few steps behind the rest of her family, and I'm grateful for the moment alone.

"Let me take you out for a proper celebration. Are you working Saturday?" We stop behind my car, and she shakes her head. "Perfect. I'll pick you up at eleven."

"Do I get to know what you have planned?"

I grin. "Nope. I'll text you what to wear the night before."

"Okay..." She glances over at her parents watching us intently in the car. "I think they're waiting for us to kiss or something."

"Do you want me to kiss you?" I would kiss her senseless in a heartbeat, people watching be damned, but I want her to *want me* to.

"I—I don't—" she stammers, and I tuck a lock of hair behind her ear and shush her.

"The first time we kiss isn't going to be in a busy parking lot with your parents watching." I tilt my head and place a kiss on her forehead instead. I may have imagined it, but I swear she leaned into it.

"They know I'm uncomfortable showing affection around them, so it won't seem strange... Thank you again, Morgan. You made tonight much more bearable." She sighs.

"Anytime, Butterfly. I'll text you tomorrow."

"Okay. See you Saturday."

"See you Saturday." She turns and walks away, her pretty dress swishing against her thick thighs.

Even though tonight wasn't the greatest, seeing Hannah always brightens my day. I can't wait until I can see her more regularly. Tonight felt like a test, and I think I passed with flying colors.

I just hope my prize in the end is her.

# CHAPTER 18

*Hannah*

The minute I got home last night I looked up the meaning behind the flowers. It took some digging to find the purple flower, but I *think* it's purple limonium.

According to Google, sunflowers symbolize loyalty, admiration, happiness, and longevity, which Morgan had already explained. The purple limonium has so many different meanings: purity, loyalty, success, love, devotion.

I would think this bouquet was just a pretty, aesthetically pleasing, thoughtful gift if it weren't for the red carnations.

Everything I read about carnations was similar. A deep, dark red is meant to convey deep love and affection. A paler red is meant to declare "my heart aches for you" and admiration.

The carnations in the bouquet are, in my unprofessional opinion, somewhere between deep and pale, so I have no idea what they mean.

This bouquet could be a declaration of feelings or just a pretty combination, and I won't know for sure unless I ask Morgan. But I don't think I want to do that.

I got into work this morning and immediately debriefed Sage about the dinner last night, gushing about my necklace and lamenting over the awkward questions from my mom. We've been debating the meaning of the carnations for the last three hours in between tasks.

"Hannah, I swear to Satan I'm going to smack you upside the head. He. Likes. You. That man is head-over-heels, weak-in-the-knees. He came to a family dinner with your serpent of a mom and didn't run for the hills! When are you going to admit you have feelings for him, too?" Sage emphasizes her points with a quick jab of her spoon in my direction.

I sigh, barely picking at my sandwich. I want to argue that she's wrong—that it was a friendly gesture and a meaningless bouquet, but Morgan doesn't do meaningless with flowers. If he were any other guy, it would be a lot easier to brush off.

I also don't want to admit I have feelings for him—to Sage or to myself. That's scary and runs the risk of me getting my heart torn from my chest. What happens if we do this for real and he realizes I'm just a weird book nerd with depression and mountains of religious trauma? What if he wants more kids? I can't give him that. What if—

Sage claps her hands loudly, making me jump out of my thought spiral. "I can feel you thinking from over here. Care to voice your concerns out loud?"

"I'm just scared," I admit, and Sage's shoulders sag while her face morphs into a sad, understanding smile.

"I would be worried if you weren't scared, babe. You've been through a lot, and there are things that could go wrong with Morgan. But... what if things go *right?*"

"I guess you're right. I'll think about it." It's the most I can promise right now.

The rest of the day goes by quickly—thank goodness—and by the time I'm headed home, I have come to terms with the fact I have feelings for my fake boyfriend. I'll ask him to come with me to Wes's show in two weeks and give him a flower that says, "I like you."

Is it a great plan? No.

But will it work? I hope so.

After I park in the driveway, I pull out my phone and call Elli.

"Hello?" she answers on the first ring, and some type of bass pounds in the background. She must be with Wes preparing for a show.

"Hey, Elli. How's it going?"

"Great! How're you doing? I hope you had a good birthday. I have your present for you! And I'm excited to see you in two weeks." She sounds happy. Elli was always quiet and reserved as a kid, and I know she struggled with some undiagnosed depression as well. Hearing her so happy makes me smile as much as it makes me jealous.

She left the church at pretty much the same time she moved to Texas, and she's been living her life authentically ever since with her hot rockstar boyfriend.

I envy that kind of freedom.

"I'm excited to see you two again. I was just calling to see if that extra ticket you mentioned was still a possibility?"

Elli gasps, "YES. Oh my God, *yes*. Are you bringing a date?"

Even though she can't see me, I cover my face in embarrassment. Emma was always the hopeless romantic one growing up, Elli and I just went along for the ride when she told us her dating stories. Now, it's like we're making up for lost time.

"I am. His name is Morgan, and we're..." God, this is embarrassing. "We're fake dating right now, but I want to make it *not* fake... if that makes sense."

Elli's silent for a minute before she squeals. "I love it. I can't wait to hear the details. Emma will actually be there too, she's coming to Utah because her family is having a big get-together for Andrew's birthday. He would've been forty."

That sobers us for a minute. Andrew was Emma's brother who passed away almost seven years ago. I know it's hard for Emma to come back because her family doesn't treat her well, but she and Andrew were close. It makes sense she'd come back to memorialize him.

"Sounds like she'll need a distraction. We should have a girls' day before the concert! We can go shopping and get ready together," I suggest. Usually the thought of going clothing shopping with anyone but Sage would make me want to cry, but Elli and Emma are both plus sized like me, so shopping with them wouldn't be tormenting.

"I love that idea. I'll start a group chat tonight, and we can make a definitive plan!" Someone says something to Elli, and I hear her mumbled response. "I have to get going, but I'm excited! See you then!"

"Bye, Elli. See you soon." I hang up, a giddy feeling bubbling in my stomach at the prospect of having some girl time with my favorite cousins.

With a family as big as ours, I'm not *supposed* to have favorites, but I don't really care. Emma and Elli are the sisters I never had, and I'm glad we're still in touch, even if it's not as often as I like.

A knock on my window startles me, and I turn and see my mom's scowling face glaring at me from the other side of the tinted glass.

I motion for her to step back so I can get out, and as soon as the door is open, she's talking.

"Why are you just sitting out here in the driveway? Whatever, it doesn't matter. My car's in the shop, and Dad's running late. I need you to come with me to pick up ice cream because the missionaries are coming over, and I have no dessert."

I completely forgot they were having the missionaries over for dinner. Or maybe I didn't know? There's every possibility someone canceled dinner for them, so my parents picked up the responsibility.

The *last* thing I want to do is suffer through a dinner with my family and the missionaries, but it's too late to pretend to be busy.

"Alright. Let's go." I motion to the car, and she gets in. I notice Jake's car is in the driveway and wonder why she isn't forcing him to go or taking his car.

Luckily for me, the grocery store is only five minutes away, but it feels like hours with only the sound of the engine running and my mom tapping away on her phone.

When she finally speaks, it's as we're pulling into the parking spot. "One of the elders coming tonight is a late bloomer. He's twenty-five."

*Fantastic.* I know exactly where this is going. "Okay? Why does that matter?"

"I just wanted you to be prepared for someone closer to your age to be there. He's very handsome."

"I have a boyfriend, Mom."

She makes a sound that's something between a scoff and a grunt but waves me off and steps out of the car.

I dutifully follow her around and give her opinions on ice cream flavors, and then we're back in my car and headed home. She's never really been in my car, so her eyes glance around the random pieces of mail and receipts that I keep stashed in one of the cup holders.

Her eyes snag on the little pink gift card Sage gave me, and she picks it up.

"What's this?" Her tone is sharp and accusatory, like I've been caught with drugs instead of a gift card.

"My birthday present from Sage."

"Why is she giving you gift cards for a lingerie store? Are you *fornicating* with that man?"

"No." I don't owe her an explanation, and I want this conversation to be done with.

She tosses the gift card down like it burns her and picks up a receipt for a coffee shop I go to every once in a while. "*Coffee?!* Alcohol, lingerie, and now this? What's next, Hannah? Are you going to pierce your nose and start doing marijuana?"

I want to tell her you don't *do* marijuana. You smoke it, or you take it in edible form, but I don't think she'd appreciate that. I want to point out that those things are normal for well-adjusted adults to enjoy. This five minute car ride has turned into an interrogation, and I'm sure if we didn't have dinner to prepare for, she'd be scolding me for my life choices.

I don't get a chance to respond because we pull into the driveway, and my dad is there, presumably with the missionaries, meaning she has to put on her mask of hospitality. "I don't recognize you anymore," she says as she exits my car.

I sit and stare out the window to get my bearings, wondering what in the *hell* just happened. A sense of foreboding sits like a lead weight in my stomach.

Something big and probably awful is going to happen, I just know it.

# CHAPTER 19

## Morgan

On Saturday morning, I take Aly to breakfast at our favorite bakery before heading over to my sister Alice's house so they can go shopping for summer clothes for my not-so-little girl. Aly said she wanted to go with someone with "fashion sense," and I pretended like it didn't hurt my feelings.

It gives me the perfect opportunity to spend the day with Hannah.

Alice and Cooper live fifteen minutes away from us in a subdivision similar to ours with their four dogs. They foster kids from time to time, but that's the closest they'll get to being parents. Alice loves her job as a teacher, and Coop works as a civil engineer for the military and has to leave on temporary duty a few months out of the year. They decided fostering and helping kids who need temporary homes was fulfilling enough for them.

Alice answers the door wearing bright orange overalls with a white tank top underneath. Her brown, chin length hair is up in two messy buns, and she's got paint on one side of her face.

"Aly! I'm so excited to go shopping with you today." Alice leans in close and stage whispers, "Good thing your dad isn't coming. He wouldn't know fashion if it bit him on the arm."

Aly laughs, and even though it's at my expense, it warms my heart. She doesn't laugh much, so I think this time with her aunt will be good for her.

"You're right, Aunt Al. He wears the same things every day."

"Hey!" I protest. "I do not."

Alice and Aly both cross their arms and pop their hips, giving me a "get real" look that must be hereditary.

"Button-up shirts with floral patterns and chino pants. And when you're not wearing those, you're wearing basketball shorts and t-shirts." Aly ticks them off on her fingers, and yeah, she's not wrong.

I like what I like, and it's hard for me to find clothes that fit and look good with my body type.

"Alright, alright. Should I wear bright overalls like your aunt, Aly?"

Aly scrunches her nose and then pretends to throw up, making Alice snort.

"I thought so. I'll be back by dinner, but text me if you need me, and I'll be here as soon as I can."

Aly nods. "I'll be okay, Dad. I promise. Have fun with your girlfriend."

I rear back, and Alice looks at me. We say at the same time, "Girlfriend?"

Aly rolls her eyes. "You've been going out a lot recently, and I saw 'Hannah' texting you one day. But I didn't read your messages! I'm okay if you have a girlfriend, Dad."

Fuck, she's going to make me cry. I thought she'd hate that I had a girlfriend—fake or not—and be upset I didn't tell her immediately.

"I'll talk to her today to see if she wants to come over for dinner sometime." My throat is clogged from the emotions rolling through me. "I love you, Bub." I pull her in for a hug, and she mumbles a "love you too" into my stomach.

Alice gives me a sharp look that means I'm in trouble for not telling her about Hannah. I just told her I was going out with a friend. "*We will be talking about this later,*" she mouths.

I have no doubt we will, and it will turn into a family affair because my sister can't keep secrets to save her life.

"Have fun, Morgy," Alice sings as she and Aly head inside.

Anticipation and excitement sizzle through my veins, like they always do when I'm about to see Hannah. I hope she likes what I have planned for today. I told her to dress casually, but with good shoes since we'll be doing some walking. It feels like it's been years since I've seen her, rather than just three days.

*Get a hold of yourself, man.*

I park in the driveway next to her car and practically bounce to the front door. Shelly answers, giving me a scathing look, but I plaster on a smile.

"Good morning, Mrs. Layton. I'm here for Hannah."

She keeps her eyes on me as she calls out, "Hannah! Your *friend* is here." The way she emphasizes "friend" makes me want to growl at the woman.

I briefly wonder if she knows we're faking it, but there's no way Hannah would tell her, and I think I've been pretty convincing thus far. Guess I just have to kick it up a notch for her mom.

Shelly steps aside, and Hannah comes out the door, nearly stealing the breath from my lungs. She's wearing another dress, but this one is a soft rose color with a gathered front, showing the *tiniest* bit of cleavage. It cinches at her waist and flows out over her wide hips. The material looks soft and flowy, and it takes all my reserve not to reach out and touch her. She has on white sandals that look like they're made of a foamy material so her feet won't kill her by the end of the day. Her hair is curled softly around her face, and her makeup is subtle, highlighting her plump lips and beautiful eyes.

The best part of her outfit is the necklace around her neck.

My necklace.

She's effortlessly beautiful, and *I* get to look at her all day long.

"Hey, gorgeous," I say, holding my hand out for her to take it.

To my utter delight, she interlaces our fingers together. "Good morning." She turns to her mom. "I'll be gone all day. I have my key." Then she drags me down the porch steps to my car.

*Strange.* Their relationship is strained on a good day, but today seems different. Worse, somehow. It's clear Hannah doesn't want to talk about it, though because after I open the door, help her in, and climb into the driver's seat, she says as chipper as she can, "What do you have planned today?"

"I thought we'd stop and get coffee at Daily Rise, then I have somewhere I want to take you to get your birthday present."

She frowns. "Coffee sounds good; I love Daily Rise. But you already got me a birthday present." She brings her hand to her neck and fiddles with the butterfly.

"That was only part one. I couldn't give you your full gift at dinner."

"Morgan..." she warns. "I said no presents."

"I already broke that rule, Butterfly. You'll find I'm quite the rule breaker." I give her what I hope is a charming smile, and she rolls her eyes.

We pull up to Daily Rise and order—a classic cold brew for me and an iced caramel and vanilla latte for Hannah—then Hannah turns to me and asks, "Are you doing anything the weekend after next?"

I go over my mental calendar. Since Aly's going to lunch with her mom next Saturday, there's nothing on my schedule other than family dinner on Sunday. I tell Hannah about dinner, and she waves me off. "I was more worried about Saturday."

"I'm free." Is she going to ask *me* on a date?

"My cousin Elli's boyfriend is performing with a big band, Keely and the Kissers. They're stopping in Salt

Lake that Saturday. Would you... Would you want to go? With me?"

I've never heard of the band, but it's been a while since I've gone to a concert. Besides, why would I turn down an opportunity to spend more time with Hannah?

"I'd love to. Let me make sure someone can hang out with Aly, but I should be good to go."

Hannah lets out a sigh like she's relieved I said yes. How could she possibly think I'd say no?

"My cousin Emma will be there, too. She lives in San Diego now, but she's visiting Utah during that time. So it'll just be you and us girls until Wes can join us. Is that okay?"

I don't think she knows her wanting me to meet her cousins means more to me than meeting her parents at this point. These are people Hannah chooses to be involved with. But it does beg the question, "Do they know we're fake dating?"

Hannah blushes. "Kind of."

*Kind of?* What the hell does that mean?

I don't get a chance to ask because we're given our drinks, and it's time to drive to our second destination.

We make casual conversation about our weeks while we drive, and the comfortable silences in between make it feel like this is a regular Saturday morning. I can imagine Aly in the back seat, inputting her own opinions while we drive to a farmer's market or head to get groceries.

The fantasy is so vivid it makes my heart ache. I want that. I want it so badly I can taste it.

When I stop in front of the store we're going to, Hannah looks over at me skeptically. "Why are we here?"

Instead of answering, I hop out of the car and open the door for her, then lead her to the door of White Lilly Books—a local independent bookstore. The bookstore is a perfectly square building painted white, with a bright blue door, and a mural of The Great Salt Lake on one side. It sits nestled between a philly cheesesteak shop and a clothing boutique.

"Morgan," she whispers as the bell above the door rings, but I ignore her still.

Jethro—the owner—a white man in his early sixties, with gray-blonde hair in two long braids over his shoulders and the kindest green eyes, makes his way around the checkout desk. He's probably only five-foot-ten, wearing jeans and an old Johnny Cash t-shirt today, along with his cowboy boots. He looks like a young Willie Nelson.

"Morgan, good to see you, my boy." He grasps my hand tightly and turns to Hannah, who offers him her hand. "You must be the lovely Hannah Morgan told me about."

"It's nice to meet you, Mr…" Hannah trails off.

"Ah, where are my manners? I'm Jethro Lillywhite. I own this place."

"Nice to meet you, Mr. Lillywhite. I'm Hannah."

Jethro waves her off. "Call me Jethro. Mr. Lillywhite sounds so pretentious. Now," he claps his hands together, "Morgan tells me you've got ten minutes. Let me show you where every genre is so you won't be confused."

Hannah looks at me for an explanation, but I don't offer one. Mainly because Jethro is dragging her around the shop pointing out the neatly organized shelves.

There are a few customers milling about, doing their own shopping, but for the most part, it's pretty quiet.

Once Jethro has shown Hannah the layout of the store, he brings her back to the front and hands her a canvas tote bag with the store's logo on it.

"Alright, Chickadee, you've got ten minutes. Morgan will start the timer, and I'll be at the checkout when you're ready." He pats me on the back and heads over to the checkout.

"Morgan, please tell me what's going on," Hannah pleads, inspecting the tote bag.

"Well, like Jethro said, you have ten minutes."

"Ten minutes for *what?*"

"Ten minutes to gather every book that caught your eye. You put them in that tote, and then I'm buying them for you." She goes to protest, but I hold up my hand. "I know you're going to say it's too much. But I saw you stop and check out at least ten books, so if there aren't ten books in that bag, I will pick them out myself."

"But, why? Why would you do this for me?" Hannah nibbles anxiously on her bottom lip.

I shrug. "Because books make you happy, and I want to make you happy." That barely scratches the surface of what I want. But it's the best explanation I can give right now. I pull out my phone and open the timer app, showing it to her I say, "Your time starts... now." And she's off.

She heads straight for the romance section, unsurprisingly. She spent the most time there with Jethro.

I meander over to the counter to wait for her, not wanting her to think she's being watched the whole time. I meant what I said, I'll add more books if she doesn't pick out at least ten.

"How did you think of this?" Jethro asks, clicking away on the computer behind the counter.

"My sister saw a viral video of a husband who did this for his wife. He did it in a Barnes and Noble, but I wanted to go local. Hannah loves books, but I would never want to just buy her some because I don't know what she wants to read. This seemed like a good gift for her."

Jethro hums. "She seems very special to you."

I watch her move from romance over to the historical fiction section, and my heart swells.

"She's the most special."

# Chapter 20

*Hannah*

I've died and gone to Heaven, but it doesn't look anything like the Celestial Kingdom.

This is a store I've been meaning to check out but never got around to. Liam never wanted me to buy books because they "took up too much space." So I got most of my reading done on my Kindle. I've bought a few physical books since the divorce, but there aren't a lot of places for me to put them at my mom's house, so I'm like a kid in a candy store right now.

I'm trying not to be greedy, but I'm having a hard time putting books back. It seems like Jethro has a lot of independent authors in this store, which is *amazing*, but it also means there are a lot of options.

Morgan said at least ten books, and so far I have six.

"How much longer do I have?" I call out from behind the shelves.

"Four minutes," Morgan's deep voice replies.

*Shit.*

I move from historical fiction to the fantasy section. There are too many to choose from, and I can't read a proper blurb, so I am quite literally judging a book by its cover. I avoid books by authors I know I don't like, which helps cut down the choices some. I swear I only spend a few seconds there, but Morgan comes around the shelves just as his phone alarm goes off.

"Time's up, Butterfly." He grins, and I have the sudden urge to kiss him.

*Woah. Where did that come from?*

I follow him to the checkout counter where Jethro scans all *eleven* of my books and throws in a gift card for $25. Morgan thanks him and tells him he'll have his weekly bouquet ready for him on Wednesday, and we exit the store.

Morgan opens my door for me, but before I get in, I wrap my arms around him and squeeze him as hard as I can—which isn't very hard because I'm not very strong, and he is *massive.* "Thank you so much, Morgan. I don't know how to repay you."

He sets the bag on the seat and wraps his muscled arms around my waist and whispers into my hair, "I don't want you to repay me, Hannah. Seeing your face light up was enough. Happy birthday, Butterfly."

He pulls back and looks at me, bringing a hand up to tuck a piece of hair behind my ear. The air sizzles around us, tension building.

This is it. He's going to kiss me, and it won't be fake anymore. I already know it's going to be an earth-shattering kiss, and I don't think I'll ever want him to stop.

His phone ringing breaks the moment, and he jumps a little and steps back, looking at who's calling.

"I'm so sorry, it's my sister who's watching Aly."

"It's okay. I'll just be waiting in the car." I give his arm a squeeze.

I try not to deflate, to put on a happy face. It's not his fault we were interrupted. He answers while I climb into the passenger seat.

His face pinches as he talks to his sister, and when he gets in the car, his jaw is clenched so hard he looks like he's going to break it.

"I'm sorry to have to cut our date short, but Aly and my sister saw Whitney while they were shopping, and Whitney pretended not to notice them. Aly's distraught, thinking her mom forgot her. I don't want to—"

I place a hand on his arm. "It's okay, Morgan. I understand Aly comes first. I have to do some apartment hunting anyway, so it's okay. I'm not upset. I'm just sorry Aly's hurting."

He blows out a long breath. "Thank you, I really appreciate that." He backs out of the parking spot and pulls onto the main road to get on the freeway when he asks, "Wait, why do you need to go apartment hunting?"

*Shit.* I shouldn't have said anything. We were having such a fun day, and Aly needs his full attention. He can't be worrying about me, too.

"It's nothing." I fiddle with the hem of my dress, which is suddenly *very* interesting.

"It's not nothing, Han. If you need a place to stay, I can help." He sounds so earnest.

"My mom said I have two weeks to find somewhere else to live because she 'doesn't recognize me,' and I'm not 'living the right way.'"

"What the hell does that mean? Why would she say she doesn't recognize you?" he asks.

"Well, she was upset about the alcohol. Then she found a receipt for coffee in my car, and Sage—my best friend—gave me a lingerie gift card for my birthday so she assumes you and I are... um... *fornicating*."

Morgan stiffens in the driver's seat, and his eyebrows almost meet his hairline. He shifts in his seat. "I—that's—well, that's shitty of her. You're an adult who can make her own choices. What's it matter to her what you drink or wear, or if you... ya know?"

I almost laugh at his avoiding the topic of sex. I would if this conversation weren't awkward enough. "I'm not following the rules of the church, and she's upset. She'll get over it eventually, maybe. But I'm honestly a little relieved. Other than trying to find an affordable place, this situation is actually taking a load off of my shoulders. I'll no longer have to pretend to be someone I'm not."

"I get that. It's easier to be who you are away from your parents." He clears his throat. "I can help with the housing situation."

"I'm not moving into your house, Morgan," I state, even if the idea is enticing.

Morgan barks out a startled laugh. "No, I wouldn't ask you to do that. There's a studio apartment above the flower shop that isn't being used. It's big enough for one person but wouldn't have worked for Aly and me."

"I won't live there rent free."

"I figured as much. But I own the flower shop outright, so I'm flexible with rent. You'd be in charge of your utilities, too, obviously, but it's yours if you want it."

I mull it over. The flower shop is closer to work than my parents' house. It's in a decent, safe area, and the shop is well-maintained, so I imagine the apartment would be as well.

"I'd like to see it before I make a decision. If that's okay?"

"Sure, we can stop by after we pick up Aly."

"What do you mean *we*? I thought you'd drop me off at home."

"You haven't eaten, Aly hasn't eaten, so I figure we'd grab some comfort food and spend the day watching movies. She asked me earlier when she could meet you. We'll just stop at the flower shop before we get lunch so you can check out the space. But if you don't want to meet her—"

"I'd love to meet Aly if you're okay with it."

"I'm more than okay with it. I can't wait for two of my favorite people to meet." He gives me a lopsided grin, and that's when I realize we've exited the freeway and made it to a nice suburb of Farmington. He turns down a manicured, tree-lined street and stops in front of a brown brick rambler-style house.

"Wow, this place is nice," I mutter, suddenly extremely nervous. I'm meeting not only Aly but his sister, too. *Shit.* I hope they like me.

# CHAPTER 21

*Morgan*

I don't think Alice was telling me the whole story when she called. I'm sure she left out some details because Aly hearing them again would just hurt her even more.

I make it a point not to talk negatively about Whitney around Aly, but right now I want to call and yell at her about being a heartless wench for ignoring our daughter.

Mother's Day is next week, and Aly has been so excited about it, but there's no telling how she'll feel now. I won't force her to go to lunch if she doesn't want to. If Aly never wanted to see Whitney again, I'd go to court and make it happen.

What a fucking mess.

Today was supposed to be about Hannah, and we were *finally* going to kiss. I was going to lean in and finally know what those plush lips feel like. Then we would have a conversation about this maybe not being fake anymore. We would see if she was ready to give a real relationship a try.

I had already planned to talk to her about meeting Aly, even though we aren't seeing each other in an official capacity, so I guess this little hiccup in our plans isn't so bad.

I think Aly is going to love Hannah. At least, I hope so. I'll do whatever is best for my little girl, and if it means letting this woman go, I would break my own heart and do it.

I pray to whatever Gods exist that isn't the case.

I didn't plan on having Hannah meet Alice or anyone from my family this soon, though. They're a lot. I love them, but they can be overwhelming.

As we get out of the RAV, my heart feels like it's going to beat directly out of my chest. I grab Hannah's hand and hold it as we make our way up the walkway to the front door. As soon as the doorbell rings, the barking starts.

Hannah jumps at the loud dogs but doesn't seem scared, which is good. They're harmless, mostly. They just get excited. Murphy, a senior shih tzu, has been known to pee in people's shoes, but Alice is pretty good at getting him outside often enough that it hasn't happened in a while.

"How many dogs does she have?" Hannah whispers. I don't answer fast enough because Alice is opening the door and trying to shove three of the four beasts back into the house. Murphy stands between her legs, his tongue poking out of his mouth as he assesses us.

"Hi, oh—hi! I'm Alice. You must be Hannah. Don't mind the guard dogs. They wouldn't know how to protect our house if someone was actually a threat. Come on in." Alice steps aside, and I lead Hannah in to take the brunt of the sniffs.

"This is Murphy." I scoop up the gray and white poof. "He's the leader of the pack, aren't you, Murph?" He yips at me in response and licks my hand before I set him down.

"Dad?" Aly says from the doorway, eyeing Hannah warily.

*Fuck.* This is probably not the best time for me to introduce them. I didn't think this through hard enough. Aly is upset, and adding a new person to the mix isn't great.

"Hey, Bub. This is Hannah. Hannah, this is Alyssa."

Hannah straightens and waves. "Hey, Alyssa. Nice to meet you."

Aly, polite as ever, waves back with a soft, "Hi."

"Do you think you could point me to the restroom, please?" Hannah asks me, clearly trying to give me a minute alone with Aly. I appreciate her ability to read the situation.

"Down this hall, last door right before the kitchen," I answer. Hannah nods and walks in the direction I told her.

"I'm sorry, Aly. I was with Hannah when Alice called, and I—"

"It's okay, Dad. I'm not mad you brought her here." Aly crosses her arms in front of her like she's trying to hug herself.

"Are you sure? Because I can take her home right now and come back for you."

She shakes her head, and her bottom lip wobbles.

I curse under my breath, kneel in front of my baby girl, and pull her into me. "I'm so, so sorry, Bub. Do you want to tell me what happened?"

Aly takes a calming breath but still stutters as she explains what happened. She and Alice were walking around Old Navy when Aly heard someone who sounded like Whitney walking by. Aly turned and recognized her and called out, "Mom?" Whitney, who was on the phone, stopped, turned around, looked at Aly, and then turned back around, walking out of the store. Aly tried to follow after her but got stopped by a store employee concerned about a child being alone.

"I texted her, too, and asked her why she ignored me, but she didn't respond." Aly angrily wipes away the tears on her cheeks. "I just don't understand why. Why wouldn't she even say hello to me?"

"I don't know, Aly. I wish I could give you a better explanation, but some people just do mean things. Maybe she has a good reason, but only she knows the answer to that. Dwelling on the what-ifs can just hurt us more."

Aly nods. "I don't think I want to talk about it anymore. I told Aunt Al not to call you because I didn't want to be a bother, but she wouldn't listen."

"I'm glad she called. You could never be a bother, Bub."

"Does Hannah hate me because I ruined your date?" she whispers, looking down at her feet.

"Not at all. Hannah understands you're my priority. She was worried you would be upset she came along with me."

"I'm not. I don't know her yet, but she's pretty. She seems nice. And she makes you smile more than you have before." She pauses to think for a second. "Is she going to hang out with us for the rest of the day?"

"Well," I say carefully. "I was going to ask if that was okay with you? I thought maybe we could go get some food from Joy Luck and watch some movies at our house. We have to stop by the shop first to show Hannah the apartment above it, to see if she wants to live there. Would that be okay?"

Aly's eyes light up at the mention of her favorite Chinese food restaurant, and she nods enthusiastically. "That sounds good. Do you think Hannah likes *Scooby-Doo*?" Aly found a bunch of my old DVDs, and my *Scooby-Doo* collection is pretty extensive. She's been hooked ever since.

"There's only one way to find out. Let's go find her before Aunt Al tells her all of my embarrassing stories." Aly leads the way as we walk down the hall and to the kitchen where Alice is talking with Hannah.

"If you want someone to go with, let me know! I'm pretty free during the summer," Alice says, and I wonder what the hell they're talking about. "Oh hi, Morgy. I was just telling Hannah about the size inclusive thrift store in Salt Lake. She's never heard of Thrift Plus, can you believe it?"

"I'll have to check it out," Hannah says with a genuine smile, and a warmth spreads through my veins seeing her bonding with one of my sisters. If she gets along with Alice, I'm sure she'll get along great with Sarah and Olivia, too.

"Not everyone is as obsessed with thrifting as you are, Alice." I turn to Hannah and place a hand on her lower back. "Ready to go check out the apartment?"

"What apartment?" Alice asks.

"Hannah might move into the apartment above the shop," Aly explains. "Can we get going soon? I'm getting hungry."

Alice's mouth forms an "o," and she nods in understanding. "If you need help cleaning the place, you let us know. The Fowler Crew has mastered the art of swift and efficient cleaning."

Hannah's smile is more nervous now but no less grateful. "Thank you, Alice. I'll be sure to let you know if I need help. And I might take you up on that thrifting company. It was so nice to meet you." Hannah holds out her hand to shake Alice's, but Alice scoffs and rounds the counter instead.

"We hug in this family," she says as she wraps her arms around Hannah and squeezes. "It was lovely to meet you, Hannah. I look forward to seeing you again."

Alice lets her go and turns to hug Aly. "Bye, girlfriend. I'll see you soon. Love you."

Aly mumbles against Alice's chest, "Love you, too, Aunt Alice."

"Bye, baby brother!" She hugs me and whispers just loud enough for me to hear, "Wrap it before you tap it." I push her off of me—gently—and she cackles. The menace.

"Goodbye, Al. Thank you for watching out for my girl."

Alice watches us hop in the car, then waves us off as we drive away—a family tradition for whatever reason.

"Alright. Quick stop at the flower shop, and then we'll order from Joy Luck. Hannah, do you like *Scooby-Doo*?"

"I *love Scooby-Doo.* It's one of my favorite childhood shows. Why?"

My eyes meet Aly's in the rearview mirror, and she smiles wide as she says, "Dad has all of the old DVDs, and I was thinking maybe we could watch them while we eat?"

Hannah turns just enough to look at Aly. "I think that's the perfect Saturday afternoon activity. I've never been to Joy Luck, though. What do you recommend?"

Some people don't know how to talk to Aly, they either treat her like she's still four, or they treat her *too* adult. Hannah doesn't sound condescending or like she's trying to get her to like her. She speaks to her like she's an actual human who has opinions and like she actually wants to get to know my daughter.

"I really like the shrimp lo mein and their sesame chicken. But Dad likes their orange chicken and Mongolian beef. We always get potstickers, cream cheese wontons, and egg rolls to share, too."

"I'm not picky, and those all sound delicious." Hannah turns back to the front, and my phone pings.

"It looks like Alice just texted me. Can you see what she said?" I hand Hannah my phone, and she hesitantly takes it.

Her cheeks flush as she reads the message, and then she hands my phone back. "I don't think I was supposed to see that." She doesn't sound upset, just a little embarrassed.

When we park behind the flower shop, I quickly read the message from Alice.

**Alice:** She's so lovely, Morgy. I think she might be my favorite person you've dated. Don't fuck this up.

I'm relieved it's not something bad, but I can see why Hannah would be a little embarrassed. We're not *actually* dating.

Yet.

But I hope that changes very, very soon.

# CHAPTER 22

*Hannah*

Morgan explains that if I move in here, this is where I'll park. There are four employee parking spots behind the store and one unmarked that he'd designate to me.

Aly wants to wait in the car, so Morgan and I make our way up the metal steps to an unmarked brown door. Morgan unlocks it and lets me walk in first.

I was expecting a small, dusty space that looks unkempt and possibly haunted, but that's not what I see.

It's a studio with enough space for a queen-size bed in one corner. There's a full bathroom, and the kitchen is big enough to accommodate one person. The floors are some type of lightly stained wood that pairs nicely with the pale blue walls and the gray backsplash in the kitchen. I walk over to the bathroom which is painted the same color blue, and the tiles on the floor match the backsplash in the kitchen. There's a decent size tub and shower combo and a vanity sink with ample storage.

Some dust lingers, like it's been empty for a while, but otherwise, this place is pretty clean and well maintained. Nothing looks one wrong move away from breaking, and cheap rent is cheap rent.

"So?" Morgan rocks on his heels, anxiously looking around.

"I think it's perfect. Are you sure you're okay with me living here?"

"I'm positive, Butterfly. I want you to have the space you need from your parents to spread your wings, and this place isn't being used." He looks like he wants to say more, but he stops.

The air around us is charged again, and if his daughter weren't waiting in the car, I would kiss him. I would say "fuck it" to my whole flower and concert plan, and we'd have the feelings conversation right now.

As it stands, his daughter *is* in the car, and I'm excited to watch *Scooby-Doo*, eat Chinese food, and get to know her better.

"We can hash out details later, let's get your girl home and watch some cartoon villains run amok."

I head out the door, and Morgan follows. I wait until he's locked the door before starting down the stairs. When we reach the car, he opens my door for me and then rounds the car.

"Alright. Let me call the restaurant, and we can go home and get my girls fed." He looks pointedly at me, and my stomach does a flip.

*His girls.*

Aly cheers, and Morgan places our order while I try to stop myself from smiling like an idiot.

The drive to Morgan's house is quick. He pulls into a suburb similar to the one Alice lives in, but this one looks older, more established than Alice's. That surprises me a bit. I know he's pretty well off, so I thought for sure he'd have a newer house in a newer neighborhood.

He clicks the garage button on the mirror of the car, and the garage door to a blueish gray house with white accents opens up.

It's *stunning*.

There's a three-car garage, and above the garage are two arched windows with white curtains on the inside. The lawn is perfectly manicured with a beautiful flower bed lining the literal white picket fence. That's all I can see from my vantage point, and I'm excited to see the rest.

Morgan pulls in, and I notice an older looking pick up truck in one of the garage bays, but the third bay is empty except for a few tools and random boxes.

We exit the car and through the garage door is a small hallway. To the left, I see a laundry room, and to the right is a half staircase that leads to what I assume is the basement. We head directly into a large family room that's painted a soft gray with gray oak floors. There's a large black leather sectional and a TV stand with a large TV on it.

There's another set of half stairs leading from the family room up to another floor where the dining room and kitchen are, as well as what looks like a small office right next to the front door.

The floors are the same as in the family room, the kitchen counters are a bright white marble over gray cabinets with stainless steel appliances. The kitchen has a massive island in the middle and plenty of cabinet space and room for cooking. There are pops of color in the form of floral accents that bring everything together.

"Wow, Morgan. Your home is stunning." I set the food down on the kitchen counter while Morgan and Aly gather utensils and plates for us.

"Thank you. I can't take too much credit for it. My mom and sisters decorated for the most part because I didn't have the first clue about what to do."

"Gigi and Aunt Livi didn't want me to live in a 'bachelor pad,' so they made sure it looked nice," Aly explains, and I chuckle at her candor.

"Should I take the food to the living room?" I ask, and Aly shakes her head.

"We're going to the movie room! I'll show you." She picks up the plates and heads down the stairs, I follow as quickly as I can. Morgan doesn't follow as she leads me down into the basement and into a dark room with a modular couch that can be put in different configurations.

"Do you want something to drink? We have juice, soda, and water," Aly asks, pulling my attention to a full-on snack bar in the corner.

"Sure, thanks. Do you have Sprite?"

"Yep!" She produces the green can. "Dad likes them, too. Can you help me set out the blankets and arrange the couch?"

She directs me how she wants the couch, and I help her lay out some cozy blankets. When we're done, Morgan comes in, having changed into an old Mustangs t-shirt and gray joggers.

I'm not an overtly sexual person. I get turned on, obviously, and I found Liam attractive, but I've never had desire course through my veins and my panties get wet or whatever the women in my books experience. Sex was always just something I knew a husband and wife should do. A way to make babies. A duty to fulfill.

But Morgan in a tight shirt and gray sweatpants apparently flipped a switch in my brain because I have to close my mouth to keep from drooling.

The t-shirt strains against the muscles on his arms and clings deliciously to the little pouch of belly on his stomach. His body is clearly an athlete's body, but it's not the kind of muscle you get from hours and hours in the gym. Parts of him are hard with muscle, but he's soft in his tummy area—right where you want to snuggle into. The joggers hug his thick thighs and show off his... package. Which isn't even hard. It's just *there*. Beckoning me through the gray fabric.

I've never wondered what a man's cock looks like, but I'm very curious about Morgan's. Which is a shocking revelation considering I'd never cared for my ex's.

"Sorry, girls, I had to go check on the kitties and change my clothes. They're safely closed away so they don't try to steal our food. Let's get this party started," Morgan says, settling into the couch and effectively snapping me out of my state of arousal.

*God that's embarrassing.*

I let Aly settle in before I do so she can have the spot she wants. I notice a small square of wood holding the food steady so it doesn't spill all over the blankets. Smart.

We spend the rest of the day eating and laughing. We make guesses on who the villain actually is and keep a tally of who wins each round. Aly wins most of the time because she's watched them more recently than I have.

I don't remember the last time I had so much fun.

I zone out during one of the last episodes and imagine this is my life. I imagine this is how we spend lazy Saturdays. I imagine helping Aly get ready for school and planning activities for her during the summer. I imagine coming home from work and having Aly help me cook dinner for when Morgan gets home.

The thought that catches me off guard and snaps me back to the present is imagining me pregnant with Morgan's baby.

I have no business imagining something I can never give him.

When Morgan and Aly drop me off that night, my thoughts swirl around me in a hazy cloud. Before I can move forward with Morgan, we need to be on the same page about our futures.

If we move forward, I need to know if he wants more kids because that's not something I can give him.

# Chapter 23

*Morgan*

Aly still wants to see Whitney the day before Mother's Day. Worried she'll forget, I text Whitney every single day between Sunday and Saturday to remind her that she has plans with our daughter.

If she finds it annoying, she should count herself lucky because I could be so much worse.

It's Wednesday, and Aly and I are shopping after school for a gift for Whitney when Hannah texts me.

**Hannah:** Sorry to bother you while you're working, but would it be possible to move in this weekend? I'm trying to book a moving truck.

I'm not letting her pay for a damn moving truck when my dad has a truck and trailer I can use.

**Morgan:** You can absolutely move in this weekend. But you're not renting a moving truck. I have access to a truck and trailer, so I'll help.

**Hannah:** You've already done so much, I can't ask you to do that.

**Morgan:** Good thing you're not asking. I'm offering! ;)

**Hannah:** Fine… *eyeroll emoji* But I'm buying you lunch. I don't have much to move anyway, so it shouldn't be too hard.

**Hannah:** How is Aly doing?

Fuck, I love h—that she's thinking about Aly.

Who am I kidding? I love Hannah. I'm not too proud to admit it. Last weekend with her and Aly cemented my feelings and made me want many more weekends with both of them.

Aly hasn't stopped talking about it, asking when Hannah is coming over again and if we can go visit her at the library.

I haven't introduced Aly to a lot of partners, just one and that relationship ended well over three years ago. Sam was a great guy but didn't love that I put Aly first. He wanted to be my top priority, and I couldn't give him that. Things ended as soon as he made his feelings known. The fact Aly is excited about Hannah makes me even more excited about Hannah.

The only bump in the road is our fake dating situation. Because hanging out with my kid and her meeting my sister doesn't feel remotely fake. It feels *very* real, and I want to make it *officially* real.

**Morgan:** She's doing okay. She still wants to go to lunch with Whitney, so we're shopping for a gift now.

**Hannah:** I hope Whitney doesn't disappoint her. Again. I'll let you get back to Aly, tell her I said hi! And I'll see you Saturday? Just let me know when you can come over, and I'll have my stuff ready.

**Morgan:** Sounds good, Butterfly. See you Saturday.

Aly is looking at a bunch of necklaces right now, try-ing to pick something to give to Whitney. Whitney is very particular about everything she owns, but I'm *hoping* she appreciates whatever Aly picks.

"Hannah says hi. Find anything you like?"

"Tell her hi back. No, I don't think Mom would like any of these... What about candles?" Aly walks out of the jewelry section of Target and towards the candles.

"Candles could work. What if we got her one of those fancy water bottles too?" I follow along, carrying the empty basket.

"I don't know, maybe. I don't know what she likes or her favorite color. I feel like a bad daughter not knowing that stuff." Aly's shoulders slump, and I tamp down the urge to call this whole thing off.

I stop in front of her so I can look her in the eyes. "You are *not* a bad daughter. It is not your fault she hasn't taken the time to let you get to know her or to get to know you. She will love whatever you get her. So get her something that means something to you."

"Thanks, Dad. I think... I think I want to just give her a candle and a bouquet of flowers with a card. Will you help me with that?"

"Of course, Bub. When we were dating, her favorite scent was cinnamon so maybe we can find a cinnamon candle."

"Okay."

By Saturday morning, Aly's so anxious she barely eats her breakfast. She paces her room over and over trying to figure out what she should wear. Bean won't leave her side, following her small path and meowing at her like he's trying to give her a pep talk. She's changed her outfit three times and is still worried that Whitney won't approve of it. She finally settled on a pink sundress with a white t-shirt underneath it and brown strappy sandals and asked me to help her braid her hair into two French braids. She's sitting on the couch now with the bouquet in her hand, waiting for Whitney to come pick her up.

Aly wanted the bouquet to have alyssum in it, since it's the flower she's named after, so we used those as filler and added some pink roses and carnations. Whitney used to love pink roses, so I hope she still does.

When the doorbell rings, Aly shoots up from the couch, but I tell her to sit tight, and I'll get it.

Whitney is dressed in what can only be described as business casual, which is weird for an outing with a nine-year-old. She has on black slacks and a sleeveless tan blouse. Her platinum blonde hair is tied in a tight ponytail, and her eyeliner is sharp and neat.

She looks like she's had some botox done, which, to each their own, but she's only thirty-one, so I don't think she actually needs it.

"Hello, Whitney."

"Morgan." She nods and comes into the house, look-ing around like she hasn't been here before. Maybe she's just forgotten everything because she hasn't been here in well over a year. "Where is your *girlfriend?*" she asks.

"Not that it's any of your business, but she's not here."

Whitney hums. "Hmm. Bummer. I wanted to give her my condolences. Shame she has so many... *issues.* I would have thought you'd want more kids."

I rear back. "What the hell are you talking about?"

Whitney's mouth upturns into a vicious grin. "Oh, she didn't tell you? Well, I can't blame her. I'd be ashamed too if my body couldn't keep a baby in it."

Hannah had alluded to having a miscarriage, but why the hell does Whitney know that? "Don't talk about things you know nothing about, Whitney," I snap.

Whitney holds up her hands like she's innocent. "I'm just saying. I know more about it than you do, apparent-ly. She lost *seven* babies, Morgan. Why would you want to be with someone who can't give you the big family you've always wanted? Someone so... *defective.* There's obviously something wrong with her if she couldn't keep a single baby alive." The way she says it makes it sound like Hannah's some type of murderer who targets babies. Not a woman with fertility issues.

"Hi, Mom," Aly says, rounding the corner before I can rip Whitney a new one.

"Alyssa! Wow, you've gotten so tall. Are you ready for a fun day?" Whitney asks, her tone changing to some-thing high pitched and nasally, like how someone would talk to a toddler.

"Yes. I—I got you a Mother's Day present." Aly holds out the bag with the candle and the flowers.

"Oh... thank you," she says tightly. "I'll open this later. We don't want to hit Saturday traffic."

Aly hugs me goodbye, and I whisper in her ear to call me if she needs me. Then she and Whitney leave, and I get in my car and drive over to my dad's to grab his truck. My parents aren't home, which is probably good since I don't have time to chit chat. I need to get to my girl.

The whole way to Hannah's, I'm wondering why Hannah didn't tell me about her miscarriages. I mean, she has kept things pretty locked down because of her trust issues, but I feel like we've shared a lot with each other.

Is she embarrassed? It sounds like her ex blames her based on Whitney's accusations and the wording she used.

The more I learn about Liam Whatever-His-Last-Name-Is the more I hate him.

I'm glad Hannah is no longer married to him, and that—hopefully—I have a chance with her. I want to show her how she deserves to be loved.

When I get to the Layton residence, I see boxes already out on the porch, and a brunette woman with a seventies style shag is hauling more out the front door.

I park on the street and open the back of the trailer, then walk to the front door right as Hannah comes out with another box.

"Oh!" she startles. "Hey. Thank you so much for coming and helping. Sage is here to help, too. I don't have a lot of stuff, so we should be able to get it done pretty quickly. I assume we'll need to clean—"

"Already taken care of," I cut her off, giving her a gentle smile, taking the box from her hands and walking it to the trailer.

"Taken care of?"

"Alice told my sisters and my mom about you moving into the apartment, and they took it upon themselves to spruce it up and make it 'homey.' Their words, not mine." I slide the box into the trailer and turn to her. "They're really excited about you living there."

Alice couldn't stop gushing about Hannah over text. The family group chat was blowing up with texts from everyone wanting to know every single detail about her. Even Kendall was ribbing me about finally finding a good partner, and he usually avoids all talk of romance, the commitment-phobe.

I didn't give in to their demands for details because I don't want to give them hope for something that might not last. We're still firmly in the "friends-who-are-fake-dating" box even though I don't want to be. I'm taking her lead on things, and she needs to be ready to do this for real.

"That's really nice of them. I—" she pauses like she doesn't want to say whatever had been about to come out of her mouth.

"You...?" I prompt, eager to hear what she has to say.

"I would like to meet them... sometime. If you're okay with that, of course."

My smile couldn't get wider if I tried. "Of course I'm okay with it. I just know they're going to love you."

Hannah nods, then nods again. "Great. Um, I'm going to go help Sage grab more boxes." She hitches a thumb over her shoulder towards the house.

Hannah turns and walks away, and that's when I notice the tight bike shorts she's wearing. They sculpt perfectly to her wide hips, bountiful backside, and thick thighs. I fail in my attempts not to ogle her, and when I finally pull my gaze away and start towards the door, the brunette—Sage, I remember-—is giving me a knowing smirk.

I'm not one to be embarrassed, but my face flushes at being caught ogling her best friend's ass.

Sage has a box in her arms, and when I reach her I say, "I can take that for you. I'm Morgan. You must be Sage."

"I know who you are, flower man. Yes, I'm Sage. Hannah's best friend and favorite coworker. And yes, I know about your... arrangement." She glances back at the door then turns back to me. "Between you and me, her ex-husband really fucked her up and messed with her head, but I can see her coming back to herself. I think a part of that has to do with you. So thank you. And... be patient with our girl. She deserves the world, but she can't see it yet."

*Our girl.*

My heart clenches. Her best friend's approval means more than that of her parents, and the fact Sage refers to her as "our girl" instead of leaving me out means I have more of a chance with Hannah than I thought.

I just need to make sure I handle her with care. I want her to know I know about the miscarriages, but I don't want her to feel like I'm accusing her of keeping something from me, or that I'm upset with her about it. It's a touchy subject, one I don't know how to broach, but maybe honesty is just the best policy.

It's unfair for Liam to share such a personal detail with Whitney without Hannah's knowledge. It's one thing to say they experienced loss, but it's another to make Hannah sound like a broken human.

"Thanks, Sage. That means a lot to me. I'll wait as long as it takes for her. She's worth it." And I mean it.

Before Sage can say anything, Hannah comes out with another box. "There are only four boxes left and my bed. I think we can get out of here in the next half hour."

"Sounds good, Butterfly. Let's get you to your new home."

# CHAPTER 24

*Hannah*

I'm glad Jake wanted to take our mom to lunch and shopping for Mother's Day because it gave me enough time for Morgan and Sage to come help me load up and move out.

Predictably, my mom was *livid* that Morgan said I could live above the flower shop. She accused me of using him for his money, "fornicating" with him, and then told me I was raised better than this. "What would Jesus think?" she had asked, and I had to keep my tongue trapped between my teeth so I wouldn't go on a rant about how I don't believe in Jesus.

The last seven months have been an emotional roller coaster, but I feel like things are finally looking up.

Since I won't have to keep up the pretenses of going to church, I can finally explore the side of myself that's been hidden underneath scriptures and garments and culty temple ceremonies.

As soon as I realized I'd be moving out, I placed an order for new underwear and even bought the red lingerie set I was imagining.

It feels silly and a little overambitious now, but maybe Morgan will see it one day.

We finish loading up the trailer—which I don't think we actually needed—in less than half an hour, then Sage and I follow Morgan in my car to my new apartment.

Sage gushes the whole drive about Morgan and how hot, helpful, kind, understanding, and wonderful he is.

She's not wrong, but it feels like I'll disappoint her if things don't work out with him. Her approval means the world to me, though, so knowing she's in my corner if things work out helps ease some of my anxiety.

When we pull up behind the shop, Sage starts planning my housewarming party, which will just be me and Sage with a charcuterie board, bottle of champagne, and all the Jane Austen movies that exist.

Morgan hefts a box of books up the steps and unlocks the door—*my* door—and when I walk in behind him, I gasp.

Not only is the place spotless, but there's an entertainment center with two bookcases on each side where there was just a plain wall last time. There's a small black loveseat sofa that looks comfy and perfect for snuggling up with a good book, and a large area rug in the space where the bed is supposed to go.

"Morgan," I whisper, "Who—what—why?" I can't even finish my sentences because I'm so speechless.

Morgan's cheeks turn a bit pink. "I figured you wouldn't have an entertainment center or a couch, and I wanted you to have a spot for your books, too. It's nothing, really. Olivia and her wife are renovating and were getting rid of some things."

"Thank you, Morgan. I don't know how I'll ever repay you for all you've done for me." Before I can overthink my actions, I wrap my arms around his squishy middle and hug him, pouring all of my gratitude into the embrace.

He doesn't hesitate to wrap his arms around me and return my affections, making my heartbeat pick up.

"You don't have to repay me, Hannah," he mumbles into the crown of my head. "Whatever you need, I've got you."

*I need you to kiss me.*

The thought comes out of nowhere, and as soon as I think it, I lean back slightly and try to convey without words how badly I want him to kiss me.

I watch his Adam's apple bob on a harsh swallow, and then he's leaning down, closing the distance between our lips. I part my lips in anticipation and—

"Alright, Hanny Bannany, where should I put your—oh!" Sage bursts through the door with a box, which she promptly drops and covers her mouth. "Sorry. Am I interrupting something?"

I begrudgingly extract myself from Morgan's arms, not so much embarrassed Sage caught us almost kissing, but more upset we were interrupted.

Again.

It seems the universe is making this the slowest slow burn of the century.

"Yes," I murmur and give Morgan an apologetic smile. "Let's get the trailer unloaded so we can order lunch."

"Oooh, I saw a nice little Indian food place on the corner. We should order from there!" Sage claps excitedly as we head back out to the trailer.

"Oh, Dosa House? It's really good. The lamb saag is delicious. Even Aly likes their chicken tikka masala, and she's not usually a fan of Indian food." Morgan hefts two boxes of kitchenware up and effortlessly takes them up the stairs.

"Damn, he's strong. Could really toss a girl around the bedroom." Sage fans herself, and I scowl at her, making her laugh. "Not me, obviously. Don't be a prude, babe. You can't tell me you haven't thought about it at least once."

I pick up the box of cookware I took in the divorce but haven't unpacked since I moved home, shaking my head. I *have* thought about it, which is a new concept for me. What if I'm bad at sex? I've only ever been with Liam, and our sex life was two minute missionary and blow jobs. He went down on me twice before deciding it wasn't pleasurable for *him,* so he didn't want to do it anymore. I don't think I've ever even had an orgasm.

Sex also hurt because there was no foreplay, and he'd start thrusting into me before I was adequately prepped. I don't even know if I can get wet, since we never explored long enough to find out. I remember asking Liam if we could use lube or something to make it less painful, but he just said a wife should always be ready for her husband. I didn't bring it up again.

"I can feel you thinking from here," Sage calls across the small studio as she places a box of bathroom stuff in the bathroom.

We walk back out to the trailer together, passing Morgan on our way, so I whisper, "What if I'm bad at sex?"

Sage gives me an incredulous look.

"I was married, sure, but Liam was so... clinical about sex. I was never even wet for him. And it was painful sometimes," I explain.

Sage rolls her eyes and mutters *fucking douche* under her breathe. "I can't say whether you're good or bad at sex, babe. But I can tell you that *Liam* was bad at it if he wasn't even preparing you for it. Something tells me Morgan wouldn't be like that. Morgan seems like the type to eat pussy like his life depends on it and say 'thank you' after."

"Sage!" I scold, glancing around to make sure Morgan didn't hear her say that.

"Oh, please." She rolls her eyes. "I bet he talks dirty, too. He seems like the type to be a gentleman in public but whisper absolute filth in your ear in the bedroom. Have you thought about what you'd like in the bedroom since leaving Liam?"

"I mean, not really. I know what interests me when I'm reading, but how do I know if it translates to real life?"

Sage tilts her head, thinking about it. "I think what turns you on when you read is a good indicator of what you'd like in real life. But you'll never know if you don't explore it."

I mull over her words while we finish unloading the trailer.

"Alright, I'll place the order for Dosa House. What do you guys want?" I ask, pulling out my phone.

After calling in the order, I offer to go grab it, but Sage says she wants to go check it out in person and offers to pick it up while I unpack the boxes. She's out the door before I can protest, leaving me alone with Morgan.

I sit down on the floor in front of the entertainment center and start unpacking my books. Morgan settles onto the floor next to me and starts on another box.

We work in comfortable silence together for a while until I remember Aly was having lunch with her mom today.

"How was Aly this morning?"

Morgan clears his throat. "She was okay. Nervous. She got Whitney a candle and some flowers, but Whitney acted like she gave her dirt or something. It was infuriating."

"I'm sorry to hear that. Aly must have been hurt." I frown, feeling a sense of familiarity. I remember giving my mom gifts I made or picked out specifically for her, and she never acted like she appreciated them.

"She didn't show it, but I can imagine she was. I hope she's okay today..." he trails off and scoots the box over until he's sitting right next to me. "Actually, there's something I wanted to tell you."

I pause my own unboxing to look at him, he looks nervous as hell. "Okay..."

"Whitney was being her usual petty self and mentioned you and Liam had some... fertility struggles."

My heart rate kicks up, and a lead ball of dread drops into my stomach, replacing any appetite I had with anxiety-induced nausea.

When I don't respond, he hesitantly continues, "She said you had... God, I feel so shitty repeating this in this way. She said you had... multiple miscarriages." I search his face for any hint of disgust, any hint of outrage at *me* because my body can't do what it's supposed to. For omitting the truth from him.

I find nothing but sympathy, which somehow feels worse, and then I can't see anything at all because tears blur my vision, and a sob wrenches out of my throat.

"I'm going to say something that might hurt, but I think you should know." He places a large hand on my knee, rubbing circles in the exposed dimpled flesh, and I brace myself for the inevitable end of whatever this is.

"Whitney implied that you were... defective. That it was your fault you miscarried. And I wanted you to know Liam is slandering you. You don't deserve the blame."

There it is—*wait, what?*

"I don't know why your ex told Whitney, why she felt the need to tell me, or why she worded it so cruelly, but I feel you deserve to know what kind of person your ex-husband is."

I bark a humorless laugh. "I already know what kind of person he is. He blamed me for the losses, saying I must not have been faithful enough, worthy enough, or wanted a baby enough to keep them. He left me alone each time I miscarried because he was squeamish and didn't want to be around the blood." I stare at a spot on the floor as tears steadily stream down my cheeks. "I wanted to go to a fertility clinic, try IVF or even IUI. My doctor even suggested an exploratory surgery to see if I had a septate uterus or endometriosis or *something*. But Liam said if we were going to have a baby, it was going to be the way God intended it to happen.

"Then, he did a complete one-eighty and said he realized God is trying to tell him not to have kids. So he started rethinking our entire marriage. He told me he was no longer attracted to me, and our marriage wasn't compatible anymore. I wanted to go to therapy to work through it, but he refused. He served me divorce papers less than six months after the seventh miscarriage."

Morgan scoots over and puts his arm around my shoulder, so I lay my head on his chest. He should stink from the heavy lifting, but he just smells a little musky with his usual spicy floral scent that adds to his appeal.

"I'm so, so sorry you went through that, Butterfly," he whispers, like he's too scared to break the tense vibe in the room.

I shrug. "I'm sorry you found out through your ex-girlfriend. I didn't think it was important to bring up, and I didn't know *how* to bring it up. So I guess now you know. I'm defective."

"No," he snaps. "You're not defective. You probably have a medical condition, but it doesn't make you defective. Have you seen a doctor about it since the divorce?"

"No, I didn't see a point. I didn't think I'd ever want to be in a serious relationship ever again, much less try to have kids." *Until you.*

"That's valid. I'm sure it'd be scary to have to go through that alone. But Hannah, you're not alone anymore. I—"

"I'm back!" Sage bursts through the door all smiles and excitement but deflates when she sees my face streaked with tears. "What's wrong?"

I give her a watery smile. "Just regaling Morgan with tales of my douchebag ex-husband. He knows about the babies. Apparently Liam told Whitney."

"What a fucking asshole. My offer to slash his tires is still open. Ooo, or key his doors. I'd love to ruin his douche-mobile a little."

"Thanks, but I don't need to bail you out of jail." I let out a harsh sigh and look at Morgan. "Thank you. For listening. And for helping me move. And for being an amazing fake boyfriend."

Morgan opens his mouth to say something but must decide against it. So he just nods and helps me off the floor.

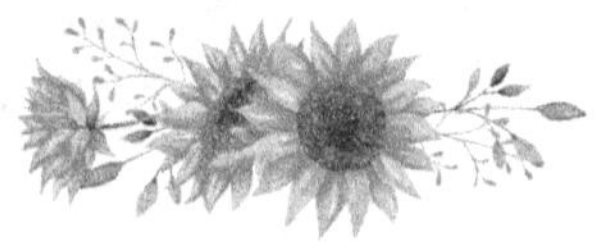

While we're enjoying lunch, Morgan's phone rings, and he takes the call without hesitation. When he comes back his face is pinched in frustration.

"I'm sorry to have to jet, but that was Aly. Something happened with Whitney. Are we still on for next Saturday? The concert?"

"Of course. I'll text you the details. I hope everything is okay. Let me know if you need anything, okay?" I give him another quick hug, and as I wrap my arms around him, he relaxes just a bit.

"Perfect. I'll talk to you soon, Butterfly." He gives me a gentle squeeze and makes a hasty exit.

Sage and I finish our lunch in silence, then clean up and continue unpacking. She's practically vibrating with the need to ask questions or scold me or something, so I finally put her out of her misery.

"Just say it, Sage."

"I think you need to tell that man you want to date for real. I also think you should hook Liam up to one of those period cramp machines, turn it all the way up to ten with no warning, and then slowly pluck every hair from his eyebrows. But first, you need to tell Morgan how you feel. That man looks at you like a sad puppy *and* like he wants to pour you into a glass and sip you slowly so he can savor the taste."

I flush at the mental image that invokes.

"But also," she continues, "you can't keep stringing him along, babe. He'd pluck the stars from the sky if you asked, but he deserves to have the same thing. I know you're scared, but Morgan is *not* Liam."

I know Morgan isn't Liam. He's already treated me better than my ex-husband ever did, and we're not even dating for real. But we never got to finish our conversation about kids. Can he get past the possibility of never expanding his family that way?

Could I handle doctors poking and prodding to figure out if there's a medical reason for my miscarriages? Could I handle the answers they might give? Could I handle another loss if we tried again?

I think with Morgan as my support system, it would be easier to handle. I don't think he'd allow me to go through it alone. I think he'd do whatever was in his power to make sure we had answers.

I assure Sage I plan on telling him after Wes's concert, and she approves of my plan. When she leaves, I sit in my new home and unpack things and arrange them the way I want, without needing to consult anyone else.

I take off my t-shirt and walk around in my sports bra and bike shorts for the first time in my life.

Today is a step forward in my journey of freedom.

I hope Morgan wants to come along for the ride.

# CHAPTER 25

*Morgan*

Aly called me from the bathroom to tell me Whitney brought Liam to their lunch, and when they went to his apartment, she was feeling left out and uncomfortable and wanted to come home.

I'm vibrating with anxiety and outrage while I drive, calling my dad on the way to let him know I'll be bringing the truck and trailer back after I pick up Aly.

Aly didn't know the address of Liam's apartment, but she dropped a pin and told me the number on the door. I drive towards downtown Salt Lake to a ritzy apartment building and park on the street in front of it because of the trailer. I walk into the lobby and am greeted by an older gentleman in a doorman's outfit.

*Liam is a pretentious asshole.*

"I need your name and who you're here to see," the older gentleman—his name tag reads "Hank"—says, clicking on the computer.

"I'm here to see Liam..." *Fuck* what is his last name? "He's here with my daughter and her mom. I'm not on whatever list you have, but my daughter wants to leave, and I won't make her stay somewhere she's uncomfortable."

"Liam…" Hank says, tapping his chin. "Blue eyes, brown hair but mostly balding? Always in a suit?"

Sure, that sounds like him. "Yes."

"Go on and get your daughter. Mr. Jensen is a rotten soul, I tell ya. Always barking at me like he owns the place. Seen him with a few different ladies in the last few months, too. Tell the mom she should steer clear." Hank presses a button, and the doors behind him *click* unlocked.

"Thank you so much, Hank." I give him a salute and head to the elevators, clicking the number three when I'm inside.

I couldn't give a fuck if Liam is stepping out on Whitney. Their relationship is none of my business. What is my business is my daughter and her well-being. For Whitney to not mention she's introducing Aly to Liam and *bringing her to his apartment* really grinds on my gears and makes my blood boil.

It may be hypocritical since Hannah was at *my* house last weekend, but that's different. If Aly gave any indication Hannah was making her uncomfortable, I would have taken Hannah home immediately. But Aly and Hannah got along well, and Aly seemed to like her. Whitney doesn't know Aly well enough to know when she's uncomfortable, clearly, or she's just ignoring it because she wants to impress Liam.

But *why?* Liam made it clear that night at Fondue Frenzy he doesn't want kids. Why would Whitney feel the need to introduce them now?

As soon as the elevator stops, I stride down the hall to 3C and bang loudly on the door.

The door swings open, and Liam flinches when he sees me, then his face turns red. "What are *you* doing here? How did you get in? Freaking Hank. Old bat isn't good for anything."

"I'm here to get Aly." I fold my arms across my chest.

"It's my day with her. You don't get to just take her back whenever you want," Whitney hisses, appearing at Liam's side.

"I had every intention of letting you have the day with her, but she called me and said she was being ignored and didn't want to be here anymore. I will *always* rescue her when she needs it."

Whitney's jaw drops, and she turns to our daughter, who is holding her shoes in one hand. Her bottom lip wobbles, and tears are welling in her eyes.

"You called your *dad?* Why couldn't you just stick it out until I took you home?" Whitney snaps at Aly.

"I—you told me to just sit on the couch and not do anything while you guys were in the other room. I wanted to spend the day with you, not your boyfriend. You seemed like you didn't want me here, so I called Dad so you guys could have your space," Aly says, her voice breaking.

Whitney scowls and turns back to me. "So you get to introduce her to your girlfriend, but I can't introduce her to my boyfriend? Seems like a double standard, Morgan."

"I asked Aly before I introduced her to Hannah. And if Aly was uncomfortable around her *at all* I would have fixed that issue immediately," I state matter-of-factly.

"To be fair, I thought Whit should have just taken her home after lunch," Liam pipes up, and it makes me want to punch him even more.

"Aly, put on your shoes and let's go," I say gently to my daughter. "You," I point to Liam, "you're a shitty person. Hannah told me about how you treated her, and Hank told me about all the women you bring around. I don't want a slimy fucker like you around my daughter."

Liam sputters, trying to make up excuses, but I hold up a hand to stop him.

I turn to Whitney. "I think we need to redo the custody agreement. Until you can prioritize Aly, I think supervised visits are the only thing I want to allow. If Aly even wants to see you at all. You'll be hearing from my lawyer."

"You can't dictate my love life! I can date whoever I want, and you can't take my daughter from me! I'll fight you for full custody!" Whitney shouts, and I hear an apartment door open down the hall at all the ruckus.

"You're right, Whitney. I can't dictate your love life. Like I said, you'll hear from my lawyers. Let's go, Bub."

Aly grips my hand as we make our way to the elevator. I hear Liam and Whitney shouting. They're probably arguing about the other women I mentioned, but we don't stick around long enough to hear.

I hope they end up breaking up. I don't hate Whitney, and no one deserves to be lied to and cheated on.

Aly and I don't speak as I get her settled in the back of the truck and pull away from the building. The only sound on the way to my parents' house is the sound of Aly's sniffles from the back seat.

When we pull up in front of my parents' I let the engine die and get out, opening Aly's door. She looks up at me, her blue eyes are a bright contrast to the red around them, and I can still see some unshed tears.

She unbuckles, and I pull her into a tight embrace. "Do you want to talk about it right now?" I feel her shake her head, so I nod, plant a kiss on her head, and pull back slightly. "Do you want to wait in the RAV while I go give the keys to Gigi and Papa?" She shakes her head again, so I help her out of the truck and hold her hand while we walk inside.

My mom is bustling around the kitchen making dinner when we walk in. "Well, if it isn't my two favorite—" she pauses when she sees Aly's face. "What happened? Are you okay, sweetie?"

Aly has always felt comfortable letting her emotions out with my mom, so she runs right to her Gigi's open arms and sobs, telling her all about what happened.

Apparently, Whitney tried to take Aly to a *bar* for a fancy lunch, but since she's a child, they had to go to a different place. Liam wasn't happy about it, and he spent the whole time ignoring Aly and only asking Whitney questions about some business deal.

"I tried to talk to him like I talked to Hannah, but he didn't answer my questions and told me to just play a game on my phone while the adults talked," Aly says, and my mom's lips thin, probably holding back a nasty retort about Aly's mom and her new boyfriend.

"I'm sorry I ruined your day again." Aly looks at me sheepishly. "Mom said you were probably glad to have a break from me, that's why she didn't want me to call you."

I bite back the urge to call Whitney and tell her off. It won't help the situation right now, and Aly needs me to be calm for her.

I kneel in front of her on the floor so she can see my eyes. "You *never* ruin my day. I was helping Hannah move today, and we were just finishing up when you called. Last week when Aunt Alice called, it only changed the plans for the day. It didn't ruin it. Did you have fun with Hannah last weekend?" I ask, and my mom's face softens.

Aly nods.

"Then it definitely wasn't ruined because Hannah had a lot of fun, too."

"Really? She isn't mad that I made you change plans with her two weeks in a row?" Aly looks down at her feet as she asks, and my heart breaks.

She's so worried about people being mad at her, and I don't know how to get her to believe that I'd do anything for her. She's the most important person in my life.

*Huh. Sounds like Hannah.* I shake that thought away to focus on Aly.

"No, Bub. Like I said before, Hannah knows you come first, and she's not only okay with it, but she wants to know you're safe, too. I won't tell her anything you don't want me to, but I think I need to tell her some of it." I swallow hard, nervous to tell her the next part. "Liam and Hannah used to be married, so she can help me know what to do to make sure you're safe."

Aly's jaw drops. "Hannah was married to *that guy?*" I nod, and she worries her lip. "He was saying mean things about his 'ex' to Mom, and I tried not to eavesdrop, but he was talking really loud."

Much calmer than I feel, I ask, "Do you want to tell me what he said?"

"He said that she was selfish. She only cared about herself, and she 'let herself go' and got fat. I wanted to interrupt him and tell him 'fat' isn't a bad thing to be. Aunt Al, Sar, Livi, and Asha are fat, and there's nothing wrong with it, but he didn't seem like he'd want me to say anything. Then he said she wasn't good in the bedroom, and I didn't understand what that meant."

My mom and I look at each other and make a silent agreement not to bring that part up.

"Thank you for telling me, Aly. I know it was probably hard to hear and hard to repeat."

"I don't want Hannah to get her feelings hurt by him anymore. It's a good thing she has you now." Aly wraps her arms around my neck.

I hope Hannah feels the same way.

# CHAPTER 26

*Hannah*

For the first time in my life, I didn't see my mother on Mother's Day.

People always argue, "That's so harsh! She's your family! Blood is thicker than water." *Blah, blah, blah.*

It was poor timing on her part to give me a two week move out timeframe right before Mother's Day. If she wanted me to pretend everything was okay and celebrate the day, then she shouldn't have scolded me like a child and kicked me out for no good reason.

It's been a strange week, adjusting to living completely on my own. I moved straight out of my parents' house and into an apartment with Liam when we got married, so I've never had a space that was completely *mine.*

I can listen to whatever music I want, I can walk around in a tank top and short shorts without getting judged for not wearing garments, and I can eat whatever I want without my mother's judgmental gaze watching my every bite.

It's Saturday, which means it's concert day. Elli and Emma will be coming over any minute to get lunch and go shopping, then we'll come back here to get ready.

Morgan wants to come to dinner with us to get to know Emma and Elli, and as nervous as I am for them to meet, it makes me a little giddy he wants to spend time with them. He offered to be designated driver tonight, too, so I could "let loose," he said.

It will be the first time my cousins and I will be together since all of us left the church, so I think a few drinks are in order. I'm not going to get drunk, though, because Morgan and I need to have a conversation, and I want to be coherent when it happens.

I texted him last week to make sure everything with Aly was okay, and he assured me she would be fine. On Wednesday when I came home from work, he was sitting outside the shop in his car so I invited him up, and he told me all about what happened on Saturday.

I was *shocked.* I'm still feeling outraged on Aly's behalf at the audacity of her mom and my ex-husband. I'm glad Morgan is an amazing dad and would protect Aly at all costs.

I'm just finishing the dishes when my phone pings from a text. I wipe my hands on a dish towel, and this time when the butterflies erupt at the sight of Morgan's name on my phone, I don't try to push them away.

**Morgan:** A package for you got delivered here by mistake. Do you want me to bring it up?

*A package? What did I—*

Oh shit.

I don't bother to text him back, just slip my shoes on and rush out the door, down the steps, and in through the back door of the shop.

I round the corner to the counter to see Morgan typing on the tablet at the front. Thankfully, the store is empty, so I clear my throat to alert him of my presence.

He turns around and grins, "Hey, Butterfly." He holds up the hot pink mailer bag, "This is for you. What'd you get?"

I'm not a great liar, and it's not *embarrassing* to order underwear. Everyone wears it.

So why am I shy about the fact I ordered it? Probably because I ordered a specific set with him in mind.

Mustering more courage than I actually feel, I shrug a shoulder and casually say, "New... clothes."

Morgan's eyebrows raise skeptically as I take the package from him. "Oh," his voice sounds a little strained. "Cool."

"Yeah!" My voice sounds unnaturally high, and I can't seem to stop the words from spewing out of me. "Now that I'm not at home, I don't have to keep the pretenses up and wear garments anymore. With summer right around the corner I'm not trying to get heat stroke, either. Can't wear sleeveless sundresses with garments! Actually, I might not even wear a bra with them." *Why the fuck did I say that?*

Morgan blinks, then runs a hand over his beard, his face turning red. "Right. Sure. Well... I hope they fit?"

Dear God, why is this so awkward?

I let out a strained laugh. "Thanks. Uh, I better get back upstairs. Emma and Elli are picking me up soon."

Right as I say it, the bell above the door rings and in walks a familiar head of blonde curls followed by an equally familiar head of dark hair.

"Speak of the devils." I smile, rounding the counter to greet them. "Hey, you two!"

Emma and Elli simultaneously turn to me and grin.

Emma looks so different than when we were kids, though the one constant has been her curly blonde hair and piercing, ice blue eyes. She's barely over five feet tall, but she's the feistiest out of the three of us. She has a gold piercing in her right nostril, her right arm covered in a full tattoo sleeve, and the rest of her body is littered with random artwork as well. She's wearing ripped denim shorts, a hot pink, cropped, balloon-sleeve corset top and matching hot pink, sparkly ankle boots.

She reminds me of a shorter, curly-haired, plus size Barbie.

Elli is dressed in a floral pattern jumpsuit with wide straps and black sandals. Her long hair is pulled back by a black headband, and she looks both the same and different. She looks happier than I've ever seen her.

"Damn, Elli, your hair's gotten so long since the last time I saw you." I give her a hug, marveling at the chocolate waves with caramel highlights. When I saw her last August, she had cut it to just below her shoulders, now it's a good six inches longer.

"Well your hair is so much shorter! I love it!" Elli fluffs the ends of my hair.

"Emma, your hair looks gorgeous as ever," I tease, hugging her next.

"Yeah, yeah. I like what I like. What can I say? I love the post-divorce bob, Hannah. It suits you." Emma glances around the shop. "We wanted to check this cute shop out before we came up. Do you know the owner?"

I may have omitted that Morgan is the owner, and that he offered me the place to live. It never came up in conversation so I just didn't say anything.

Morgan steps up next to me, "I'm Morgan, the owner. And Hannah's... friend." He extends his hand to Emma, who tilts her head and gives him an assessing look while she shakes it.

"Emma," she says. "Morgan... Fowler? Like the Mustangs' wide receiver?"

Morgan just gives her a nod, and she gives me a wicked grin.

Elli gives me a smirk and shakes his hand as well. "Nice to meet you, Morgan. I'm Elli."

"A pleasure, ladies. I'll let you all catch up, and I'll see you at five to pick you up?" Morgan looks to me for confirmation, and I nod. "Perfect. Have fun, Butterfly." He gives me a squeeze on the arm as he walks back to the counter.

*Butterfly?* Emma mouths with a quirked eyebrow.

I huff a laugh. "Come on, let me grab my purse, so we can get lunch and you can ask me your questions."

They follow me out the back and up to my apartment where they "ooo" and "ahh" about all the little details. I tell them how Morgan and his family cleaned the place and set up the shelves and entertainment center, and they swoon. Once I grab my purse, we head down to my car and pile in to head to Sweet River for lunch.

Emma explains she has a work event when Wes's tour stops in San Diego, so she decided to come to the Utah show since she's here for a family event anyway. Though her smile remains bright, it falters slightly at the mention of her family. Elli and I don't press for more information.

Elli tells us about what life on a tour bus is like, and how she and Wes have become really great friends with the members of the band. She sounds like she's having a blast traveling with the love of her life, and I couldn't be happier for her.

Once we sit and order our food, Emma folds her hands in front of her and says, "Now, Hannah. Tell us what's going on with Hot-Football-Player-Flower-Shop-Man."

Elli nods her head in agreement, so I spill and tell them everything.

"I don't want it to be fake anymore," I admit at the end of my spiel and both of them are staring at me slack-jawed.

Emma shakes her head. "Damn, girl. Your life could be a soap opera. I mean, what are the *chances* that your ex-husband is dating his ex? I don't blame you for wanting to make it real, either. That man is F-I-N-E *fine*. I'd have climbed him like a tree the moment I saw him. I bet he fucks hard."

I almost spit out my lemonade. "Emma!" I scold, looking around to make sure no one heard us, but she just laughs. I should introduce Emma to Sage. They'd have a blast ganging up on me.

Elli giggles. "It's weird to hear sex talked about so openly after being in the church so long, huh?"

I just nod my agreement.

"What's your plan to make this thing not fake?" Elli asks as our waiter brings our entrees.

"I thought I'd tell him the truth tonight. We've had two almost-kisses, and I swear I can *see* the tension between us sometimes. I just worry I'm imagining it."

"I can assure you you're not imagining it. That man's yearning so hard, I could tell in the two-minute interaction we had," Emma says, and Elli nods in agreement.

"I'm just scared, you know?"

Elli gives me an understanding smile. "I get that. I was nervous to start dating Wes because of past relationships. Our situations aren't the same, but I'm glad I gave him a chance. He proved to me he was different even before we started dating."

Emma nods. "I don't do serious relationships, but if I were to settle down, I would want it to be with someone who looks at me the way Morgan looks at you."

"*You* don't do serious relationships?" I don't believe that. Emma has always been the hopeless romantic of the three of us.

She waves me off. "Feelings are too messy. I'm focused on my career right now, so I only need a partner for orgasms."

Elli looks just as shocked as I do about this little revelation. "The serial monogamists of the world are weeping at the lost opportunity to lock down Emma Price."

"Well maybe if I found a sexy rockstar who followed me like an adorable lost puppy, or an ex-football player who looked at me like I hung the fucking moon it would be different." Emma shrugs. "As it stands, you two seem to have found the last good men in the world."

"What about women?" I ask, since I know Emma's bi.

"I love women. Women are beautiful, lovely, and perfect, but I still don't want to settle down. My ex-girlfriend is one of the reasons I swore off serious dating. She wanted to get married three months in, started talking about adopting kids or doing IVF, and when I told her I wasn't ready to get married and I wasn't sure I wanted kids, she broke up with me and told me I should have been up front with her—which I *had been.* So now I make sure it's crystal clear I don't want a serious relationship, just sex."

"Oh shit. That really sucks, Emma. I'm sorry." I don't know what else to say. Emma's been through more shit than I would ever wish on even my worst enemy, so the fact she's still so happy-go-lucky is astounding.

Again, Emma waves me off. "It's all good. I'm happy with my life. Besides, there's no time for sadness! We have to go find you the perfect outfit for confessing your feelings. One that says 'take me, Morgan. I'm yours.'"

Once we've finished our food, we head out. I thought about taking them with me to the size-inclusive thrift store Alice told me about, but I don't want to go without her, so we end up at the mall instead where there are—shockingly—*three* stores that carry plus size options.

The first store is a bust, but it's nice to have people who understand the struggles of clothes shopping as a fat woman. Sage understands, too, but she makes a lot of her own clothes so we don't spend much time shopping together.

At the second store, Elli finds a black bodysuit with lace long sleeves on it and a denim mini skirt that's frayed slightly on the edge. It's simple, but it looks like it was made for her.

The third store is where Emma and I find our outfits. Emma picks an army green cargo skirt that she's paired with a plain black baby tee and picks out some black platform sandals to go with it.

The dress I pick is unlike anything I've ever worn. It's tight, short, and doesn't have sleeves. But when I try it on, I immediately try to picture Morgan's reaction to me in it. Will he like it? Will he hate I'm showing so much skin? Will it make him want to shove me against a wall and kiss me senseless?

I guess I'll find out soon enough.

# Chapter 27

## Morgan

I don't know why I'm nervous knocking on Hannah's door. It's hardly the first time we've hung out, and we're not even going on a date. We'll be surrounded by at least two other people at all times.

Maybe it's because I'll be spending time with people who are extremely important to her or because they're all much younger than I am, and I worry I won't be cool enough for them.

Maybe I'm nervous because I looked up the company of the "new clothes" she got today because I was curious and discovered it was a lingerie store, and I'm wondering if she's wearing any of it tonight.

Are they lacy? Plain? Printed? Did she buy thongs, boy cut, cheeky? It really doesn't matter, honestly, because the thought of Hannah in any kind of underwear has my blood rushing down south immediately.

The blonde cousin, Emma, opens the door and smiles wide. "Come on in, your girl is almost ready. Elli's just finishing up on her hair."

I don't know why I feel the need to clarify, "She's not *my* girl." It sounds weak though.

Emma snorts. "Sure, big fella." She pats me on the shoulder. "Whatever you say."

"So, you're from San Diego?" I ask as she slips on sandals that look three inches thick.

"Well, I'm technically from Cottonwood Heights over in the Salt Lake Valley. I've just lived in San Diego for the past eight years."

"That's cool. Do you like it?"

"I love it there." She gives me a wistful smile. "You don't have to make small talk with me, I'm not going to think you're rude. I can tell you're nervous enough."

*Oh, thank God.* "Thanks. I appreciate your honesty."

"I prefer to be blunt. Saves everyone time in the long run, even if it hurts feelings in the beginning." She flicks some of her curly blonde hair over her shoulder.

We sit in amicable silence, listening to the muffled chatter of Elli and Hannah from the bathroom. Then Elli comes out of the bathroom and gives me a wave.

"Hey, Morgan. Hannah's just changing into her outfit and then we can go!"

We hear the door to the bathroom *click* open, and when Hannah emerges from behind the door, I swear my jaw falls to the floor.

The black dress with little red flowers embroidered on it looks like a corset on top, lacing up in the front and pushing up her breasts in a way that makes me drool. Her lush lips are painted a bold red to match the flowers on her dress, and I try three times to look away from them before I actually succeed.

I notice she's once again wearing the necklace *I* gave her. My inner caveman is pounding his chest with pride and telling me to fully claim her.

"Wow, Hannah you look..." What word describes the way she looks? She's great every fucking day, but today she looks... "There's not a word in any language to describe how beautiful you are."

She pulls her bottom lip between her teeth. "Thank you Morgan."

I don't know how long we stare at each other, but it's long enough that Emma claps her hands together and brings our attention back to the other two members of our party. "Alright, love birds. You can ogle each other from across the table or fondle each other under the table. I don't really care, but let's get going so we're not late for Wes's show."

"Emma!" Hannah scolds, which just makes Elli giggle and Emma smile wickedly.

"We'll meet you out in the car," Emma says, dragging Elli out the door.

Hannah slips on a pair of black combat boots and grabs her purse, but before she can get out the door, I place an arm above her to keep it closed, forcing her to turn and look at me. Her chest heaves with each inhale, and it takes everything in me not to mess up her pretty red lipstick.

"I'm no good with words, Butterfly, but you look good enough to eat," I say in a husky whisper. "If you weren't wearing that lipstick I'd..." I trail off, not wanting to push her boundaries. I don't know if she wants this. Wants *me.*

She turns fully so her back is pressed against the door frame, her chest pressed against mine. "You'd what, Morgan?" When I don't respond, she runs her fingers up my chest and over my shoulder, her hand shaking slightly, like she's as nervous as I am. "It's a lip stain, and it's transfer-proof. So tell me, what would you do?"

I lean down so our lips are only a hairsbreadth apart and whisper, "I'd devour you, Butterfly. But if I do that now, I don't know if I'd be able to stop, so we better get out to the car before I hand my keys to your cousins and decide to keep you in here for myself."

Goosebumps rise along her arms as I pull away from her, and she inhales a shaky breath, then we head out the door. While she locks it, I subtly adjust myself, grateful the dark jeans somewhat hide the semi I'm sporting.

*God, that was a close call.*

Elli and Emma insist Hannah sits up front with me, since she's the tallest, and on the way to the restaurant, they all chatter while I ask and answer questions where needed.

We're seated fairly quickly at Colby's, and Hannah and I are ushered into the same side of the booth. It's both a blessing and a curse I won't be staring directly at her all through dinner, but it's a special kind of torture to have her arm brush mine when one of us moves or to feel the heat of her thigh so close to my own. When I cross my ankles, my foot nudges hers, and she startles a bit but nestles her foot close to mine instead of pulling it away.

I don't know why that gesture makes my heart race faster.

It's hard to focus on anything other than the close proximity of our bodies, but I manage to still be part of the conversation as we order.

They're talking about a baptism and it makes me wonder, "You were all in it growing up, then left the Mormon church?"

Emma answers first, "Yep." She pops the "p." "I was the first to leave, as soon as I graduated high school. There was a lot that made me leave, but I honestly don't think I ever really believed in it. As soon as I was old enough to legally remove my records, I did."

"I only left last year. I'd been questioning it for a while after reading certain literature and finding out the true history of it. I also just wasn't happy in it. I'm much happier now that I don't have to base every life decision on arbitrary rules made up by old white men who say they can talk to God," Elli explains, and Hannah and Emma murmur their agreement.

"Sage is the one who brought all the history and stuff to my attention. What really broke my shelf though, was how people talked about miscarriages. They made it seem like God was trying to teach me something every time I lost a baby, and I was angry. Why would an all-powerful being force me to endure things like that for no reason? People also *heavily* implied if I couldn't have a baby I was unworthy of being a mom, which was hard to hear," Hannah states, and I place a comforting hand on her thigh.

"What do you mean, 'broke your shelf?'" It's a phrase I've never heard before.

"It's a phrase used by the ex-Mormon community. I don't know if other religions use it," Emma explains.

"Basically it means you find out all these issues or lies out about the church but because you want to be a faithful member, you put them on a metaphorical shelf."

"Then," Elli continues "The shelf starts cracking from the weight of all the things on it, and that *one last thing* you just can't look past gets put on there, and it breaks."

Hannah finishes off the explanation with, "That's the point people usually leave. Or, in my case, just go through the motions."

"Damn. That sounds like a lot to go through. Are your families okay with it?" I ask Elli and Emma. I already know how Hannah's mom feels about her decision.

Emma lets out a sardonic laugh. "I come back once a year if I'm able to because things with my family are so tense. My parents are extremely displeased with all of my life choices."

Elli nods. "My parents act like I don't exist anymore. I only have contact with my little sister, Izzy, who's going to graduate in a few weeks and move to Texas and live with me."

"I can't imagine Aly doing anything that would make me cut her off. Unless it was like, murder or something." Is parenting within the confines of religion really that much different?

"That's because you love her unconditionally," Elli says sadly, and my heart hurts for her.

Oblivious to the deep conversation we're having, the waiter chipperly brings our food, helping to ease some of the tension.

Once we all have our food, the topic shifts to things a bit lighter like work and romantic partners. Elli gives me a brief summary of her love story, all the miscommunications and bumps in the road, but how their souls are intertwined, and she can't imagine not having him in her life.

I can relate. I feel that way about Hannah.

"Ugh. If you guys weren't so freaking cute I'd gag over how sweet you are." Emma twirls her pasta around her fork almost angrily.

"No special someone for you, Emma?" I can't imagine she's single. She's feisty, but I can see a sensitive center underneath that bubbly exterior. And I may only have eyes for Hannah, but even I can appreciate that Emma is gorgeous.

"Nope." She pops the "p" again, but doesn't elaborate further.

"Emma's sworn off any serious relationships," Hannah explains.

"Orgasm-ships only for me!" Emma puts her fist out for a fist bump from Elli, and Elli rolls her eyes but obliges.

"I have a feeling someone is going to change that attitude sometime soon. Right when you least expect it." I grin, and Emma scoffs.

"Highly doubt it, Flower Daddy. But I appreciate your enthusiasm."

I look at Hannah and mouth, *Flower Daddy?* She just shrugs, shakes her head, and continues eating her burger.

"You're a flower shop owner and a father, Morgan. Get your mind out of the gutter," Emma chides, and I can't help but laugh. I don't think that's at all what she meant, but what do I know?

It's nice to have adult conversations with people I'm not related to, and Emma and Elli don't seem awkward or wary with me at all. They ask about Aly, but not in a way that seems like they feel obligated to. Neither of them want kids, so I find it endearing they want to know about my little girl.

All three of them try to fight me when I offer to pay the bill, but I don't budge on it. Emma huffs about being an independent woman who doesn't need a man, but I point out now she can spend more money on drinks, and it seems to appease her.

When we make it to the concert venue, Elli leads us around the back where she bumps fists with a gentleman with long brown hair in a braid down his back, two different colored eyes, wearing a navy blue chevron print blazer over a white tank top and high waisted jean shorts.

"That's Misha, the manager. He's an interesting guy and one of kindest people I've ever met," Elli explains as she leads us through a hallway to what I assume is the green room.

I've never been backstage at a concert unless someone was performing at half-time, so I'm not sure what I expected, but it wasn't this.

The room isn't green, for one, it's got black walls and multi-colored furniture scattered around. There's a table with snacks and drinks, and I can see some clothing racks and vanities along the edges.

As soon as we walk in, a dark-haired man with a sleeve of floral tattoos jumps off the couch and practically skips to Elli. "Baby! Did you have a good day? I missed you." He peppers little kisses all over her face, and she giggles. This must be Wes.

"I missed you, too. But it was good to catch up with Emma and Hannah." Elli clasps their hands together and turns to Hannah and me. "This is Morgan, Hannah's boyfriend."

"Oh, I'm not—" I try to say, but Wes interrupts me.

"Nice to meet you, Morgan. Hannah, good to see you again."

"Thanks for having us, Wes. It's good to see you, too." Hannah's giving him a shy smile, and I tamp down the excitement at the fact she didn't correct him about me being her boyfriend.

My own smile is huge as I express my own gratitude, and then he's taking us along to meet the rest of the band.

I looked up Keely and The Kissers last night so I could listen to some of their music. They're good, a little indie, a little rock and roll.

The lead singer, Keely, is sitting on the lap of a brunette that looks slightly out of place among the tattoos and piercings of the other members. Wes introduces her as Mikala, and the other two members as KC and Leah. Emma sits down next to Leah, and they immediately start flirting.

"Wait a minute," Keely eyes me, "You're Morgan Fowler. You played for the Mustangs!"

I nod. "I did. Big football fan?"

Keely scoffs. "Hell no. My brothers are, though. We grew up in Estes Park, so they *obsessed* over the Mustangs. Made me watch every game. I was more interested in the cheerleaders." She gives Mikala a saucy wink. "But I picked up a few things. Shame about your injury. They were super bummed about you having to retire. They're going to be so jealous they didn't get to meet you."

I laugh. "Thank you, I appreciate that. I'm more than happy to sign an autograph if it'd lessen the jealousy."

Keely waves me off. "Nah. I don't get many wins over them, so I'll take this one and milk it for all its worth. Thanks for the offer, though."

The door to the room opens, and someone with a clipboard comes in and tells everyone Wes's set will start in ten minutes.

Elli gives Wes a kiss on the cheek, and we head out to grab drinks before we settle in for his set.

# CHAPTER 28

## *Hannah*

I've never been to a concert before, unless you count "The Tabernacle Choir at Temple Square" formerly known as "The Mormon Tabernacle Choir."

This is *definitely* not the same.

The crowd is a good size for an up-and-coming band, and while there are a few places to sit, we're going to be standing off to the side and at the front of the stage so Elli can ogle Wes during his set.

Emma's sipping on a gin and tonic—that she didn't pay for. Leah, the bassist, followed us out to the bar and bought Emma the drink and gave her her number.

"How does she do that?" Elli whispers to me as we wait for our own drinks. Morgan is pressed close behind me with his hand on my hip because the space is filling up with concert-goers.

His touch is searing my skin through my dress. The moment at the apartment has left my blood feeling fizzy all night, and I'm anxious with anticipation. I wanted him to kiss me more than I've ever wanted anyone in my life. I wanted to let him give his keys to Elli and Emma so we could stay in my apartment and release this pent up tension that's been building since the first time we met in his flower shop.

"Do what?" I ask, trying to get my thoughts back on track.

Elli circles her finger in the direction of Emma, who's now talking to some stranger covered in tattoos. "Just... flirt with random strangers. I wish I had her confidence."

"You want to flirt with random strangers? I think Wes would object," I tease, nudging Elli with my shoulder.

She huffs out a laugh. "I don't want to flirt with random strangers *now.* But dating was so fucking hard, and I think it would have been easier with confidence like hers."

I never thought about that. How Elli must've felt dating in the church at her age. I was married before I could legally drink, and Emma left before she was persuaded to get married young. But Elli was considered "old" even at twenty-four.

Morgan cuts in before I can say anything, "I don't know Emma very well, but to me it looks like she's too scared to let anyone in more than surface level. I do think she's genuinely a confident and friendly person, and obviously she's pretty, but how deep can their connections really be if she doesn't give them more than a night?"

"That makes a lot of sense. It's kind of weird to see her so adamant about not having a serious relationship. Growing up she was always planning her dream wedding and going on and on about how excited she was to have a husband—before she came out as bi, obviously. I think there's more to the story behind her swearing off relationships." Elli nods in agreement, and Morgan squeezes my hip, in what I assume is acknowledgement, right as the bartender drops off our drinks.

Morgan ordered a plain Dr. Pepper while I added coconut rum to mine. I wanted to get something stronger, but I want to have a clear head when I tell him how I feel.

Emma leaves the person she was talking to, and Elli leads us through the crowd to the front right as Wes walks out on stage. The crowd cheers, and he grins, waving to everyone as he settles in.

"Hey there, Salt Lake City! Thanks for the warm welcome. I'm Wes Jones, and I'm excited to play for you tonight. This first song is one you may know. It's dedicated to the most special girl in the world and the love of my life."

Wes sings *Love Bug,* his eyes locked on Elli's the entire time. The crowd sings along with him, practically drowning him out, but he doesn't even seem to notice. He's so focused on my cousin, it makes me want to tear up.

When he strikes the final chord, Elli blows him a kiss, which he pretends to catch and put in his pocket. He starts playing another original song, this one a bit more upbeat than the first.

Morgan stands behind me while we slightly sway to the beat. He leans down so he can speak in my ear, "He's really fucking talented." His breath ghosting across my ear makes me shiver.

"Yeah, he is. I think he's going to go pretty far."

The last song he plays is a cover of *gentle* by Lexi Jayde, and even though I've heard the song before, the lyrics feel like a punch to the gut.

*Could you please be gentle with me?*
*My heart is fragile, don't you see?*
*I can't take another break, take another burn*
*I don't want another lesson learned*
*Could you please be gentle with me?*

I turn to look at Morgan, who's already looking at me, and it feels like I can't take a full breath. I want to stay and support the band, but I want to tell Morgan how I feel, too. I turn back to face the stage, and Elli nudges me.

*Go,* she mouths with an understanding smile. I wrap her in a hug and whisper thanks into her ear.

I look over at Emma, who comes and wraps me in a hug next. "You've got this, Hannah. And *please* call me tomorrow to tell me if he's big everywhere." She waggles her eyebrows suggestively, and I smack her lightly on the arm.

"I will not be doing that."

She sticks her bottom lip out in a pout but holds a hand out to Morgan. "It was nice to meet you, Morgan. Take care of our cousin."

Morgan shakes it but looks confused. "Are you leaving?"

"No, uh, I'm ready to go if you're okay with it." My cheeks flush, and I wish it was just from the alcohol.

Morgan nods. "For sure, Butterfly. Are you two going to be okay?" he says to Elli and Emma. God, this man is so fucking kind.

My cousins share a look, and Emma speaks for them. "She's got Wes, and I'm probably going to have a night of orgasms with Leah, so yeah, we'll be perfectly fine."

Morgan gives them a solid nod, then grabs my hand and leads me out of the venue. He doesn't let go of my hand until I'm getting into the car and he absolutely has to.

"Are you okay?" he asks once he settles into the driver's seat.

"I don't want to fake date anymore," I blurt out.

Morgan's eyebrows furrow. "Okay. Um, that's fine. I thought we... Never mind. I'll respect your wishes, Hannah. I still want to be friends though. Is that okay?"

*Oh God. He doesn't get it.*

I shake my head. "No, I don't want to be friends either. I want to be... I *like* you, Morgan."

"I like you too, Butterfly."

He's always been open and honest with me. He deserves the same.

I take a deep breath, suddenly wishing we weren't in his car right now.

"No, I *like* you, like you. I want you. I want to date you for real. If you want that, too, obviously."

"Hannah, are you positive? It's not just me you'd be committing to. Aly and I are a package deal."

"I know. And I want to be in her life, too. I want more lazy Saturdays watching *Scooby-Doo* with both of you. I want to be as involved as you both want me to be. I fully understand she's your primary concern, and I would never do anything to jeopardize your relationship with her."

Morgan searches my face, like he's searching for a lie. He's not going to find one. I'm more than okay with him putting her first. It's one of the things I love most about him.

"This isn't just the alcohol talking, right?" he asks softly, like the moment is fragile, and he doesn't want to shatter it.

I reach across the console and grab his hand, mentally sighing in relief when he doesn't pull away.

"I only had one drink, and there was barely any alcohol in it. So no, it's not the alcohol talking. I had a whole plan with flowers and a grand gesture—"

"What do you mean?" he cuts me off.

"I—I was going to give you a bouquet with yellow daffodils and aster to convey my feelings for you." It sounds stupid now, I'm glad I didn't go with it.

"Did you look up the meaning of the flowers in your birthday bouquet?"

I nod.

He nods.

"Can we go now?" I ask quietly.

He starts the car, still holding my hand, and drives us away from the venue.

# CHAPTER 29

## Morgan

*She wants to date me. She wants our relationship to be real.*

My head swims with those three little words, the ones that would be too soon to say. My mouth aches from the force of holding them back.

*She likes me.*

Asters and yellow daffodils: Two symbols of love. She was going to give them to me to convey her feelings.

*She wants to be with me.*

I was going to take her to her house, give her a kiss goodnight, and leave. But now—now I'm thinking half with the head on my shoulders and half with the head in my pants. Aly's sleeping at Olivia's tonight, so I don't need to worry about her.

"Um, Morgan? This isn't my exit," she says, still gripping my hand.

"I know. I'm taking you to my place, Hannah. We're going to talk." *And then, I might finally get a taste of you.*

"Okay."

The rest of the drive is silent, and when we pull into the garage and I put the car in park, the tension becomes so thick I swear it could be spooned out of the air. I exit the car, open Hannah's door, and lead her into the house. She toes off her shoes by the door and sets down her purse, then stands there, looking up at me.

Her lip stain is a bit faded, and her hair is a little more wild, but she still looks absolutely gorgeous.

I step forward and brace a hand above the wall like I did at her apartment. Only this time, I bring a hand up to cup her jaw. I watch her throat work on a swallow as our eyes lock.

"I thought we were going to talk," she whispers.

"We are. Tell me again you want to do this for real."

"I want to do this for real." Her voice doesn't waver one bit.

"I want that, too." I drag my thumb across her cheekbone, watching her little pink tongue drag across her lips. "Can I kiss you, Hannah?"

She tilts her face up to mine in silent agreement, and I lower mine to meet her halfway.

The instant our lips touch, it feels like a puzzle piece fits into place. A piece of my heart that had been rattling around waiting to be put back by the right person.

I kiss her slowly, wanting to memorize everything about this moment. Savoring her like a fine wine, I take long, luxurious sips so I can discern every flavor and let my palate memorize them.

I tease the seam of her lips with my tongue, gently asking if she'll open up for me, and she eagerly does, our tongues dancing in a way that's so new, yet so familiar..

She tastes like coconut rum and my future wife.

I want more, want to take this slow, want anything she'll give me.

I press my body against hers, bringing the hand on the wall down to grip her hip and groan into her mouth at how amazing she feels.

She's so fucking soft, so lovely. I want to feel her everywhere.

I pull back, and she *whimpers*. But I need to ask her. Need to know if she's feeling as desperate as I am.

"I know we just made this official, and I don't want you to think I only want you for sex but—"

*Meow!*

"What was that?" she asks, peering around me. "Oh!" She startles when the black void of fur rubs against her legs.

"That would be Bean. Resident black cat asshole." I sigh, trying to pick him up.

He hisses at me and swats at my hands.

"Awe, he's just a baby. Aren't you a sweet baby?" she coos, bending down to let him sniff her hand.

The little demon rubs himself on her leg like they're lifelong friends and lets her pet him. When she tries to pick him up, *he lets her.*

"Are you made of catnip or something? He'll only let Aly pick him up. No one else in my family is even allowed to touch him besides her." I watch as Hannah cradles him like a baby, and he nuzzles into her breasts.

*I'd really like to do that, too, you little beast.*

"That can't be true. He's such a sweetheart. Aren't you, Bean?" She plops a kiss on his head, and I swear if cats could smirk, he'd be smirking at me right now. Like he *knows* I was trying to get intimate with Hannah and decided it would be fun to intervene.

*Meow.* Bagel ambles in, and Hannah gasps. "Oh, the other one! Are you and your brother best friends?"

Resigning myself to letting her love on the cats for a little bit, I make my way over to the couch and sit down, motioning for her to sit by me. She does, and Bagel immediately hops onto the back of the couch to sniff her.

When he's done his sniff-spection and deemed her safe, he curls up into her lap while she still cradles Bean.

I didn't think anything could make me love this woman more, but watching my asshole of a furbaby cuddle into her makes me want to drop to one knee right the fuck now.

"Sorry, I got distracted by the cats." She sighs, looking a little timid.

I give her an unimpressed look. "Are you really? Because you look pretty comfy over there."

"I had a cat growing up—Cheddar. My mom spent a fortune on a Siberian cat because they're supposedly hypoallergenic. She would have him groomed to look like a lion. He was kind of dumb, but he was the sweetest thing. He would curl up on my lap while I was studying or when we'd watch a movie. I think he could tell I needed a friend, so he would get on the end of my bed and sleep there some nights. I was devastated when he died, and my mom wouldn't let me get another cat.

"I wanted to get a cat with Liam, but he always refused. Said we should save our money for more important things. We always conveniently moved to places we couldn't have animals, or he'd say we should focus on having a baby instead."

I grab her hand and squeeze. "You can come cuddle these two anytime. Or you can get your own cat. I think your landlord would be lenient."

She stiffens a little and stops petting Bean, who lets out a *meow* in protest. "Can we even date if you're my landlord? That's got to be a breach of lease—"

"We don't have a lease—"

"Oh God. What if we break up and you don't want me to live there anymore?"

"Hey." I gently squeeze her hand. "Look at me." She turns and meets my eyes. "I don't plan on breaking up. Okay? And if for some reason we did, I would *never* jeopardize your living situation. If you'd like my lawyer to draft up a lease, I will do it. But know your living arrangement is safe."

"Sorry, that was probably overly dramatic, but I just *really* don't want to have to live with my parents again."

Apparently bored with our serious conversation, Bean and Bagel simultaneously leap off the couch and dart from the room.

Hannah continues, "I don't need a lease. I trust you."

I nod, unsure of what else to say. I love that she trusts me, and I hope I never lose that trust.

"So... before we were interrupted," she turns and faces me, using her sock-covered foot to run up my leg, "you were saying something about wanting me for sex?"

Just like that, the tension in the air is back, and my cock stirs, remembering how perfect she felt against me.

I run a hand up her thigh. "I was saying I don't want you to think I want you *only* for sex, but if you were interested…" I trail off, feeling the heat of her skin under my palm. If I slid my hand up just three inches my fingers would be able to feel the heat of her pussy, too.

"I've only ever been with Liam. I might not be… good," she whispers, like it's a shameful thing.

I shake my head. "First things first, Hannah. I never want to hear that douchebag's name—or any other person's name for that matter—when my hand is so close to your pussy. Second, that doesn't bother me. I want to pleasure *you*. I want *you*. Exactly as you are."

Hannah pulls her bottom lip between her teeth while she thinks about it.

It feels like hours before she finally grabs my face in her palms and says, "Please be gentle with me." Then she brushes her lips against mine.

# CHAPTER 30

*Hannah*

Morgan kisses me in a way that can only be described as meticulous. Like he wants to know every ridge of my lips and every taste bud on my tongue. It's equal parts hungry and savoring, and it's something I've never experienced before. I've never been kissed by someone who wants me so badly.

"I'll be so gentle with you, Butterfly," he says between kisses. "Does that mean I can take you to my bedroom?"

"Yes, please."

He stops kissing me, stands, and takes my hand, leading me up the two sets of stairs to the top floor of his house. I didn't come up here last time, and it's dark, but with the little strips of lights running along the floorboards, I can make out picture frames hanging on the walls. There are two doors on the right and two doors to my left. On the left, I can tell one belongs to Aly because it's painted a bright teal. I assume the other is Morgan's office, and the one on the right is a bathroom.

Morgan leads me to the last door and opens it to reveal his bedroom. When he turns the light on, I can see it's painted a soft gray color, has the same flooring as the rest of the house, and the bedding on the king-sized bed matches the color of the walls. Two matching side tables sit on either side of the bed, and there are pictures all over the walls.

Morgan steps toward me to kiss me, but I stop him. "Wait!"

"What's wrong?"

"Do we have to keep the light on?"

"No," he says slowly, "but is there a reason you don't want me to see you?"

I suddenly feel extremely self-conscious. "My ex never left the light on during sex, and he told me it was because he didn't find my body attractive, so I just... don't want you to think the same thing."

He moves around me to turn the light off, and I feel equally relieved and disappointed.

But then he goes to the bedside and turns the lamp on. "I find every single thing about you attractive, Butterfly. We can keep the lights off, but I'd really like to see what I'm eating."

*Oh. Oh!*

The ache between my hips grows. "I've never..."

"Don't tell me that prick never gave your pussy the attention it deserves."

I shake my head, mortified now at my lack of experience.

Morgan sighs, and I think he's about to tell me he doesn't want to do this anymore, but instead he strides to me in two steps, grabs my waist, and turns me around.

"I'm going to take your dress off now, Hannah. Is that okay?"

"Yes."

He slowly undoes the zipper in the back and pulls the dress down so it pools at my ankles. "Goddamn it, Hannah." He runs his hands gently over the delicate red lace of my bra, the dips in my hips, and the waistline of my matching panties. "This color is so fucking tantalizing against your skin. I can't decide if I want to leave it on or rip it off with my teeth."

I turn around so he can see the way the cups of my bra hold my breasts, and his eyes immediately fall to my chest. "Fuuuuuuuuck," he groans, cupping them in his palm almost reverently. My nipples poke through the lace, and when he swipes his thumb over the hardened nubs, I gasp. He does it again, and I moan.

"You make such sweet sounds, Butterfly. I wonder what sound you'd make if I did this." In a seamless motion he pulls the lace of my bra down and pulls one nipple into his mouth. I immediately arch my back, offering myself to him.

One of his large hands splays across my lower back while the other cups my free breast. Then he switches his ministrations to the other nipple, and with his hand on my back, he deftly unclasps my bra.

The pleasure coursing through me makes my clit throb unlike anything I've ever felt before, and I'm greedy for more. Sex with Liam never felt like this, and Morgan's barely even touched me.

Morgan pops off my nipple, kneeling to gently pull my panties from my body, and sets them on the floor.

"Are you wet for me, Hannah?" he rasps, planting gentle kisses along the soft swell of my belly, his hands running up and down my dimpled thighs.

"I..." I trail off, unsure of how to tell him I'm so aroused I might combust, but I might not be wet.

"Maybe I should just see for myself." His hand trails down until his fingertips brush over the curls on my mound, but before he can feel my vagina, I grab his wrist.

"I don't get... wet," I murmur.

Morgan blinks, then blinks again. He stands and cups my face. "That's okay, Butterfly. There's plenty of other ways we can get you ready to take my cock." He kisses me hard but pulls back too soon and gives me a wolfish grin. "Lay your sexy body on the bed, I'm going to enjoy a late night snack."

I slowly follow his directions. When I turn, he gives me a gentle swat on my butt, and I find I don't... hate it. It's not something I'd ever thought about in the bedroom, but maybe I'd be open to exploring that more later.

I lay down on the soft comforter, and he follows, the tent in his boxers—*when did he get undressed?*—makes my brain short circuit a little bit.

My eyes greedily roam over the expanse of new skin I can see. He's so strong, muscles defined from all the years playing football, but he's got a little stomach pudge that makes my mouth water. I like that he doesn't look intimidatingly toned.

My eyes snag again on the large erection he's sporting. He's a large man, so it makes sense he'd be large there, too. Anticipation zips through me as I wonder how it'll feel as he slides inside me.

I spread my legs, ready to let him try and stick that thing inside me, but instead of shucking off his boxers and thrusting into me, he settles his shoulders between my thighs, forcing me to spread my legs wider for him.

I try to close them, and he tuts, "Now now, Butterfly, it would be rude of you to not let me feast when I've been craving a taste of you since the first moment you walked into my shop." He kisses the crease where my thighs meet my hips, then down one thigh and up the other. "If you don't like what I'm doing, you tell me to stop, okay?"

"Okay," I agree, and as soon as the last syllable leaves my mouth Morgan licks up my center in one long stroke, ending at my clit.

*Oh. My. God.*

I bow off the bed, but Morgan's strong arm is right there, holding me down.

"You're definitely wet for me, Butterfly, I can taste it. You just need extra attention on this delicious pussy, and I'm more than happy to give it to you."

He cups my ass with both hands and tucks in to my pussy like it's a dessert. His beard scratches my sensitive inner thighs, his nose bumps against my clit while his tongue spears into me over and over. I don't know what sounds I'm making, but they seem to spur him on, and he doubles down on his efforts.

He moves his tongue up to flick rapidly against my clit, sending sparks of arousal up through my entire body, a low ache in my belly expanding and pulling taut. One thick finger gently prods against my opening and slowly enters me. He moves it back and forth a few times, then pulls it out completely, then I feel a second finger join the first.

He crooks them to some secret spot that's never been touched, and I cry out at the burst of pleasure threatening to consume me.

His lips wrap around my clit, and he sucks, his fingers keeping a steady rhythm inside me. Within a few strokes of his fingers, my lower body tingles, and the band inside me snaps, releasing a pleasure so intense I can't even make a sound. My whole body tenses, but Morgan's clever fingers and expert mouth work me through until the overwhelming pleasure is just a dull ache.

He removes his fingers and his lips from me and looks up at me from between my thighs with a proud smile on his face. His beard looks wet, and I have a startling realization it's because of *me*.

"How—what was *that*?" I pant.

"What was what?" He quickly stands from the bed and discards his boxers, his cock bobbing free and jutting thick and long from his body. He strokes it once, twice, before getting back on the bed and hovering over me.

I haven't seen many penises, but that can't be a normal sized one, right?

"The... the wetness and the intense feeling I had. That's what an orgasm feels like?"

# Chapter 31

## Morgan

I'm equal parts proud and sad that I gave Hannah her first orgasm. She's twenty-seven and was married for over seven years for God's sake!

"Yeah, Butterfly. That was an orgasm. Want to have another one?"

She nods, so I reach over and grab a condom from the bedside table.

"I'm on birth control," she blurts out, her cheeks flushing a deeper red. "And obviously I haven't been with anyone in almost a year. I got checked at a doctor's appointment to be sure, and the tests were clear so..."

*Fuck.*

"I haven't been with anyone in six months, and I get checked after every partner. I'm good to go, too... Are you sure you're okay without a condom?"

"I want to feel all of you, Morgan." Again, her voice doesn't waver.

I toss the condom unceremoniously to the floor and settle my hips between her glorious thighs. Feeling them wrap around my head will be ingrained into my psyche until the day I die. I could live and die there happily.

"I'm going to go slow, and if you feel at all like we need a little extra lube, you let me know okay? It's totally normal to use lube," I assure her, gripping the base of my cock and nestling the head at the entrance of her sex.

She nods, and I push the head in, the warmth of her pussy sending a shiver of need down my spine. The urge to drive into her hard and fast to get her off creeps into my head, but I push it away.

This isn't a quick fuck.

I push in deeper, and despite her saying she doesn't get wet, it's easy to slide into her until my balls are flush to her ass, and she's wiggling to adjust to me.

"How do you feel, Butterfly?" My voice is strained, every muscle in my body tense as I wait for her to be ready.

"So full. Fuck," she moans.

I slowly pull out, leaving only the tip in before I thrust slowly back in, repeating the motion three more times.

"Morgan, please," she cries, her hands gripping the comforter.

"What do you need, Hannah?"

"I don't know! Just, *more.*" She thrusts her hips up rapidly to try and get the friction she needs.

"Needy girl," I tut, "fucking yourself on my cock. Such a pretty sight. Do you need me to go faster or harder, Butterfly?"

"Both!"

"I wanted to go slow." I thrust hard and fast, loving the way her heavy tits bounce. "I wanted to take my time with you." I thrust again. "I wanted to make love to you, Butterfly. But you want to be fucked hard, huh?"

"Yes, yes, yes!" she chants, clawing at my back. I'll wear her scratch marks as a fucking badge of honor.

"Fuck, Hannah," I groan, continuing to thrust hard and fast while gripping her perfect pink nipple between my teeth.

"Morgan! It's happening again!" she screams, and I feel her pussy clench around me in a vice grip as she comes again.

"Hell yes, Butterfly. You take it so well. That's it, I'm going to come, too, so if you want me to pull out tell me now," I grit out through clenched teeth.

"Let me feel it, please," Hannah moans, wrapping her legs around my waist as if that will keep me inside her.

As if I'd pull out after she begged so beautifully.

Two more thrusts, and my hips stutter as my balls tighten, and I fill her.

With no barrier between us, it doesn't feel like a regular orgasm, it feels like we just joined parts of ourselves together forever.

I don't want to leave her warmth, but my dick is softening, and we're both sweaty, so once I've caught my breath, I gently pull out of her.

I stand to grab a washcloth, and as she sits up, a bit of my cum drips from her swollen pussy. My mind flashes with images of a pregnant Hannah, *my* ring on her finger, her belly round with *my* baby. My hindbrain grunts in approval, even as the logical part of me knows she doesn't want that.

I rush to wet the washcloth and clean her up as best I can in the moment, all while picturing a life with the woman in my bed.

I never really thought about having more kids—Aly is more than enough for me—but suddenly the urge to have a baby with Hannah, to tie her to me forever in that way, works its way up my throat, and I feel like an asshole.

"I'm going to get the shower started, Butterfly. Come join me when you're ready."

She nods, looking a little shy, and I can't have that.

I stalk to the bed and tilt her chin to meet my eyes. "I've seen every inch of your magnificent body, and there's not a single part I don't like. Don't get shy on me now."

She nods again, letting me help her off the bed and to the bathroom where I turn on the shower.

My bathroom is one of the only parts of the house I had renovated. I wanted a big enough shower to fit two people, and there's a bench along one wall. Two shower heads and a rain shower head mean you're getting hit with warm water from every direction.

It's one of my favorite places in the house.

I guide Hannah under the warm water, and she tilts her head back and lets it wet her hair. I grab a shampoo bottle and start washing her hair.

"This smells like my shampoo," she mumbles as I massage her scalp. Once she's rinsed, she opens her eyes and blinks as she sees the shower products lined on the shelf next to mine. She turns to me with a bewildered expression.

"I, uh... just picked the ones that smelled like you," I admit, knowing that it sounds weird as hell.

"I—why?"

"Because I was being hopeful. I wanted you in my bed, in my shower. In my *life*. So I was *manifesting* as the kids say. I wanted to be ready in case we got to this point."

Hannah gapes at me. "You weren't just trying to be sexy when you said you've wanted me since I walked into your shop, were you?"

"No, Butterfly. I wasn't."

"So this whole time you've just been playing my boyfriend when really..."

"I've been trying to earn your trust. I know that asshat was—well—an asshat to you, and I wanted to show you how you should be treated. How someone who... wants every part of you would treat you." *How someone who loves you unconditionally would give you the whole world on a platter if you asked.*

"Thank you, Morgan. For being patient with me while I realized what was right in front of me. I'm sure it wasn't easy."

I pull her wet body into mine. "I would wait a thousand years for you, Butterfly." I seal my promise with a kiss, one I hope conveys every emotion I'm too scared to say out loud to her.

When we finish our shower, I slip into some underwear and give her a pair of my boxers and a t-shirt so she doesn't have to put on her dress. When she asks me if I'm taking her home, I give her my best *get real* look and motion for her to join me in my bed.

As I turn off the lights, the room is bathed in darkness. Hannah tries to keep her distance on the king-sized bed, but I pull her body flush against mine.

"Come to lunch at my parents' tomorrow. Well, today, I guess. I want you to meet the rest of the family," I whisper.

I expect her to decline or say it's too soon, but she agrees.

I stay awake long enough to feel her breathing even out, and when I close my own eyes, I fall asleep immediately, feeling happier than I have in a really long fucking time.

# CHAPTER 32

*Hannah*

There's something hard and hot pressed up against my back as I stir from sleep, but when I try to wiggle away, a firm arm bands around my belly and pulls me back.

"Don't you dare. I'm enjoying the cuddles," Morgan's deep voice commands, raising goosebumps on my skin despite his body heat.

"Good morning to you, too," I tease, earning me a quick squeeze. "Don't you need to get Aly soon?" I try to sit up to look at the time, but he rolls so he's caging me underneath his body.

"Olivia and her wife, Asha, are spending the day with Aly. We'll meet them all for family lunch," he explains through kisses peppered along my jaw.

"Okay," I breathe. "I need to go home so I can change into something that's not your clothes." He continues kissing me, down my neck, biting gently.

"Hmmm. But I like seeing you in my clothes." He sits us both up so he can pull his shirt over my head. "I like you even more with no clothes at all." He trails his lips down my chest and kisses the swell of each breast.

"Morgan…" I warn. "I really need to get ready so I can look presentable for your family. I don't know if we have time for—oh!" He cuts me off by biting my sensitive nipple.

"We can be fast, Butterfly. Let me make you come. I need it."

"Okay." It's hard to resist when I know the pleasure he can bring me.

"Fuck, yes." *My boyfriend* moves off of me just enough to reach into a bedside drawer and produce a bottle of lube. He pulls the boxers I'm wearing down and tosses them, then discards his own.

He *clicks* the bottle cap open and drops a small amount of lube onto his fingers, then rubs small circles around my aching clit.

"Oh, that feels good." I reach for his cock, wanting to feel the weight of it in my hand.

It's hard and hot, but the skin is soft, almost satiny. I give an experimental tug, and he grunts.

He increases the pressure on my clit, and the tension in my core builds and builds, but just when I'm about to come, he stops.

I whine in protest but stop when he pulls his cock from my grasp. He puts a little more lube on his cock and slides into me easily.

"Fuck me, Hannah. I swear you were made for me. Your pussy grips me so well," he groans, slowly thrusting in and out of me.

The swollen head of his cock rubs along my G-spot, and the weight of him on top of me adds a delicious pressure to my clit when he thrusts in as deep as he can go.

Last night felt like a frantic need to be as close as possible, at least on my part, but today the desire to have him hard and fast isn't there. The leisurely way he thrusts and the loving way he's looking at me are enough to bring me to tears. I'm coming sooner than I thought I would, and he follows quickly after.

Last night felt like we were consummating our relationship with fucking, but this morning feels like making love.

The words *I love you* are on the tip of my tongue, but I swallow them down so I don't scare him away when I just got him.

*You won't scare him away.* A small voice in my head tells me, but I still keep it to myself.

We shower again quickly because it's later than he thought, and he takes me to my apartment so I can get dressed.

I have no idea what I'm supposed to wear to a family lunch where I'm meeting the family of my boyfriend of less than twenty-four hours. He said it was casual, but I want to make a good impression.

I decide a sage green jersey swing dress is comfortable but casual, and since we're running low on time, I twist my short hair into a semi-messy bun.

When I emerge from the bathroom, Morgan looks up from his phone and groans. "How am I supposed to keep my hands off of you when you look so good?"

"It's just a dress!"

He stands and stalks towards me, easily closing the distance between us. When he reaches me, he wraps his arms around my waist and pulls me flush against his body. "That dress is hiding my new favorite meal, Butterfly. All day I'm going to be thinking about how easy it would be to lift it up, pull your panties to the side, and feast on you."

*My goodness.* I thought dirty talk was only for the bedroom. Liam certainly never said such sexual things in *or* out of the bedroom.

"What color are they?" he asks.

"What?" I blink up at him.

"What color are the panties you're wearing?" He slides his hands down my back to grab my ass in a bruising grip.

I must not answer him fast enough because quick as a whip, he has my dress hiked up around my waist and is running his thumb along the lace of my cheeky panties.

"Black," I whisper.

"Hmmm. I think the red is my favorite so far. I can't wait to see the rest." He gently rights my dress. "Let's go, Butterfly. We don't want to be late." He plants a swift kiss on my lips and drags me to the door, barely pausing to let me get my shoes on and grab my purse.

On the drive there he gives me a brief rundown of his family tree. Olivia is the oldest and is married to Asha.

Alice is next, and I already met her and Cooper. Then it's Morgan and his twin sister, Sarah. She is married to Justin, who Morgan says looks like a Republican hillbilly but is actually one of the nicest, most accepting people ever. The youngest Fowler and only other boy, Kendall, is the only one of his siblings that doesn't live in Utah. He lives in Pennsylvania and plays for a Rugby team.

"And no one else has kids except for me. Unless Kendall's knocked someone up and doesn't know about it, which isn't out of the realm of possibilities."

"Bit of a player?" I ask.

"He's hot, and he knows it. Bit of a commitment-phobe. He and Emma are very similar, I would say."

"Ah. So he's had his heart broken and doesn't want to try again yet." I get that. But I'm glad I'm moving past it and taking a chance with Morgan.

"Bingo. Alright, Butterfly." He pulls to a stop in front of a lovely red brick ranch house. "Are you ready to meet the Fowler crew?"

"As ready as I'll ever be."

Morgan opens my door and walks us to the house, not bothering to knock before he steps inside. A bunch of different voices chatter when we walk in, but they all come to a halt when the door shuts.

We walk through the entryway and down the hall to the kitchen where multiple smiling faces greet me.

"Hannah! Aunt Liv said you were coming. I'm so excited to see you!" Aly bounces to me and wraps me in a hug.

"Hey, Aly! I'm excited to see you, too." I feel like I'm about to cry, which would be extremely embarrassing.

"Oh! Hannah, it's so good to meet you!" A woman with short brown hair streaked with gray and the same eyes as Morgan wraps me in a hug as soon as Aly steps back.

"Mom, you didn't even introduce yourself," Morgan teases.

"Oh, where are my manners? I'm Iris, Morgan's mom, but you can call me Gigi or mom, if you'd like."

"*Mom*," Morgan groans.

"It's lovely to meet you, Iris." I don't remember the last time my own mother gave me such a warm embrace, and getting one from someone who so clearly loves her kids makes me a little misty-eyed.

Iris loops her arm through mine and walks me around the room introducing me to everyone.

Morgan's dad, Axel, is *tall*. Taller than Morgan, if only by an inch, and he towers over Iris, who's at least two inches shorter than my five-foot-seven. I would find it an odd pairing if they weren't so in love.

I'm pleasantly surprised to see that all of Morgan's sisters are plus size, and so is Olivia's wife. It's nice to not feel insecure about existing in my body.

When Iris stops us to meet Olivia and Asha, Olivia gasps. "I know that necklace. I *made* that necklace!"

I instinctively touch the butterfly around my neck. "It's gorgeous, I wear it every day," I say shyly.

"It looks so pretty against your skin tone. I'm glad it found a home with you because a lot of people like peach moonstone," Asha says, and Olivia nods.

"Peach moonstone can promote emotional healing and enhance intuition. It's a powerful stone and very sought after," Olivia adds on.

"Oh, well, that's very fitting for my situation then," I say with a small laugh.

"Ah, yes. Aly filled us in on the drama with your… *gem* of an ex-husband."

My stomach drops. How much do they know? Do they think less of me because I'm associated with Liam? How does Aly feel about it? Does she hate me for being associated with him?

"He's a real piece of work, isn't he? I'm glad you got out of that relationship," Iris tsks, shaking her head.

"I think it was a mutually beneficial divorce for sure." I don't like talking bad about him, even if he probably deserves it.

"Well," Aly's small voice startles me, I didn't realize she was on my other side, "I don't like him. I'm glad you're in love with my dad now."

She says it so certainly, like she's privy to my inner thoughts about her dad.

The tips of Morgan's ears are pink when I look at him, and he just gives me a small shrug as if to say *I'm not going to correct her.*

"Your dad treats me way better than my ex-husband ever did. I'm very lucky to have him in my life," I say in response to Aly.

Before anyone says anything else, the front door slams shut, and a deep voice bellows, "I'm home!"

Aly gasps, "UNCLE KENNY!" then runs to the man entering the kitchen.

# CHAPTER 33

*Morgan*

"**K**endall Eugene Fowler, what on earth are you doing here?" Mom sets her hands on her hips and scowls, trying to look intimidating. It still works on us even though we're almost a foot taller than her.

Kendall grimaces at the use of his middle name but flashes Mom his best golden-boy smile.

It doesn't work on her.

"Can't a guy crash his family lunch and come see his beloved mother?" Kendall asks, setting Aly down on the ground and giving Mom a bear hug.

"Considering you didn't call or text to tell me you were traveling all the way from Pennsylvania, I don't think this is a good-will visit."

"Well, I have some big news to share with everyone, so I—" he stops when his gaze lands on Hannah. The change in his demeanor is instant as he turns on the play-boy charm. "Hello," he croons. "I don't think we've met before. I'm Kendall." He extends his hand to Hannah who takes it in a firm handshake.

"I'm Hannah."

"Hannah. Lovely name for a lovely girl," he says, and all three of my sisters gag.

"She's Dad's girlfriend, Uncle Kenny. Get your own," Aly, my sweet angel of a daughter, says, standing in front of Hannah like she can protect her from my brother.

Everyone laughs at Aly's declaration, including me and Hannah.

Kendall's head whips around to me, at least having the decency to look a little apologetic as he mouths, *sorry.*

I walk over and wrap my arm around Hannah. I know there's nothing to worry about, Kendall would never try to steal her, and I can tell Hannah has no interest in my brother.

"How long have you been together? Why didn't I know about it?" Kendall asks as he doles out hugs to the rest of the group.

"We made it official last night, actually. And you would know things if you ever checked your freaking phone."

"Well, congrats, bro. I'm happy for you. As long as this isn't another situation like Witch-ney where you're only with her because she's knocked up." Kendall winks at me, and I feel Hannah stiffen beside me.

As much as I want kids to be in our future, the topic is a sore spot for Hannah after everything she's been through, and my baby brother just had to go and put his foot in his mouth.

To take the spotlight off of Hannah, I say, "I think we're all more interested to know about your big news."

"Yes, yes, let's all get a plate filled, and Kendall can give us the news." Mom claps, ushering us to serve ourselves buffet-style.

Once we've loaded up our plates and gathered around the table, Kendall tells us Utah is the new home to a Major League Rugby team, and he's been recruited to join. He's here looking for a place to live while he trains for the upcoming season.

"Doesn't the Union season start in September? That's a pretty quick turnaround," Asha points out.

"While waiting for the facility to be completed here, we've been training in PA for the last few months. We only have two weeks off to find housing and get situated," Kendall explains.

"Well, you're more than welcome to stay here until you find a permanent place to live, honey," Mom offers.

Kendall gives her a grateful nod, and the conversation switches back to my girlfriend.

Everyone asks Hannah a thousand questions about herself. How many siblings does she have? Where does she work? Did she grow up in Utah?

Once Hannah mentions she grew up Mormon, the questions come even faster. My family isn't unfamiliar with the church, but none of us have ever considered joining. Being surrounded by the culture is fascinating in the way a car wreck is fascinating. You want to know more information, but you're glad you're not part of it.

"So your parents are still members of the church even though you're not?" Dad asks, and Hannah nods.

"They're not happy about it. They even kicked me out when I started dating Morgan because he's not a member, and they think he's a bad influence on me,"

Hannah explains. I squeeze her thigh under the table, letting her know I've got her.

"What the hell does that matter? Morgan's not a bad person just because he doesn't believe whatever the Mormons believe," Alice scoffs.

"I know," Hannah sighs. "But there's a certain standard in the church people are expected to uphold, and non-members are looked down on unless they show an ounce of interest in joining. I married my ex when I was eighteen because he was a respectable member, and I thought that's what I was supposed to do. I would never encourage an eighteen-year-old to get married so young."

Everyone's jaws drop at that bit of information.

"Can I ask a personal question about something I saw on Tiktok?" Sarah asks.

Hannah nods.

"Is it true there are secret ceremonies done in the temple? Where they strip you naked and pour oil all over you? And you vow to cut out your bowels if you deny the church or something?"

Hannah nods again, fiddling with her necklace anxiously. "The oil ceremony changed around 2006, where they had you completely naked. When I went through before I got married, I was naked underneath a cloth that looked like a pillowcase with the head and arms cut out of it. Instead of pouring oil all over my body, they just poured it on my head. They would do it a few times, ring a bell, say some words, and then I got to put on my church-appointed garments.

"The bowel thing is real. They even make you do a slashing motion over your stomach to solidify the whole thing. They make a lot of veiled threats about what will happen to you if you deny the gospel, but I honestly have so much of it blocked out because it was so traumatizing."

I'm grateful Aly finished her food and went to play outside for a bit. This is not a conversation I want her to hear.

"That sounds like a super scary violation of privacy." Asha shakes her head.

Everyone murmurs their agreement, various levels of disgust and horror on their faces.

"Is it true you don't get to wear your own wedding dress when you get married in the temple?" Sarah pipes up again.

Hannah's leg bounces anxiously, so I set my palm on her thigh to try and calm her. "It depends on what your dress looks like. It has to be white as paper—they even hold up a piece of paper to compare it—and long-sleeved. There are other articles of clothing you have to wear during your sealing ceremony over the dress, too, so the dress is covered anyway. Taking pictures or videos isn't allowed in the temple, so it's not like anyone knows."

"What kinds of things do you have to wear over it?" I ask.

"Well there's a robe that looks like a half toga, a white sash, an apron that's made to look like it's made of fig leaves to represent Adam and Eve in Eden, and women get a veil while men get a hat that looks like a chef's hat. For shoes, the men have white loafers, but the women get literal slippers to wear in the temple, all with white socks."

"So basically you have to cover the expensive dress you bought or not wear it during the ceremony? That seems like a waste of money," Mom says, shaking her head.

"Yeah, it can be. For me, I just picked out a simple white dress that didn't cost a lot. My ceremony was made of only close family members that had temple recommends, and the reception took place in the gym of my parents' church. Not exactly my dream wedding, but I didn't know I had any other options at the time."

When we get married, she will have the wedding of her dreams. If she wants to have a big party with an expensive-ass dress and a live band—it's hers. If she wants to have a destination wedding in Ireland—done. Whatever she wants, I will give her. She deserves to have the wedding *she* wants.

The conversation luckily changes from Hannah's religious trauma to lighter topics, and before we know it, it's time for me to get Aly home and to bed.

My mom sends Hannah home with a grocery bag of leftovers and makes her promise to come over again soon so they can get to know each other further.

Alice, Olivia, Asha, and Sarah coordinated a lunch date and shopping with my girl so they can get to know her without me or my mom around.

When Hannah runs to the restroom before we leave, Mom pulls me in for a hug and whispers, "I can see why you're so smitten. She's amazing, Morgan. I'm so happy for you."

"Thanks, Mom."

Kendall gives me a hug next, saying we need to grab lunch so we can catch up, and I make him promise to answer his damn phone next week so we can.

Once we're in the car, Aly talks our ears off the whole way to Hannah's apartment, telling us all about the jewelry she helped Aunt Olivia make and how she made Bean and Bagel matching collars.

As badly as I want Hannah to spend the night again, I haven't talked to Aly to see if she's okay with us having sleepovers, so I'll be patient and wait.

Aly agrees to wait in the car while I walk Hannah to her door. When we reach the top of the stairs, I double check to make sure Aly can't see us before I push Hannah into the door and smash my lips against hers in a frantic kiss. It's been too long without her lips on mine.

It's messy, desperate, and over too quickly for my liking.

"Thank you for coming today, Butterfly. My family loves you already." I trace the slope of her nose, the swell of her cheeks, the line of her jaw.

"They're great, Morgan. Thank you for inviting me."

I nod. "I don't want to leave you," I whisper.

"I know." She cups my face. "But you and Aly need to have clear expectations and boundaries, and she deserves to have a say in whether or not I sleep over. So go spend time with your daughter, and call me tomorrow, okay?"

Fuck, this woman is amazing.

"God, I love you." *Oh shit.* That was supposed to be an inside thought, but I don't apologize for the outburst, waiting to see how she reacts.

I *won't* apologize for loving her.

"I love you, too, Morgan," she whispers, tears brimming behind her glasses. "It feels a little crazy to say it so soon, especially since we only made things official last night, but if you can be brave enough to tell me, I can be brave enough to say it back."

"You love me?" My own voice is thick with emotion. I'm so relieved she didn't go running.

"So much it scares me."

I kiss her again, tenderly this time, and taste the salt of her happy tears on my lips as they trail down her face.

I reluctantly pull back. "Now I really don't want to leave you."

She smiles. "Go. Text me when you get home. I'll talk to you tomorrow."

I sigh. "Okay. I love you."

"I love you, too, you big goof."

Aly asks why I have a big grin on my face as I settle back into the car, and when I tell her it's because Hannah loves me, she rolls her eyes and says, "Duh."

I text Hannah when we get home, then call her once Aly's in bed, promising myself that I'll talk to Aly tomorrow after school about Hannah spending the night.

I can't believe this is my life now.

# CHAPTER 34

*Hannah*

I'm floating when I walk in to work the next day.

*Morgan loves me.*

Sage is in the break room when I go in to drop off my lunch, and when she sees me, she gasps.

"Hannah No-Middle-Name Layton. Did you get *laid?*"

How the *hell* does she know that?

Grateful we're alone, I nod my head enthusiastically, and Sage squeals, jumping up and down excitedly.

"Oh my God, girl. Tell me *everything.*"

"I'm not going to tell you *everything.*" Sage pouts, and I roll my eyes. "I've never shared anything about my sex life with you before, I don't think I'll start now."

Sage waves my protests away. "I wasn't interested in your sex life with a vanilla, missionary-only, bor-ing-ass-douche like Liam. But now? With a football star, strong-as-fuck, smitten Morgan? Hell yes, I want to know everything." She sighs. "I bet he fucks dirty, even though he's so sweet."

I can feel my cheeks growing hotter by the minute. I wish I could tell her she's wrong so she would drop the inquisition, but she's not wrong. He's equal parts caring and dirty.

"I didn't know sex—*orgasms*—could be like that," I whisper. "It was amazing. He made sure I was totally comfortable and ready and was always checking in to make sure I was okay. I had to actually beg him to—"

The door to the break room swings open, and our boss, Janine, walks in. She's a good boss and super chill, but I don't really want her to hear about my sex life.

"Howdy, girls. Get up to anything fun this weekend?" Janine starts the kettle for her morning tea.

"I read most of the weekend. It was nice to be able to relax, but nothing too exciting," Sage says.

"I spent time with my cousins, and we went to a concert on Saturday." *And then had the most amazing sex ever. And met my* real *boyfriend's family and confessed I was in love with him.*

But Janine doesn't need to know that.

"Oh! That sounds fun. What concert? Anyone I'd know?"

"Keely and the Kissers? My cousin's boyfriend is their opener for this tour."

"What a strange band name. I haven't heard of them. I can't keep up with all the new music people these days."

Janine is only forty, but she acts like a crotchety eighty-year-old sometimes. Sage and I often have to explain pop culture references to her. When romance books started getting really popular on TikTok, people started coming in, asking if we had any "BookTok" books. She decided she wanted nothing to do with it because she can't keep up with the latest trends.

"There are a lot of them," I agree. "I better get to work. I have lots of books to shelve today since Lisa's on vacation."

Sage says the same, promising we'll talk on our lunch break, and then I spend a blissful morning at the resource center recommending books to kids and adults alike.

At lunch, I recount the weekend's activities for Sage, leaving out the dirtiest details, much to her dismay. I gush over how kind and welcoming Morgan's family was, the weird moment when his brother flirted with me, and how they peppered me with questions about the church.

"I'm glad they aren't members, babe. I think that would do more damage to you," she says between bites of pasta salad.

"I'm glad, too. Telling them about the temple ceremonies and the disaster that was my wedding was really hard, and all I could think was 'I'm glad Aly will never have to go through that.' She's so unconditionally loved by all of those people, and while I'm extremely happy for her, it makes me feel a little jealous, too. Is that bad?" I hate feeling jealous of a nine-year-old. It feels icky. I want that kind of unconditional love and support from my own family.

"I don't think that's bad. I think if you wished she were suffering, *that* would be bad. But you're one of the people who can support her now. You can wish you had the same support and love she does and still love and care for her."

I am, aren't I? Now that I'm part of Morgan's life, I'm going to be a part of Aly's life. Loving Morgan means loving Aly, and even though it's a different kind of love—and I've only met her twice—I do love her. I hope with time, she'll come to love me, too. I can never replace her mom, and I'd never try to, but I hope she'll see me as someone she can love and trust.

"Thanks, Sagey. Your support means a lot to me."

"How ever can you repay me?" She sighs dramatically. "Oh! I know. You said Morgan has a brother who plays rugby, right? Is he single?" She waggles her eyebrows.

"Kendall is perpetually single. He doesn't do monogamy."

"Ah, playboy. You know 'playboy reformed' is one of my favorite romance tropes. I think I can fix him."

"You don't even know what he looks like!"

"I know Morgan is hot and Kendall is an athlete. There's no way he's not attractive. Come on, Hannah! We can be sisters-in-law!"

I shake my head. "No way! I don't want to be responsible for your heartbreak. If you guys meet and hit it off, fine, but I will not be instigating it."

Sage rubs her hands together like an evil villain. "I shall make him mine!"

God, she's weird.

The rest of the day flies by after that, and when I get off of work, I head over to Morgan's house for dinner.

Has he talked to Aly already? Am I spending the night?

I pack an overnight bag to leave in my car, just in case.

# Chapter 35

*Morgan*

I wanted to talk to Aly alone about Hannah staying over, but then I reconsidered. If Hannah is going to be a big part of our lives, then I think it's a conversation the three of us need to have together.

I asked Aly if I could invite Hannah over for dinner to talk about something important, and she gave me an enthusiastic yes.

Aly and I are in the middle of chopping vegetables when the doorbell rings, signaling Hannah's arrival.

"I'll get it!" Aly drops her knife, and it clatters to the counter as she sprints to the door. I fight the urge to follow her to get a glimpse of Hannah.

It's only been twenty-four hours since I've seen her, and that's already too long.

I hear Aly and Hannah chattering away as they come down the hall, but I can't make out what they're saying. They sound happy, though, and it makes my heart soar to hear them getting along.

"...and then Josh K. said I wouldn't be able to read *Goosebumps* because it's too scary and I'm a baby," Aly huffs.

Josh K. is a kid in Aly's class who won't leave her alone. He picks on her for anything he can, and when I tried to talk to her teacher about it, she just brushed it off as "kids being kids" and "boys being boys." Apparently, Josh just has a crush on Aly, and *that's* why he's being mean. But I don't want Aly to grow up thinking people who are interested in her romantically will be mean to her, so I have never once said that to her.

"It sounds like he might be speaking from experience. Maybe those books were just too scary for him. Do you want to read them?" Hannah asks.

Aly wrinkles her nose. "Not really. I like to read about princesses and mysteries. Not scary things like that."

"*Magic Treehouse* is a good series. Have you read those yet?"

"I read those last year. I liked them! I've also read *Junie B. Jones.*" "Read" is an understatement. More like devoured. There are fourteen *Magic Treehouse* books and twenty-eight *Junie B. Jones* books. She read all of them so fast, and she's been struggling to find other books she likes as much.

"Oooh, *Junie* is a classic. If you like those books you could try *Judy Moody* or *Ramona and Beezus.* If you want more mysteries, *The Boxcar Children* is a good one or *The Secret of the Hidden Scrolls.* If you want mysteries and princesses, *The Rescue Princesses* is really good, too," Hannah says, still focused on Aly, even though they're in the kitchen now, and she could have easily switched her attention to me. The fact she's giving Aly her undivided attention makes my heart soar, and I have to stop myself from dropping to my knee and proposing right now.

"That sounds like a long list. Can you write it down for me?" Aly asks, heading to the junk drawer for a pen and paper.

"What if you come to the library sometime and I help you pick them out? That way you can see them and read the descriptions before you decide."

Aly looks at me. "Can we go this Saturday, Dad?"

"Sure, Bub. If it's okay with Hannah."

Aly looks at Hannah in anticipation. "Of course it's okay. I don't work Saturday, but I'm more than happy to meet you there."

"What if we made a fun day out of it?" I suggest. "We can go to the library, pick out books, grab lunch, and then come home and have a read-a-thon."

Read-a-thons are something Aly and I started doing when she started reading. It helps us have something special to do in the winter when we can't get outside. We get a bunch of snacks and fun drinks, cozy up on the floor with blankets, and spend the day reading.

"Yes!" Aly claps. "Does that sound fun, Hannah?"

"Of course it does—no better way to spend a Saturday." Hannah finally looks at me, her smile wide and excited, and it's a punch straight to the gut in the best way.

*Hi, gorgeous,* I mouth to her while Aly starts making a list of snacks.

*Hey, handsome,* she mouths back.

God, I want to round the counter and kiss her.

Once Aly's satisfied with her snack list, Hannah asks how she can help with dinner, and I direct her to chop the vegetables Aly abandoned while I start on the rice and sauce.

"What are we making?" Hannah asks while I whisk some soy sauce, brown sugar, and spices.

"Dad's famous stir fry. I don't think it's actually famous, but it is good," Aly answers.

"It's totally famous, you little stink. I made it all the time for the football team, and they begged for my recipe. I think that makes it pretty famous." I poke her side, and she jolts and giggles.

"I don't know, Morgan, I've never seen it in a cookbook," Hannah teases.

"Yeah, Dad. If it's not in a cookbook, it's not famous," Aly agrees.

I gape at them. "Is this how it's going to be from now on? You two ganging up on me all the time?"

Hannah scoffs. "Of course—girl power and all that."

"Yeah, girl power." Aly and Hannah high-five.

If I'm going to be battling anyone, I'm glad it's these two.

*Meow,* Bean announces his presence to the kitchen and heads directly for Hannah. She scoops him up, cooing and giving him pets like he's an angel, and Aly's jaw drops.

"He lets you hold him? He only lets me hold him!"

"I can't believe it either," I agree.

Aly giggles. "Looks like it's just you, Dad."

"No, remember how none of your aunts or uncles can hold him either? They all tried."

"Oh, yeah. Guess that means Hannah is just a good person, and Bean wants her to stick around." Something tells me this is Aly's way of saying *she* wants Hannah to stick around.

"Yeah, Bub. I guess so."

Bean protests loudly when Hannah sets him back down so she can finish helping with dinner, but I throw his mouse toy down the stairs, and that seems to distract him enough.

Once everything is finished, we plate up our chicken, rice, and veggies and sit at the dining table to eat.

Hannah makes a point to include Aly in our conversations, and Aly chatters away happily, answering every question Hannah asks.

When we're about done, I set down my fork and clear my throat. "I wanted to talk to you about something, Aly, and I wanted Hannah to be here because it affects her, too."

Aly and Hannah set down their own forks to give me their undivided attention. A mix of worry and anticipation on their faces.

"As you know, Hannah and I are dating."

"Yes, you're all gross and in love." Aly rolls her eyes.

"Yes, gross and in love. Great synopsis, Bub. Anyway, when people are dating, they want to spend a lot more time together. That sometimes means having sleepovers."

Aly nods. "Okay…"

"Would it be okay with you if Hannah slept over sometimes? Not all the time, obviously, but just a few times a week?"

"Does that mean I'd have to go somewhere else?" Aly asks quietly.

"Oh, no, Aly. Not at all," Hannah jumps in. "I would *never* do something that means you can't be in your own home. It would just mean I'd be here, too."

"So you don't think I'll be a bother if I'm here, too?"

"No," Hannah says vehemently. "I want to hang out with you just as much as I want to hang out with your dad."

"Hannah and I will want to go out alone on dates sometimes, but I'll always check in with you, like I do now, and make sure you're okay to go to someone else's house. Hannah's not just part of my life, she's part of *our* life now." Hannah squeezes my hand in a comforting gesture.

"Does that mean I can ask you questions about girl stuff?" Aly asks Hannah, her voice full of hope.

Hannah looks at me, and I give her a small nod.

"Of course you can, Aly. I don't want you to think I'm trying to replace your mom, but you can come to me with any questions you have, okay?"

"Okay. Can you sleep over on Friday? That way we can all drive together to the library."

"I think that's a great idea." I can't help the smile taking over my face.

When we're done with dinner and our ice cream sundae dessert, I send Aly up to get ready for bed, and Hannah helps me with the dishes.

I wash while she dries, and the task takes less than half the time it would have taken me if I did it myself.

When we're done with that, I cage her against the counter and kiss her senseless, trying to show her how much I appreciate her and love the way she treated Aly tonight.

I nip at her bottom lip, and she whimpers, but I swallow the sound with my mouth.

"Fuck, Butterfly. I've been dying to kiss you all night. If Aly weren't here right now I'd bend you over this counter and fuck you. Take my time with you. Tease you with my mouth," a nip at her jaw, "my fingers," I lick up her throat, "until you're begging for my cock." I bite that sensitive spot where her shoulder meets her neck, and she writhes against me.

"I want that," she whimpers, and I press my hard bulge into the softness of her belly.

"I'll be thinking of you in the shower later, Butterfly. When my hand is squeezing my cock, I'm going to imagine it's your warm pussy. When I come on the shower floor, it'll be with your name on my lips."

I kiss her again hungrily but pull back when I hear little feet on the stairs.

Hannah's eyes are a little glassy when I step away to adjust myself. She shakes her head like it will clear the lust from her brain.

"Teeth are brushed, pajamas are on. I just wanted to say goodbye to Hannah," Aly says as she enters the kitchen, Bean and Bagel hot on her heels. Bagel plops himself down at my feet, and Bean starts twirling between Hannah's legs.

"Thank you for having me over for dinner. I'm excited for Friday and Saturday," Hannah says, her gaze darting between the two of us.

"Even if you don't sleep over, can we have dinner together again this week?" Aly asks shyly.

"I think that's a great idea. Why don't you two come over Wednesday for Indian food?" Hannah suggests.

"Dosa House? Yes!" Aly pulls her arms towards herself in a celebratory gesture. "Can we, Dad?"

"Sure, Bub. That sounds great."

"Fantastic. I'll see you two then." Hannah goes to walk out of the kitchen, but Aly stops her just before she can.

"Can I... Can I have a hug goodbye?"

Oh damn it, now I'm going to cry. Aly's always been an affectionate kid, but she's a lot more reserved after everything with Whitney.

Hannah looks a little choked up herself as she nods and bends down so Aly can wrap her arms around her neck.

After Aly lets Hannah go with a "See you Wednesday!" she darts back upstairs, the cats following her like she's their leader.

I walk Hannah to the door and give her one last kiss that hopefully conveys how much I love her.

"Thanks again, Morgan. I'll see you Wednesday." Hannah smiles as she walks down the steps.

"Hey, Butterfly?" I call when she reaches the bottom. She turns around. "Yeah?"

"I love you."

"I love you, too." Her smile is soft and grateful before she turns around. I watch her get into her car and don't close the door until she drives away. I shoot her a reminder to text me when she gets home so I know she's safe.

The house doesn't feel as cozy or complete without her here. It's still home, but it feels like it's missing a vital piece.

She'll be back here Friday, in my bed where she belongs.

# CHAPTER 36

## Morgan

Kendall and I have lunch plans the next day, so I meet him outside our usual cheesesteak place while Olivia keeps an eye on the shop.

The man lived in the cheesesteak capitol of America and still insists this hole-in-the-wall place in Utah is the best he's ever had.

He's not wrong, it's pretty fucking good.

Once we've ordered and sat down at our table, I ask him about his decision to move. Apparently the owner of the Knights—Utah's official Major League Rugby team-—had been scouting out club teams for potential players, and he really liked Kendall's skills.

"The team has a contract with some apartment complex near the stadium, but since I'm single I'd have to live with two other dudes. I don't want roommates. I like having a space that has nothing to do with rugby. Something to call my own," he explains.

"That makes sense, but the alternative is living with Mom and Dad, which seems like it would cramp your style."

"Yeah, it would, which is why I wanted to talk to you. The apartment above the flower shop—can I live there? I'll pay you rent and utilities, and I can even watch the shop sometimes if you need me to."

"Well, Hannah's living there. If she weren't, I'd let you move in for sure."

Kendall blinks. "You're dating your tenant?"

I roll my eyes as the waitress drops off our sandwiches and sides and explain the whole roller coaster that is mine and Hannah's relationship.

I tell him everything, only sparing the explicit details.

"That sounds like a fucking romance novel, bro," Kendall mumbles around his massive sandwich.

"What the hell do you know about romance novels?"

He shrugs. "I read. They're honestly better than porn sometimes. So imaginative. It's basically a guide on how to pleasure women. The ladies *love* a man who knows what he's doing."

Like Kendall didn't already know what he was doing. Cocky fucker.

"Anyway," he continues, "I think you should just offer to have her move in, and then I can live in the apartment above the shop. Win for everyone."

I roll my eyes. "If it were that simple, I would have done that already. But I have Aly to think about, and she *just* gave us the okay to start having sleepovers. Besides, we've only been official for like two days."

"Hell yeah! Sneaky sex for the win." He holds his hand up for a high-five, but I give him an unimpressed look.

"Don't be gross, dude."

"Sorry."

"Whatever. I think you should take the apartment with the other guys to get out of Mom and Dad's, then when Hannah moves out, the place can be yours."

"I'll figure something out. Now, tell me more about Hannah."

# CHAPTER 37

## Hannah

I stare at the calendar, then at my birth control packet, counting the days again. I've done the calculations four times, and I get the same answer.

My period is two weeks late.

It's been a month since Morgan and I had sex for the first time, but I swear I've been taking my birth control at the same time every day and haven't missed a pill since I started it six months ago.

This cannot be happening.

We've had the most amazing month. In the beginning, I only slept over on the weekends because Aly was in school, but now that she's not, I sleep over a few nights a week. She comes to Morgan's flower classes at the library every Thursday, and sometimes I bring her to work with me when I think she'll like the activity for the day.

Morgan and I have gotten really good at being quiet during sex, and on the nights Aly wants to spend with someone else when we have the house to ourselves, we're insatiable.

And now that's all going to change because I might be pregnant.

He's going to think I lied to him about wanting kids. He's going to think I'm trying to baby-trap him, and he's going to hate me.

I don't want Morgan to go through the heartbreak of losing a baby, and if my body has proven anything, it's that babies are not safe inside it.

I take a sick day from work and rush to the nearest drugstore to get three different types of pregnancy tests.

When I get back to my apartment, I follow the instructions to a T, like I have so many times before, and anxiously wait for the results.

It feels like hours when my timer finally goes off, but before I can go back into the bathroom and see the results, there's a knock on my door.

Dread bleeds from every pore on my body, my stomach falling to the floor because I know who's there before I open it.

I open the door just a crack to find a concerned Morgan. "Hi, Butterfly. You feeling okay? Shouldn't you be at work?"

"Sick day. Don't want you to get sick," I say, my voice hoarse from crying.

"Can I come in and check on you, please? I don't care about getting sick. I care about you."

He sounds so earnest, so concerned, I can't say no. I step back and let him come in the door, and he rushes around me, looking for signs of illness. He places a hand on my forehead to check my temperature, then on my cheeks.

"You don't seem to have a fever. What's going on?"

Tears well in my eyes, anxiety crawling up my spine. I don't want to tell him. I don't want him to be mad at me.

But I have to.

Wordlessly, I walk to the bathroom and pick up the three tests I took and pad back to where he's still standing right inside the door. I don't even look at them, just hand them to him and step back, wrapping my arms around my midsection like that will protect me.

He blinks at me a few times before looking at the tests.

"You're pregnant." He doesn't say it as a question. He takes a big breath, "*We're* pregnant?" This time it *is* a question.

My thoughts spiral a little because his tone is unreadable, and I refuse to look at him right now.

He walks over to the couch and sits down, then stands back up and comes over to me, dragging me over to sit with him.

"Hannah, please look at me."

"I'm so sorry," I sob, my voice breaking on the last word.

"No, Butterfly, no. You have nothing to be sorry about." He rubs a hand up and down my spine, but it does little to soothe my anxiety.

"I swear I was taking my birth control religiously. I don't—I don't understand how this happened! I promise I'm not trying to baby-trap you. I don't even know if this pregnancy will last longer than a few weeks, and I don't want you to hate me or have to go through the pain of a miscarriage. You don't deserve that."

His hand stills on my back, and he's pulling my hands to his so I'm forced to turn and look at him. There's a sheen of tears in his own eyes as he speaks, "I don't hate you, Hannah. I could never hate you. I don't think you're trying to trap me with a baby. This isn't your fault. Birth control is never one-hundred percent effective, so there was always a chance this could happen. As far as me not deserving to go through the pain of a miscarriage, *you* are the one who doesn't deserve to go through that again."

"You're not mad?"

"Of course I'm not mad, Butterfly. I'm shocked, but I'm not upset. We do have to make some decisions, though. Mostly you. You have the hardest choice to make."

"What choice is there to make?"

"Whether or not you want to keep this baby. If you decide you want to terminate so you don't have to worry about potentially losing the baby later on, then I will drive you to the clinic and stay by your side. But... if you want to keep the baby, I will do everything I can to support you and make sure you and this baby are healthy and taken care of. We will see the best doctors, and I'll research the best prenatal vitamins. Whatever you choose, though, I will be here for you as your *partner*. Because you didn't get pregnant by yourself. I was an active and willing participant."

The tears won't stop flowing down my face, a mixture of intense relief, overwhelming anxiety, and an abundance of love sit heavy in my chest.

Morgan's words rattle around in my head and settle into my heart, and I know without a shadow of a doubt he means what he says. He truly would take me to the clinic if it was what I wanted, but...

"I want to keep the baby," I whisper. The decision settles into my chest, and I feel at peace with it. I know there's still a chance I won't carry to term, but it's a risk I want to take with Morgan.

Morgan nods. "Then we'll keep the baby. I'll make a call to the best OBGYN in the state and get you an appointment. And I want you to move in with me."

"What? No, that's too much," I protest, even though the thought of moving in together makes my heart soar.

"It's not, Butterfly. I want to be able to keep an eye on you as much as possible. If I thought you'd quit your job and stay by my side twenty-four-seven I'd ask you to do that, but I know how important your job is to you. I want to tell Sage, if you're comfortable with that, so she can help keep me updated."

"I'm not fragile, Morgan. I don't need you to watch me all the time." The words hold very little fight because his protectiveness feels good. It doesn't feel suffocating or demeaning. Do I think he needs to keep tabs on me all day every day? No. But the thought that he cares so much about my health and the wellness of this baby makes me love him more than I thought was possible.

"I know that, Butterfly. But your health and the health and well-being of this baby are my priority."

"What about Aly?"

"I think she'll be ecstatic you're moving in. I don't want to tell her about the baby yet, though. I think telling her about it prematurely might be confusing if the worst happens."

I nod. "She's your daughter, so I'm following your lead on that front."

Morgan shakes his head. "You may not be her mother biologically, but you've been more of a mom to her in the last month than Whitney has in nine years. We're a team, Hannah. We do this together. Got it?"

"Got it."

"Good. Now, tell me how you're feeling. Any nausea or headaches or anything?"

"Nothing yet, but I'm probably only about four or five weeks if I base it on my last period."

"When did it usually start in your last pregnancies?"

"Usually around ten weeks, but I only made it past twelve weeks once so sometimes I never even felt sick, just bloated."

"God, Hannah. I am so fucking sorry you went through that. You're one of the strongest people I know." He places a gentle kiss on my forehead. "I'm going to go call my parents and have them bring Aly here so we can tell her about you moving in, and then we're getting you moved this weekend. Okay?"

"Okay."

"I love you, Butterfly. So much."

"I love you, too."

Morgan steps out of the apartment to call his parents, and I finally glance at the pregnancy tests on the coffee table. The digital one has a bold **pregnant** in the little window, and the others have two very dark pink lines. Weird, when I took tests before, the line was barely visible.

I place my hand over my stomach and whisper to the little pea-sized baby inside me, "I want you to stay right there for at least thirty-six weeks. Please don't leave me."

# CHAPTER 38

## Morgan

*I*'m going to be a dad.

Well, okay—I'm already a dad—but I'm going to be a dad *again,* and Hannah is going to be the one carrying our baby.

I'm still reeling.

The day we found out she was pregnant, my parents brought Aly to the shop, and we all went to Dosa House for dinner and asked Aly if she was okay with Hannah moving in.

I swear she's more excited than I am; she wanted us to move her that same night. We waited until the weekend when we could have the rest of the family's help, and it went very smoothly.

Now, Hannah's clothes are hanging next to mine in our walk-in closet, her skin care products have a permanent spot on the shelves in the bathroom, and her books are mingled with mine on the bookshelves in my office.

I'm planning on turning the office into a nursery, but I don't want to get ahead of myself, so I haven't told Hannah, yet. I think it would be too hard to see the space for the baby and then lose it, rather than scramble to get it put together.

God, I hope we don't lose this baby. Not just for my sake but because I don't think Hannah would have it in her to try again. Which is totally understandable and not something I'd ever consider trying to push her on, but the excitement of a new baby makes me realize how much I want another child with Hannah.

We haven't had sex since we found out, mostly because we've been busy with moving and settling into a new routine, and I miss the warmth of her body. I don't want to push her to have sex if she's not feeling well, but I think we need some alone time to at least snuggle and talk without nine-year-old ears around.

Sarah and Justin are taking Aly camping this weekend, so Hannah and I will be alone in the house for the first time in two weeks. I asked Olivia to cover for me at the flower shop so I could spend the day cleaning the house and setting up the movie room for a romance movie marathon.

Hannah hasn't had any cravings yet, so I bought a bunch of different snacks I know she loves, a new cozy pajama set, and sparkling apple cider in lieu of champagne. There are six different takeout menus for her to choose from for dinner, and I hope at least one sounds good.

Sage texted me ten minutes ago when Hannah left the library, so when the garage door opens and shuts, I'm ready at the bottom of the stairs with a bouquet made up of white lilies—a symbol of peace and fertility—dark pink gerbera daisies—gratitude—and pink roses—love, and happiness.

"Welcome home, Butterfly." God, I love saying that. I love that this is her home, *with me*.

"Hi… Those are stunning. What's the occasion?" She slips off her shoes and sets her purse on the hook next to the door.

"No special occasion, we just have the house to ourselves this weekend, and I want to pamper you. I have a new pajama set in the dryer, six takeout menus to choose from, and an array of snacks while we have a romance movie marathon."

Hannah gapes at me like I just told her something outlandish.

"What… why?"

"Because things have been go, go, go, this last week with moving in and adjusting to a new routine. We only have time for each other before we go to bed, and we're too tired to really connect. I want to spend time together and just relax. Is that good with you?"

"I'm so sorry if you feel like I've been neglecting you. I've been so worried about the baby and feeling more tired because of the extra stress and all the things that need to be done and—"

"Shhh," I cut her off and press a kiss to her lips. "I'm not feeling neglected at all, Butterfly. I know there's a lot going on, and the stress isn't good for you and the baby." She's not showing yet, but I rub my hand over her belly anyway. "I want to give you a weekend to just sit and relax and not have to worry about anything other than what food you want to eat. I'm not expecting sex, okay? I do expect cuddles, though, so be prepared."

"Are you sure?"

"Positive. Now, pick a place to order from, then go get changed. Shower if you want to and meet me in the movie room." I hand her the menus, and she quickly glances at the names.

She immediately hands me back the Thai food menu with a scrunch of her nose, then the Mexican food, then the Indian food, sandwich shop, and burger place. She's left with the Italian menu and asks if she can get two different things off the menu.

I'd buy her the whole damn restaurant if she asked me to.

Once I have her selection, she heads upstairs, and I place the order while she's getting ready. Then, I go to the kitchen and prepare the flowers for their vase. I set the blooming pink bouquet on the dining table where it will get a good amount of sunlight but not so much that it will wilt too soon.

Twenty minutes later, the food arrives just as Hannah comes down the stairs in the floral print cotton cami and matching shorts, her hair still a little damp from her shower. Her face is completely bare, and I can see the few light freckles she has.

She's so goddamn beautiful.

I can't believe she's mine, and she's carrying my baby. The sudden urge to get down on one knee and propose is so strong it nearly bowls me over.

I've been having that feeling a lot lately.

Wordlessly, she helps me take the food downstairs to the movie room where the snacks and drinks are laid out on the small counter there.

Keira Knightly's version of *Pride and Prejudice* is already queued up and ready to begin while we situate ourselves on the large couch.

"Where are the kitties? I didn't see them when I went upstairs," Hannah asks as we settle in.

"I gave them some catnip and put them in the office so we could have some peace tonight. They're fed, have water, and I put on some bird videos on my computer so they can be entertained while they're high."

Hannah giggles and shakes her head. "Oh, to be a cat, watching bird videos while blazed."

"They're spoiled little creatures, that's for sure."

Once we've settled, I press play on the movie, and we watch while we eat. Once we've had enough food, we move the containers to the side, and I settle myself into the couch cushions with Hannah pressed up against my side and laying her head on my chest.

We stay like that during the whole movie, and I'm positive Hannah's fallen asleep by the end of it, but when I glance down to check, she's already looking up at me with hooded eyes.

"Morgan?"

"Yeah, Butterfly?"

"Have you ever... fucked someone in here?"

*Oh boy.* My cock stirs immediately at that dirty word coming from her pretty mouth.

"You're the only person I've ever had sex with in this house, Butterfly."

"Want to christen this couch?" She runs a hand down my chest to tease the waistband of my basketball shorts.

"Are you sure, Hannah? I don't want you to feel like you have to—*oh fuck.*" I can't even get the rest of my sentence out because Hannah slips her hand into my shorts and squeezes my cock gently. The warmth of her hand feels so damn good around my shaft.

"I'm sure, Morgan. I feel fine, but I want you to make me feel *good* in a way only you can." She pumps me once, twice. "Please."

The "please" does me in. In one swift, fluid motion, I have her delectable body pinned beneath me, and I'm devouring her mouth like it's the only source of sustenance I'll ever need.

It's a hungry kiss, all lips, tongue, and teeth, and the noises she's making are going to make me come in my pants like a damn teenager.

I need to make her come first. At least twice.

"How do you want me to make you come first, Butterfly?" I kiss a path down her jaw, following the path of bare skin exposed from her askew pajama top. "On my fingers?" I cup her pussy over her shorts, and she gasps. "Or on my tongue?"

"Surprise me."

"Hmmm. I think I'll do both. Why don't you take off your pretty pajamas so I don't ruin them?"

I move so she can sit up and take off my shirt while she removes hers, then I help her shimmy out of her shorts. "No underwear, Butterfly?"

She shakes her head, biting her bottom lip. "I don't wear underwear to bed."

"You mean to tell me when you're looking so pretty in those little nightgowns you wear, you haven't had any panties on underneath?" Fuck, those nightgowns look like something a grandma would wear, but on Hannah—God—they make me feral in a way I've never felt before.

"You think those are pretty? I wear them because they're comfortable, not because they're sexy."

"Those goddamn dresses make me feral, Butterfly. When you wore one the first night you officially moved in, I had to jack off in the shower before coming to bed. Something about them..." I trail off and run a hand down her curvy sides.

"Guess all the lingerie I've bought was a waste of money, then," she teases.

"Not at all. You could wear a burlap sack and I'd still want to devour every inch of you. It's not what you wear, Butterfly. It's *you*. I want you, all the time. I love you."

"I love you too, Morgan." She sits up a little and captures my mouth in a slow, enticing kiss that makes me feel like I'm melting into a puddle.

When she finally pulls away, I trail my mouth down her chest, carefully kissing each peaked nipple because I know her breasts are starting to get more sensitive. I trail down her stomach, leaving extra kisses and silently telling our little embryo to stay where they are. Then I shimmy down and kiss my way to where her thighs meet.

"We may have already had dinner, but I'm starving. So let me enjoy this decadent dessert."

I don't dive in like I'm craving to, instead I start with slow circles of my tongue on her clit, adding pressure with every completed circle. She writhes beneath me, arching into me to get more friction, but she's not in charge right now, I am. I want to take my time and enjoy the taste of her.

I lick up one side of her pussy and down the other, nibbling gently on the lips in a way I know gets her even closer to an orgasm.

"Please, Morgan. I want you," she whines.

"I want you too, Butterfly, but I want to make you come on my tongue and fingers and then on my cock. So be good, and let me play." I punctuate my command by pushing one finger inside her. She's already wet for me and not just from my mouth being on her. I slowly pump my finger in and out, then add a second one, and curl them to find her g-spot.

"Oh fuck!" she moans loudly as I rub against her. She must be more sensitive now that she's pregnant, because while she's enjoyed this before, I've never gotten such a visceral reaction from her.

I'm certainly not going to complain about an increase in her pleasure.

She humps herself against my fingers while I flick her clit with my tongue. "That's it, Hannah. Ride my fingers and my face. Take your pleasure. I want to watch you come apart."

"Fuck, I'm going to come!" she moans, clamping down on my fingers as a rush of wetness coats my hand.

I work her through her orgasm, and when she pushes my head to signal she needs a break, I slowly pull my fingers out.

I shuck my shorts and boxers and position myself at her entrance, but she shakes her head.

"I want you to fuck me from behind."

Who am I to tell her no?

She turns and rests on her elbows, presenting her ass to me, and I groan appreciatively at the tantalizing sight. Her ass wiggles while she situates herself, and I have to tamp down the urge to take a big ole bite of it.

I position the head of my cock at her entrance and slowly push in. The way her pussy grips me and molds perfectly to my cock makes my head spin. This position gets me deeper inside her, every soft part of her wrapping around my hardness like the best kind of glove. Once I'm fully inside, I ask, "How do you want this, Butterfly? Fast and hard or slow and sweet?"

Hannah props herself up on her elbows, looking at me so sweetly as she says, "Fuck me hard, Morgan."

"Whatever you ask for..." I pull out and push back into her hard and fast, relishing in the way her ass ripples with each thrust. I've been so pent up from the stress of everything that my orgasm is right at the base of my cock, ready to explode.

"Fuck, Butterfly. I'm going to need you to reach down and play with your clit so you can come with me. I'm going to get there embarrassingly fast."

She follows my directions, the first swipe of her fingers causing her to clench around me. She's getting close.

"Come! Now!" I need her there first.

As the first drops of my cum release from my cock, she clenches around me and moans my name, squeezing out every last bit of my orgasm.

I stay inside her until my cock softens, then I pull out and wipe up our combined releases with my discarded shirt.

"Come on, Butterfly. Let's get you cleaned up, and then we can watch *You've Got Mail.*"

"Okay," she sighs, looking completely spent and relaxed for the first time in weeks.

We watch two more movies before we're both yawning and ready to call it a night. When we settle into bed, she curls up like a cat at my side and kisses me tenderly before falling asleep against my chest.

# CHAPTER 39

*Hannah*

I'm freaking out because today is the day we go to the doctor to see the baby for the first time. According to my last period, I should be nine weeks now. Morgan called and got us an appointment with the best OBGYN in Utah, even though my insurance doesn't cover her.

I have good insurance through the library, but Morgan wouldn't budge on this, so here we are in the waiting area while I fill out a new patient questionnaire.

The office looks like any other medical building from the outside, but on the inside it's like we've stepped into a cozy luxury cabin. The side tables look like they're made from logs, and there's a big fireplace that's turned off since it's almost July. The leather sofas and waiting chairs are actually pretty comfortable to sit in and wide enough to accommodate my plus size body, which I appreciate.

I quickly fill out the questionnaire, and not five minutes later, we're being called back by the medical assistant—Kiley—who takes my weight and blood pressure, then sends me to the bathroom for a urine test. She asks the standard questions about my pregnancy history and symptoms, and leaves us so I can change into a hospital gown.

I hate the initial visit with a provider. I had three different doctors because of insurance changes when I was with Liam, but each one was an older white man who told me I was too "unhealthy" and that was why the babies weren't making it to term. I asked them to do whatever blood tests they needed to cement that answer, but they all just told me I needed to lose weight.

"I'm sorry you have to relay so many details about your miscarriages, Hannah. I can't even imagine how hard it is." Morgan squeezes my hand from where he's sitting next to the exam table.

"Thank you. It's one of the harder parts of all of this. I already feel more comfortable here than I have with other doctors, though. I like that they have different gown sizes for people with different size bodies."

Morgan's brows furrow. "I never realized that could be an issue."

I nod. "Some places only have one size, and it's not nearly big enough to cover a bigger body."

"That's stupid. They're a medical office, they should accommodate and accept all body sizes."

I smile at the new found outrage for the bias of the American healthcare system.

"I agree. Now, just to prepare you, some doctors will make blatant comments about my weight and body in regards to my health. I know you want to protect me, but please let me handle this."

"Fine. But I won't be happy about it," he grumbles right as a knock sounds on the door.

A woman in a white lab coat comes into the room, her long brown hair pulled into a chic ponytail. "Hello, Miss Layton, I'm Dr. Azadeh Badar. It's nice to meet you." She holds her hand out, and I shake it.

"Nice to meet you too, Dr. Badar."

"Is this dad?" She nods to Morgan.

"I am. Morgan Fowler, nice to meet you, doctor."

"You as well. I'm glad you have a supportive partner with you, Hannah." She claps her hands. "Alright. We're going to be doing a transvaginal ultrasound to see if we can see the baby, and that will give us a more accurate idea of how far along you are. According to your chart, you should be about nine weeks, but the ultrasound will help us confirm that. Then, once we're done, I'll send you over to the lab for some blood work. I noticed you have had quite a few miscarriages in the past; have any of your previous providers done any sort of testing to see if there's a medical reason?"

"No. They just said it was because of my weight."

She frowns. "Well, sometimes weight can be a determining factor, but there's usually an underlying issue that goes along with it. I don't see a history of diabetes or cholesterol issues, so I don't think your weight is the problem. I'd like to run some additional blood tests..." She types something on the computer. "We'll test your hCG levels, of course, as well as blood count levels, and I want to do an AMH test which will tell us your egg count and egg reserve. If that comes back abnormal, there may be additional testing we want to do."

"Okay, that sounds good."

"Perfect!" She snaps on some hot pink gloves, pulls out the transvaginal ultrasound wand, sheaths it in a protective cover, then puts the ultrasound goo on it.

"That's going inside her?" Morgan's face is twisted in confusion and a little bit of horror.

Dr. Badar chuckles. "Yes, Mr. Fowler. I assure you it's safe. Hannah, have you had one of these done before?"

"Yes."

"Great. A little bit of discomfort isn't uncommon, but it's not nearly as painful as a pap smear or a cervical biopsy."

Morgan nods, looking a little paler now. Poor guy.

Dr. Badar turns down the lights and props my feet up in the stirrups, then gently inserts the wand into my vagina. The big screen facing us shows up in black, white, and gray as Dr. Badar wiggles the wand, checking both of my ovaries. She moves the wand up a little bit more, and there it is.

The tiny little bean-shaped thing in a sac.

Our baby.

But this ultrasound looks a little strange compared to the other ones I've had. I just can't pinpoint why.

"There they are! I'm just going to turn the sound up to check the heart rates..." Dr. Badar turns a dial, and the *whoosh whoosh whoosh* of a tiny little heartbeat fills the room.

Morgan squeezes my hand as we listen and tears spring to my eyes.

"Wait, did you say heart *rates*?" Morgan says, and my eyes snap back to the screen.

"Oh, yes. Here." Dr. Badar zooms in on the monitor. "This is baby A, and their heart rate is about 168 bpm, and this is baby B whose heart rate is about 165 bpm. That's exactly where they should be. You're measuring at about nine weeks and two days. That puts your due date at February 15th."

"We're having *two* babies?" My blood is pounding in my ears. I just came to terms with the fact I am pregnant with one baby, but now there are *two*?

"Will they be fraternal or identical?" Morgan asks, sounding much calmer than I feel.

"Fraternal. They have different sacks. Do twins run on either side of your family?" Dr. Badar asks.

"My aunts are identical twins, but they're the only ones," I whisper.

"I'm a fraternal twin, and my mom's sisters are fraternal twins," Morgan says.

"Ah, well, that explains it, then. Alright, I'm going to pull the wand out now and clean you up—okay, Hannah?"

I can't speak, so I simply nod.

Dr. Badar hands me the ultrasound pictures and a pregnancy welcome bag, tells us to schedule an appointment in a week to go over test results and for another ultrasound, and sends me to the lab to get blood drawn. Morgan heads to the waiting room while the nurse pokes my skin and takes the blood needed, and then I'm sent on my way.

The drive home is quiet, both of us still processing the news. When we pull into the garage, we just sit there in silence.

"Twins," Morgan whispers.

"Twins," I echo.

"Holy shit."

"Holy shit, indeed." The back of my eyes begin to burn. "I can't lose two babies at once. I won't survive it."

Morgan rushes out of the car and flings open my car door, looking at me at eye level. "Nothing is going to happen to these babies." He puts a hand gently on my stomach.

"You can't promise that. You don't have any control over it," I sob.

"You're right, but I'm manifesting this. These babies are going to grow and grow inside you, and when they're fully grown and ready, they will come out and be loved unconditionally. Aly is going to be so excited to be a big sister, and my siblings are going to lose their shit because there will be two babies to dote on. Sage is going to be the best bonus aunt ever, and we are going to be the best parents."

"How can you be so sure?"

"Because I love you."

I want to believe him, I want to believe he can see into our future and it's exactly the way he painted it, but I've done this song and dance before. I've gotten hopeful, only to have my hopes crash and burn.

I can't tell him I don't believe him when he sounds so sincere and so hopeful, so I simply nod.

Only time will tell if he's right.

# CHAPTER 40

*Hannah*

One week later, we're back in Dr. Badar's exam room, waiting to discuss the test results.

I've been a mess the entire week. I haven't slept well, I've been getting more nauseous, and the foods I love are slowly starting to repulse me. My breasts hurt all the time, and I'm uncomfortably bloated.

Ten weeks is about the time the babies stopped growing during my previous pregnancies, so when I'd go in for my twelve week ultrasounds, there was no heartbeat.

Except for one instance when I made it thirteen weeks—that one was the hardest because we had made so many plans.

I'm scared she'll tell us there are no heartbeats today.

Dr. Badar knocks on the door and waits for my confirmation to come in.

"Good morning, Hannah. How are you feeling today? Any new symptoms?"

I shake my head. "Just some nausea and craving a lot of salty snacks."

"That's totally normal. With your increase in blood volume it can make you crave salt, so as long as you're drinking plenty of water you should be fine."

She sits down on a rolling chair and types away on her computer. "Now, we got your test results in. Your hCG levels are perfect, blood cell counts all look good, and we have the sex of the babies if you want to know."

"I think I'd like to know the results of the other test first. And make sure the babies are okay before I get too attached," I say quietly, and Dr. Badar nods understandingly.

"Well, your AMH test came back looking perfect as well. Your eggs are healthy and viable, and your reserve is standard for someone your age. Now," she turns to Morgan, "were you the provider of the sperm for her previous pregnancies?"

Morgan shakes his head.

"Okay," she twists her lips, "I wanted to take a sperm sample to test the vitality of sperm, but if that wasn't you, it wouldn't be conclusive for the past pregnancies. Sometimes the sperm aren't viable or strong enough to help the embryo grow past a certain point. My guess is, since your blood tests came back normal, there's some sort of medical condition with whomever you were conceiving with previously. There's no way to tell unless I do a sperm test on them, but it's highly probable."

"So what you're saying," Morgan interjects, "is Hannah's not the problem?"

"Like I said, I can't confirm it without running tests on the other party, but with the test results we have, it doesn't seem like there's any overlying issue with Hannah."

*There's some sort of medical condition with whomever you were conceiving with previously.*

I know she said it can't be determined for sure unless she tests Liam, but it stands to reason that if my blood tests came back normal, then *I'm not the problem.*

Morgan holds my hand while Dr. Badar lifts my shirt and squeezes gel onto my stomach. She turns on the machine and starts pushing on my belly looking for the strawberry-sized babies.

Her silence is deafening, and I'm steeling myself for the terrible news, when two little tadpole-esque blobs wiggle on the screen.

"There they are! Let's check their heart rates..." She turns the sound up, and two distinct heartbeats fill the room, and hope inflates my chest. "Perfect. They sound amazing and are measuring right on track."

"Do you think I'll still miscarry?" I ask quietly.

"There's still that possibility, but since all of your tests look good and the heartbeats are within a healthy range, I would say the chances are low. If it would make you feel better to come in again in two weeks instead of the standard four, we can make that happen. We want to ease your stress as much as possible."

"I think that would make me feel better."

"Great! I know it's tempting to get a fetal doppler so you can hear the heartbeats yourself between appointments, but the FDA discourages it because of the risks it can cause to both mom and baby." Dr. Badar wipes the excess goop off my belly and helps me sit up, handing me the black and white pictures of our babies.

"Would you like to know the sexes of the babies?" she asks, pulling up her laptop.

I look over at Morgan, who shrugs, clearly letting me lead.

"I... yes. I think I would like to know."

"You will be having two little girls! If the blood tests had come back with 'Y' chromosomes, we wouldn't be able to tell both genders, but since there was no trace of male DNA, we can confidently say you are having two girls."

*Two girls.*

*Two.*

*Girls.*

*I'm going to be a mom.*

When we get to the car, the dam breaks, and I start sobbing. Morgan holds my hand and lets me sob until I'm ready to talk, and once I've calmed down enough, I rant.

"The entire time, Liam blamed *me* for losing our babies. He made me feel worthless and useless and like I was broken, when the whole *fucking* time it was most likely *him?!* I wanted to go get tested. I wanted him to get tested, too, so we could cover our bases, but he ignored the request because he refused to think he could ever be a problem.

"My mom, his mom, and other people at church heavily implied I wasn't worthy enough to have a baby and made my miscarriages out to be a 'lesson from God.' I was suffering so badly, and no one ever checked on me to make sure I was okay. Everyone just expected me to grin and bear it and move on like I didn't lose a part of myself with each baby. It's not *fair* I was ignored and blamed for something that could have been easily diagnosed. And now, I'm going to be anxious for the rest of this pregnancy—however long it lasts—because I'm so fucking traumatized! It's not fair!" My voice breaks on a sob, and I take a calming breath before I continue.

"I never knew the sex of the babies before. I never wanted to know. But now I know I have two little girls growing inside me, and there's still a chance I could lose them. Knowing will make it so much harder. I want to be positive and hopeful, but it's so hard to do that right now."

It feels good to get that off my chest. It feels good to be able to confide in Morgan and not worry he's going to call me overly dramatic and chastise me for being negative.

"It's not fair you went through that and went through it pretty much alone. You didn't deserve any of what happened to you. But you won't be alone if it happens again. We will get through this together, and I'll follow your lead with everything. If I need to call Dr. Badar and tell her we're coming in every day to check the heart-beats, I will. *We are a team,*" Morgan vows, and I love him all the more for it.

"I want to tell Aly as soon as you're ready to. I want her to know in case something happens, so she doesn't feel like we kept a secret from her. Then, I would like to tell your family if that's okay? I think that having their support would be helpful."

"Anything, Butterfly. Anything for you. Anything for Aly. Anything for our girls. I just have one thing I want from you."

"What?"

"Marry me."

"Wh-what?" *Surely, I heard him wrong.*

"Marry me. Tomorrow, in a week, in a month, in three years, I don't care, but I want you to be my wife, my true partner. Aly already told me I should have proposed by now, but I don't have a ring—"

"Yes," I interrupt. "I don't care about a ring. I want to be your wife."

Morgan kisses me, and it's a little awkward over the console in the car.

When I pictured him proposing—and I have—I didn't picture it in the parking lot of an OBGYN office, but I don't care. I don't need a big proposal from him, knowing he wants to be with me forever is enough.

"I love you so much, Hannah. Whatever we go through, we'll go through it together."

"I love you, too. I'm glad you're the one I'm on this journey with."

# Chapter 41

*Morgan*

Hannah is officially fourteen weeks, and the time has flown by this last month. We've had two more appointments to see the twins, and they're growing beautifully, the doctor has no concerns thus far.

It's become a standard routine for me to lay on Hannah's belly and talk to our girls every night, and now that Aly knows, sometimes she tries to talk to them, too.

We told Aly the day after we got the blood results. We took her out to her favorite bakery for breakfast, and while we were sitting outside basking in the mild summer morning sunshine, we told her she's going to be a big sister in February to not just one baby, but two.

She was more excited than I thought she'd be, but a big part of me still worries she'll feel like we're trying to replace her. Hannah and I both assured her we would never do that, and she is still our top priority, but the babies will become a top priority as well.

Hannah gently explained she's been pregnant before, but the babies didn't make it to the end, and it's a possibility something could happen to the twins, but we wanted to celebrate them as long as we could.

Aly had a lot of questions about miscarriage, and Hannah answered them as best she could while still keeping it light. She didn't treat Aly like a dumb kid, which I appreciated. Hannah talks to Aly like a little adult, and I am awe-struck at her ability to speak so eloquently about something that was so traumatic for her.

Aly's been brainstorming names and helping us pick out colors for the nursery. She asks Hannah every day if she's feeling okay and if she can help with anything, and when she goes to the library with Hannah, she makes sure Hannah is eating small snacks frequently.

We wanted to tell my parents so they could be aware if we needed to make an emergency hospital visit, but they don't know the genders. We decided to wait to tell my siblings until Hannah was fourteen weeks. We're headed to family lunch today to deliver the good news.

Hannah ran to the store to pick up the gender reveal cake—she wanted something fun to tell everyone we're having two girls—and Aly is upstairs reading in her room.

My phone rings, and when Whitney's name flashes across the screen, I want to press ignore. I haven't heard a peep from her since the lunch fiasco over a month ago.

Against my better judgment, I answer, "Hello, Whitney."

"You got that fat bitch *pregnant?*" Whitney screeches. "What the hell, Morgan? You're trying to replace our daughter? You're not going to have time for Alyssa if you're having fucking *twins* with your little gold digger.

And you *moved her in*? Without telling me about it? What about how this will affect Alyssa? What about how this affects *me*?"

*There it is.*

I don't know how she found out, but it doesn't really matter. I don't know how this would affect her at all. If she were a more active participant in Aly's life, maybe it would affect her a little bit, but as it stands, this has nothing to do with her.

"First of all, watch your tone and how you speak about Hannah. I will not stand for you slandering my fiancée and calling her petty, malicious names."

"*Fiancée?!* Are you fuckin—"

"Second of all," I cut her off, "Aly is excited to be a big sister, and she's well aware of how things will change, but she also knows she will remain a priority to us. Third of all, this *doesn't* affect you, Whitney. You are not involved in this in the slightest. You're barely involved with Aly. I don't care if you don't want Hannah to live here, it's not your choice. I talked to Aly about it, and she was more than okay with Hannah moving in, so your opinion means literally nothing to me."

"Alyssa is *my* daughter, and I should have a say in who is involved in her life," Whitney spits at me through the phone.

"If you made any effort at all over the last few years to be involved in Aly's life, maybe that would hold more weight. You all but abandoned her, Whitney, and treated her like she's a bother rather than your own flesh and blood. On the one day she wanted to spend with you, you took her to your boyfriend's house and ignored her."

"I have a life, Morgan! I'm busy and don't have the time to be a full-time mom! You know this."

"I have a life, too, Whitney. The difference between us is I've made the time to be a full-time dad because that's what Aly deserves. I've given you a pass in the past because I didn't want to put Aly in the middle of petty drama, but I'm done. I will be taking you to court for full custody. Any communication between us from here on out will be done through lawyers. Goodbye, Whitney."

I hang up the phone without waiting for a response. I don't know how she knows about the pregnancy when we've only told three people so far, but she has no right to be upset. There was never any indication we'd get back together, and her fake concern for Aly's well-being makes me see red.

"Dad?" Aly croaks, and I turn around on the couch to see my sweet daughter with tears in her eyes.

"Hey, Bub. What's wrong?"

"I heard you on the phone... with her..."

"Oh, Aly, come here." I motion for her to snuggle into me on the couch, and she sobs again as she settles. "How much did you hear?"

"All of it. I couldn't hear what she said, but... I'm so sorry. I texted her and told her I was excited to be a big sister to twins. I thought she'd be excited for me, you, and Hannah, but she texted me back and told me I would be forgotten because of the babies. She also said Hannah would never love me like she loves her babies."

I'm not a violent man, and I'd never even think about hurting a woman or a child, but the audacity to say that to a nine-year-old girl—your own fucking child—makes me want to punch a wall.

"I'm not upset at you for telling her, Bub. I'm so sorry she said those things to you. It was unkind and unfair. Do you believe her?" I stroke her bright blonde hair.

"No," she whispers. "Hannah is very nice, and she's never made me feel like a dumb little kid. I know she's not my real mom, but she's been nicer to me than Mom has and..."

"And what, Bub?"

"I don't think I want to see Mom for a while. She obviously doesn't want to see me, and I don't want to keep getting my feelings hurt." Aly sounds resolute and absolutely devastated. I don't blame her for not wanting to go through the pain anymore, but my heart aches for her all the same.

"You're old enough to make that choice, and I won't push you either way. If you wanted to keep trying with your mom, I'd help you as much as I can."

"I know... but... I feel like if she actually loved me, she would want to see me more. She says Hannah won't love me because I'm not her daughter, but I *am* Mom's daughter, and she still doesn't love me."

God, I hate that she's so smart, so observant. I wish this weren't happening and she wasn't going through this shit with Whitney.

Hannah comes in from the garage carrying the cake and sees Aly curled up at my side, her tears staining my shirt, and she immediately sets the cake down and comes to sit in front of Aly on the coffee table.

"Hey, you okay, sweetheart?"

Aly nods but starts crying again, and after asking Aly for permission, I relay the whole story for her. Hannah's jaw drops when I get to the part where Whitney told Aly that Hannah wouldn't love her. I can see the anger in her eyes, but she doesn't direct any of it towards Aly.

"I'm so sorry, Hannah. Do you hate me?" Aly asks sadly.

"*No.* Absolutely not. I could *never* hate you." She leans forward and grabs Aly's hands as Aly looks at her with tearful eyes. "I love you, Aly. You may not be my biological daughter, but I love you just as much as I love these babies. I could never forget about you, and I hope you know that. If you're ever feeling like you're being left out when the babies come, you just need to talk to me or your dad, and we will fix it."

"Promise?"

"Promise, sweetheart."

"I love you, too, Hannah. I'm glad you're part of our family." Aly leaps forward and wraps Hannah in a hug that makes tears spring to my eyes.

I join their group hug, all of us crying now.When we finally pull back, I notice it's time to leave.

"Alright, girls. It's time to go give everyone the good news. Are we ready?"

# CHAPTER 42

*Hannah*

I don't know why I'm so nervous to tell Morgan's family we're expecting. It probably has to do with how my ex in-laws were never happy for us when we announced we were pregnant, so by the third miscarriage I stopped telling them.

Liam only has one sibling, an older sister, so I thought they'd be excited to have grandkids, but they were harsh about it and never treated me well.

My own mother was never excited, either.

Morgan's mom cried happy tears when we told her we were expecting, and then sobbed uncontrollably when we said it was twins. His dad even got a little misty-eyed and made Morgan promise he'd let him help with the nursery renovations. I cried, too, at the overwhelming support they've already given.

Iris texts me at least every other day to check in and ask if I'm craving anything she can make. So far, my cravings have been snacks and drinks, but she's offered to pick up anything I need, any time.

We still haven't told anyone we're engaged, mostly because I don't have a ring, but also because we want the focus to be on the babies.

We'll tell everyone when we decide on an actual date.

We're greeted by big hugs and warm welcomes when we walk into Morgan's parents' house. Iris fusses over me holding the cake and scolds Morgan for making me carry it, even though I'm the one who insisted on bringing it inside.

"Ooo, you got the cake with the...good...frosting..." Olivia stutters as she reads the words on the cake and looks up at Morgan and me. "SHUT UP!" she yells. "Tell me this isn't a joke!"

That gets the attention of everyone else in the room, and they come over to read what's written on the cake. "Fowler Twins: Due February 15th" written in yellow frosting. Everyone starts talking at once.

"*Two* babies?" from Kendall.

"Hell yes! More baby cuddles," from Asha.

"I told you this would happen." Alice punches Cooper in the arm.

"I call dibs on being godmother!" Sarah declares.

"Okay, okay, you wild bunch. Do you want to find out the genders?" Morgan asks, and it shuts everyone up.

"Not until after dinner, dear. I want to keep everyone in suspense," Iris says with a mischievous look in her eyes. She takes the cake and puts it in the fridge, ignoring the disappointed grumbles of disagreement.

"That's really rude, Mother. And why aren't you acting surprised?" Alice accuses with a pointed finger.

Iris lifts one shoulder. "Gigi privilege. I get to know before everyone else."

That causes an outcry from Morgan's sisters, who turn their attention to me to pepper me with all the questions from my due date, to my cravings, to all the symptoms I've been experiencing.

When Iris finally gets everyone back on track and we start dishing up dinner, Morgan leans into me to apologize for everyone's bombardment of questions. I guess Whitney didn't want anyone involved with the pregnancy, so everyone wants to be involved, and they're all just really excited to get to be part of this big life event.

That makes my hormonal self tear up a little. I can feel the love and excitement from everyone, and it's so genuine. I feel bad they didn't get to be part of Whitney's pregnancy.

The chatter during the meal revolves around name ideas and color suggestions for the nursery, baby shower plans, as well as a tentative meal rotation and babysitting schedule. Everyone is so eager to pitch in and help out, it makes me feel both less and more anxious about the potential of losing these precious miracles.

"Hannah, should I coordinate with your mom for a baby shower so we don't do one on the same day? Or should we just do a joint one?" Iris asks, and the delicious chicken I'm chewing turns to ash in my mouth.

After a harsh swallow, I shake my head. "My mom... doesn't know."

"Hannah's mom still hasn't talked to her since their falling out." Morgan reminds them.

"My brother is leaving for his mission soon, and his big farewell is two weeks from today. I haven't decided yet if I want to tell her. I'd like to tell him before he leaves, but I don't want to ask him to keep it a secret."

I expect for them to be upset and tell me the usual "family is blood" and to just get over it, but they surprise me.

"I'm so sorry, Hannah. I can't imagine the pain you've experienced," Iris says sadly.

Everyone offers words of support, and it's honestly so healing to have Morgan's family welcome me with open arms, to support my decision instead of ridiculing me for it. I have no doubt these babies will be loved unconditionally and will never wonder if they're wanted.

Once everyone's pitched in to clean up lunch, we get the dessert plates and cake back out for the gender reveal.

"I hope it's boys. We're outnumbered." Kendall nudges Justin playfully.

"Well, I hope it's girls so we can keep outnumbering you." Alice sticks her tongue out at Kendall, who then tackles her into a headlock and ruffles her hair. He may be the youngest, but he easily towers over everyone else and is much stronger.

"Children, please. No rough-housing or no cake." Iris points the knife at the two, and they separate quickly.

"Go ahead and cut it, Gigi," Morgan prompts, and Iris slowly slices into the cake.

Everyone leans in closer to see the inside color of the cake, and Iris is milking the suspense. She goes millimeter by millimeter until the pink inside the cake is showing, and everyone cheers.

"But wait, does that mean they're both girls?" Kendall groans, and Alice slaps his chest playfully.

"I'm excited to have more granddaughters to spoil rotten," Axel says, putting his arm around my shoulder.

"Thanks, *Papa*," I tease as I hug him back.

"Aly girl, how do you feel about having two little sisters?" Axel asks Aly, who's helping Iris dish up slices of cake.

"I'm really excited!" Aly seems to be in a better mood than when we left the house, thankfully. This morning was heavy.

"Do you guys have any names picked out yet?" Sarah directs the question at Morgan, but he looks to me for the answer.

I clear my throat. "We obviously want to stay with the flower theme—"

"Hell yeah! Gladiolus. Primrose. Gloxinia. Dude, Mistletoe would be sick. Misty for short," Kendall interrupts, holding up a finger for each name. I'm honestly a little shocked he knows what a gloxinia is.

"Gloxinia? Honestly, Kendall?" Iris tsks and shakes her head.

"I think it's a great name!" Kendall defends.

"Those are not good names, Uncle Kenny. I don't want my little sisters being bullied because they have silly names. I think Poppy and Daisy are cute," Aly suggests.

"I like those a lot. Those are in our top five." I smile at Aly, and she gives me a beaming grin in return.

"The other three on the list are Marigold, Cleo, and Violet." Morgan comes and stands behind me, wrapping his arm protectively around my waist and settling a hand on my stomach.

"Those are all very pretty. Whatever you decide to name them, they'll be so loved. Sometimes you just don't know until you see them." Iris looks at me with a mixture of sad hope and excitement. She knows about my miscarriages, and she's been so helpful and supportive it makes me tear up just thinking about it.

I don't understand how a woman I barely know has treated me better in a few months than my own mother has my entire life.

# CHAPTER 43

*Hannah*

We've officially made it to sixteen weeks, and I'm starting to show a little bit.

It's not as obvious as it would be on a thinner person, but I know my body, and I can tell. Morgan can too, apparently, because as I was showering this morning, his gaze was locked in on my stomach, and when I asked him what he was looking at, he hopped in the shower—still in his boxers-—and knelt to the floor to press tender kisses all along the swell of my stomach.

He proceeded to give me two orgasms to "show his appreciation for carrying our twins"—his words, not mine.

I've never made it this far into pregnancy before, and I had to look up if being extra horny was normal. It is, apparently, and I'm not complaining.

Morgan isn't either.

I was never the one to initiate sex with Liam, but I don't have that problem with Morgan. He makes me feel confident, sexy, and *safe*. As soon as I see Morgan walk in the door I have to give my vagina a scolding because it wants to be filled *immediately*. If Aly isn't home, I give in to my hormones and jump on him, sometimes we don't even make it up the stairs. One time, we were halfway up the stairs, and I couldn't wait so he just fucked me right on the staircase. When she is home, I have to stand in front of the freezer to cool myself off so I can function properly.

I swing between only wanting to eat salty snacks and only wanting to eat candy, but I haven't had any strange cravings yet.

Today is Jake's farewell, and he texted me to personally ask if I was going to be there. I wasn't sure if I wanted to go, but I couldn't say no to him.

It's been over four months, and I'm not excited to see my mom. I'm hoping I can avoid her as much as possible. There's always a luncheon after the church meeting, and I plan on showing up long enough to say hi to Jake and then leave.

I told Morgan he doesn't need to come, but he refuses to let me go by myself. Aly said she wanted to come because she's never been to a church before, and she wants to see what it's like, so she's coming too.

I gave them a rundown of what a sacrament meeting entails, how someone will be passing around bread and water, and we aren't allowed to take it because we aren't worthy.

Aly and Morgan both think that's a mean thing to do, and they aren't wrong.

Dressed in a simple jersey swing dress and gladiator sandals, I'm pulling Aly's hair into a french braid down her back. Her hair's gotten long this summer, and she looks so grown up. It's wild to think she starts school again in a few weeks.

"Your hair's gotten so long," I comment as I plait the strands together.

"Yeah..." Aly's shoulders slump a little.

"Do you not like it long?"

Aly shrugs. "My mom told me girls look better with long hair so I've never cut mine more than a little bit."

"Do you want to cut it short?"

"I think so. I like the way your hair looks. And sometimes my hair feels too heavy for my head," she pauses, "Do you think I'd look good with short hair?"

"I think you would look beautiful with whatever length of hair you want. If you think your head would feel better with shorter hair, we can make an appointment to get it cut." I finish up the braid and tie off the end, and Aly turns around and gives me a hug.

"Thank you, Hannah. I'll think about it."

Damn hormones. Every time she hugs me I almost burst into tears.

"You're welcome, Aly. Do you want help picking out a dress?"

"No, I already picked one out."

"Perfect. Your dad and I will be waiting here for you. We need to leave in twenty minutes, okay?"

"Okay!" She rushes up the stairs to get changed.

I sit on the couch and scroll through social media while I wait for my baby daddy and my future step-daughter to get ready.

Elli's been posting about the tour, and I can see how happy she is in every picture. I briefly wonder if I look happier than I did before, so I scroll through some of the pictures I've taken recently on my phone.

I take "bumpdate" pictures every week, even though there's not much of a bump yet. In the beginning, I wasn't smiling in the pictures. Still scared these babies wouldn't make it past a certain point, but in the last three weeks, my smile is slowly starting to show along with my belly.

I'm still extremely anxious I'll miscarry, but that anxiety lessens at every new milestone. Morgan's been amazing about talking me through the steps of what would happen in worst-case scenarios. He cooks or orders whatever I'm craving, he massages my feet every night, and helps me remember to take my prenatals.

I love him so much.

Morgan comes down dressed in pressed black dress pants and a crisp white button down with the sleeves rolled to his forearms.

Mmm. I've never found forearms attractive, but I want to lick his while he fucks me.

*Woah! Calm down, girl. You're headed to a family event.*

"See something you like, Butterfly?" Morgan drawls while giving me a devastating smirk.

"Do you know how hot you look right now? It should be illegal to look that good in a white shirt." I can feel my cheeks heating with embarrassment that I was caught ogling him.

"Well, it should be illegal to look that good in a simple green dress, but you look delicious." He joins me on the couch and gives me a chaste kiss on the lips.

"Thank you," I sigh, snuggling into him. I want to do this all day. Laze around with him and Aly. Not go to church or deal with my mother.

"Are you going to be okay today?" Morgan absently rubs a hand over my belly, as he always does when we're cuddling. It's like a magnet for him, he can't help but touch it.

"I'll be fine. I still haven't decided if I want to tell my mom about the twins, though."

"I'm making the executive decision we won't. Not today, at least."

"I feel like Jake deserves to know, and he leaves tomorrow. It would feel shitty telling him in a letter when we've known for over two months."

Morgan nods. "That's true. I guess if you think Jake can keep it to himself, you could tell him, but it's completely up to you. I'll support whatever decision you make."

"Thank you."

"I'm ready!" Aly comes down the stairs wearing a cute green dress that almost entirely matches mine.

"I love your dress, Aly. Are you okay with us matching? I won't mind if you want to change."

"No, I'm okay."

She's not thinking about this as hard as I am, so I'll leave it be, but it makes me tear up a little bit.

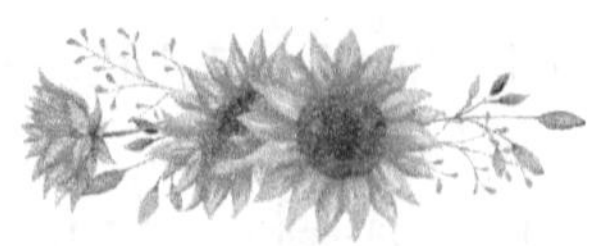

Once we get to my parents' church building, we usher inside and find an empty bench in the back away from the rest of my extended family. I was hoping to see Izzy, but Wes's tour ended at the beginning of this month, and they helped Izzy move to San Marcos last week so she can start school soon.

Wes and Elli got engaged soon after they got back, and I'm hoping we can make it out to their wedding, once they've set a date.

Grandma and Grandpa Monson see us walking in, and Grandpa gives me a look that says he'll want to meet Morgan and Aly later, making me more nervous than anything.

Grandpa wants all of his grandkids to get married and have babies, and he makes it known that is his goal. He is constantly trying to set up the single grandkids with servers at restaurants, or members of the college ward he's the patriarch over. If he finds out someone over the age of twenty is single, he goes right into matchmaker mode.

I swear if it weren't illegal to marry your cousin he'd set us up with our own relatives.

I scan the rows of familiar faces when a tap on my shoulder grabs my attention.

My cousin Talmage stands in the aisle with a sheepish grin. "Hey, Hannah. Good to see you. Can I snag this seat next to you? I don't need Grandpa pointing out all of the single women the entire meeting."

I chuckle because he totally would do that. "Sure." I nudge Morgan. "Can we scoot over, please?"

His eyes flit to Talmage and must deem him non-threatening, so he scoots himself and Aly over, and Talmage folds himself into the pew.

Morgan extends his hand. "I'm Morgan."

"Talmage, Hannah's cousin. Nice to meet you!" Talmage shakes his hand with more enthusiasm than I was expecting. It's not like Talmage and I were super close growing up.

He's two years older than me and always found sports more interesting than sitting around and chatting, which is what Emma, Elli, and I tended to do at family gatherings. We preferred to lock ourselves away in a basement bedroom rather than interact with everyone else.

"Are you just visiting Utah? I heard you were out in California," I ask quietly as the prelude music starts.

"I was, I was helping with the summer fires, but I'm back for good. I work for the Springville Fire Department now."

"That's cool. I'm guessing from your earlier statement, there's no rumored fiancée either?"

Talmage shakes his head.

I don't get to ask any further questions because the meeting gets started, but color me curious about Talmage's life.

I watch Aly and Morgan for their reactions to certain things during the meeting, and when the sacrament is passed to our row, Talmage looks at me, I shake my head, and he declines it as well.

*Interesting.*

I wonder what that's about. Talmage has always been one of the golden boys of the family. I thought for sure he'd be married with a gaggle of kids by now, but I guess you never really know.

It's none of my business, so there's no way in hell I'd ever ask him. If he's no longer in the church, good for him. I hope he knows he's not the only one, though.

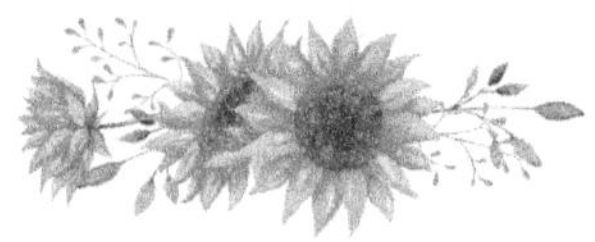

By the time the closing prayer giver says "amen," I'm ready to get out of here. These benches are uncomfortable as hell. Aly looks bored out of her mind, and Morgan looks like he's about to fall asleep. Even Talmage is scrolling through Instagram when I glance over at him.

Talmage gives me a quick "see you later" as he rushes out the door, and my little family follows quickly after. I don't want to go to the luncheon, but while we were sitting there, I had time to think. Seeing Jake look less like a little boy and more like a man made me realize he's grown up now. For some reason I feel the need to tell him about the twins. It would be unfair to tell him after he left he's going to be an uncle and miss the first two years of his nieces' lives.

We drive the short distance to my mom's house, park down the street, and sit in the car for a minute while we wait for more people to get here. I don't want to go in there and be yelled at as people are arriving. My mom won't say anything with a crowd present.

Once I feel like there are enough people, we pile out of the car, and I brace myself for the inevitable chaos about to ensue.

# CHAPTER 44

*Morgan*

Hannah's nervous, which means she's stressed, which isn't good for her or the babies, and I'm in overprotective dad mode.

Aly is hungry and a little cranky, so I'm hoping we can get in, get out, and go get some food for my girls.

Aly clings to Hannah's arm as we walk into her parents' house. It's filled to the brim with people I don't recognize. I catch the eyes of the cousin who sat with us—Talmage—and he gives me an acknowledging head nod while he intently listens to the older gentleman who's gesturing wildly while he talks.

That grabs the older man's attention, and he abandons Talmage to hobble over to us with a grin stretched across his weathered face.

"Hannah, it's so good to see you." He wraps his arms around her in a hug and squeezes her so hard I worry she can't breathe.

"You too, Grandpa. This is my boyfriend, Morgan, and his daughter, Alyssa. Alyssa, Morgan, this is my Grandpa Monson."

Grandpa Monson's bushy eyebrows shoot to his non-existent hairline, and he appraises me quickly.

"Well." He clears his throat. "Lovely to meet you, Morgan and Alyssa. I didn't know Hannah was seeing anyone. Do I hear wedding bells on the horizon, then?"

Hannah's hand finds mine, and I give her a reassuring squeeze.

"*Grandpa*," Hannah groans. "We're taking things slow."

"Never too soon to think about eternity, Hannah. Wouldn't want you to be left out of the Celestial Kingdom because you're waiting." Grandpa Monson gives Hannah a reassuring pat on her hand.

It hits me then. He probably doesn't know she left the church.

Before anyone can respond, Grandpa Monson says, "It was nice to meet your new family, my dear. I need to finish telling Talmage about a nice girl in our ward so he can get married!" Grandpa hobbles back over to Talmage and sits down, immediately placing his hand on Talmage's shoulder, and Hannah's own shoulders relax.

Jake is talking to a group of kids his age, leaning in pretty close to a brunette girl wearing a yellow dress. I wonder if that's the girl he wanted to get flowers for.

"I'm going to see if Jake will come talk to us downstairs really fast," Hannah says and makes her way to her brother.

He turns to her and wraps her in a hug. She whispers to him, and he nods his head quickly, then we all head down the stairs and close the basement door.

"Hannah, I'm sorry for what Mom did. I told her she was wrong for doing it, but she didn't want to listen. She's been so mean lately, and she's been talking badly about you behind your back," Jake rushes out as soon as we're alone.

"It's okay, Jake. It's not your fault, and I don't blame you at all, okay? Mom and I have our issues, and that's between us. I wanted to tell you some things before you leave, and I'm sorry I'm doing it literally the day before you go, but I didn't want Mom to have more time to bully you into telling her." Hannah takes a deep breath, waiting for Jake to nod before she speaks again.

"I've left the church. I don't want a lecture on it, but I think it's fair that you know. Morgan and I are unofficially engaged, and I'm pregnant. With twins. Girls."

Jake's eyes turn into saucers at the news, and he looks down at her belly, then back to her, then up to me. "How far along are you?" he whispers.

Hannah gives him a watery smile. "Almost seventeen weeks."

Jake's own eyes fill with tears, and he makes a choked sound in the back of his throat. "I know you probably didn't think I noticed things, but I remember how excited you were when you got pregnant the first time. I remember how devastated you were at the losses. I was so happy you divorced that douchebag. I wanted to help you so badly when you were locked in your room for a week after you moved in. I know we aren't super close, but I want you to know I'm so happy for you, Hannah. I don't care if you've left the church. I just care that you're safe and happy. I'm so excited to meet my nieces."

Jake looks over at Aly and kneels down to be at her eye level. "I don't think we properly met, but I'm Jake. I guess I'm going to be your uncle. What's your name?"

"Alyssa. But... all of my aunts and uncles call me Aly. You can call me Aly, too," Aly whispers with a shy smile.

Jake grins. "Nice to meet you, Aly. I can't wait to get to know you better." He frowns and stands. "Now I really wish I weren't going," he says more to himself than to anyone else.

"There will be plenty of time to get to know her and the twins when you get back. I promise to write letters and send pictures. You have more freedom with phone calls, so call when you can," Hannah says, wrapping her little brother in a hug.

"I won't tell Mom, promise," he whispers before they break apart.

"I think we're going to head out, I don't want to see Mom right now, and I just wanted to talk to you." Hannah sniffs. "Be safe out there, please. Don't get yourself in dangerous situations."

"I won't. Love you, Hannah."

"Love you, too, Jake."

Jake rushes back up the stairs to greet the rest of the party while Hannah takes a second to compose herself.

"Alright, I'm starving. Let's get lunch," she says after a minute, but before we can get up the stairs, Shelly bursts through the basement door.

"Were you even going to introduce me?" Shelly snaps in lieu of "hello."

"Hello, Mother. We were just leaving."

"You can't stay to celebrate your brother? That's self-ish of you, Hannah." Shelly shakes her head.

"Jake is aware we aren't planning on staying. I already spoke with him and wished him luck." Hannah inches closer to me, and Aly moves to stand behind my back. She's never seen someone speak to their child this way, and Shelly gives off intimidating vibes.

My mom is always gently scolding us or joking with us when we're at her house. If she needs to have a serious conversation, she always makes sure it's in private, and even then, she's kind and gentle.

"You won't even introduce me to my own future grandchild? I heard you are *engaged.* Don't you think that's something I should know?" If looks could kill, Hannah would not be standing right now. The look Shelly gives her is so full of indignation and hatred.

"I made the choice not to introduce Alyssa to you, Mrs. Layton," I interject, and Shelly turns her acidic look on me instead. "I refuse to stand here and let you spit vitriol towards my future wife, and I would never subject Alyssa to your hateful words and ugly attitude."

Shelly rears back as if I've slapped her. "How *dare* you come to my house and insult me?"

"I didn't want to tell you about the engagement. After the way you treated me I wasn't going to allow you to be part of my life. If you want any part in my life or your grandchildren's lives, you need to seriously rethink how you treat me and my family." Hannah's eyes widen when she realizes the slip up. I hope Shelly doesn't catch it.

She does.

"You're pregnant?" Shelly gasps and *literally* clutches her pearls while shaking her head. "I knew you were living in sin with him, but this? It'll take a lot to save you, Hannah. What makes you think this baby will survive when the others didn't?"

Hannah looks at me, and I nod imperceptibly to let her know I'm okay with whatever she wants to tell her.

She takes a big breath before she says, "I'm almost seventeen weeks. The doctor ran multiple tests, and it's most likely Liam was the issue before, not me. The babies are growing as they should, and I haven't had any problems."

"You're having more than one?!"

"Two girls," Hannah confirms. "And they will *not* grow up the way I did. They'll grow up in a house knowing what unconditional love looks and feels like. Like I said before, if you want to be part of their lives, you will need to rethink how you treat me and my family."

Shelly sputters but can't say anything before Hannah is up the stairs, and we're following her closely behind. Hannah ignores the people calling her name and wanting to talk to her, choosing instead to rush to the car.

Once we've pulled out of the neighborhood, Aly says very quietly, "You and I are a lot alike, aren't we, Hannah?"

"Why do you say that, sweetheart?" Hannah asks.

"We both have moms who don't love us the way they should."

Hannah sighs. "No, they don't. But you know what we have?"

"What?"

"We have each other." Hannah looks over her shoulder at Aly in the backseat and gives her a sad smile.

"I'm glad we have each other."

"Me too, sweetheart. I'm also glad we have your dad."

"Yeah, he's okay," Aly jokes, and I glare at her in the mirror, making her and Hannah burst out laughing.

"Alright, troublemakers, what are we having for lunch?"

"Pizza!" Hannah and Aly say in unison, and we all laugh.

I'm pretty glad to have these two by my side, too.

# CHAPTER 45

*Hannah*

I haven't heard from my mom since the farewell almost three weeks ago. I'm taking that as a sign she doesn't want to be part of my life anymore.

We started renovating the nursery, since I'm almost halfway to my due date. Dr. Badar explained twins usually come before thirty-seven weeks, so technically, I'm more than halfway. We're hoping I can make it to the thirty-two-week mark.

I'm on my lunch break at work, writing thank you notes to the participating vendors for the summer program when I feel it.

I thought I was having gas pains, but I don't think that's what this is.

The babies are moving.

I stand abruptly from my desk and walk quickly outside while I dial Morgan.

"Hannah? Is everything okay?" he answers frantically.

"I felt them move!" I practically scream.

"Felt...? Oh my God, the babies? You felt them move?!"

I'm nodding my head excitedly even though he can't see me. "Yes, the babies. I felt them move."

"Hannah!" Sage rushes out to me. "Are you okay? Is something wrong?"

"I'm fine, Sage, I felt the babies move and wanted to call Morgan to tell him." I point at the phone.

"Oh, thank goodness," Sage sighs in relief. "That's so exciting! Tell Morgan I say hi."

"Tell Sage thank you for checking on my girls," Morgan says, obviously able to hear Sage.

"He says hi, and thank you for checking on us."

"You're welcome!" Sage shouts as she walks back inside.

"We're having babies, Morgan," I whisper as more tears of joy fall down my cheeks.

"We sure are, Butterfly." A bell dings in the distance on his end of the phone. "I'm sorry to cut this short, but I've got to help a customer. I'll see you in two hours. I love you."

"I love you, too, bye." I hang up and head back to my office where Sage is waiting for me with a big grin on her face.

She helps me finish the notes while she rants about her latest boy drama. Sage is very prone to making snap judgments when it comes to men and not giving them a chance to prove her wrong.

One time, Liam tried to set her up with one of his friends so we could have someone to double date with. Sage didn't even make it past the appetizers before she decided he was a pretentious douchebag not worth her time and spent the rest of the night ignoring his many attempts at a conversation.

She wasn't wrong in her assessment.

Liam refused to set her up on a date again, which is probably a good thing because his friends are assholes.

Not that Sage needs any help in the dating department. Men trip over themselves to get her attention.

"I can ask Morgan if he has any friends to set you up with if you want. I'm sure he doesn't surround himself with finance bros like Liam. I'm sure we can find you someone great. Oh! I can ask Kendall if any of the rugby guys are single?" I suggest.

Sage's cheeks turn pink as she shakes her head. "No rugby players."

Hmmm... Sage isn't telling me something. She was very into the idea of a rugby player just a few weeks ago. "Why not?"

She waves me off. "I don't have time for a sports dude. Plus, they're so... sweaty and massive. I don't want a caveman. I want a nice smelling, gentle lover."

Sage and I both burst out laughing because the last thing Sage wants is a gentle lover. She has... *particular* bedroom tastes, and gentle is not part of the description.

"When you're ready to tell me why you've changed your mind about rugby players, you let me know," I say with a pat on her hand.

"Nothing—"

"Hey, ladies!" Janine bursts into the office without knocking, interrupting Sage's denial. "Hannah, your ex-husband is here, asking to speak to you. Do you want me to kick him out?"

*Ugh. Fucking Liam.*

"No, I'll go talk to him." I stand from my chair and make my way to the front of the library.

I text Morgan *Liam is here, and I'm speaking to him, but I'm okay.* Then I round the corner, and there stands my ex-husband.

"To what do I owe the displeasure, Liam?" I ask quietly but harshly.

He gives me a thorough onceover, his gaze locking on my stomach before finally bringing his eyes back to mine. "Can't a guy just visit his ex-wife at work?"

"No. But I don't want to have this conversation here. Follow me."

Liam sighs like I'm being unreasonable, and it has me straightening my spine and putting more guards up. He follows me without a word into a conference room that almost never gets used.

He barely waits for the door to close before he says, "Twins, huh? Weird how you can keep this pregnancy, but you killed every single one of our babies. It's like you were *trying* to lose them so I would divorce you," Liam spits with a tone used to scold a child.

"The fact you think I would actively put my body through that pain not once or twice, but *seven* times shows just how out of touch with reality you are, Liam."

"It's just strange, Hannah. Makes me think you weren't actually fully committed to our marriage." He shrugs.

"I was more committed than you were! I wanted to get testing done, Liam. I wanted to go to couples counseling. I was willing to try. *You* were the one who called it quits. You gave up when things got hard because *you* were looking for an out."

Liam scoffs. "Why should I get tested when it's clearly *your* fault you can't stay pregnant?"

"It's *clearly not* my fault. I got tested when I found out I was pregnant with the twins. The doctor hypothesized it was mostly likely a problem with the previous *sperm donor.* That whoever was getting me pregnant before didn't have strong enough sperm to help the embryo grow."

His jaw clenches at the blow to his fragile ego, but I'm just stating facts.

"You can't possibly prove that," he says through gritted teeth.

"Not one-hundred percent, no. Not unless you go and get tested. But the only difference between my previous pregnancies and this one is the father. Now tell me why the hell you're at my place of work, Liam. I'm done with this petty conversation."

"Whitney told me you were pregnant with twins, and I wanted to confirm it for myself. I also wanted to tell you to call off your guard dog. He can't take full custody of the kid, it would look bad for Whitney."

"I'm not going to tell Morgan what he can and can't do when it comes to Alyssa. Why do you even care? You've made it clear you don't want anything to do with her."

He shrugs. "Like I said, it would look bad for Whitney. She can't afford the legal fees it would take to fight him, and I sure as hell am not going to be fronting that bill. She's been trying to convince me to get *her* pregnant so she can rub it in Morgan's face, and I think she'll back off if she doesn't lose custody of the brat."

"Liam, I couldn't care less about what's happening in your personal life. Your and Whitney's issues are none of my business, and what Morgan does with custody of Alyssa is up to him. I'm not going to tell him what to do."

"You just want to see me suffer."

I throw my hands up in the air. "This isn't even about you! If you don't want anything to do with a woman who has a kid, then break up with Whitney! Don't bring your relationship drama to me because you and I? We're over, Liam. *You* made that clear when you handed me fucking divorce papers. My life is none of your business, and frankly, I don't give a shit about yours. I don't want to see or talk to you ever again, so please just leave."

Liam scoffs again. "You always were a bitch. I don't know what he sees in a fat, selfish, defective—"

"You better not say another word about my fiancée," Morgan's deep voice interrupts, and Liam and I both whip our heads in the direction of the open door.

"What are you doing here? How did you know where we were?" I ask as he comes and wraps an arm protectively around my waist.

"I was already on my way when you texted me he was here. The woman at the front desk told me she saw you come in here. This kind of stress isn't good for you or the babies. I'll take it from here." Morgan places a kiss on my forehead, then turns to Liam. "If I need to take out a restraining order because you're harassing Hannah, I will. You have no reason to be here, so leave. And do not contact her again."

Liam puffs up his chest, trying to stand tall, but he's not as big as Morgan, so he only reaches his chin. "Back off from Whitney, and I'll back off from Hannah."

Morgan gives a condescending chuckle. "Whitney is the one who keeps contacting me. I've already told her any contact will be done through our lawyers from here on out. If I need to get lawyers involved here too, I will. I will protect what's mine at all costs."

It's got to be the pregnancy hormones making me all tingly at the way he growls "mine." Overprotective Morgan is hot as hell, and I'm seriously wishing we weren't in public right now.

"Whatever, man. Enjoy my sloppy seconds," Liam spits, then turns to walk away.

Morgan speaks just loud enough for only the three of us to hear, "Oh, I enjoy her very much. And she sure as hell enjoys me if the way she screams my name every night is any indication."

Liam freezes, and I watch his hands ball into fists. I think he's going to take a swing at Morgan, but instead he just stomps out the front doors of the library like a petulant child stomps out of a room.

"Was that necessary?" I whisper, turned on as hell.

"Hell yes it was, Butterfly. He should know how much more... *satisfied* you are now."

My cheeks heat to a million degrees. I should be feeling upset and hurt by what Liam said, but I've heard it all before. If anything, it cements that the divorce was the best thing to happen to me, even if it was extremely difficult at the time.

These damn pregnancy hormones have made my libido sky rocket, so instead of feeling upset, I'm feeling horny at the show of Morgan's protectiveness.

"That was very hot. I really wish we weren't at my place of employment." I sigh, and Morgan's eyes darken, even as his brow furrows with a hint of worry.

"You're not... upset by what just happened?"

I shake my head. "I know I should be, but Liam's told me the same things over and over. I feel... relieved I don't have to deal with him anymore. I also feel like I want to jump your bones."

"Yeah? My fiancée's feeling a little hot and bothered?" He leans in and whispers in my ear, "Is your pussy needy for me?"

I can't help the whimper that escapes my throat. *Yes. Yes, I am needy for him.*

I nod my head in response worried what might come out of my mouth if I speak.

Morgan gives me a rakish smirk. "You're off the clock in ten minutes. Then I'll take you home."

"What about my car?"

"I'll bring you back tomorrow to grab your car, don't you worry about it, Butterfly."

Morgan takes a seat in the lobby of the library, and I head back to my office, wishing time would go just a little bit faster.

Janine and Sage are waiting for me when I get back and insist I tell them the details of what happened, even though I'm pretty sure they were watching the whole thing go down. Sage offers, again, to slash his tires, and Janine says she knows a witch who can put a spell on him to make him impotent.

As tempting as those offers are, my brain is solely on the man waiting to take me home and ravish me, so I decline and ask Janine to leave a few minutes early. She agrees, so I clock out, gather my stuff, and rush out to my future husband.

"Janine let me leave early, let's go." I grab his hand, pulling him out the door and to the car.

"Someone's eager to get home," Morgan teases. We make it to the car, and I wait for him to unlock it, but instead he cages my body between his and the car, framing my jaw with his big hands.

God, I love his hands.

"What if I planned to take you out on a date, Butterfly? Wine and dine you then take you home and make love to you slow and sweet."

"I need you now," I whine.

"Get in the car, Hannah. We're going out on a date." He steps back and unlocks the car, opening my door for me as I pout. I get in and buckle.

Morgan rounds the car and gets in, then starts pulling out of the parking lot.

"Show me."

I turn and look at him, confused. "What?"

"Show me how needy you are for me, Butterfly. Spread your legs, and show me if your pussy is wet."

"But you're driving," I protest, even as I inch my dress up my thighs.

Morgan thinks about that for a second, then turns off of the main road and down a street that leads to—of all things—a Mormon church building. He pulls into the empty parking lot, and I'm grateful this area is surrounded by trees. "I would never risk you or our girls' safety, but I can't wait long enough to take you home and lay you out properly. You'll have to get off on my fingers now, then I'll fuck you properly later."

Fuck me, this man is all sorts of hot. How did I end up with such a sweet, gentle man who talks so fucking dirty?

I scoot my chair back as far as it can go and prop one leg up on the dashboard, hiking my dress up further to show him my underwear with a tiny wet spot on it. It's not easy with my big belly, but I'm determined to make it work.

"Mmm. That's my girl. Move your panties over." He slides a hand up my bare thigh, his fingers toying with the edge of my panties.

I slide them to the side, and he swears under his breath. His fingers trace the seam of my sex, gathering the bit of wetness there and dragging his fingers back up to my clit.

"What made you so wet, Butterfly?"

"Seeing you be all protective. But I've been horny all day thinking about how good you make me feel." I gasp as one thick finger slowly circles my clit.

"You like that I'll take care of you? You like me claiming you as mine?"

"Yes!" I moan when he increases the pressure.

"Good. Because you are *mine*, Hannah. I'll never let anything happen to you. Spread your legs a little further for me, Butterfly."

I do as he says, and he slowly inserts two fingers into my pussy, the palm of his hand grinding into my clit.

"Ride my fingers, make yourself come. If you don't come soon, you'll have to wait until we get home tonight."

I start to grind against his hand, picking up speed while he matches my rhythm stroke for stroke. He keeps the pressure on my clit with his palm, and my orgasm crescendos quicker than I thought it would.

"That's it, Butterfly. My pregnant fiancée riding my fingers looks so fucking pretty. You gonna come for me? Make a mess on my hand?" Morgan groans.

"Yes, Morgan. Please!" I don't know why I'm begging, he already told me it was up to me to come.

"Let me see you fall apart," he demands.

"Oh God, I'm coming!" I shout as the waves of pleasure crash over me, and I come around Morgan's fingers.

"Fuck yes, that's so fucking beautiful, Butterfly." Morgan works me through my orgasm and pulls out his fingers slowly once I've stopped writhing against his hand.

I whimper at the loss then watch with rapt attention as he brings his fingers to his mouth and sucks the arousal from them, moaning like he's eating the most decadent dessert.

It's much hotter than it logically should be.

Morgan opens the center console, pulls out a pack of baby wipes, and hands them to me to clean up as best as I can. I discard them in the little trash can he keeps in the car, and put the wipes away.

"Why do you have diaper wipes even though Aly's nine?"

"You'll soon find out diaper wipes are a godsend with kids of all ages, and it's crucial to have them *everywhere*," he explains.

We pull back out onto the main road, drive for a few minutes, and pull up in front of a little strip mall.

"What are we doing here?"

"You'll see. Come on, we have an appointment."

# CHAPTER 46

## Morgan

I was nervous Hannah wouldn't like this surprise, but after what happened with Liam, I think it's going to be a good thing.

Hannah and I get out of the car, and I intertwine our fingers, leading her to the door with a peeling sign for Gemma's Gems.

The jewelry store may not look like much, but it's owned by the kindest couple. They make sure all of their gems are ethically sourced or lab-made and specialize in custom rings.

"What are we doing at a jewelry store?" Hannah whispers.

"We're getting you an engagement ring."

"Are you sure you don't want to wait?"

"We've waited long enough, Butterfly. I need there to be no doubt in anyone's mind you're mine, and I want to spend the rest of my life with you and our girls." I place a protective hand on her belly. I'm dying to feel the twins move, but if she only felt them move today, I probably won't feel them from the outside for a few more weeks.

When she called me earlier to tell me she felt them, I teared up. It's a big milestone, and I hope this makes her feel less worried about losing them.

We're soon greeted by Gemma and Joseph, the owners, who talk us through the process for creating a custom ring. Hannah's eyes dart around at the displays of jewelry, different metals, and different gems to choose from. She looks a little overwhelmed.

Once they've finished their spiel, they tell us to look around and get an idea of what we might like, and then ring the bell when we're ready to start the process.

Hannah finds a case with one-of-a-kind rings, and she immediately zones in on the ones with a peach colored stone in the middle.

"This gemstone is so pretty. I think I want one of these," she says in awe and points to a pear cut gem on a gold band with a halo of diamonds around it. "That's the ring I want."

"You don't want to look around more? Design one yourself?" I clarify, just to make sure she's getting exactly what she wants.

She shakes her head, then freezes and places a hand on her belly. "The girls agree with me. That's the one."

"They kicked just now?" I place my hand next to hers, willing them to do it again.

"Yeah, they did. I think that's a good sign."

"I think so, too, Butterfly. I'll get Gemma and Joseph to come out here and see if this one is available."

I leave Hannah, ring the bell, and Gemma comes out immediately.

"Are you ready to design your ring?" she asks brightly.

"I think my fiancée would like one of the ones already made, if it's available."

"Oh! Sure, let's take a look."

We walk over to the case, and Gemma unlocks it. She takes out the ring Hannah pointed to and slides over the little box it's in.

Gemma explains it's a lab grown peach champagne stone, and the halo of diamonds are lab grown as well.

Hannah takes the ring and carefully inspects it, then hands it over to me. It's stunning and definitely something I would love to see on Hannah's finger.

"There's a matching band, as well, if that's something you're interested in," Gemma says.

"Yes, we're interested. What do you think—is this the ring?" I ask Hannah, who grins as she nods.

"I'll grab my notepad and keyring to measure so we can resize both," Gemma says, then shuffles to the back.

"Are you sure this isn't too much money? I'd be okay with a $50 ring from Etsy," Hannah whispers.

"Nothing is too much for you, Butterfly. Besides, I want you to love your ring. Not just be okay with it. You'll be wearing it for a long, long time."

Gemma comes back, measures Hannah's finger, and tells me it should be done in about a week.

"Wait, where is Aly?" Hannah asks as we pull into the driveway after picking up dinner.

"She's sleeping over at Alice's house so we can have some alone time. It was her idea to take you ring shopping."

Aly told me I needed to hurry up and get a ring for Hannah so she doesn't change her mind about getting married. Not that I was worried that would happen, but she was right.

"That's so nice of her. I think we should hit up the last farmer's market on Sunday so we can spend some time with her, too."

God, I love this woman. I love how easily she's integrated into mine and Aly's lives and how she loves Aly like she's her own.

"That's a great idea, Butterfly. You've had a long day, so let's get you into bed."

We make our way upstairs with Bean and Bagel hot on Hannah's heels. Bean refuses to leave her alone, I think he knows she's pregnant and wants to protect the babies. Bagel is less concerned about Hannah but still cuddles up to her belly whenever she's sitting down.

I can't wait until Bean is cuddling her stomach and one of the babies kicks him in the head. I don't think he'll hurt Hannah, but he'll be pissed for sure.

I corral the cats out of the bedroom, much to their dismay. Then, joining Hannah in the bathroom, I take the time to help her wash off her makeup, then shampoo and condition her hair. She lets me clean her body with a washcloth, and I quickly run through my shower routine, ignoring the way my cock throbs from touching her soft body.

I hop out and dry myself off before helping her out of the shower and drying her off. She goes through her skincare routine, and we brush our teeth before she dresses in one of those goddamn nightgowns, and I slip on a pair of boxers before I hop into bed and settle behind her under the covers.

I know she's probably tired from the day's activities, so I'm not expecting her to scoot her ass into my crotch and wiggle it back and forth across my erection.

"Hannah," I groan. "You can't be rubbing that sexy ass on me, or I'm going to think you want me to fuck you."

"I do want you to fuck me."

Damn it. "You need to rest."

"I'll sleep better if you take care of the ache between my thighs first." She turns her head back to look at me like it's an innocent request.

I slide the hand resting on her hip down her thigh, then slip in under the fabric of her nightgown and run it back up her smooth skin.

"You still feeling needy, Butterfly? My fingers weren't enough?" I know she's not wearing any underwear because I watched her get dressed.

"Need more," she whimpers as my fingers tease the crease where her pussy meets her thigh. She opens her legs wider.

"Greedy thing." I nip at her earlobe. "Do you want my mouth? Or my cock?"

"Your cock, please."

"Well, since you asked so nicely." I pull my boxers down and fist my cock, gliding the head against her wet pussy. She's been getting wet so much easier since she got pregnant, and I'm loving it.

"Do you want it slow and sweet, or hard and fast, mama?" I notch the head at her entrance and grip around her thigh to spread her thighs wider.

"Hard and fast," she moans, and I enter her in a swift stroke. "Oh God!"

"I'm probably not going to last long," I admit. I'll make sure she comes, though, before I even think about coming myself.

"I'm almost there. You touching me in the shower got me all wound up."

"Up on your hands and knees, baby." I pull out of her, and she follows my directions, arching her back and pressing her ass into me.

I give her ass a spank and watch the way it ripples before entering her again. I set a hard but steady pace, which apparently isn't fast enough for my girl because she starts pushing herself back onto my cock faster.

I spank her again. "Look at you, fucking yourself on my cock. Always so fucking needy for me, aren't you? You need me to fuck you faster?"

"Yes, please, faster. I need you to make me come," Hannah moans.

"Anything for you, Butterfly." I pick up the pace, my cock hitting her G-spot with every thrust. She chants the same words over and over again, and I feel her getting close.

I bring my hand around her belly to press hard, fast circles on her swollen clit, and it only takes a few more strokes for her to detonate and throw me over the edge with her.

"I love you so much." I press a kiss to her shoulder before pulling out.

"I love you, too," she sighs, already on her way to sleep.

I step into the bathroom to clean myself off and grab a wet washcloth to wash her off, but when I come back to clean her, she's already closed her eyes. They pop open when I wipe the sticky release from between her thighs, but she settles back again.

I discard the cloth in the laundry basket and turn off the bedside lamp before curling around my fiancée and draping an arm over her stomach.

Maybe it's my imagination, but I swear I feel the twins move underneath my palm.

# Chapter 47

*Hannah*

The last few months have flown by in a blur of doctor's appointments, tests, and holidays.

The twins looked perfect at the twenty week ultrasound, and I passed my glucose test with flying colors.

Morgan talks to them every night, and as soon as they hear their daddy's voice, they kick like crazy.

My belly is huge, and I've been living in oversized sweaters and comfy pants since my stomach popped at twenty-four weeks. Bean hates it because he can't snuggle up against me as easily anymore, but Bagel doesn't seem to mind as much.

We spent Thanksgiving with Morgan's family where Iris made the best turkey I've ever had.

Christmas morning was just the three of us exchanging presents and eating crepes, then we spent Christmas evening with his family, playing board games in matching pajamas.

New Year's Eve was a week ago, and we stayed up until midnight watching *Scooby-Doo* and eating snacks to our hearts' content.

I haven't heard from my mom much since Jake's farewell, but I've been writing to Jake every week.

He hates his mission. His companion has been instigating physical altercations, and he wants to come home. He's spoken to the mission president, and all he tells Jake is he should have more faith. The companion isn't getting reprimanded for hurting Jake, and Jake won't supply any other information than a vague explanation of what happened. I hate not knowing more, but it's frowned upon by the church to complain about anything when you're on your mission, so I doubt Jake will elaborate.

Jake doesn't explicitly say in his letters he's starting to doubt the church, but that's the vibe I'm getting from him.

I wouldn't be surprised if he came home early, and I don't blame him.

Morgan started the process of getting full custody of Aly in September, and one day in November, a courier brought us a yellow envelope. Inside was Whitney's voluntary termination of her parental rights, signed and notarized, along with a letter to Aly and a letter to Morgan.

We read Aly's letter first to make sure it was safe for her to read, and it was almost the same as the letter to Morgan. They were short and simple. Whitney doesn't want to be dragged through court or pay the legal fees, and she doesn't want the responsibility that comes with being a mom. She thought it would be better for everyone if she wasn't involved anymore.

Morgan seemed unsurprised at his letter, but he was shocked Whitney terminated her parental rights—especially on her own. We've barely discussed next steps, and I'd never dream of offering to adopt Aly, even though, in my heart, it's what I want.

I want her to see me as a mother figure and someone she can rely on. Someone who loves her as she is and wants to watch her succeed. Even if I don't legally adopt her, I hope one day she can see me that way.

We gave Aly the letter shortly before Christmas when she asked if her mom would be coming around for the holiday. She took the letter to her room and didn't come out for two hours. I asked Morgan multiple times if we should check on her, but he was adamant she needs to process this on her own.

Eventually she came down, her eyes puffy and red from crying, and told us what her mom wrote.

It still makes me mad when I think about how easily Whitney dismissed Aly.

Morgan started taking her to a therapist so she could talk to an unbiased third party, and it seems to be helping, but I know it will take time for her to feel okay again.

Morgan's family has been extra attentive with Aly to make up for her mom abandoning her.

Iris, Sarah, Alice, Olivia, and Asha have planned a baby shower for this weekend because I'll be thirty-six weeks and could go into labor any time, and when they asked if they should invite my mom, I told them no.

Part of me wonders if it's a shitty thing for me to do, but another part of me is proud of myself for sticking to my boundaries and holding my own.

Morgan and I have had long discussions about what we're going to do about childcare and my job, and I think we've come up with a solid plan.

I have three months of paid leave, and then I'll continue to work full-time, and Morgan is going to ask Olivia if she'd be willing to take over more of the flower shop's daily operations. Morgan's mom has offered to help watch the twins so I can work, and I couldn't be more grateful to have everyone's support.

Morgan moved his home office downstairs, and we turned the room upstairs into the nursery. Kendall, Morgan, and Axel spent a long weekend painting and assembling all the furniture, so the only thing left to do is organize the thousands of clothes we have and wash all of the bedding.

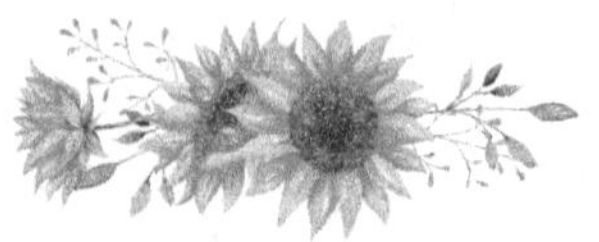

I've been feeling off for the last two days. This morning I've felt so nauseated I haven't been able to eat more than a few saltine crackers. I've been having Braxton Hicks contractions, but they haven't been consistent or painful. I have so much anxiety about losing these babies that my mind automatically jumps to something being wrong.

If I have the babies now at thirty-six weeks, they'd probably have to be in the NICU for a while, but they would most likely survive, and that's the only thing keeping me from rushing to the hospital.

Iris and Morgan's sisters refuse to let me help with the setup of the baby shower and have insisted I sit on the couch and relax.

I'm not used to just... sitting and waiting for an event to start. I'm always the one helping to get everything ready.

I'm also not used to the men helping out, but Kendall, Axel, and Morgan are all happily setting up the decorations and moving furniture around. Aly's the one telling them where things should go.

I don't know how it is in other families, but in mine, the men aren't allowed at the baby or bridal showers. Morgan scoffed and said there was no way he was missing a party for his babies, so he, Kendall, and his dad will be hanging out, too. I think Justin and Cooper will be here as well, but they've been tasked with getting last minute utensils and ice.

The urge to pee hits me like a truck—a fun side effect of growing two humans. I stand from the couch, start walking to the bathroom, but then I feel the gush of wetness soak my pants, and I gasp.

"Hannah? Are you good?" Morgan jumps off the stool and comes over to see the puddle of liquid under my feet. "Do we need to go get you a change of clothes?" he speaks softly, soothing me because he thinks I peed my pants.

"Hospital."

"What?"

"Water broke," I manage to say, clutching my stomach as a wave of anxiety pummels into me, and tears fill my eyes. It's too soon. I'm not ready yet. They aren't fully cooked!

Morgan pales, and it takes him a good thirty seconds to process what I said. Meanwhile, I'm still dripping onto the floor.

Iris rushes in with towels and a change of clothes. "Change into these, and I'll have Axel drive you and Morgan to the hospital. Aly will stay with us, and we'll take care of everyone coming for the shower. We'll grab your bags from your house and meet you at the hospital, okay? Don't you worry about a thing. This isn't uncommon with twins, everything will be okay. Morgan, help her get dressed then get Hannah to Dad's truck. Now."

"Dressed. Truck. Got it," Morgan rasps as he gently takes my hand and leads me to one of the spare bedrooms to change out of my wet clothes.

"Are they going to be okay?" I ask when he kneels down to help me slip out of my leggings.

He kisses my stomach reverently. "They're going to be perfect, Butterfly."

The drive to the hospital felt excruciatingly long and super short at the same time, and now I'm on the labor and delivery floor being checked in. Morgan is irritated.

The nurse checking us in asked if we were sure my water broke, confirming I didn't just pee my pants, and Morgan snapped at her that I would know my body.

I guess it's protocol to test it no matter what, so when she pulled the strip of paper away from me and confirmed it, Morgan rolled his eyes.

Then they had trouble finding my veins for the IV, and Morgan looked like he was going to pass out with how many times they poked and prodded at my hands. They finally got it with a vein finder and a seasoned nurse, and now I'm in a room with a band around my belly and a fetal monitor for each twin attached to it.

Dr. Badar walks in and gently explains that because the babies are early, a vaginal birth may not be the safest route to go, and she highly suggests they do a cesarean section to make sure both me and the babies have the safest delivery.

I knew this was a possibility, so I sign the papers agreeing to have the procedure done, and they prep me for surgery.

# CHAPTER 48

*Morgan*

*I*'m going to be a dad today.

Well, I'm going to be a dad *again*.

I swear my heart fell out of my butt when Hannah said her water broke, I barely remember getting here. I'm glad my dad drove us because it was probably safer than if I had.

We had to wait a few hours to do the cesarean procedure because Hannah had eaten today, and they didn't want to risk aspiration.

Now, I'm waiting outside of the operating room in a white jumpsuit, mask, gloves, and a hat while I wait for Hannah to be prepped for her c-section, and I'm agitated because *I* want to be in there. They're doing a spinal block to numb her, and they won't let me be there to comfort her or hold her. I can hear her pained whimpers from the other side of the door, and it's killing me.

Dr. Badar peeks out the door and guides me into the room, telling me to keep my hands to my chest so I don't touch anything. I'm directed around the anesthesiologist to sit on a stool the size of a dinner plate at Hannah's head.

She looks half asleep, most likely from the anesthesia and stress of everything happening with her body. Her eyes keep blinking open and closed, and she looks paler than ever. She gives me a small smile as I sit down.

I'm handed a bag in case Hannah feels like she needs to throw up—which feels like something that should absolutely *not* happen when she's being cut open—and they've put up a curtain over her stomach so we can't see what the doctors are doing on the other side.

Good, I don't want to watch that.

The doctor narrates everything she's doing, and part of me wishes she wouldn't. I just want to know if the babies are okay.

Hannah winces, and I look over to see why. From my vantage point, I can't see anything surgical happening, but I can see the doctor from the hips up pushing herself on top of Hannah trying to push one of the babies out. It looks like the doc is doing deck-ups out of a pool on Hannah's stomach, *Jesus Christ*—but I'm assured it doesn't hurt, it just feels like a lot of pressure, and then tiny little cries fill the operating room.

"Here's baby number one, and she sounds great. Dad, you can follow the nurse over to the vitals station and watch her get cleaned up."

I'm torn because I don't want to leave Hannah while she's still being operated on, but she gives me a small nod, so I follow the nurse with our first baby to a small room off of the operating room where she sucks the goop off of the baby and then checks her vitals.

"She's four pounds, nine ounces. Which is a pretty good weight for twins born this early. She seems to be doing well..." The nurse keeps telling me things about the baby. Things I should probably listen to. She keeps gushing about the head of blonde hair matted to her head, but my attention is pulled back to the operating room wondering if Hannah and our other baby are okay.

I don't know how long I stand there, staring at the tiny human under the blue bili lights, but after what feels like an eternity, another nurse brings in my second daughter, and she isn't crying as much as her sister.

"Is she okay?" Worry clogs my throat, making it hard to speak.

"She's having some trouble breathing, but she let out a cry when we pulled her out, so she'll be okay. Mom's just getting stitched up, and we'll bring her to where you and the babies will be waiting in the room.

My stomach turns because I don't want to leave Hannah alone, but I swallow back my protest and focus on my daughters. I trust Hannah is in good hands with Dr. Badar.

"Baby B weighs four pounds seven ounces," the nurse says as she continues to wipe the baby clean.

"Do you have names picked out yet?" the nurse tending to Baby A asks, and I shake my head.

Hannah and I decided to wait until we saw the girls to name them, and even though I want to give them names now, I won't be doing that until she meets our daughters.

We're guided back to the recovery room where they administer shots to the babies. Baby A screams bloody murder for a good three minutes when she's poked, but Baby B just lets out a sad yelp of discomfort then goes back to sleep.

Hannah's rolled in a few minutes later, looking exhausted. Once she's been situated in the bed, the nurse hands over Baby A to Hannah who bursts into tears. I'm handed Baby B.

I sit on her bedside and kiss the side of Hannah's head while we look down at our daughters, my own eyes blurring. I'm relieved everyone is okay, and so overjoyed at the gift Hannah has given to me. To us.

"I'm so fucking proud of you, Butterfly. I love you so much."

Hannah lifts her watery eyes to me. "I love you, too. I can't believe my body made them."

"I can. You are incredible. They're so perfect. But... we need to name them."

Hannah glances between the two babies then strokes the chubby cheek of the girl in her arms. "This is Poppy Fowler. And this," she places a hand gently on the baby in my arms, "is Violet Fowler. What do you think?"

"I think those names are perfect for them. Violet is already much calmer than her sister. Poppy is fitting for this feisty little thing."

"When will Aly be able to meet them?"

My heart fucking soars. She's just come out of a major surgery, and she's already thinking about when Aly can come see them. If I didn't already have a plan in motion, I'd ask her if she wants to adopt Aly right now.

"Tomorrow morning. It's late, and you need to rest, Butterfly."

Hannah pouts. "Fine. I'm starving, too."

"Let's find some food for you."

# CHAPTER 49

*Hannah*

The next morning, after the least restful night of sleep I've ever had due to the nurses checking on me every couple of hours, Aly, Axel, and Iris shuffle into the room with bags in tow.

The nurses kept the twins in the NICU last night to monitor them, but the girls didn't seem to need any extra help or attention, so they said we can keep them in here tonight if we want to. I missed them last night, as crazy as that sounds.

"Are you okay, Hannah?" Aly asks as soon as she sees me, making me want to cry.

I've cried a lot in the last twenty-four hours. It still feels surreal to have not only one, but *two* babies that Morgan and I made together here with us, safe and sound.

I'm holding Violet, feeding her a bottle, while Morgan feeds Poppy. I didn't want the anxiety of guessing how much they would be eating while breastfeeding, and bottle feeding will be easier for us when I go back to work, so I opted to not breastfeed.

"I'm feeling very tired, but I'm okay, Aly. Do you want to hold one of your sisters?"

Aly nods her head enthusiastically, and Morgan directs her to use the hand sanitizer before sitting on the couch next to him.

He finishes burping Poppy and teaches Aly how to cradle her head and hold her steady.

"This is Poppy, and the other one is Violet," Morgan says quietly.

"She's so tiny," Aly whispers in awe.

I finish burping Violet and see a sheen of tears in Axel's eyes. "What do you think, Papa? You want to hold your granddaughter?"

Axel clears his throat. "I won't say no to that." He sanitizes his hands and takes the tiny, bundled up human.

"Hi there, Violet. I'm your Papa. You and your sister already have everyone wrapped around your fingers," Axel coos, swaying back and forth.

Iris sits over by Aly, who's still staring wide-eyed down at her sister. "Oh look, Aly, Poppy's opening her eyes. She wants to see you."

"Hi, Poppy. I'm your big sister, Aly. I promise I won't let anything bad happen to you or Violet." She looks at Morgan. "Can I kiss her?"

"Sure, but only on the top of her head. We don't want anyone to kiss her face because she can get sick very easily."

Aly places the gentlest kiss on her head, then hands her over to Iris who happily takes Poppy and coos to her about how pretty she and her sister are.

My eyes meet Morgan's from across the room, and we smile at each other. I know the road ahead with recovery is going to be long and difficult, but I can't help but think it'll be easier with these people by my side.

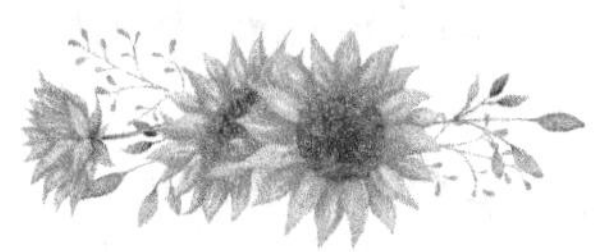

Four days after giving birth, the doctors cleared us to go home, so we packed the car seats into the back of the RAV. Aly sat between them, giving us updates on how the girls were doing and every move they made.

Iris and Morgan's sisters went over to stock our fridge and clean our house yesterday so we could just relax when we got home, which made me cry again.

All of the Fowler crew has stopped by to meet the babies and help out around the house, each of them taking turns spending the night at Morgan's request so I can rest and heal.

The first night we got home, Iris slept over. I tried to fight her on it, saying I was capable of doing the nighttime feedings, but Iris tutted at me and told me to stop being so stubborn and to accept the help. Not an easy feat when you're used to doing most things on your own.

After two weeks of being fussed over, I insisted I was fine to handle the nighttime routine, so everyone started slowly backing away and letting me take over. I appreciate that they didn't fight me.

It's been an adjustment trying to get a new routine going with the girls. They sleep in a pack 'n play in our bedroom on Morgan's side, and he insists on waking up when they do. More often than not, we're both awake cradling a baby and giving them bottles until they settle back to sleep.

There's no one I'd rather lose sleep with.

Our days are filled with never-ending diaper changes, feedings, and rocking them to sleep. Violet has remained a very calm baby, only crying when she's super hungry or when she got her shots. Poppy, on the other hand, is a very outspoken girl. If she's upset, we will know about it immediately, and it takes a bit more to get her settled.

Bean is extremely curious about the babies but refuses to get too close to them. If they're crying and Morgan is holding one of them, he meows angrily at Morgan until they quiet. When they're crying and I'm holding them, he rubs his head on my legs like he's giving me moral support.

Bagel is the silent protector of the twins. He sits next to them when we have them on their blankets on the floor and curls up next to them when they're crying. He doesn't seem bothered by the extra noise or baby items scattered around the house.

I'm going in for my six-week postpartum appointment today, and Morgan is staying home alone with the twins. I'm not nervous to leave them, I have complete trust in Morgan to handle it on his own, but I'm sad to leave the twins. I'm worried I'll miss big moments if I'm not with them all the time, even though there won't be any big milestones for a while.

I go through the routine of checking in at Dr. Badar's office, and before long she's knocking on the door and coming in to greet me with a smile.

"Hello, Hannah. No babies today?"

"Morgan wanted some alone time with them."

"It sounds like he's a very involved father."

"He is. He's the best."

"I'm glad to hear it. How has recovery been?"

"Good. I'm feeling much better than I was at my two-week appointment. The stitches have dissolved, and my scar no longer itches, so I assume that's a good thing."

"That is a very good thing. If you don't mind, I'd like to look at the scar just to make sure everything looks good, then we can talk about birth control options."

I nod, laying back on the table and lifting my sweater so Dr. Badar can examine the scar on my pelvis. She confirms the stitches have dissolved, and it's healing well, then asks if I've thought about going on birth control.

I explain Morgan's already got an appointment set with a urologist for a vasectomy, but I would like to be on birth control pills until the procedure is completed.

I'm sent home with a prescription for birth control, instructions to still take it easy with lifting, but I'm cleared for sex and light exercise.

When I get home, I find Morgan shirtless, with the twins sleeping on his broad chest covered in a cozy blanket.

The sight makes me want to cry tears of joy and jump his bones.

"Hey, Butterfly, how was your appointment?" he asks in a hushed whisper.

"It was good. Dr. Badar said my scar has healed nicely, and I can start lightly exercising." I bite my lip. "She also cleared me for sex."

Morgan's eyes meet mine as a slow grin takes over his face. "Good thing my mom and dad agreed to sleep over so we can go on a date."

"You don't think it's too soon?"

"We won't be going anywhere except to dinner and then coming back here. We could both use a break, and it's only one night. We'll still be here with them, just not in the same room. Now, go get ready." The command in his voice sends a shiver down my spine and pulses at the spot between my hips.

"Thank you." I give him a chaste kiss and run upstairs.

I don't know how long I have, so I rush to get ready. I curl my hair and put on makeup for the first time in over six weeks. I brush on a lip stain, then put on a proper bra for the first time since having the twins and look at myself in the mirror.

Pregnancy changed my body. It added more stretch marks, more extra skin, and I haven't lost all of the weight I gained. A large part of me worries Morgan won't find me as attractive.

I take a deep breath, reminding myself that Morgan has seen me in every stage of pregnancy and he still finds me attractive. He's seen my body at every stage of post-partum recovery, helped me shower when I could barely stand, and helped me change when I couldn't bend over. He hasn't given me any indication he doesn't like the way my body looks.

I'm about to step into the closet to get dressed when Morgan comes in, typing on his phone. When he looks up and catches my reflection in the mirror he drops his phone to the floor.

"God damn, Hannah," he groans.

"You don't think my body looks bad?" I whisper.

Morgan stands behind me, his hands tracing up and down my sides, gently running over the cotton underwear at my hips. "This body? The one that grew not one, but two babies? The one that houses the heart of the woman I love so much I ache? A body so fucking sexy I'm about to come in my fucking pants?" He punctuates his point with a slow grind of his cock to my ass.

I don't answer. I can't answer as his fingers gently pinch my nipple through the fabric of the bra.

"No, Butterfly. I don't think your body looks bad. I think it's perfect. I think if we didn't have reservations, I'd toss you on the bed and spend the entire night showing you just how much I *love* your body." Morgan places a gentle kiss to the sensitive spot behind my ear. "Now get dressed before I do just that. We have to leave in fifteen minutes."

I pick out a pair of black leggings and a forest green sweater dress, since I know Morgan and our date won't just be a quick run through the drive thru.

When I come out of the closet, Morgan's changed into black chinos and a forest green cable knit sweater. I roll my eyes at his need to match me, but I will admit I secretly love it.

Iris and Axel are sitting on the couch talking softly.

My anxiety flares at the thought of leaving the girls again so soon, but I know Iris and Axel will take good care of them. It's not like this is their first time with twins.

Aly's on the couch talking to Violet and Poppy about her day, both of the babies wide-eyed and listening intently to their big sister.

"Alright, kids, don't you worry about a single thing, okay? I have experience with twins, so I know what I'm doing," Iris says, pulling me into a hug. "You two just enjoy yourselves."

"Thank you so much, Iris."

She gives me a wink, then Morgan and I are off on our first date night as parents.

# CHAPTER 50

# Morgan

As Hannah and I sit in a booth at Fondue Frenzy, I reminisce about the first time we were here. It feels both like decades ago and yesterday that we went on our first fake date and ran into both of our exes.

I still can't believe my once fake girlfriend is going to be my real wife, and *soon* if I have anything to say about it. That's part of the reason I wanted to bring her out tonight. Now that the girls are here, I want to iron out the details of our wedding.

I can't wait much longer for her to have my last name.

We order the same things we did on our first date, and luckily, we don't run into either of our exes this time.

Before the dessert course comes out, I turn to Hannah and set the ring box on the table between us.

"What's that?"

"I have a very important question to ask—two, actually."

She rolls her eyes. "I already agreed to be your wife. I was wondering when you'd let me wear the ring. You've had it long enough."

"I want to set a wedding date. If you want to have a small ceremony now and a big party later, we can do that. If you don't want to do a big thing and just go to the courthouse, that's fine, too. I just want to marry you. So what do you say?"

"I think we should get married on the one-year anniversary of the day we met at Silver Spoon. Just a small courthouse ceremony, and when the twins are older, we can have a bigger party to celebrate. I want Sage to be a witness."

"I love that idea, Butterfly. Can I ask Kendall to be the other witness?" I flip the lid on the box and slide the ring onto her finger. She grins at me, and I plant a chaste kiss on her lips.

"Of course. I think that would be sweet. What was the other question you wanted to ask me?"

"Well, Aly and I have been talking. She's opened up more about the Whitney stuff, and her therapist says she's done really well processing things. I wasn't going to bring this up until Aly did, and two weeks ago..."

"Brought what up?" Hannah looks wary but also a little hopeful.

"Would you like to officially be Aly's mom?"

"What?" she gasps.

"Aly wants this too, I promise. She's the one who came to me and asked if you'd want to adopt her. I told her I would ask. She told me to tell you she loves you, and that you're a good mom to the twins. She wants you to adopt her, so you can be her mom, too."

Hannah's eyes fill with tears as she nods. "I would love to be Aly's mom. I love her so much. If this is what she truly wants, I'd be honored to adopt her."

I didn't think Hannah would say no, but the relief I feel makes me feel ten times lighter.

When dessert comes, we happily eat and talk about everything, reminiscing on the past and excitedly planning our future.

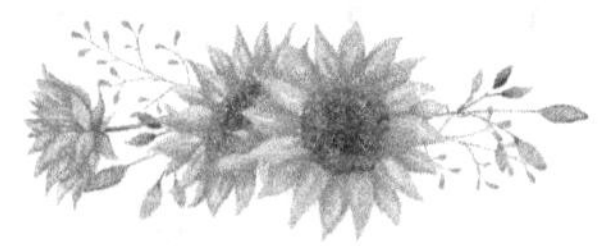

When we get to our room when we get home, I practically attack Hannah. Going six weeks without sex wasn't a hardship because I know she needed to recover, and I would never put her health in jeopardy. I missed my fiancée, though. I missed her softness, the way she responds to me.

Watching Hannah become a mom has been the hottest thing anyone's ever done, and I want to show her how much I appreciate that her body gave us two of the most precious gifts ever.

She tastes like chocolate when our tongues mingle and fight for dominance, and my girl seems just as pent up as I am if the way her hips push into mine is any indication.

"Morgan," she mutters between harsh presses of our lips together. "Need you."

I pull back and slowly peel up her sweater dress, my cock grows even harder at the sight of her gorgeous breasts.

"You need me, Hannah? Where do you need me?" I tease, cupping her breasts in my hand and squeezing, brushing her nipple with my thumb.

"I need you in my pussy," she moans, arching into my touch.

"What part of me do you want in your greedy little pussy, hmm? My tongue?" I flick her nipple with my tongue. "My fingers?" I grab a handful of her ass. "Or my cock?"

"All of them! Please! I just need you."

"Get on the bed so I can lay you out properly."

We undress quickly, and I follow her as she lays on the bed, holding myself above her so I don't hurt her incision. Fuck, she feels so good, even though just our chests and legs are touching. I've missed the touch of her skin on mine these past few weeks.

I kiss my way down her belly, paying extra attention to the silver and red stretch marks on her skin, but avoiding her surgical scar. The mark reminds me how fucking strong she is, and a wave of gratitude washes over me.

I channel that gratitude into the slow licks and sucks around her pussy lips and clit, paying extra attention to the hard little nub. I insert two fingers, and she bows off the bed with a cry when I find that sensitive spot inside of her, gently rubbing it while I continue to flick at her clit with my tongue.

She comes after a few meticulous strokes of my fingers, moaning as quietly as she can as her legs shake. While she's coming down, I flip her over onto her hands and knees, relishing the way her ass jiggles when I spank it.

Not wanting to risk her getting pregnant again, I slip a condom over my length and notch the head at her entrance, barely pushing in.

"Fuck, Morgan. I need it. You feel so good. Missed you."

"I missed you, too, Hannah. So fucking much. God, you feel amazing."

I grip her hips, sliding in all the way, and I nearly come as the heat of her surrounds me. Fuck, I'll never get tired of this feeling.

"I'm not going to last long when you feel this good, Butterfly," I groan. "Play with your clit so you can come with me." I start thrusting slowly, gradually picking up the pace while her fingers work her clit. I feel her pulse around me and know she's getting close.

"That's it, Hannah. Squeeze my cock. Fuck, you feel so fucking good. Come for me."

We tumble over the edge together as I fill the condom, and she squeezes around me.

I pull out, discard the condom, then drag my future wife to the shower so we can shower off the day. We end up slowly fucking on the shower bench, Hannah riding my cock, before we finally get out and dry off.

That night, I fall asleep tangled up with the mother of my children, happier than I've ever been.

# EPILOGUE

*Hannah*

*Two and a half years later...*

"**P**oppy, no! You're supposed to eat your oatmeal, not put it in your hair," Aly groans from the kitchen table. "Mom, I think we need a dishrag."

My heart still soars when she calls me that, even almost two years later. I love being her mom. We finalized Aly's adoption six months after the girls were born, and the same day, she shyly asked if she could start calling me Mom. I was so excited, I burst into tears.

"I think Poppy is going to need a bath, what do you think, Vi?" I ask her twin sister, who's meticulously spooning oatmeal into her mouth. She still gets a little messy, but she's not nearly as chaotic about it as her sister.

"No bath!" Poppy protests, pounding her hands on the high chair tray and splattering oatmeal on the wall.

"Poppy bath," Violet agrees, placing her spoon in her mostly eaten bowl and holding it up for me to take. "All done."

"Aly, would you mind helping Violet get dressed for the day while I go put Poppy in the bath really quick?"

"No problem, Mom. Come on, Vi. What color dress should we wear today? Pink or purple?"

"Pink!" Violet yells excitedly as Aly takes her up to her room.

"Alright, Pop. Let's get you a quick bath so you don't have oatmeal hair when we take you to Gigi and Papa's." I wipe most of the oatmeal mess up before taking her out of her high chair and carrying her upstairs to the bathroom.

"Gigi! Papa!" Poppy claps excitedly.

Iris and Axel are watching the girls for a week while Morgan and I go to Texas for Wes and Elli's wedding. They're having a small, intimate ceremony for their closest friends and family, and I'm honored to be on the guest list.

It's a childfree wedding, mostly because no one else has kids in their friend group, otherwise we'd bring the girls with us. It's hard to leave them for this long when we've never been apart for more than two days, but it'll be nice to have some time with just the two of us.

I hear my husband's footsteps on the stairs and the patter of Violet's feet padding down the hall before I hear a screeching, "DADDY!"

Poppy splashes the water and chants, "Daddy! Daddy! Daddy!"

"How are all my best girls?" Morgan says from the bathroom doorway, scooping up Violet and propping her on his hip. Violet wraps her arms around Morgan's neck and nuzzles into him.

The sight makes my ovaries explode, but we will not be having any more babies. Morgan had a vasectomy four months after the girls were born, and even though we know there's still a small possibility we could get pregnant, we haven't had any issues.

"Pops put oatmeal in her hair, but other than that, we're good," Aly answers, coming to hug Morgan from the side. I love that the girls hug him when he gets home, even if he's only been gone for an hour.

"Poppy, oatmeal is for eating, not for your hair," Morgan teases, and Poppy gives him a toothy grin.

I finish up Poppy's bath and help her get dressed for the day while Morgan loads up the suitcases into the van. We upgraded my small sedan for a minivan when we realized how hard it was for Aly to climb in between the girls and how uncomfortable it was to be squished between two bulky car seats.

Once everything is loaded into the car, we put the girls in their seats and head over to Iris and Axel's. The twins make us play *B-I-N-G-O* on repeat the entire way there and sing along the whole time.

Thank God the drive is less than ten minutes.

"Oh, it looks like Uncle Kenny is here too, girlies," Morgan says as we pull into the driveway.

"Uncky Kenny!" Poppy and Violet shout in unison.

The girls love their aunts and uncles, but Uncle Kenny and Uncle Jake hold special places in their hearts. They come over to play almost every week, and they take Aly out for ice cream or other special treats pretty often. Jake and Aly play video games together, and he helps her with the math homework Morgan and I don't understand.

Jake ended up coming home from his mission two months after the twins were born because he was being so badly beaten by his companion. He won't give me many details about how bad things were, even now. I know he's in therapy for it, and is working through the trauma he endured. The best I can do is hope he comes to me in time.

When he got home, we went to lunch to catch up, and he told me he was questioning things about the church. We spent over four hours talking, with him asking me about things he was questioning and me answering them as neutrally as I could. In the end, he decided to leave, too.

My mom blamed me, of course, but Jake stood up for me and told her he came to the decision on his own. He told her if she wanted to be involved in our lives, she should rethink the way she treated us growing up.

We haven't really heard from her since. The only time I saw her was at my grandpa's funeral the October after the girls were born.

Kendall, Axel, and Iris come out the front door to help us unload the girls and their luggage, and the twins squeal as Kendall takes turns tossing them up in the air like they don't weigh anything.

"Hey, Han, how's Sage?" Kendall's body language is nonchalant, but his voice sounds eager.

*Interesting.*

"Hi, Kenny, I'm good, thanks. Super excited for the trip. How are you?" I tease, watching his cheeks stain pink.

He huffs. "I'm good...?"

I roll my eyes but decide to put him out of his misery. "Sage is doing well, I think. We haven't had a chance to hang out as much because she's been busy with her new boyfriend."

Kendall's jaw clenches at the mention of Sage's new boyfriend. Dale is... well, he's a douchebag. I don't like him very much, but Sage seems... kind of happy. I think she just wants to be done dating, so she settled for Dale. She hasn't asked for my opinion on him, and I haven't given it unsolicited.

Dale works for Kendall's rugby team, but I'm not sure what he does. I know he doesn't *play* the sport, just works in the office.

Kendall and Sage have been acting weird toward each other ever since our small courthouse ceremony where they served as witnesses. Sage acts like she doesn't even know Kendall exists, but Kendall asks about Sage whenever I see him—which is a lot.

I don't know what's going on there, but if Kendall's interested in Sage, he's kind of shit out of luck. She knows his reputation and doesn't want anything to do with it. Sage doesn't do no-strings-attached sex like Kendall. He'd have to work really hard in order to even get her to give him the time of day.

"Good for her," he grunts before his demeanor changes to the happy-go-lucky guy we all know and love. He takes off in a gallop, making Violet giggle.

"He asked about Sage again, didn't he?" Iris asks as soon as I've breached the doorway.

"How did you know?"

She shakes her head. "That boy hasn't stopped talking about her since your wedding. I don't know why he's still denying he likes her. Did you know he's over here most weekends when he doesn't have a game? I don't think he's been out with a girl in over a year. Odd behavior for him."

My eyebrows shoot into my hairline. "That can't be true. Kendall doesn't want to settle down."

Iris shrugs. "Sometimes when the right person comes along your whole perspective changes."

"That's true. I guess stranger things have happened."

I give Iris and Axel a rundown of the girls' schedule, even though they're very familiar with it. I tear up a bit when Morgan reminds me it's time to say goodbye and get to the airport.

I give the twins and Aly a hug and a kiss on the cheek before we leave, and they wave us off as we drive away.

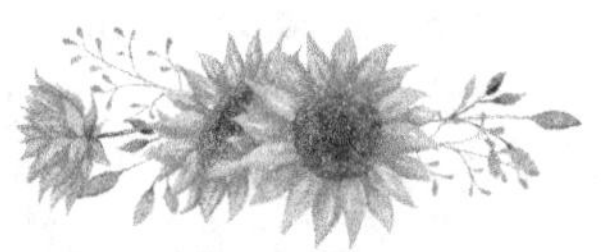

Wes and Elli's ceremony is held in a lovely botanical garden in Austin, right in front of a waterfall. There are less than twenty people here, but the love pouring from everyone is palpable. Keely and the rest of the band are here, along with Wes's close-knit friend group, and Emma and her fiancé flew in, too.

Izzy walks Elli down the aisle, beaming at her sister. Elli looks so beautiful and so happy, it makes me tear up a little. It's not flashy, just a white satin dress with spaghetti straps that hugs her curves and has a slit running up the thigh. Her hair curls in long waves down her back with half of it twisted back and decorated with baby's breath.

Wes gets emotional when he sees her walking in, falling to a crouching position and covering his mouth as tears stream down his face. He has on a plain black dress shirt, rolled to his elbows, and black dress pants. His long hair is pulled back into a neat bun.

Wes's best friend, Robin, is officiating the ceremony, and she can barely get the words out because she keeps tearing up.

When they get to the vows, Wes tries to compose himself, but he still cries when he promises Elli forever, and Elli blubbers her way through her own vows as she promises him the same.

I find myself a little misty-eyed by the end of the ceremony. It reminds me of the small party we had to celebrate our marriage on our one-year anniversary. Morgan and I exchanged vows in front of his family, my brother and cousins, and Sage. I had already done the big wedding, and Morgan didn't care about having a big party. It was small and intimate, just like Elli's, and it was perfect.

Wes's friend, Matt, knows a guy who owns an exclusive fancy restaurant in Austin—where he apparently took Elli on a date before she started dating Wes—so we head there for a small reception after the ceremony.

The rest of the night is filled with dancing, drinks, laughter, and good food.

"It's wild to see how far the three of us have come, isn't it? Especially you and Elli. You two were much deeper into the church than I was," Emma muses from next to me. Wes and Elli just cut their cake, and now they're feeding each other bites in between kissing and laughing.

"It's nice to finally be able to be ourselves."

"'Live for truth.' Isn't that what Grandpa always said? I don't think *this* truth is exactly what he meant, but it's our truth. That's what matters."

"Probably not what he meant," I agree. "But I hope he's proud of us anyway."

I like to think that whatever the afterlife has to hold, Grandpa Walter is looking down on us and smiling at the fact we're happy. We may not be part of the church anymore, but we're living for ourselves and our loved ones, and I think that's the best thing we could do.

## The End

# Acknowledgements

I want to start out by thanking my husband, because he's been my biggest supporter and cheerleader. He's let me talk endlessly about plot ideas and helped me through anxiety attacks. He's talked me out of wiping out my entire existence and quitting this writing thing more than once, and I wouldn't be where I am without him.

I also want to thank Jen and Brit at The Author Experience for their amazing work. They have been incredible to work with and have been so patient and kind with me while explaining the editing process.

Thank you to my Beta readers for helping me make this story better!

I want to thank you, reader, for taking the time to read Hannah's story.

# About the Author

Daisy Wren lives in the Utah Valley with her husband and three kids. When she's not writing her next book (or working her corporate job), she's reading, cooking, and spending time with her family. Daisy's love of writing has been prominent since childhood, and she's always felt a call to share her stories. A hopeless romantic since she first saw *The Phantom of the Opera* at age eight, she's been writing her own love stories ever since. Daisy is a former member of a high demand religion and hopes to bring light to the issues of the church she was raised in, while also telling beautiful stories about life after leaving. Please visit her at www.DasiyWren.com or on social media for updates about upcoming releases and for bonus content!

TikTok: @daisywrenauthor
Instagram: @daisywrenauthor
Threads: @daisywrenauthor